Jenna
one of your tried
and true

RED AS BLOOD

EVERBEACH
BOOK 1

SORBONI BANERJEE
DOMINIQUE RICHARDSON

WISE WOLF
BOOKS

WISE WOLF BOOKS
An Imprint of Wolfpack Publishing
wisewolfbooks.com

This is a work of fiction. All of the characters, organizations,
publications, and events portrayed in this novel are either products of
the author's imagination or are used fictitiously.

Cover design by Wise Wolf Books

ISBN 978-1-957548-14-2 (paperback)
ISBN 978-1-957548-15-9 (hardcover)
ISBN 978-1-957548-13-5 (ebook)

*To anyone who has ever looked in the mirror
and wondered about your worth—we see you.*

RED AS BLOOD

RED AS BLOOD

PART ONE

"You godless child," cried the sorceress. *"What am I hearing from you? I thought I had removed you from the whole world, but you have deceived me nonetheless."*

—*Rapunzel*, Grimm Brothers

CHAPTER 1
THE SHOW
RAVEN

Apple-red lipstick should be banned from candlelight vigils. If I wrote the rules, I would make this the number one, you get stopped at the door and sent home rule, and then I'd give the reasons why: Tone deaf. Obnoxious. Attention stealing. Wrong.

But I don't make the rules. *She* does. My stepmother, Vera, applies the gaudy hue over her collagen-puffed lips. I rest my head on the cool of the glass window, turning away from her show. I wish the limo would hit a bump and mess up her calculated, red swaths.

Red is the color of love, hearts, fiery passion. And lava —melting and destroying as it moves. Red can be the last edge of a sunset. A kiss.

Or it can be a warning. Stop. Go no further—danger.

Today, red is the color of Penny missing.

Tomorrow, senior year starts, and Penny's locker will stay shut, her seat at the lunch table empty.

Our limo turns onto a palm tree-lined, private drive, the road slithering back and forth until it meets an intricate iron gate, crowned in the center with a golden *S*. The sight of the Steele estate coils around my churning gut.

Penny's vigil should be at the *real* beach where we spend every summer on the hot sand, playing volleyball, swimming in the turquoise surf. Not here. At *his* house.

The guard waves us in, and we park in a lot next to the carriage house.

"Here, Raven, put some on." Vera waves the offensive lipstick at me.

I turn only slightly toward her. "No, thanks."

"Even when we're sad, we must always put our best face forward. This will do wonders for your peaked complexion."

"Some color might look nice," my dad says. Surprise. He's taking her side again.

My dad catches my gaze. Reflected in his stare is the strain of being caught in the middle again, and my annoyance ebbs. His eyes are an almost translucent green, a mirror image of my own. My light skin color is from him, too, in stark contrast to the midnight curls I inherited from my Jamaican mother. I touch my ruby heart necklace, remembering her warm, brown hands fastening it around my neck years ago. Hers, but she gave it to me. Now, it's all I have left.

"Here. Let me just—" Vera twists toward me, grabs my chin, armed with the godawful lipstick.

I want to pull away, but I know I'll end up with red smears and a stepmother who will only try again.

"There." Vera sits back, caps the lipstick, and stashes it in her purse. "Such an improvement. You'll thank me when you see it." Vera offers her mirror—she's gloating. I stare at my lap, biting my tongue.

Vera gives me one of her closed lip smiles. "I know how you feel right now. I've experienced loss, too."

"That was different." I grit my teeth trying to stay small. Self-preservation.

"Loss is loss. It hurts. We manage the pain. And then, we move on."

Move on from Penny. Like that's an option. Not when Penny could still turn up. *Will* turn up.

I don't care if it's been six weeks since she disappeared from the psychiatric hospital. I don't care that the searches only uncovered a faded hoodie—Penny's favorite. It used to be green, but the beach and endless use had turned it a sort of sage gray.

She is somewhere safe. I choose to believe that. Even after the other thing they found...

The memory is bright, like I'm standing in the search tent again. When the detective came back with the evidence, the air froze like I'd stepped into a morgue. He carried a plastic bag, its contents haunting: Penny's long, blonde signature braid—chopped off and left behind, next to her hoodie.

What did they do to her in that hospital to make her want to run, to change her appearance drastically enough to disappear? Because that was the theory the detectives had gone with after they couldn't find evidence of a kidnapping.

She left us. But why?

Or was it something *someone* didn't do? Guilt edges against my chest, the ever-present shadow of how I let a best friend down.

I force air into my lungs and can almost feel one of Penny's floppy sweatshirt hugs, the sleeves stretching over her fingers as she bounces on her toes. I swear I smell her coconut oil and jasmine scent—she's always coming or going from the beach.

Will I ever see her again? Ever get a chance to explain?

No. Just because everyone else is giving up doesn't mean I have to. Once I get away from Vera and my dad, I'll have space to think, and I will figure out what to do next for Penny.

Vera eyes my hair. "Are you sure you don't want my mirror?"

"I'm fine," I bite out a little too harshly.

"The frizz is worse since we left the house. And your roots, they're curly again." Vera picks up her phone.

I know what comes next. And if it is what I think it is, I'm too close to the line to deal with this. I tense, hands in fists, bracing, but my control is frayed.

"Hello? Oh good. I caught you," Vera says into the phone. "I need to book Raven Snow an appointment. Yes, soonest available. For a Keratin treatment."

My tether snaps. "Seriously? Today, right now?" I say, my tone broken glass. "Why can't you ever back off? You're unbelievable."

Vera whips around wearing her mask of shocked hurt —eyes wide, mouth dropped open. The only thing she's missing is her hand flying to her mouth, then the look would be complete. I can hear the person on the other line asking if everything is okay. "I have to go...I'll call you back." Vera slides her phone into her purse and looks at me. Her chin quivers, tears pooling in her eyes, and when she speaks, her voice cracks, the show hitting its crescendo.

"All I'm ever trying to do is help you. We're on the same team. Then you treat me this way." She looks at my dad. "And Clive. You...you—never mind." Vera flings the door open and pours out of the car.

My dad lets out a long breath. "Raven."

"Dad." I mock his tone.

"Hey. Is that necessary with me, too?"

I cross my arms in response.

"I know you're going through a lot. I get it. But is there any way you can try a little harder?"

"Because she's making such an effort?" I fidget with my necklace.

My dad puts his hand on mine. "She really is trying. I mean, just now. She extended an olive branch. But you didn't reach back."

"Is that what that was?" I keep my eyes trained on his hand.

He heaves a long sigh. "This puts me in a tough spot."

"Then don't leave."

"You know I have to."

"Why?"

"Raven." His voice is soft this time, too soft against my jagged anger, making this terrible day worse. He *knows* what leaving means.

"We've gone over this." He shifts in his seat. "You know I have to go for work. There are some things in Jamaica. I just...I need to be there. It's only for a few weeks."

Things. Never details. "You said that last time and you stayed half the year." I pause, resting back in the seat. "I thought...the business, your company—didn't it go under?"

My dad flinches. And my anger evaporates. We never talk about his unspoken failure. And the real reason I need to make peace with Vera. Why I have no choice but to endure. *Money.*

"I'm working on it," he says.

"But I'm going to be alone with her again." Hurt lodges in my throat.

"It will be different this time. I promise. Can you try and keep the peace...for me?"

I refuse to meet his eyes. "So, you need me to be the bigger person, say I'm sorry."

My dad squeezes my hand but doesn't say anything. He doesn't have to.

The driver opens my door.

"I'm going to make a quick call," my dad says. Of course he's going to hide. Doesn't matter. Might as well start my punishment.

At the front of the limo, Vera stands tall in her red-bottomed wedges, blonde hair pulled back in a tight bun at the base of her neck. Her black sheath dress hangs on her waiflike frame. I walk to her and when I stop, I smooth my emerald, A-line dress over my curves.

"I'm sorry."

Vera raises her head higher, like she's the queen and I'm her subject. Her gaze is hidden behind oversized sunglasses, even though the sun is almost gone. Another power play.

I force the words out. They taste like poison on my tongue. "I shouldn't have spoken to you that way. I was upset about Penny, and I didn't—"

Vera cuts me off with one finger under my chin, her long nail scraping against the delicate skin, lifting my face so my eyes meet hers. Trepidation rings through me.

"You're right. You shouldn't have. Your friend Penny is the one you should be upset with. She chose to run away and turn everyone's lives upside down. Yet, after everything I've done for you, I'm the one who gets your disrespect. I will continue to tolerate you for him, but—" My dad's door opens, and Vera's harsh features soften. "But, honey, I accept your apology. I know you're going through a lot. We'll get through today and be better for it."

My dad joins us, taking his place next to Vera. "It

sounds like you two made up?" He puts his arm around his wife and gives her a peck on the cheek.

"Of course, we have. Right, Raven? We had a nice little chat, and I forgive her."

I let Vera manipulate the conversation. The vise on my stomach since we drove onto the estate tightens until all emotion is clamped, and I'm the picture of docile obedience.

My phone buzzes with a text. Aarya.

> What's taking so long? Ditch your dad and wicked stepmother and get down here.

"Aarya's waiting. Can I go?"

"Yes, of course. But come over here and give me a hug." My dad opens his arms, and despite everything, I lean into his embrace. "I have to head out before the vigil ends. Do you want to come with me?"

"I was thinking of going home with Aarya?" I say it as a question, my submission on full display.

"That's fine. I'll come back to the Steeles after I drop Clive off," Vera says.

"I'll miss you, darling," my dad says into my hair, squeezing me tighter. "I'll call you when I land."

"I'll miss you, too."

He releases me and I leave them by the limo.

Dread rises in my chest as I make my way down the manicured grass, past lighted trees, and across a wooden bridge over sea oat covered dunes. The salty, humid air envelops me. I step into the soft sand and trek to the large crowd gathering oceanside near rows of white chairs. Torch lights flicker around the perimeter. There are hundreds of people—classmates, parents, teachers, community officials. A woman stands holding a bouquet of flowers tied with a yellow ribbon blowing in the ocean breeze. The small, white, bell-shaped flowers bring me to an abrupt halt: lilies of the valley.

I shudder. The last time my dad left me alone with Vera—

Nope. Bury it. Don't think of the flowers. What they mean.

I have to be stronger than I was today. More in control. There's no room for mess-ups, not when I'm alone with Vera. I will fly under the radar, dance when she tells me to dance. Because what happened four years ago cannot happen again. I shut my eyes and touch my necklace.

Today is Penny's day. Not mine. And I will not let anything else distract me—not fear, not sadness, not guilt.

I open my eyes, resolve in place, and scan the crowd.

Aarya Samudra waves, new fluorescent red highlights illuminate her short, angled, jet-black hair. Her parents sit next to their long-time family friends, the Grimsleys.

I shake my head at how dramatically Aarya is leaning to not be shoulder-to-shoulder with the Grimsley's son, Punkaj, in the narrowly placed seats.

"How's your dad handling the hair?" I ask as a greeting while shooting a sidelong glance at Mr. Samudra.

"Mmm." Aarya makes a face. "Better than the spikes."

I cringe, remembering. "The rats comment."

She shrugs. "There was no insinuation a rodent was my stylist this time. So, there's that. However, there *was* a whole take-away-my-car-for-the-weekend thing that happened. You're going to have to drive me home from the afterparty."

"First, you can't call the reception an afterparty. Second, my ride home is Vera. Pick your poison."

"*First,* Penny would have called it that. And *second,*

the wicked witch drives us home on her broom masquerading as a limo or I acquiesce to my chastisement and let my dictator parents drive us?" Aarya looks up, tapping her chin, like there is a real decision to be made. "Fine, so much for my protest. I'll take the tyrants over evil incarnate."

Punkaj Grimsley narrows his eyes. "Shh."

Aarya squints back dramatically, imitating his expression. "He's a senior going on senior citizen," Aarya says. Punkaj straightens his posture, clearly hearing her, but Mr. Maturity isn't taking the bait.

"You're not wrong," I confirm.

"Hey. There's Logan Steele," Aarya says, drawing my attention to Penny's on-again, off-again boyfriend. "I still don't understand why he of all people would be hosting."

I look around nervously. "Shh. Don't talk about him when we're on Steele property."

"Let them hear me," Aarya says, taunting.

Logan looks up and meets my gaze. His blue-gray eyes hold the heaviness of this day, almost like he's looking for a lifeline, but whatever this act is, I'm not falling for it. I cut my eyes away, making sure I don't glance in his direction again.

Detective Anderson, who organized the searches for Penny, grabs the mic and calls Penny's parents, Mr. and Mrs. Zale, to stand with him under an archway decorated with sunflowers.

"That's my cue." Aarya takes her candle and walks up to them.

Mr. Samudra snaps to attention, back rigid. His wife places a hand on his arm and murmurs something in his ear. Clearly Aarya hasn't told them she's singing tonight. I'm not surprised. She always brushes it off as "Indian parent problems," like it doesn't hurt they consider her music a waste of time. Even though I disagree with them, it *is* their way of caring. Unlike my dad who can't even see that leaving me with Vera is the worst idea ever.

Aarya's voice, clear and searing, pulls me back to the vigil. She's turning "Amazing Grace" into something that sends frissons through my body. I wish her parents understood: a voice like hers is *not* a waste. Others join in singing, and I'm surrounded by a muffled chorus echoing with sniffles and sorrow.

Tears sting and everything blurs. Images come at me in pieces: my friend Dawn, standing next to her dad Pastor Thorne; the prayer he says; Penny's mom sobbing and her father like stone. Would my dad be stone, too? What would my mom have been like? A buried ache rises, and I can't stop it. My mother's absence. Deep pain pours over the wall I hide it behind. I'm gripping my ruby heart hanging from my neck again.

I look at the ocean. Waves lap against the horizon, the sun dips below. With everything in me, I will my pain to go with it.

Someone tips their candle to light mine, bringing my focus back to the crowd. Why does it feel like the light goes through me? Flames flicker. Wishes to see Penny again. I'm terrified they won't come true. Because Penny is no normal runaway. She's a risk to herself. Without her meds and psychiatric care, she will spiral.

Wax overflows from the candle's wick, and the sharp burn snaps me out of my thoughts. There is a girl staring at me from between the dunes. When our eyes meet, a shiver prickles my skin, and she darts between the trees into the shadows.

"Are you alright?" Aarya asks, suddenly next to me again.

I blink. Almost everyone is gone. I must have really

zoned out. Did I imagine the girl? I blow out my candle, shaking off the eerie feeling. "I'm as good as I can be." I follow Aarya up the beach to the boardwalk leading back to the Steele mansion.

"What's he still doing here?" Aarya points to Punkaj, slowly walking up from the beach.

He catches our gaze and makes a beeline toward us. "Hey, I had a question about Penny."

"Is this on the record for your big bad internship at *The Mirror*, or are you asking me as a *friend?*" Aarya puts her hands on her hips. "Because I never heard you say, how are you?"

Punkaj falters. "Never mind. And...sorry. It sucks they called off the search."

"Understatement of the year." Aarya looks like she's going to pounce.

I can't deal with this right now. "Can we just catch up later?" Without waiting for an answer, I steer Aarya away.

When we reach the carriage house, the girl I saw in the dunes is walking toward us. So she *was* real. "Do you know her?" I discreetly motion toward the girl.

"Never seen her in my life."

"Why is she staring at us?"

Before Aarya can respond, our paths meet. "Are you Aarya Samudra?" she asks.

"Have we met?"

The girl ignores Aarya's question and looks right at me. "And you're Raven Snow?"

I nod. "I'm sorry, I missed your name."

"Elle. Elle Glass. I'm a friend of Penny's."

I study the girl in the waning light. She's a natural beauty, with long ash brown hair framing her oval face and hazel eyes with flecks of amber. "How do you know Penny?"

She pulls out a manila folder from her crossbody bag, ignoring another question. "These came in the mail with no return address. The instructions said to find you both and your friend Dawn."

I take the folder. Inside are four envelopes with names written on them: Raven, Aarya, Dawn, Elle.

I recognize the handwriting. The air holds its own breath. "They're from Penny."

CHAPTER 2
A WORLD APART
AARYA

Letters from Penny.

Seeing Penny's loopy handwriting hits like a heavy base chord, buzzing in my chest and throat.

I've felt this sort of throb before—when your heart beats everywhere but where it's meant to. The time my mother almost crashed our car in the rain. The time my brother ate a peanut and his throat closed. Every time the starter gun claps at my swim meets. Whenever my father says my name, in that way—*Aarya*—and I know the next words will tell me what I've done wrong. Again.

Fear hums. It vibrates through your body and tells you not to move. Which is why you have to move. And keep moving. Become the melody fear can't catch.

I dart from possibility to possibility of what these letters from my missing friend might say.

I ran away with a beautiful boy, and I'm living on an island beach.

I accidentally joined a cult.

I'm on drugs hiding in a homeless camp.

I flit to these to avoid thinking about the one possibility that has my hands shaking and heat spreading through my face. I look to Raven, hoping for an anchor, but she's got the faraway look I've come to know. She's going down the same dark path, but if mine ends in a cliff where I stop, hers is a landslide that can bury her.

"Hey," I reach out and touch Raven's arm, make her focus back on me. "Breathe."

She's had panic attacks for as long as we've been friends, but they got worse after eighth grade summer.

Raven's shoulders stiffen. She searches for refuge in the gaze I force steady. For her. "It's okay. You're okay."

The new girl—Elle—glances back and forth between us. "I'm hoping it's good news not..." She trails off, her jaw clenching.

"Not...suicide notes." Raven's voice catches.

"They're *not*." I say with a force so unwavering I convince myself.

Raven gives the smallest of nods and exhales.

Helping Raven lets me shelve my own quivering nerves. Taking care of someone else's feelings is better than feeling anything yourself. It's like swimming in the ocean in the rain, the needle cold droplets from the sky distract you from the churning currents beneath.

I turn to Elle. "Let's open them."

"No."

I startle at her answer. "What do you mean, no?"

"We can't." Elle points to Penny's writing. "It says open them *together*, you, me, Raven, and Dawn, who's not here."

Who does this girl think she is to call the shots?

"How exactly did you know Penny anyway?" I scan her expression.

"Our moms knew each other," Elle says.

"And you were *that* close Penny mailed the letters to you?" This doesn't add up.

"We became friends over time." Elle shrugs. "I'm really not sure why me though."

A tingling starts to crawl from my face to my fingers like a deep itch. Impatience has voltage. I shake it off.

"Fine. Let's go find Dawn."

I walk toward the mansion, but when we reach the base of the sprawling white marble steps leading up to the terraced lawn and pool, Elle stops. She pats down her hair against the ocean air and smooths her sundress.

"I wasn't expecting to have to go inside."

"You're fine," I say. "No one cares what you look like, they're too worried about what *they* look like. Let's go."

"It's...giant," Elle breathes.

"Always throws me, too," Raven reassures her.

I try to imagine I'm seeing the Steele estate for the first time. "The house that sugar built," I say flatly.

The Steele's angular mansion rises in front of us. Old-fashioned streetlamps illuminate the path from the carriage house. It circles around a statue of a dragon coiled in a fountain, head reared, steady streams of water arching out of its mouth right before the porte cochere.

"That's new." Raven cocks her head at the dragon. "Kind of creepy."

"Kind of powerful," I say. "I like it."

"You would," Raven answers.

"I like dragons, too," Elle says. "They're the unicorns of lizards."

Unicorn lizards, ha. That's like something Penny would say. I wave for Elle to pick up the pace. Doormen stand at the entry checking names before letting people into the reception.

"It's like they're royalty," Elle murmurs. "Protected from the world."

"Or it's like Jurassic Park. Protecting the world from *them*," I say. "Interchangeable really, raptors, trust fund babies...unicorn lizards."

Elle shoots me a small smile and scans the scene. "Let's get in and out. Find Dawn. Done."

"I like your thinking. The sooner we find her the sooner we know how to help Penny."

We cross the long lawn to the door and a butler escorts us up more marble stairs, guiding us through stained-glass French doors into the majestic foyer. Heavy industrial chandeliers contrast dramatically with their cascading crystals. Two staircases spiral up, leading to the east and west wings.

We head straight back toward glass doors facing the waterfront. In the center of the patio the winding pool shimmers, surrounded by cabanas and high-top tables with floating votive candle centerpieces. Stairs dip to a grassy area where the guests gather, and waiters serve hors d'oeuvres. Stationed to the left, a chocolate fountain is surrounded by fruits and cakes. To the right, a bar, and beyond, the beach and waves whispering in the dark.

Everything is meticulous. I feel like I'm watching a choreographed scene—kids from school, my parents talking to the Grimsleys, hotel mogul and skincare empress beside famed news anchor and pro golfer. Perfect Punkaj standing up too straight beside them—the ultimate super son. Dawn's father, the pastor, making his rounds. Vile Vera, at the elbow of her boss Harvey Steele.

And the Zales. Penny's parents look shipwrecked, stranded in a sea of people gathered here for their missing daughter—or to see who they can see. Or be seen.

At the center of this gathering of Everbeach's finest

stands Logan Steele. His sandy blonde hair, piercing blue-gray eyes, and perfectly tailored suit culminate into a presence that shouts, *here is the heir of the estate*.

Logan sees us, too. That polite smile. It's there for everyone but us, for those watching the interaction from afar.

"What Penny sees in Harvey Steele's baby raptor, I will never understand," I say.

"So *that's* Steele light," Elle says.

"Steele light?"

"Penny started calling him that when she got tired of all the on-again-off-again drama. Said he was the half-assed edition. All billionaire, no balls. But...he's *really* hot."

I snicker at the nickname. All this time and I never could quite come up with one for him. "He's hot as hell. But—"

"But a total player. Thinks he can have whoever he wants, whenever he wants," Raven finishes for me.

Raven's not usually that blunt. I like it. "That pretty much nails it."

She shrugs. "Unfiltered me today, I guess."

Elle looks like she's not sure. "Penny always said he was different than what everyone saw."

"Logan's only redeeming quality is that Penny loved him." I raise an eyebrow at her as Logan approaches. "You'll see."

"Thanks for coming," Logan says, then he turns to Elle with a curious squint. "I'm Logan."

"Elle."

He nods a standard greeting. Zero recognition. Suspicion bubbles up again. How is this girl holding the only piece of Penny and none of us had any clue she existed until tonight? Everbeach isn't that big.

We're all standing around awkwardly looking from

each other to the floor. So I blurt, "Sorry you had to do all this?"

Logan gives me a how-dare-you stare. Maybe it would work on someone else. "Are you actually expressing sympathy or insinuating how I feel?"

"What do you mean?"

"You said it like a question."

"The punctuation was purely ornamental." I've never been good at hiding how I feel.

"*Sorry you had to do all this?*" Logan mimicked. "Like it's not something good."

"*You* said it. Not me." I go for the kill. "Sorry you had to host a big party when your girlfriend is missing. Or wait. Ex-girlfriend. What exactly is she to you anyway?"

"More than she'll ever be to you," Logan says. "And it's not a party. We just wanted to give people somewhere to go after the vigil. To say thank you. For their help and support."

Before I can respond, Raven warns me with a curt tilt of her head that Mr. Steele is approaching.

"Girls. Thank you for being here."

I feel myself shrink. Even now, with Penny's letters pulling at me, I notice the sheen of his black suit, the crisp cuffs of his shirt, gold watch at his wrist. Harvey Steele has the sort of presence that makes you want to thank him for the air you're breathing. Because he's sharing it with you. Because he owns it. Because he owns everything.

It's not even about his sugar empire. It's simply *him*. Stony authority layered with magnetism. I want to do what he does. I want to command a room right down to the oxygen.

No one would ever be able to tell me what to do or be or *not* be ever again.

"I hope this night, everyone being here together, helps

us hold on to hope." After a brief pause, he nods indicating the end of his foray into human emotion. "Logan, there are some people you need to thank for coming. Meet me by the bar once you're finished here."

"Yes sir," Logan says. "Well, I clearly have some things to attend to. As always, Aarya, it was not nice catching up with you."

"Hopefully, we don't do this again any time soon," I say.

"My sentiments exactly."

He walks away, and I immediately turn to Elle. "When did you meet Penny again? It's weird she never mentioned you."

But Elle is looking past me.

"Is that her?" she asks. "Dawn?"

I follow her gaze and spot honey blond barrel curls across the room. Every other thought evaporates, replaced by only Penny's letters. "Sure is." I grab Raven's arm, practically dragging her, Elle keeping pace.

Dawn gives us a little wave hello. "I'm so glad to see you. I'm just wandering around in a blur like it's a bad dream." She notices Elle. "Hi. I'm Dawn Thorne."

"Elle." She fidgets with the manila folder.

"Apparently she's a friend of Penny's," I say. "And has some news."

"Penny mailed me letters," Elle says. "There's one for each of us, including you."

Dawn's hand flies to her mouth. "She *wrote* to us! She's okay?"

"We don't know what they say yet." Elle looks around and ducks her head a little. "Can we maybe go somewhere else? Less in the middle of everything?"

"Agreed," I say. There's a game room upstairs on the opposite side of the mansion where Logan and his younger brother throw parties. It should be empty right now. "Follow me."

Our steps echo through the long marble corridors lined with paintings of generations of the Steele family on one wall, floor to ceiling windows on the other.

I open the door to the game room, revealing pool tables, vintage pinball games, foosball, and a wall-to-wall screen with rows of gaming chairs. Signed memorabilia from all sorts of famous people hang on the walls.

"Are you serious?" Elle stands mesmerized by framed photos of Steele with celebrities and politicians. "Harvey Steele at the *White House*?" Elle shakes her head and leans in. "Is that an original signed record from Jett John?"

"Yeah, only the biggest pop star in the whole world." I point to the picture beside it, of Jett John and the Steeles next to their yacht, the Sea Dragon. "That's Logan's uncle, R.P. beside him. He runs Ursula Productions." My pulse jumps. Imagine signing with a giant label like Ursula, singing, *performing*, for a living. Praised, not punished, for my passion.

"Do you really have no idea how next level rich the Steeles are?" I nudge Elle along. "Come on. Are we opening the letters or what?"

We sit down at a card table. It feels somehow appropriate. A high stakes gamble.

Elle opens the packet and puts a letter down on the smooth green felt surface in front of each of us. No one moves.

The letters might hold good news. Or they might say goodbye.

The fragile possibility that Penny is alive and well is only guaranteed for as long as the letters stay sealed. Hope is inside these envelopes, and it lives or dies when we open them.

"I don't understand how it got so bad," I say softly. "I thought she was good with her meds, then, High Tower. Out of the blue."

Dawn fiddles with her letter. "Was it out of the blue? She got so distant. She stopped wanting to hang out. Was it just with me?"

"No," Raven says. "She cancelled on me left and right. And I was so busy, I just let it happen."

"Same," Elle says softly, picking at the seal of her envelope.

"I hope it's good news," Dawn says.

"Me, too." I take a deep breath and rip mine open.

The other girls follow suit. If someone asked what hope sounded like before, I would have said chimes, or a flute. One strain of a violin. But now, I'd say it's the sound of tearing paper.

Racing to get to Penny's words, I take them in. "It's...a poem?"

"Mine, too," says Dawn.

"Should we read them out loud?" Elle asks.

"Yes." I wait and when no one starts, I read mine. "Aarya Samudra: *Take a deep dive...raise your voice in support. Docks clocked by day, false reports that night cheats.*"

Elle clears her throat. "Elle Glass: *Hearts...turned to steel...a long time ago. To survive, walk on glass, pretend you don't know the deceit.*"

Dawn reads next. "Dawn Thorne: *Go to their church. Wake and ring the grand bell! The taste of success is a spindle from hell...and sweet.*"

Raven goes last. "Raven Snow: *Portraits in mirrors make it much clearer. They point at nightmares...and ask you who's nearer...and discreet.*

Silence falls, confusion condenses.

"Any idea what any of this means?" Elle asks.

Raven shakes her head. Dawn looks equally baffled.

I feel like this is all on me. I should know what she means. Penny loves playing with words in poems like I love doing with song lyrics.

But it's been a long time since I've written a song. Not since my dad's massive freak out when Mom found my YouTube channel. Because trying to be some "American rock star" is not respectable or responsible, and therefore banned.

For a while the lyrics still came—you can't turn off your brain—but I stopped writing them down. I was too mad. I let them dance out and away and evaporate. What isn't there, as strong, if not stronger than what is. Penny. Forever powering the space between the words.

And I'm failing her. Because this time, I don't know what she means.

No one says a word. We just sit there in the stillness.

Penny has something she wants us to know, something she's not comfortable saying straight out, whether she ran away or it's more complicated—darker.

Not being able to decipher it feels like being pulled under water, the faraway sky shimmers, and I'm reaching, trying desperately to get fingers around something solid. All I want is the crisp breath of answers, to crack the surface and see the real world. The one where Penny isn't missing. The one that's gone.

I make a decision. "Let's go find our parents and take these to the police."

CHAPTER 3
SPINNING WHEELS
RAVEN

One call and Vera had a meeting with the police. At least I'm not the only one to ask how high when she says jump. I guess it helps when you're Harvey Steele's attack dog. I follow Vera into the police station. Dawn and Aarya trail behind with their parents. Vera glides right up to the front desk.

"May I help you?" the receptionist asks.

"We're here to meet with Detective Anderson," Vera says.

The receptionist peers over her reading glasses. "Name?"

Vera looks a little stunned that someone doesn't instantly know who she is, but recovers quickly stating her name and adding, "It's about Penny Zale."

"Ah yes, he did tell me to expect someone soon. But my goodness, I didn't anticipate such a big group. And look, there's more of you now."

Elle walks toward us with a man dressed in jeans and a t-shirt. Ash brown hair and hazel eyes, definitely her dad.

The woman hands us clipboards with forms attached

to them. "Here's some paperwork to fill out. We'll call you back shortly."

We take seats in the waiting room. Vera stands talking to the Samudras, so I can at least fill out my form without her peering over my shoulder.

Name. Address. Phone number. Simple enough. But then I get to *the question*.

My pencil hovers over the box next to "Black/African American." I glance at Vera chatting away. It would be so easy to draw an X. The little box stares at me, taunting.

I touch my necklace, then fidget with my hair. It's smooth and straight and lifeless. I know what everyone sees when they look at me. Only one side. My dad's. Exactly what Vera wants.

I may as well be white as snow.

And still, for Vera, it's never enough.

Vera sits down next to me, and the decision is made. I draw an X on the box next to "White/Caucasian."

Vera leans in and whispers close to my ear. "I spoke to your father. He knows we're here, and I told him not to worry. I've got it handled." She preens like a peacock.

I fish around in my purse. Vera presses her lips together in a flat line and hands my phone to me. "You left it in the car earlier."

"It must have fallen out."

"Perhaps you should take better care of your things."

"I'll be more careful."

"Without me, your and your father's lives would be quite different. So how about we appreciate what we have a little bit more, instead of carelessly leaving things strewn about?"

"Sorry," I mumble like a robot. I scroll through my missed calls and messages. Not a word from my dad. Why hasn't he reached out? He said he'd call when he landed in

Jamaica. Instead, he talked to Vera. He's busy, and I know I shouldn't take it personally, but knowing doesn't stop my thrumming pulse. He can't even send a quick text saying, *I'm here if you need me* or how about something easier, three words, *I love you*.

Fine. I don't need him either. I can handle this on my own.

But my breath trips. Uneven, tumbling.

Over my dad.

Over Vera.

Over poems and Penny and my helplessness.

Everything I cannot fix. My thoughts become an unstoppable whirlwind.

My throat tightens. I need air. Breathe. Pressure builds in my chest. My heart is beating fast. Too fast, a rushing rhythm.

I grasp my mom's ruby necklace. Stay present. Fight.

Slicing through the tornado of fears, a persistent breeze circulates—*Accept what I cannot change*. A piece of my calming mantra.

Again and again, I repeat it. Until my breathing no longer stumbles.

My next breath is deep and steady and fills my lungs with a sawdusty smell, pulling me back to the room. The recently remodeled police station. Vera's checking email on her phone. Aarya's talking with her parents. I'm okay.

I scan the walls, searching for something to ground me, and my gaze lands on a thank-you plaque to Steele Sugar. For the millions they donated to the new building. The Steele's have their hands in everything in Everbeach.

And there goes the Queen Wasp of Steele Enterprises. Vera interrupts the receptionist on the phone and not so quietly asks what's taking so long.

"Such a shame." Dawn's mom catches my attention,

drowning out Vera's questioning. "This is why it's so important to read your Bible. Surround yourself with good Christian friends. The devil's always waiting to tempt you."

Oh great, another one of Mrs. Thorne's holier-than-thou speeches. I try to catch Dawn's eye, but she's focused on her mom.

"You don't know if Penny was reading her Bible or not," Dawn says.

"I know I hadn't seen her at church in a long time. And only God can know someone's heart, but their actions are telling."

"Maybe now's not the time to—"

"When's a good time? Someone has to say it. She was skipping church and youth group and doing who knows what. That's why I'm so proud of you, honey. You're there every Sunday, a Bible study leader. I don't have to worry about you ending up like this."

"Mom..." Dawn's voice trails off. Her lips move but no words come out, like she's struggling for what to say next. I wish I could jump in and save her, tell Mrs. Thorne how ridiculous she sounds, but Vera would have my head for disrespecting the oh-so-important-wife of Everbeach's star pastor.

"You can't give sin an inch or it will take a mile."

Mrs. Thorne may as well have thrown a bucket of cold water on me, equating Penny's disappearance with sin. Like Penny somehow deserved this?

Dawn shifts her eyes from her mother to the floor, squinting like her head hurts. "We don't know. We're not sure what happened." Is that what I look and sound like when I yield to Vera?

"Well, I'm not convinced these poems point to anything new. If she would've turned back to God...had more faith, she could have beat her depression. Those doctors and medications were just Band-Aids."

Okay, that's it. I can at least rescue Dawn from this conversation. But just as I'm about to get up and walk over to her, the large door on the opposite side of the room opens.

"Thanks for your patience," Detective Anderson says. "Please join me in the conference room."

Vera is first through the door with everyone filing in behind her and taking their seats. I spin back and forth in my chair, an almost soothing motion. Vera grabs my knee, hard. I stop moving, but she clings on, digging her nails into my skin. I clench my jaw, refusing to acknowledge the pain shooting up my leg. I glance at Vera sitting there straight backed, as if nothing is amiss.

Aarya whispers, "What's wrong?" I guess I didn't hide it as well as I thought.

Vera quickly releases her grip.

"Alright, let's see what you have." Saved by Detective Anderson.

Aarya stares at me a moment longer, and I can see her frustration in the furrow in her brows and rise of her chest. But she backs down and turns to the detective.

Elle slides the manila folder over to him.

Detective Anderson reads each letter, then looks at us with raised eyebrows. "And who was it that initially received these letters?"

"I did," Elle says.

"And how do you know Penny?"

Elle's dad looks like he's going to answer, but Elle cuts him off. "My mom knew Penny's mom."

"When did you get them?"

"Yesterday. In my mailbox. The package wasn't postmarked"

"So, someone left it there. Did anyone see someone out of the ordinary at your house?"

Elle shakes her head no.

Detective Anderson tucks our only remaining pieces of Penny back in the folder. "Do these poems mean something to any of you?"

Silence.

"Okay. Well, you might need some time for them to trigger something. I'll keep the originals, but I can make copies for you all." Detective Anderson pauses, tapping the folder on the desk. "There's been a change to the investigation. And with the arrival of these letters, there's something you should know."

He clears his throat and continues. "Penny is no longer classified as a runaway. Her disappearance is now being investigated as an abduction."

Abducted.

Devastation settles in my bones.

"Was it someone from the hospital?" Vera asks, concern lacing her tone.

"We aren't discussing our leads at this time," Detective Anderson says. "If you think of anything related to the poems, anything at all...any reason for you to think someone wanted to hurt Penny, we need to know."

He looks at Elle, Aarya, Dawn, holding their gazes long enough to convey his authority, and when his eyes meet mine, a grave sense of peril surges through my veins.

"Now it's important you listen carefully to what I have to say next. We have reason to believe it was a violent abduction. The risk is too great for you to poke around on your own. I know these letters came to you, but you must leave this investigation to us. Do you understand?"

I think I nod. But I don't know. When he speaks again, his voice is muffled, like he's far, far away and I'm buried under abduction, violence, danger, heaped one on top of the other.

"Reach out immediately if someone tries to contact you again."

I look to Aarya and see the same inner turmoil. Confusion, shock, fear, all mixed in a spinning wheel of new information. It's luring me. Closer to the spindle. Stop.

But I can't. I won't.

Half of me feels sick, stomach roiling over the depravity. Someone took her from that tower, cut off her braid against her will to make it look like she changed her appearance and disappeared into the night. But the other half of me is steel. Penny needs me. She needs *us*. Because she is not a runaway.

She is a victim. And she left a message for each of us. Messages that make no apparent sense yet manage to scream one thing.

Help.

CHAPTER 4
THE PUNCH
AARYA

Abducted strikes a different punch than *runaway*. The whispers wind through the halls on the first day of school like an electric eel. Some of my classmates look down when I pass. Others give me watery looks of sympathy but still keep their distance. I honestly can't take it. I have no idea how I'm going to get through this day.

Swim. I will swim my way through it.

I count down the time until lunch when I can get away. There's no way I can handle sitting in the cafeteria, with the gossip simmering. Instead, I swing open the heavy door to the pool, breathe the familiar smell of chlorine, the sticky heated air enveloping me in much needed silence. I'm alone.

Except...for Punkaj Grimsley.

He sits against the cement wall reading a book. "I'm going to kick your ass at practice today," Punkaj says without looking up.

I snap his book closed by way of an answer. I feel like I can breathe again. *Someone* acting normal. Who knew seeing Punkaj would ever be something I'd welcome? He narrows his eyes at me, stands up, peels off his hoodie and rolls down his warmups. I do a double take. Since when does Perfect Punk have a perfect six-pack? It's bad enough he always manages to eke out a higher GPA than me. Now he's suddenly all built, and might swim faster than me, too? Punkaj catches my eye and smirks. "Checking me out?"

I pretend to vomit. "Don't mistake observation for attraction. What did you do? Spend the whole summer working out so you could keep up with me?"

Punkaj raises an eyebrow. "You talk a big game. Round of Sink or Swim before practice?"

"This again?" I roll my eyes, but inside, I'm grateful for the momentary break. Whatever keeps me from the reality of the day. "Afraid you're going to lose?" Punkaj presses.

I flip my hair, grasping at anything that feels familiar. "I've been beating you since we were six. I always stay under longer." I do an about-face and dive into the pool. When I surface Punkaj is right there, ready.

"One. Two..." We each take a deep breath.

I close my eyes and drift down, hands hanging at once heavy and light, dead weights pushed back with a softness. My knees graze the cement at the bottom. When I leave my eyes squeezed shut like this, it's like I'm deep under the ocean, somewhere layered with indigo and turquoise, where schools of fish flick and flash, as fast as the myriad things that could have happened to Penny.

The possibility of an abduction shouldn't be such a blow. Penny is *not* a runaway. Penny runs *to* things. She always told me to do the same—to run straight through emotions. Blow them up head on. Life is manageable that way, tiny flecks of pain like dew glistening, instead of the flood that can drown you.

Except—the flood still came, chasing or dragging Penny out of Hightower.

Penny's poem whispers. *Take a deep dive, raise your voice in support...* A dive where? Whose voice? Hers?

Suddenly bubbles churn around me, arms are beneath me, and I'm yanked to the surface and hauled to the side of the pool.

"What the hell Aarya!" Punkaj sputters, letting go only after placing both my hands firmly on the ladder.

"What's your problem?" I try to get my bearings.

"You win, okay? You win. Don't ever do that again."

"Do what?"

"Stay down there like that. That was crazy long. You... you scared me."

"It was *that* long?" It couldn't have been. But Punkaj is flustered. That never happens.

"I held my breath longer than I ever had," he says. "And you were down there like three times as long."

"Sorry. I was caught up in my thoughts."

"Penny?"

"Always."

"I know." Punkaj's voice doesn't hold its usual edge.

The silence that follows isn't empty.

"Can I, uh, help at all?" Punkaj sounds like he's trying on the words for size.

"Are you being *nice* to me?"

"Come on. I'm not that big of an asshole."

"Ehhhh." I make a face, mostly teasing, but also a little bit not.

Punkaj's forehead creases. "Hearing my mom on TV all, *breaking news at eleven, shocking twists in the case of*

Penny Zale..." He shakes his head. "It's completely surreal; that she was talking about someone we know."

Frustration with the police simmers, and I find myself doing something unusual. I ask for Punkaj's opinion. "Do you feel like we're getting the whole story?"

"Not sure yet," Punkaj says. "*You* certainly don't."

"What makes you say that?"

"You look like you're a volcano about to explode." He doesn't say it in his usual all-knowing way.

But he's right. I do feel like I'm about to erupt. Lava is an emotion. Punkaj pushes his wet hair off his forehead. "Hey. When I tried to talk to you at the vigil... I do want to do a story for *The Mirror*. But not about Penny, not exactly. More on how a facility of that level loses a patient."

"Mistakes happen."

Punkaj's dark eyes scan my face. He doesn't let me off the hook. "You have questions."

Why is he always so perceptive? "No. I just can't believe it's reality. It's like a movie. Friends aren't supposed to get...*taken*."

Punkaj is silent for a moment, then says, "There's a word my mom uses. In Bengali. *Mon kharap*."

"I know it. It means *sad*."

"Not just sad. She said it's more of an overarching feeling like something is keeping you down. Abstract gloominess. The feeling of weight on the mind."

I glance over at Punkaj to find him already looking at me. I swallow a lump in my throat at the constant, abstract, heaviness of Penny's disappearance.

Mon kharap it is.

"Yeah. So I'll let you know if I find out anything interesting," Punkaj says.

"Thanks."

"You're welcome for saving your life," he adds.

"I wasn't drowning."

"Could've fooled me." Punkaj pulls himself out of the pool and ties a towel around his waist, water beading on his broad, brown chest.

"Hate you," he says.

Our usual goodbye. "Hate you more."

"Hate you the most," we say at the same time.

As Punkaj walks away, I feel an odd tug. I *like* hating Punkaj Grimsley today. It gives me something to feel that is straight forward. Hating Punkaj is as orderly as swimming laps.

———

Order is hard to hold. I see and feel Penny everywhere.

She leans against a locker, tossing her golden braid over her shoulder, grinning with excitement. She reaches for my arm, to steer me through the crowded hallway. She only exists like this—in my tortured imagination.

Where is Penny Zale? The question grates down my spine like a succession of black piano keys, all the sharps and flats. I reach into my pocket to touch the letter, paper already softened from being folded and unfolded, read and reread.

"Hey." Someone taps my shoulder. Dawn. Her face is like a wilted flower. "This is awful," she says.

"I know."

"Where are you going?"

"Drama. You?"

"Journalism." She gestures to the fancy camera that's almost always hanging from her shoulder.

I nod. There's nothing to say, and that says so much. Dawn squeezes my arm and her fingers trail away.

I look up from where she was touching me to see Elle Glass. "Since when do *you* go to school here?"

"Since today," Elle says.

"Today sucks."

"Yeah. I can't believe—"

I cut her off. "Not here. Elle nods in agreement. She's somehow made our preppy uniform look edgy by untucking the back of her shirt and popping her collar. She's wearing homemade looking sea glass earrings, and her hair spills in messy, natural, beach waves down her back. She does *not* look like she's from Everbeach.

"Where did you transfer from?" I ask.

"Public school."

So vague.

"Public school," I repeat, waiting.

"I'm here for the art program," Elle offers. "It's got a really amazing reputation."

"Um, cool." I mean, I can't force her to tell me more. "Well, welcome to the Academy. Sculpting the bright minds of Everbeach's future. Do you know where you're going?"

"Drama class?"

"Lucky you. That's my next class, too. And Raven's." I gesture for Elle to follow me to the auditorium.

I spot Raven in the second row and head her way.

"Look who I found." I point to Elle.

Raven looks as surprised as me. "You're a student here?"

Elle gestures to her uniform. "It would appear so."

"Here we all are then, I guess," I say.

"Here we are," Raven echoes.

Without Penny. With this new girl. Other students start filling the seats.

"Can I sit here?" Dawn's boyfriend Grayson McKinley swoops in.

"Of course. Grayson, this is Elle. She's new."

"Nice to meet you Elle." He sits down next to her. "Where are you from?"

"Ash...ville," Elle answers.

I narrow my eyes. "I thought you said public school?"

"Right." Elle doesn't seem fazed. "Not here though. Ashville."

"Ashville? Love it there." Grayson grins widely.

Elle flashes a poised smile back. "You look like someone who would love it there."

Grayson frowns. "What's that supposed to mean?"

"It's full of uptight people pretending to be artsy," Elle says.

I burst out laughing at Grayson's crestfallen expression. Elle had Mayor McKinley's rule following, perfectly put together, preppy son pegged in a whole two point five seconds.

A lilting voice interrupts us. "I cannot *wait* to meet the new drama teacher."

I cringe. The Tremaines.

I lean in close to Elle. "Meet god's gifts, Nikki and Katarina Tremaine. Identical twins, equally obnoxious."

Elle squints. "They look familiar."

Their faces remind me of little girl shoes, bulbous chins like a rounded toe, blank square buckles for eyes. But they're always immaculately put together, with glossy hair, perfect nails and makeup—a not-pretty-pretty.

I motion for Elle to lean in so we can gossip with Raven. "They're vultures. Whenever Penny and Logan broke up Nikki was there, hovering. Watch out. They'll go after you just because you're new and pretty."

"Remember the yacht we saw in the picture?" Raven

asks. "Logan and Hunter took the twins out to the Bahamas and did who knows what? And of course, he begged for Penny to forgive him right after."

"Straight up takers," I say. "Their mom married into money, got divorced and kept the change. Bought a trailer park of all things. I mean great, go her. But it's not like she earned it."

"She owns a trailer park?" Elle looks like she swallowed hot coffee too fast.

"You okay?" Raven asks. "Don't worry, we've got your back. They've been like this forever. Literally since kindergarten, when they made fun of the bright cotton dresses my dad would bring back from Jamaica so badly I stopped wearing them."

"And they used to tell me I smelled like curry." I roll my eyes. "They only have power if you let that crap bother you."

Elle absorbs this information. "Thanks. At least I know to have my guard up."

"Okay class settle down! I'm Mister Alpine, honored to be joining the faculty here and beyond excited to make Everbeach Academy renowned for its theatrical prowess."

Just as the lanky new drama teacher launches into roll call, the doors in the back of the room swing open and close with a double bang. "Logan Steele, present." As if we were all waiting for him. *Please*.

Raven throws her sweater over the seat next to us to make it look taken, while Nikki quickly clears her bag from the seat next to her to make room. Logan takes the bait and sits down between the twins.

"Logannn," she purrs. "I thought the vigil was stunning. What a show of support for Penny." Nikki says in a whisper loud enough that we all can hear.

Katarina sticks out her lower lip in sympathy. "Do you like, need anything?"

I lock eyes with Raven. Are the twins seriously hitting on Penny's man? She's just been classified as abducted. Raven scrunches up her nose like it smells as rotten as it feels.

"Okay class!" Mr. Alpine tries to wrangle everyone's attention. "I thought for our first day we could play some icebreakers. All right? All right!" He bounces from foot to foot.

"Our first ice breaker is all about how convincing you can be when delivering a line. It's called two truths, one lie."

Okay, Drama Dude, *terrible* idea.

"Isn't that a drinking game?" someone calls out.

"I'm sure anything can be," Mr. Alpine's face furrows, an eleven appearing between his eyebrows. "But let's try to approach this as actors, 'kay?"

"Kay!" a couple students sarcastically repeat. We all walk to the stage and sit down in a circle on the floor facing each other.

"All right, uhhh, let's see." Mr. Alpine points to me. "Why don't you get us started? Three things, one of which is not true."

Of course, he's chosen me first, today of all days. "Uh...I like opera. I'm vegan. I'm...heartbroken."

Katarina answers. "The lie is you're vegan. I see your food on social media all the time and there's totally meat. You sing, so opera makes sense. And, heartbroken, obviously. Penny."

"Right." My voice sounds small, even to me. Hearing Penny's name and heartbroken together out loud, in Katarina's singsong voice, makes every joint in my body lock up. I clench and unclench my fingers, like that will remind the rest of me how to move.

We continue around the circle. Elle's turn.

"Hmmm. I can ride a motorcycle, I clean houses for a living, and I have a tattoo."

"You cleaning houses is the lie," Grayson answers.

Elle smiles brightly. Too brightly. "Right."

"So that means the rest is true. You can ride a motorcycle?" Grayson sounds amused.

"Can't you?" Elle scoffs.

Logan's interest is piqued. "And you have a tattoo?"

"Don't *you*?" Elle evades Logan's question.

I try not to glare at Logan by default as he takes his turn. More like ball breakers. This poor teacher is toast. He's not going to survive a week in the teenage jungle that is Everbeach Academy. Rich kids versus dewy-eyed drama teachers. Might as well stuff him in the proverbial locker and give him a wedgie.

"I'm a billionaire..." Logan's eyes flash with mischief.

Case in point. "I can fly a plane..." He stares pointedly at Elle, the new girl, fresh meat, and makes a pouty fake innocent face. "I'm a virgin." Logan smirks with satisfaction at the snickers this elicits.

"Logan," Mr. Alpine warns.

Elle ignores the bait. "The lie is...you can't fly a plane."

"Wrong," Logan shoots back. Smug. So frickin' smug. "I've had my pilot's license for a year."

Wait. *What*?

My head snaps around. Raven looks equally appalled. We both know that he and Penny hadn't slept together yet. At least that's what Penny said.

"Don't be like that, Logan," Raven mumbles. It's soft, but Logan hears her.

"Like what?" he asks.

"Never mind," Raven replies.

I'm not about to let it drop so easily. "Like you're *not* still a virgin," I snap at him.

"Okeeeeey how about we move on to a new icebreaker," Mr. Alpine suggests. Logan turns to me with a smirk. "How would you know?"

"I know it wasn't Penny. So, if you're *not*, then...you suck even worse than I already thought." I wish I could shoot laser beams from my eyes.

Mr. Alpine tries again. "Ladies and gentlemen this is inappropriate!"

Logan ignores the floundering new teacher. "Maybe you didn't know Penny as well as you thought."

A face comes into focus across the circle from me. Elle's furious expression could be my own. Her hazel eyes flash amber, and she turns on Logan. "Are you for real right now? Penny is *missing* and you're talking about her like that?"

"Enough!" Mr. Alpine begs.

"Leave him alone," Nikki cries, as if Logan is somehow the victim.

"Since when do *you* know Penny?" Logan sneers at Elle.

"Since when do *you*?" Elle coats the word like an oil slick right back at him. "All you ever did was cheat on her."

Whoa. She went there.

"Cheat on her?" Logan's face closes. "Says who?"

"Penny," Elle answers.

"Yeah, well. Penny's *crazy*."

"Don't..." Elle warns.

"Just saying." Logan shrugs, with an unaffected ease that makes me seethe. "Penny got locked up for a reason."

I'm still trying to process his words when Elle's fist

connects with Logan's face. It's the most satisfying sound I've ever heard.

Nikki and Katarina gasp, covering their mouths in overdone horror.

"Are you *crazy*?" Logan holds his face, wincing. And then Mr. Alpine is standing between Elle and Logan, guiding her a few steps back. "You are both going to the principal's office immediately!"

"Gladly." Elle stalks off the stage.

Logan mumbles a string of curse words before skulking down the aisle, and says to no one in particular, "Where the hell did *she* come from?"

The door closes behind them. The collective shock leaves silence for a few seconds and then everyone explodes, buzzing in reaction.

As my heartbeat slows, Logan's words replay.

Where the hell *did* Elle come from?

Two truths. One lie. Maybe it isn't just a game. Maybe people right in front of me know more than they're letting on. Elle did come out of nowhere. With messages from Penny. And Logan is, well, Logan.

Punkaj is right. I have questions. And one of them is this: Am I watching two liars hide one truth?

CHAPTER 5
BROKEN PRINCE
RAVEN

need to get out of here. Fortunately, my last class is study hall, easy to sneak out unnoticed. I hurry down the hall avoiding eye contact with everyone I pass. One single thought on repeat.

Elle. Punched. Logan.

What the hell made him say something like that about Penny? It isn't his style to be such a blatant ass.

And the new girl, so savage, delivering the clap back of the century. Definitely someone I want to be friends with. She made Academy history today.

When the bell rings in five minutes, everyone will flood the hallways talking about it. To avoid the surge, I practically sprint to the parking lot.

I hop in my car and instant déjà vu.

The last time I skipped out early was with Penny, and it's like she's right there in the car with me. She made fun of me for never rolling down the convertible top. I explained she didn't understand one disastrous word and what said word did to my hair: *humidity*. Penny responded that I didn't understand another word: *carefree.*

Right now, this moment, I need carefree like a wish needs a star.

I push the button, and the convertible top drops back. The sky and sun greet me. When I see students pouring into the parking lot, I take off; humidity be damned.

I make a quick stop at the florist to pick up a bouquet of sunflowers, then get back on the highway.

An urgent ache grows in my chest. Penny's words echo. I've memorized them already, writing and rewriting her cryptic lines while pretending to take notes in class all day. *Portraits in mirrors make it much clearer. They point at nightmares...and ask you who's nearer...and discreet.*

What is Penny trying to say? Is the poem a clue or could it mean something else...something specific to me, something I should have told her but didn't?

Heaviness settles creating a deep hollow in my stomach. Pedal to the floor, I gun it to the highway, faster and faster, but I can't outpace my guilt.

I lift my foot, and my car coasts to the speed limit.

Mirrors and nightmares and discreet. Maybe Penny found out what I was keeping from her. Maybe she knew instinctively. Maybe I shouldn't have avoided her until it was too late.

The incessant pit spreads from my stomach to the tips of my fingers.

No. Four of us received letters. It can't be about that.

After easing my car around a bend, I take a right down a desolate side road. My tires kick up the sand blown onto the street. I pull off into the bike lane and park in a place I wish I didn't have to be.

When I go to close my roof, I hesitate. Puffy clouds dot the sky. Penny drove around in her Jeep with the top and doors off constantly, never caring if rain was coming. So today, neither will I.

I grab the flowers and head toward the entrance sign, which reads, *The Villas at Hightower: The premier shining light to heal mood and anxiety disorders.* In the distance, the looming white stucco institution sprawls out on both sides across the meticulously maintained hospital grounds. A hexagonal structure juts several stories higher than the rest of the building. *The Tower.*

Rows of small rectangular windows line the exterior walls. It looks more like a prison than a beacon of any kind of light. I shudder at the contrast of what Hightower claims to be to what it was to Penny. The road to her hell.

At the base of the sign is a makeshift memorial for Penny. The wind carries the scent of freshly mowed grass. Colorful flowers rest next to a toppled teddy bear dressed in the Academy's uniform. Votive candles burnt down to the wick dot the perimeter, and...there's someone lying in the grass.

His tan, muscular arms are folded behind his head. A t-shirt hugs his lean frame. Off to the side there's an Academy sport coat, button-down shirt and tie. As I get closer, I recognize the stranger's disheveled sandy blonde hair, and icy rage freezes my veins.

"Not who I expected to see." The nerve of Logan, to show his face here after what he just said.

"Trust me, I wasn't looking for drama round two either." He looks away, jaw clenched. "I can't believe that girl punched me."

"How's your eye?"

"Still there."

I lean in to get a better view. "It's already starting to get a little purple. You'll have a nice black eye." I probably sound too excited and brace for his reply.

"Guess I deserved it."

I stare wide-eyed. Since when does Logan own his behavior?

He laughs, then winces, clearly in pain. "I can be a jerk sometimes."

"Sometimes? Try most, or better yet, all of the time."

"Wow, tough crowd."

"What you said was low. Even for you."

Logan is silent—the loudest part of our conversation yet. He wraps his arms around his knees and bends his head. When he sits up and his gaze locks with mine, sorrow glistens in his smoky eyes. A rare vulnerability. If I didn't know better, I'd think he's trying to stop tears before speaking again.

"Why did you say what you did?"

Logan regains his composure and looks right at me, sharp. "It's what assholes do. And I'm an asshole. Remember?"

I'm caught by the edge in his voice, and I purposely ignore his pointed reference. We are not talking about *that* today. "Are you trying to say you're not? That you really love Penny?"

"Maybe it's both. I'm an asshole *and* I love Penny."

"Could've fooled me. Did you even visit her when she was in Hightower?"

He cocks his head. "Did you?"

"I wasn't the one dating her," I say.

"And I was?"

"Weren't you?"

"There's a lot you don't understand," Logan says.

"And I don't care to. She's gone, you're still here, and I barely spoke to her before she was locked away." I want to add *because of you*, but I don't. He knows.

Logan stares at the grass in front of him. "I never had

a chance to talk to her again either. After her parents brought her here. I was already in New York for my internship. And, well...I guess it doesn't matter now why I didn't come back and visit. Only that I didn't."

"I don't understand why she was in Hightower," I say.

"Her mom told me it was a mental breakdown."

"Was it really so bad they brought her here?" I motion to the monstrous hospital behind us.

"She didn't give me much information. Only that it came on suddenly."

"I should have been there," I say.

"You can't blame yourself."

"I could have done more."

Logan turns to me and holds my gaze when he says the next words. "And maybe things could have gone down differently, but they didn't."

He's not talking about Penny's disappearance anymore. But it's nothing I want to discuss. Not now. Probably not ever.

I grab my flowers and stand. It's unfair of him to bring this up. I need to change the subject and get out of here.

"Hey, Steele?" I say.

"Hey, Snow."

"You got beat up by a girl." There. Right back in the place where he belongs.

"Yeah, I think I did." Logan picks up his flowers and joins me next to the memorial. "Sunflowers were her favorite." He nods to our matching selection.

"Sunny and bright. Like her." Silence stretches while we both stare at the mementos for Penny. "I'm so worried about her. I can't stop asking myself where she is. If they'll find her in time."

"I am, too. My dad's pulled out all the stops, too. Has his people on it. And still, nothing."

I glance sideways at him. With Harvey Steele's pull and connections with the police, would they have told him about the letters? They wouldn't have, it's classified, right? I slide one hand into my purse and grasp the poem. "I hope the police are doing something," I hedge, seeing if maybe he'll offer up whether he *does* know about them.

"It feels like they aren't, now that we don't have the daily searches." He glances past the memorial to the open field where the police tents were set up for all those endless weeks.

If he knows, he's not saying a word. "I thought the same thing. It's weird, this place feels so empty now."

"Yeah. Everything feels...off. School. Drama. The things I said I know I shouldn't have." Logan places his sunflowers on the memorial. Raw emotion spreads from his eyes across his chiseled face.

He admitted he was wrong again. He brought her favorite flowers. And he's clearly hurting, missing her—like I am. I don't know what to do with this Logan, so I simply nod toward the flowers and say, "That was nice of you."

He offers me a crooked smile. "Well, don't tell anyone, wouldn't want that getting around."

"What, that Logan Steele might *actually* have a heart?"

"Definitely not for anyone to know." Logan runs his fingers through his hair, and my attention is drawn to the tight fitted sleeve around his muscled arm. My eyes trail down his broad chest to where his shirt lifts a little to reveal a hint of his abs underneath.

Unwelcome heat rises to my cheeks. Time to leave. I set my sunflowers down next to the teddy bear. "I need to get going."

"Yeah, I'm heading out soon, too."

I say good-bye and walk to my car. When I glance back, Logan is watching me. He waves, and I return it, before shrinking into the front seat.

A sleek, black car pulls up behind me, and it clicks why I didn't know anyone was here when I parked. Of course there wasn't a car. Logan never drives himself anywhere. He has a personal driver always on call.

I need to put legit physical distance between us. Yes, Logan is hot, and yes, he is still an asshole, even if he admitted he was wrong for once. I hit the gas, needing to find *carefree* again.

Being out here, in the open expanse where we searched endlessly for Penny, seeing the Tower again, realizing the possibility that she could truly be gone—it pulls at something familiar: a ravenous void feeding on my deepest fears, powered by my greatest loss. I touch my mom's necklace and then kick my car into sixth gear, racing my thoughts again.

The detective's warning echoes. *Dangerous. Violent. Abducted.*

I push the pedal down harder, and the needle inches around the speedometer.

Images flash. The search tent. Penny's braid. Her hoodie.

With each wild turn down the highway, the wind stretches and pulls my tightly wound threads taut. It feels like I'm at the edge of a cliff and Penny's out there, battered on the rocky shores, beckoning me with whispered truth. I'm ready to take the leap, and I whisper back, words that feel like I'm shouting from the rooftops, *Penny, I'm here, I will find you, and I will never let you down again.*

CHAPTER 6
HOLDING COURT
RAVEN

All my resolution comes to a screeching halt when I get home and see Vera on the back patio and remember what day it is.

I close my eyes and steady my breath. What was I thinking coming straight home? I know better than this. I always make plans with Aarya to stay away from home today, to avoid my triggers and Vera's wrath, but with Penny's disappearance, I completely forgot.

Vera kneels in the garden, hunched. Her normally controlled hair cascades around her shaking shoulders, and I can tell she's crying. My gut twists, and I'm surprised by the tug I feel to comfort her.

I find myself opening the French doors and stepping out onto the patio, despite instinct telling me to run. I walk over to Vera and place a hand on her shoulder. She flinches.

"Are you okay?"

"What do you think?" Vera wipes her face with both hands and stands. Her tone isn't harsh, despite the bite of her words. She gives me a small nod and looks over at the five gray stones with flowers planted behind each one. "Today would have been the last baby's birthday."

"I know." She didn't say it in an accusatory way like I expected. More solemn, broken, and it softened my edges, but only a little.

"I took the afternoon off. I'm on my way to the spa." Vera smooths her dress. She looks at me with raised eyebrows and a questioning gaze. "Would you want to join me?"

I startle. Step-daughter-and-mother bonding time is not our thing. At all. Ever. Especially when my dad isn't around. "I, uh, have to study. For drama." Good one. Who studies for drama class?

"Study. For drama." Vera's chin quivers, and it seems real. Not her normal show. "I'll just head on out then." Vera twists her hair up into a bun. This is closer to the Vera I know. "By the way, Detective Anderson called. They couldn't authenticate the poems. Anyone could have written those letters. They're a dead end."

"What?" I try to keep my composure, but I'm flooded with anger. "I *know* they're from her. It's her handwriting and—"

Vera holds her hand up, cutting me off. "Listen. He reiterated the danger of the situation. He wants me to make sure you girls are staying out of it. Please tell me you and your friends are leaving the poems alone, letting the police handle it?"

"Sure..." I should have said it a little bit more convincingly and maybe not rolled my eyes at the same time.

"I'm serious, Raven. Your father will be livid if I don't protect you from doing something stupid."

I cross my arms. "How could helping Penny ever be stupid?"

"When you ignore the authorities. This isn't a request. Even beyond your father, think about what I do. I'm chief counsel for Steele Enterprises. How will it look if you ignore what the police say and get yourself in trouble? We have a reputation to uphold."

"I don't care about reputations when Penny is—"

"We all care about finding Penny. But this is a job for the police. What do you think you can do that they haven't?"

"Like they've done such a great job so far."

"Raven, clearly, I'm not getting through to you. I don't want to have to do this, but..." She pauses, rubbing her temple and looks up for a moment. "If you go against what I'm asking, you can forget basketball this season."

"No...you can't—my scholarship offers. If I don't play, they'll be rescinded."

"I most certainly can and I will. If you can't be trusted to do what's expected, then you leave me no choice. The ball's in your court, quite literally." And there's her tightlipped smile again. "So, are we in agreement?"

My dad's not here to protect me. He still hasn't called or returned any texts. At this rate, by the time I get ahold of him to plead my case, the season will be over, and all of my plans ruined.

I'm stuck and she knows it, so I have to agree for now. "Understood."

For a second, Vera looks like she's going to hug me good-bye, but instead, she puts on her sunglasses.

I don't know what's more shocking: Vera threatening to take basketball away or actually-maybe-almost hugging me.

"By the way, I got something for you." Vera pulls a prescription bottle from her purse and hands it to me.

I swallow, a thick, stabbing sensation like a jagged

lump of coal is stuck in my throat. I can't even look at the bottle. "What are these?"

"Anti-anxiety meds. I called your psychiatrist and got them filled for you."

"But I can't...I don't need them." I try to hand the bottle back to her.

"I talked it over with your doctor. She thinks you're in a much better place now, and you can handle having them on hand. Don't think I didn't see what happened at the police station."

So she did notice my panic attack. I thought I held it together better. "I pulled myself out of it on my own. I'm fine. Really."

"I've seen the stress Penny's disappearance is putting on you. I'm trying to be preventative here. These are only on an as-needed basis. Okay?" She smiles at me, like a real smile that looks like she genuinely cares, and my resistance fizzles.

I nod and she heads out the door, leaving me clenching the bottle like it's a lifeline and my worst nightmare all wrapped up in one.

Vera seemed worried about me, and she went out of her way to talk to my doctor. Am I reading everything wrong? Like in the limo. My dad said Vera tried, but I shut her down. And now...is she threatening basketball to trap me, or does she really care and want to keep me safe?

Maybe I'm missing cues. Or maybe I know better.

I can never forget what happened.

Everyone has that moment. Where you look in the mirror and what you see is not what you get anymore. When everything changes and you are never, ever the same again.

For me, it was *that* summer after eighth grade, on my

thirteenth birthday, the last spa day Vera ever planned for us.

I look over at the painted iron table, with intricate swirl patterns now chipping slightly at the edges. I remember the tea pot and tower of pimento cheese sandwiches, lemon scones, and blueberry muffins—my favorites—a ruse for Vera's true plans that day. No, I couldn't go with Vera to the spa today or any day.

Right now feels too much like four years ago. When I sat at that table waiting for Vera to join me. The day I saw the flowers and stones for the first time.

"I have something special planned for you." Vera's tone dropped on *you*, as if the word tasted like a rotten apple. "Come over here and see."

I joined her by the garden, where she motioned for me to take a closer look. White bell-shaped flowers hung upside down on green branches. Just in front of the plants were five gray stones with a single name etched on each one. Names I didn't recognize.

"Do you see the names on the stones?"

"Yes..." My voice trailed off. A whispered dread of understanding.

Vera was eerily calm as she nodded. "I think you'll want to sit down for this." She took her seat at the table, and I followed. "Do you know why we would need a graveyard back here?"

I shook my head no, afraid to speak.

"Have you ever wondered why your father and I haven't had any children?"

"I thought maybe it wasn't...you know, your thing, with your career and all."

"You thought wrong. We've tried." She leaned forward. "I've been pregnant five times, and every single one ended prematurely. Five children. Five deaths."

I sucked in a breath. "I didn't know."

"Of course you didn't. Your father never wanted to tell you. He didn't want you to suffer." Vera scowled and looked away. When she spoke again her voice was distant. "He protected you over me. I had to endure the pain privately, silently, while you just went about your life, knowing nothing different."

"When was the first..." I couldn't say the words.

"Right after Clive and I married."

"I was seven." Confusion and shock thrummed through my veins. Did Vera really expect my dad to tell me when I was so young? "I was just a little girl."

"You were never just a girl. You've always been *her* daughter. My constant reminder of what your father did to me."

"I don't understand."

"You will."

"Do you know why I picked these flowers to plant for my babies? They're called lily of the valley. Some people call them our lady's tears." Vera took a sip of her tea, like we were having a casual conversation and she wasn't squeezing my heart with her words. "The name suited my pain, for the tears I've cried over something I've desired all my life."

"But you have me," I whispered.

"You are *not* mine. These five babies, these five little lives that never came to be...I'll always mourn them. And you'll always be nothing more than a painful reminder. Make no mistake about this, you stole every chance I ever had at being a mother."

I had no words. But Vera didn't seem to care.

She pulled out a small wooden box wrapped in a red ribbon and pushed it toward me. "Open your birthday present. It's time you know the whole story."

That coffin-like box contained the last, shattering truth, the final nail sealing my heartbreak.

I push down the memory of what I learned next, refusing to allow any more of that terrible day into the present.

Because what I learned next destroyed my understanding of who I was in this world. It means I deserved everything Vera said to me and probably more. It was the blow that sent me spiraling down into a wasteland of blue pills and empty prescription bottles and a deep belief I should never have been born.

I look down at the bottle in my hand, my grip so tight my knuckles are turning white. The chasm opens wide and my pulsing blood seeps and pulls, panic taking hold, looking for a release. It would be so easy to take one right now.

No. I drop the bottle.

I dart out the front door, grab my ball from the garage, and sprint across the driveway, dribbling hard and fast. I shoot up to the hoop, right arm, right knee lifting in unison. The ball slams against the corner of the box and swishes through the hoop. I take shot after shot like this, driving hard and banking the ball, refusing to stop until my limbs are shaking and my thoughts are still.

Wearing myself out on the court is its own kind of medicine. Only then do I allow myself to process what just happened.

Though her behavior today could have fooled me into thinking she cared, the reality is, Vera has me trapped in her web. I can feel the threads tightening, choking, while she waits, biding her time for my slip up, her moment to strike. She'll drain me of all life, taking away my one and only escape: basketball.

Obeying Vera means failing Penny. Defying Vera means failing my dreams.

But only if I'm caught.

I put the ball away and go back inside. With my head in a better place, I grab the prescription bottle off the ground and stash it in my purse, knowing I need to play her game to pull this off. If she really thinks she's helping me with these pills, I'll go along with it to keep the peace. I can leave them there and never take a single one.

I can't do anything to piss Vera off. I need to fly under her radar, dot my i's, cross my t's, and make it look like I'm obeying her commands—all the while doing what I need to do for Penny. It's a huge risk that could end any hope of escape through playing college basketball on scholarship and getting out of my Vera-controlled hell.

But it's a risk I'm willing to take because who's going to get Penny out of *her* hell? If the police refuse to investigate, then it's on us. It's as simple and as complicated as that.

We're Penny's only hope, and it doesn't matter what the police say, what Vera says, what *anyone* says. Penny is alone and vulnerable, possibly in the hands of someone intending to do her harm. Who maybe already has, who maybe has done the unthinkable, who maybe...

Control the things I can.

I take in a deep breath despite how it snags on my erratic, racing pulse, and let it out in a slow, controlled count down from ten...nine...eight...

I cannot and will not let fear and doubt takeover because we *can* win.

The letters are a gift—and not just one, but four, directly from the source. We have a chance, but we must make a move. Now.

Three...two...one...my breathing evens, my pulse slows, and my determination settles in. I know, without question, that I will do whatever it takes and risk it all to save my friend.

CHAPTER 7
TWISTED THREAT
AARYA

The crowd in the hall parts like the sea and Elle appears, fresh off her one-day suspension. Dawn and Raven exchange a look as she heads straight for us.

"Sooo," I say.

"Sooo?" Elle says back, like she's not sure where I'm going with this.

"Do you feel like the hero you are?"

A relieved smile creeps onto her face. "My hand hurts like hell. No one tells you that part. I probably don't know how to throw a good punch."

"Oh no, you threw a good punch," Raven says. "He has a black eye."

Elle's face falls. "For *real*? Oh man, I wanted this to all go away."

"Logan has a black eye?" Dawn exclaims.

I frown. "Wait...I've been with you all morning Raven. How did you know that?"

Raven shuffles a bit. "He was um, at Penny's makeshift memorial a couple days ago." She flicks a shiny strand of hair off her shoulder. "It was no big deal. He was leaving when I got there."

"Of *course* it's a big deal," I say. "Logan Steele just got whacked in the face! How dare he even go there anyway? After saying what he said about Penny. That's so ballsy and callous and..." I trail off.

A guy walking by holds up his hand to Elle for a high five. The girl next to him gives her a double thumbs-up.

"Half the school worships you," I tell her.

Elle looks worried. "And the other half?"

"There's always going to be a Team Logan," Dawn says, focused on the door.

A low murmur, punctuated by laughter, picks up the volume in the hall. Everyone stares at the main entrance as Logan walks in, a few books casually tucked under his arm, right eye rimmed in purple and red.

Raven fiddles with her necklace. I don't know what's worse, that she didn't mention the black eye, or is acting like the omission is somehow normal. Raven and I are constantly in touch. My mom teases me that we're intravenously connected by texts, even about the little things: which shirt to wear, the taste of a new lip gloss, quotes from a book, nail colors, news articles, songs. Bad dreams, good dreams, what time we went to bed. First to say good morning. Last to say goodnight. Our messages are like sprinkles on ice cream decorating the days, all day, every day. Logan Steele's black eye is *not* something you forget to tell your best friend about.

Logan runs a hand through his tousled blond hair looking right at Elle. He brings his middle finger to his pouty lips, eyes gleaming as he flips her off from a distance.

Oh, please.

His two best friends flank him as he approaches.

Ryan's curly brown hair sits on top of his head like a cabbage, and David's pasty face lives perpetually in the sneer of a D horror movie marionette.

"Morning sunshine," Logan says.

Elle opens her mouth and closes it again. I take a deep breath ready to unleash when Elle places a hand on my arm and addresses him herself. "Look. Logan. You know you were out of line. But...I'm sorry for hitting you. My emotions were running high."

"Right," Logan drawls. "Because you and Penny were *so* close, I never even heard of you the entire time I was with her? It's funny how when something bad happens to someone everyone suddenly becomes their best friend. How did you know her anyway? Or are you just pretending?"

"Come on, Logan, leave them alone," Grayson steps in. "Knock it off."

Dawn touches his arm, but the tension quickly fizzles when Logan just laughs and rolls his eyes.

"Get over yourself, Grayson. Don't you have some straws to ban from the cafeteria? Sea turtles to save? A social justice protest to organize?"

"I think you're walking proof of social justice in action," Grayson quips pointing to the black eye.

Good one.

"Walking proof of an asshole," I add.

"Whoa. Settle down Sea Witch." A guy with the same sandy hair and chiseled jaw as Logan tousles my hair. What the—I duck out from under it. Logan's younger brother? What's *he* doing here?

"Sea witch?" Elle looks back and forth between us.

Hunter Steele grins. "It goes way back. Our big sugar harvest party. All the kids were playing together in the pool. This one..." He points to me. "Surfaces dramatically, flips her hair, and announces with flair that she's a mermaid before bursting into song. I said 'Mermaid? Please, more like Sea Witch.' It stuck."

Ugh. Of course it did. I distinctly remember it stuck because he made it stick.

Hunter's arms widen. He's not...going to...I try to squirm out of his awkward boy-hug. I'm suffocating in the smell of surf wax and his fancy man-lotions. Death by lime verbena.

"I'm so sorry about the news. What they think happened to Penny." Hunter at least sounds sincere.

I smooth out my hair and uniform. "What are you doing here? I thought you were doing the pro-surfer thing with tutors this year?"

"Change of plans," Hunter says.

Logan scoffs. "He came back because he didn't make the cut."

"It's more complicated than that." Hunter steps in front of him. "In the surfing World Qualifying Series, you gain points per competition. You need enough points, you know, to advance. And there was an issue about a guy, whether he dropped in on me." He shrugs. "So—"

"So, he's home." Logan's voice is flat. "Going to school like the rest of us."

Wow. I almost feel sorry for Hunter. All that time invested. For what? To end up back here like everyone else.

"I'll be working, too," Hunter says. "For your mom, Raven."

Raven's eyes flash. "Vera's *not* my mom."

Hunter shrugs. "Stepmom whatever. I'm going to be her intern, learn the legal ropes. For when I run Steel Sugar one day."

Logan snorts. "That's funny. We know I'm the only one Dad trusts to take over."

Hunter ignores his brother but only because he's sidetracked. By Elle. He gives her a long, slow grin. "Hi. I'm Hunter. Hunter Steele. You must be the lightweight champ everyone's talking about."

Elle regards him suspiciously.

"We should hang out some time." Hunter angles toward her. "Get a bite to eat or something. Maybe a knuckle sandwich." He laughs at his own cheesy joke.

"You're *so* funny Hunter." Logan shakes his head. "I think we're done here." He walks away. Ryan and David follow like the good little puppets they are.

Hunter laughs some more. "See you around Sea Witch," he says. His eyes trail over Elle. "And *Slugger*, I'm serious. Anyone who gives my brother what he deserves, deserves a night out on the town."

"Give it a rest Hunter," Grayson intervenes again. But Hunter is already sauntering away.

Dawn smiles at her boyfriend. "Thank you, Grayson."

"Yeah, thanks Mr. President," I say to Grayson once the Steele brothers are gone. "We were handling it. But I guess some back up is never a bad thing."

"Mr. President?" Elle asks.

"He's class president," Dawn says proudly. "And one day he'll be president of the United States."

Elle cocks her head. "Oh really?"

"Do you not find me to possess presidential qualities?" Grayson teases.

"*I* do," Dawn says.

"All I need," Grayson kisses her on the cheek and flashes one of his signature grins.

"I mean, with a smile like that you're destined for

either politics like your dad...or toothpaste commercials," I say. "Come on. We're going to be late for class."

Late August thunder rumbles in the distance off and on throughout the day, like the sky can't decide if it wants to commit to a storm or not. It's not until Raven and I are walking out to our cars that it makes up its mind with a straight up deluge.

"Ugh. Perfect timing." We break into a jog. "My car is way in the back lot."

"Just hop in mine. It's right here," Raven says. "I'll drive you over to yours."

We dive for cover.

"Ew your seat is all wet. You left your window open."

"No, I didn't."

"Umm?" I point to the cracked window and push the seat down with my hand and water oozes out of it like a soggy sponge. I lift my butt to show her my soaked uniform.

Raven laughs. "Guess I forgot."

"Kind of like how you forgot to tell me you saw Logan the other day?"

Heavy raindrops tap against the windshield like fingers impatiently drumming.

"Aarya. It's not like that. I have a ton on my mind between Vera and Penny. I feel...trapped."

I let out a sigh. "Yeah. I get it. It's...all consuming."

A crack of thunder rattles the car.

"It's like this." I point outside. "One minute you're walking along and then *boom*. You think of Penny and suddenly you're drowning in a downpour, questioning what just happened."

The thunder rolls as if in agreement.

"What was that?" Raven asks.

"Uh, *thunder*." I laugh and gesture to the clouds, but Raven shakes her head no with conviction.

"It sounded like...it was from in here. In the car. Listen."

We both go still to focus on the sound—a low, eerie thrumming mixed with scraping and hissing.

"Ummm." Raven's voice rises, her eyes locked in the rearview mirror. "There's something back there."

I steel myself and follow her gaze. Whatever it is...it's moving. Eyes glisten. A tongue darts out. With an elegant slink, it weaves around itself.

"Holy shit! It's a *snake*!"

I grab my door handle as the snake slithers forward. Raven fumbles with the car door, screaming. Both doors open and we tumble out our respective sides, scrambling away from the car.

A crowd of students quickly gathers despite the rain, classmates venturing toward the open doors for a closer look, and their reactions swirl.

"What's going on? Are you okay?" I hear Punkaj's voice over everyone's.

"That's a *python*!" Logan says.

"Where?" Hunter pushes the crowd back and steps between us and the car. "Lemme get him." He grabs some random guy's lacrosse stick and jabs into the open door.

"Someone get the principal!" Punkaj says. "Aarya, Raven, stay back."

"I'll go," Elle says.

"I got this," Hunter says, trying to get the massive snake to coil around the lacrosse stick, but it lunges toward him. He jumps back, dropping the stick, and the snake retreats into Raven's car. "Orrr, not." He laughs.

The principal and some teachers push us all back to wait for animal control. Raven's fingers dig into my arm, and I can hear her trying to steady her breath.

"What happened?" Grayson pushes his way through the crowd with Dawn.

"Florida life," Hunter says. "Snake in the car."

"No kidding. That's what you get for leaving your window open," I joke, pushing my rain plastered hair off my face. But my heart is pounding.

It feels like we're standing out here forever before animal control finally arrives. Dawn pales at the sight of the snake as two officers work to get it out of the car. They keep its head at a safe distance with a big two-pronged fork looking thing, and deftly tuck a long pole against its body. The python wraps around it in messy loops, and they gently dangle the reptile over a plastic container, trying to get it to fit. Applause and cheering break out as the snake is dropped into the box. The excitement fades as the officers drive off, and the crowd quickly dissipates.

Even though the snake is gone, the idea of getting back inside the car makes me skittish. The two of us stand alone in the now empty parking lot.

"Well, that was...something," I say, with a big leftover shudder.

Raven's phone dings. She checks the message, and her mouth drops open.

"What's wrong?" I ask. "Who is it?"

Raven's expression is a mix of horror and confusion. "It's from an unknown number. And..." Her voice trails away.

I peek over her shoulder. "What the hell?"

Someone texted a picture of a penny, the eyes of Abe Lincoln blacked out with a sharpie like some sort of sketch of a zombie.

"That's straight up twisted," I say, swallowing a cold pit as I take in the image of the defaced coin.

Raven's voice wavers. "Is someone trying to mess with us about Penny?"

Her phone dings again and a text comes in.

> Step back. The truth bites.

A sense of dread coils around me.

Yes. Someone is.

CHAPTER 8
THE SUMMIT
AARYA

Fog swallows the spires of the Maharaja Resort. It's not unlike how I feel, confusion and unease creeping in like the mist off the ocean. Raven and I stand at the main entrance of my parent's hotel waiting anxiously for Elle and Dawn, so we can fill them in.

Dawn arrives first. "Sorry, I was at ballet rehearsal. I got here as soon as I could." She tugs nervously at a bright yellow tee shirt with *Faith in Action* across the front. "I'm skipping youth group for this. My mom will be so upset with me if she finds out."

"This is important," I reassure her.

A sputtering engine shreds the air. Elle pulls into the guest drop off circle in the ugliest truck I've ever seen. It's so rusty it's practically orange, paint flaking off in such big chunks it looks like a rotting log shedding bark.

She rolls down the window. "Where do I park?"

"Um...the valet's got you. Just hop out here. We need to show you something stat."

Elle notices me scanning her truck. "I like old things.

The aesthetic and all." She smiles the too bright smile again. "Meet Pumpkin."

"You named it?"

"I named it. And she got me here just fine after your S.O.S. text. What's going on?"

"We'll talk when we're in my room." I gesture to the hotel. "And away from prying ears."

Elle takes in the hotel's grand entrance. "You *live* here?"

"My parents own it. Follow me."

I wave them into the lobby.

"Ummmm, hold on." Elle turns in a circle with her arms up. "Are you for real? Tell me you never get used to this."

"I don't think anyone would ever get used to it. Come on." I don't slow down as I acknowledge the towering multi-story aquarium glimmering like a skyscraper of water under the glassed-in roof. Its blue light gleams out against the dark, oriental rugs.

"I mean yes. Obviously. But also...them." Elle points.

Oh. Right. *Them.*

The hotel lobby is full of life-size carved statues of Hindu gods and goddesses, smiling demurely even as they do all sorts of bizarre things. Some ride lions and swans. Some grip lutes and books in their many hands. Others, weapons. One holds up a bleeding head.

"These are amazingly ferocious," Elle murmurs.

"Meet the fam." I lightly touch each of their hands as we pass. "That one you're staring at is Kali. She looks like a monster if you don't know her story, all covered in blood, heads hanging from her neck."

"But she's um...not, right?" Dawn always looks at Kali like she's alive and completely untrustworthy as she passes.

"Nah, she kills demons. And just got carried away on

her rampage for revenge. She's misunderstood." I point to the next one we walk by. "And this is Ganesha. When someone chopped of his head, his dad saved his life by hacking off an elephant's to stick on him."

"Right place, right time?" Elle jokes.

"Unless you're the elephant," Raven says. She pushes the button for the penthouse, and I hurry the girls inside.

The doors open into our sprawling living room. My little brother glances up from his video games. I barely noticed him at first curled inside the giant leather chair. Raj gives me a look of scrutiny topped off with a sly smile. "Do you have a reservation?"

"Go back to your games." I grab an aptly named throw pillow and chuck it at his face as we walk by.

He laughs as it misses completely and lands sideways on the floor. "Should have had Raven handle the free throw."

I hurry the girls along into my room before my parents can emerge and start asking too many questions about the homework project we aren't really doing. Raven closes the door for me, shaking her head. "I love how Raj can play video games whenever he wants, but they give you such a hard time about music."

"My brother and I have the same parents. But mine are stricter," I deadpan.

I motion for everyone to grab a fuzzy, hot pink beanbag; the only things in my room I picked out. They clash horribly with the mustard and maroon paisley and heavy dark carved wood of my parents' chosen décor. We pull them in a circle in front of the floor to ceiling windows, the ocean below turning over on itself.

"Okay. We're good now," I say. "We can tell you."

"We think someone put the snake in the car on purpose to scare us," Raven says.

"Why?" Dawn asks.

Raven hands Dawn her phone. "This came in right after...from a blocked number."

Dawn's face twists as she takes in the disturbing picture and threat. Elle leans over her shoulder. "That's really messed up."

"Clearly someone doesn't want us asking questions about Penny," I say.

"The police said it could be dangerous," Dawn says.

"Vera got an update on the case," Raven says. "They're giving up on the poems!"

"What? Why?" Elle asks.

"The police said they can't trace them to Penny," Raven says.

Dawn unwinds her ballet bun with nervous energy. "The police really aren't going to help us?"

"I mean, they'll keep investigating however they do things, right?" I say. "But the poems, they're on us."

"And if you're going to be a part of this, you have to keep it a secret from all of the adults," Raven says. "Vera explicitly told me to leave the poems alone. You won't see me for the rest of the year if she knows I went against her orders. And I won't be able to play basketball this season. I'll lose everything."

I squeeze Raven's hand in solidarity, and she continues, "But I'm willing to take the risk for Penny."

"Well?" I turn my attention to the others. "You in or out?"

Elle doesn't hesitate. "I'm in."

Dawn twirls her hair around a finger, winding it up, letting it go. "Maybe it's actually as dangerous as the police say it is," she says. "Maybe everyone has our best interests at heart."

"That's cute." I glance at my guitar, untouched for months. *Sure* they do.

"Sorry," Dawn says. "But I'm worried there are thorns we can't see. The snake with the creepy message—that's an actual threat to us."

"So, are you saying you're out then?" I ask.

Dawn drops the hair she's twirling and pauses before looking me in the eyes, a steely determination there I'm not used to seeing. "Let's please agree to be careful, okay?"

Raven nods. "Of course. There's a lot at risk. Pissing off parents and police is one thing. Finding the truth about Penny is another level. Someone who abducts a teenager is...evil."

"All the more reason to not give up," Elle says softly.

"Exactly." I place my poem on the floor between us and wait.

Elle puts hers down. Raven follows suit. Then Dawn. It feels like a pact where people cut their hands and exchange blood—Penny's words, the veins of truth, tying us all together.

Elle

Hearts... turned to steel... a long time ago. To survive, walk on glass, pretend you don't know the deceit.

Dawn

Go to their church. Wake and ring the grand bell! The taste of success is a spindle from hell... and

sweet.

Aarya

Take a deep dive... raise your voice in support
Docks clocked by day, false reports that night
cheats.

Raven

Portraits in mirrors make it much clearer. They point
at nightmares... and ask you who's nearer... and
                                        discreet.

Dawn's brow furrows and her pink glossy lips purse. Raven lets out a little burst of air—*pfft*—which fits the feel of the room.

Elle speaks up. "Hang on... Hearts turned to *steel* a long time ago."

She barely gets the line out and I know where she's going. How had we not seen it immediately? "Holy shi—"

"Shmonkies. Holy shmonkies." Dawn tries to censor me.

"Shmonkies up your ass." I bulldoze forward. Dawn's mouth opens and closes. "Elle, read it again!"

"Hearts...turned to steel...a long time ago."

My heart pounds. "Steel! Steele! *Logan* Steele. Penny's trying to tell us he has something to do with it!"

The only sound in the room is our various inhales and exhales.

Raven takes a ragged breath. "You don't think he *did* something to her?"

Elle weighs in. "Their relationship was toxic, and so is

Logan. I obviously am not a fan. But what exactly are we getting at here?"

"I'm not saying he *abducted* her," I explain. "But Penny is basically calling him out on paper: walking on glass...trying to deal with deceit. Whatever happened to her, he has something to do with it."

"If she's saying anything real at all," Raven murmurs. "She sounds drugged. Delusional."

"Maybe," Elle says. "But also, maybe not."

"I say maybe not," Dawn blurts out. "Penny had her issues. But humans have a body and a soul, right?"

"If you believe in god," Elle says.

"If you believe in God," Dawn repeats. "*I* believe God created mankind to exist in each of those realities—physical and spiritual. What worries me is the dichotomy Penny lived in."

"What dichotomy?" I ask.

"Soul versus body. You can't reduce all problems to one or the other. Penny was so extreme in nature that it's easy to assume her issues were physical—that she had some sort of chemical imbalance. But I worry for her soul."

"Of course you do." I can't help but roll my eyes.

Raven motions for me to be quiet. "Go on," she says to Dawn.

"I'm just saying, what's medical and what's a crisis of faith? What if poor Penny was trapped in Hightower with only a medical diagnosis when what she really needed was *hope*?"

"You think she was in there because her soul needed a hug?" My doubt cuts the air.

Dawn holds steadfast. "I mean, read the poems. She sounds *ruined*. Someone broke her heart."

The observation rings painfully true.

And painfully obvious.

"*Logan* broke her heart," I say.

"Well, if you're that sure, should we tell the police? They said come to them with any ideas," Dawn says.

Raven shakes her head. "No way."

"Why?" Elle asks.

"First, they don't believe the poems are real, and our theory right now is based off that alone. Second, the Steeles can do no wrong in anyone's eyes," Raven says.

"They're the emperors of Everbeach," I add. "Not everyone goes around punching royalty, Elle."

"I feel nervous hiding it though," Dawn says.

"I'm nervous *not* hiding it," Raven says.

Maybe there's a compromise. "My dad said everything goes through our team of lawyers. So, we tell *them*. Once we have more proof than a couple of poems," I offer.

"Okay," Dawn agrees.

"You all have some impressive back up," Elle says. "Aarya's 'team' of lawyers, the pastor of Everbeach, and Steele Sugar's top dog? I've got...my dad." She lets out a wry laugh.

"What does he do?" Dawn asks.

"He's in...domestic shipping. Not exactly helpful in this case."

"What about your mom?" I ask.

Elle stills. "My mom is...dead."

Leave it to me to put my foot in my mouth.

"Car accident."

"I'm so sorry to hear that," Raven says gently.

We all wait for Elle to speak again. She turns her letter over in her hands. "Penny, Penny, what are you trying to tell us?"

Raven looks pained. "What is she trying to tell *me*? To

look in the mirror? To look at myself? Does she think *I* did something?"

"I mean, she's apparently telling *me* to go deep sea diving and Dawn to ring a giant bell," I point out. "We can't think surface-level. We are missing her real message. Obviously."

Dawn twirls her hair again. "Let's all think about it tonight. See if anything makes more sense in the morning. We should probably all get home. We don't want to get on parent-radar right out of the gate."

"Yeah," Raven says. "Especially Vera."

"Of course," I say. "So, I guess, see everyone in school."

Even after I walk them all out, I drift back upstairs, desperately needing time to think. Instead, when I open my bedroom door, an ambush. My parents. They perch on the edge of my bed.

"Aarya, we need some talks," says my mother.

I go with hope first. "Did the police call? Is there good news?"

Their faces don't give me what I'm searching for. They're looking at me the way they look at beggars in India when we visit; misfortune they want to plow by as quickly as possible.

"No news. Sorry." My mother tightens the braided bun at the nape of her neck. "But we want to know. Was Penny doing drugs?" Her accent catches the "*r*" making it sound like dah-rugs.

"You *know* she was on medication."

"But was she taking more than she should? Or dabbling in some type of...recreational drugs?" my father asks. "Were any of you?"

"No! What? Are you serious right now?"

"This is not an unreasonable conclusion. Penny was in

psychiatric care. Then, we hear runs away. Now we learn, maybe taken. By who? Teenagers who do drugs meet bad people," my father says. "Raven, too, had her own troubles. She isn't doing such things again, like grade eight, is she?"

"Raven? Come on." The room feels like it's pulsing. "She was going through a ton back then. You have no idea."

"When teenagers get in trouble it usually is dah-rugs." My mother backs him up.

"Penny wasn't doing drugs. Raven isn't. I'm not. None of us are. This is ridiculous!"

My mother stands up, walks to my dresser, and starts opening drawers. Not this again.

"Ma!" I push the drawer closed.

"Aarya, you'll let us take a look." She reopens it. I fade back. I may as well not even be in the room.

My father lifts each corner of the mattress on my bed, and finding nothing, lies down flat on the floor, sweeping his arm as far as he can under the bed.

I lean on the door frame, arms crossed. "Well? Happy?"

My father hauls himself to his feet with a grunt and holds out his hand. "Phone and computer."

"*What*?"

"Unlock them. We are going to go through your emails and texts."

"I cannot believe you're doing this to me when my friend is *missing*."

"That's exactly why we're doing this," my mother says. "We're not trying to violate your privacy. We're doing our job as your parents."

"We look now, together, or we take the phone away completely. Your choice."

"Go for it." I hand him the phone and gesture to my desk where my laptop is charging. "Search away. I have nothing to hide."

My guitar leans against the wall. I grab it, sit down on the floor and start strumming, daring them to tell me to stop. They know I'm trying to bother them, so they don't react. They're good at these games.

But I'm better. They'll find nothing. No internet history. No old text streams. My browser's set to clear immediately on closing. I delete texts almost as soon as they come in for exactly this reason. When you're not allowed to do anything, you get creative. A date with a guy at the movies? Going with friends. A big party on the beach? Easy, sleeping over at Raven's. An all-weekend concert? Building a house for Habitat for Humanity. I know what to say and how to make a lie parent proof. Indian parent proof.

I never make the same mistake twice.

To think, I allowed myself to believe, for even a second, that maybe just maybe they'd be impressed by my channel, my songs. That seeing it, hearing me, would make them realize, being a singer isn't a choice, it's a calling. You're so talented, I thought they'd say. *We were wrong. We support you. Go for it.*

I should have known better.

Of course, it went exactly the way it did.

I will never forget my dad's face when he scrolled, saw all the views, the thousands of "likes." Disgust. Disappointment. And shock that I would do such a thing. And then forbid me to post anything else. His eyes bugged so wide they went from his careful side part all the way to his thick black mustache.

Right now, that mustache is curled into a furry upside-down caterpillar.

When they dig up nothing, my mom's expression softens into an apology. But my father snaps the laptop shut with an arrogance that makes me want to fling it across the room.

"Thank you for letting us ease our worries," my mother says. "The police will get to the bottom of this, *bheta*."

Darling. Hardly.

I flinch out from under her formal, forehead kiss.

My father gives a curt nod. "Yes. We leave it to the police now."

"You mean Sherlock Samudra didn't find anything?" I widen my eyes in mock surprise. "Is this episode of CSI Maharaja over?"

He ignores my sarcasm. "Goodnight Aarya."

I slam the door behind him. My parents are wrong. The police are wrong. Penny isn't some drugged out runaway mixed up with the wrong crowd. If something bad happened to her, it was by no fault of her own, this much I know.

I recite her letters over and over while strumming the guitar, trying to make sense of them. The melody I pluck sounds dissonant, dull. And after a while, Penny's words feel like they're floating through the air in a tangle, and I'm about to swirl away with them. I wish I could stretch the guitar strings to tie the corners of my room to each other, hold all the lines in place.

Lines are safe. Spaces scare me. Space is...*space*, outer space, vast and dark, past weather and atmosphere...or tucked in the trap door of my mind. To come up against blankness is new for me. Holes and spaces, lost places, whole and spacious—Penny's spirit, sweeping as ever, even when locked in lines of poetry.

My guitar looks like it's tilting its chin up at me in a

challenge, as if it knows I have nothing. I'm frayed—tethered and frayed from all the talking that solves nothing. At some point even endings, end.

What good is all this discussion if it isn't helping find Penny any faster? Talking is simply how we measure losing, how we *stay* tethered, *become* frayed. All we have to go on...are some words in ink. For the first time in a long time, my mind spirals into what could almost be the lyrics of a song.

> *The ink that wells is for wishing.*
> *The wish that gives is for breathing.*
> *The breath that sighs is for giving.*
> *And the pause and the cry is just living.*

Maybe Dawn is right. Maybe there is such a thing as dying of a broken heart like all the fairy tales say.

PART TWO

Looking-glass, Looking-glass, on the wall, who in this land is the fairest of all?

—*Snow White,* Grimm Brothers

CHAPTER 9
BAD DECISIONS
RAVEN

stare at the chair across from me while Aarya goes on
about something with the poems. But it's the chair
that has my attention—Penny's empty seat.

Since freshman year we've sat here together, at a four
top in the corner of the cafeteria—me, Aarya, Dawn, and
Penny.

No one has tried to use the seat, knowing who it
belongs to, and Elle never makes it to lunch because she's
using the extra time in the art studio. So, for the past two
weeks, it's been the three of us going around and around,
trying to hammer out a plan to investigate Logan with
that empty chair staring back at me, my guilt lodged in my
throat.

Aarya snaps her fingers in my face. "Have you heard a
word we've said?"

I blink. "Did you really just snap your fingers at me?"

"Yes, and I'll do it again if I have to. You've been
checked out since we got here."

"Wow, testy much?" This is not normal Aarya behavior. Then again, I haven't exactly been myself. "You were saying?"

"We were talking about the Sugarcane Festival on Saturday," she replies.

"I'm not going to be of much help," Dawn says. "I'm in the pageant that afternoon."

"Yeah, so am I," I say. If I didn't have to, I would have bowed out long ago.

"The pageant isn't all day," Aarya says. "There's time in the morning. Logan will be there, and we need to come up with a plan to get closer to him."

I am not volunteering for that plan. It's the exact opposite of what I've done since I saw him at Penny's memorial. Nope, deflect. "You could still enter you know."

"I wouldn't dare take the title away from you," Aarya says.

"Hello. I'm in the pageant, too. You'd have to beat us both," Dawn says.

"Hate to break it to you," Aarya says, "but Raven won last year, and there's nothing to indicate she won't win again unless you say a few extra hello Mary's."

"It's *hail* Mary's. What's wrong with you?" Dawn laughs and shakes her head at Aarya. "And we don't even say those. That's Catholic. I'm nondenominational."

I shift in my seat. "It doesn't matter who wins. I kind of don't want to this year."

"That's crazy talk," Aarya says. "I know *I* want you to. There's ten thousand dollars in scholarships on the line. And the look on Vera's face when you can finally say, I don't need you anymore? Priceless."

"It's not that I don't want the scholarship money. I need it. It's just..." I glance around making sure no one is paying attention and lower my voice. "I feel like we're not getting anywhere and Penny is still out there and more than likely in danger and after the snake in my car..." I shiver and trail off, thinking of it hissing from my backseat.

Dawn places her hand on my knee and squeezes. "I can't forget the threatening text. It all scares me, but then makes me even more worried for Penny."

Aarya lowers her voice, too. "That's why we need to make a plan for the Sugarcane festival. We can work around the pageant, but it's the perfect time to get close to—"

The cafeteria door swings open and the entire room's attention shifts. I casually glance up because I know who just walked in.

Logan's shirt is untucked, tie loosened, hands in his pockets, a sultry pout on his lips. He could have walked right off a movie set looking like that. Love him or hate him, Logan Steele has the *IT* factor down. His entourage trails behind.

"Speak of the devil," Aarya says.

Logan's smoky eyes meet mine, and damn if it doesn't make my heart speed up a little. He must have sensed it because his lips turn up in a smirk. But instead of looking away, he holds my gaze. He's messing up my avoidance strategy by continuing to stare and oh no—now he is walking toward me which is not acceptable at all.

"I need to go practice." I stand up, grab my bag and lunch tray, and leave without giving Dawn or Aarya time to respond. I don't look back.

I get to the gym as fast as possible and start right in on free throws—three dribbles, spin the ball, eyes on the hoop, dip, and release. The ball swishes through the net.

I do the same ritual again.

And again.

I take shots from the paint. From the three-point line. Drive in for lay-ups, drive out for long shots. Run lines. Back and forth.

Stopping at the free throw line and back. *Don't think about Logan.*

Midcourt and back. *Forget that night, the balcony.*

Opposite free throw line and back. *Let go of the guilt.*

Full court and back. *We will decipher these clues.*

We will find Penny.

In twenty minutes, I've worked up a sweat and cleared my mind.

My next shot bounces off the backboard and rolls down the court toward the entrance. Running full speed after it, I stop midstride when someone picks up the ball and dribbles toward me.

Logan.

He walks casually, dribbling with slow and controlled measure. Like everything he does.

"Can I have my ball back?"

"Depends."

"On what?"

"Did you say please?"

I put my hands on my hips and shake my head. "I was in here minding my own business, and you strolled in and stole my ball."

"You're at the disadvantage seeing how I'm the one with the ball." His smirk is back.

"Fine. Keep it." I turn away from him to head to the lockers.

"Wait. I wanted to talk to you."

The sincerity in his tone makes me stop and face him again, but I still say, "I don't have time."

Logan looks at his watch. "Fifteen minutes until next period starts."

"I'm sorry. You misunderstood. I have time to practice, not talk."

"I'll practice with you." He holds the ball with both hands, one foot back, ready to play one-on-one.

I raise an eyebrow. "You want to play in your uniform?" I look down. "And those shoes? What are those, designer loafers?"

"You sound like someone who's scared they'll lose."

Oh, he has it coming.

I post up in front of him, legs in position, arms out. Logan drives to the basket, and I shuffle keeping step with him. Right outside the paint, he pulls up short to shoot and I jump, slamming my hand into the ball and knocking it down the court. I run, grab it before he does, and beeline for the hoop, landing an easy lay-up.

I spread my arms out wide in triumph, beaming. "That's how it's done!" I say, and then freeze. This is not how this was supposed to go. "Why did you follow me?"

Logan looks at me intensely. A storm of heat. That's how it started last time. With Logan following me onto that balcony and me asking him why.

"You've been avoiding me for weeks."

"No, I haven't."

"Sure. That's why every day when drama class ends, before I even look up, you're gone."

"Probably because you're too busy talking to Nikki and Kat." Why did I say that? I don't care who he talks to.

Both his eyebrows rise but he lets my comment go. "I don't even bother coming over to your table in the cafeteria because you refuse to ever glance my way. That's why today, when you looked up, I thought maybe you were ready to talk."

"What's there to talk about?"

"That night."

If I could erase that night like a dream forgotten upon waking, I would.

It was one of the Steele fundraisers I went to with Vera and my dad, and I dealt with yet another one of Vera's subtle attacks.

"Raven, honey, that dress is not appropriate for this evening." She tsked, and like oil running down a pipe, Vera's eyes swept over me from head to toe—a drip, drip, drip of her disapproval. "I do apologize, Harvey. She's usually much better at putting herself together."

The way Vera spoke to me in front of the Steeles was hurtful and demeaning and made me want to disappear alone in a safe cabin in the woods where she couldn't get to me again. But who was I kidding? She'd probably hunt me down even then.

I looked down at my bright blue dress, with its asymmetrical chiffon skirt, cinched at the waist with a silk, fitted bodice and sweetheart neckline. It wasn't a floor length, flowing ball gown like Vera had on, but the invitation said cocktail attire. I was in line with what other girls from my school were wearing. But the damage was already done.

When Vera's martini glass was almost empty and my dad had stepped away, she shifted the spotlight back to me.

"You know, Harvey, I'm always impressed with how well-mannered and put together your boys are." Vera motioned toward me. "We all know how hard I've tried with Raven, but I'm not sure if she'll ever quite measure up to what you've done with your young men. I guess some things you have to be born with."

Harvey laughed—probably knowing how Vera feels about me—and said, "Time will tell how the Steele genes play out with these two..."

He may have said more, but I couldn't hear him. I mumbled some excuse to exit the conversation, and as soon as I turned the corner, I sprinted down an empty corridor and burst onto the balcony at the end of the hall, letting the door slam behind me. I didn't stop until I hit the railing, hands firm on the edge, gripping it tight, tight, tighter.

I couldn't get enough air.

I would never be good enough for Vera's approval. For Harvey's approval. For anyone's approval.

To fit in here.

Around these people.

In this world.

Vera's charity case. They laugh at me. In front of my face. Probably behind my back, too. *Not enough, never enough.*

The balcony door opened and shut. Quietly.

I squeezed my eyes shut, breath coming in jagged bursts.

"Breathe." A touch, gentle, grounding.

"Hey. I'm right here. Look at me." His voice soothing when it shouldn't be. Logan lifted my chin, brought my gaze to his.

"Why? Did you? Follow me?" My words matched my erratic breath.

"Vera was an asshole to you."

He was here, not laughing with Vera and his dad; an unexpected anchor tethering me to the shore. My breathing slowed. "I didn't think anyone noticed."

"Come on. Like attracts like. She's my dad's go-to for a reason."

Logan took my hand. "May I?"

"Why?"

He flipped my palm up, pressing different points. "My

mom used to do this when I was little. They're trigger points. It helped me calm down. When my dad yelled at me, she'd do this and say, *make a wish and say it out loud. Make the world what you want it to be.*"

"It must be nice. To have a mom like that."

He was quiet a moment, eyes on where he was gently squeezing parts of my hand. "What's the deal with you and Vera?" He asked quietly.

"Long story. But what you just saw...that's the G-rated version."

His molten blue-gray eyes locked on mine, his hand, no longer pressing. Instead, his thumb rubbed back and forth over my palm. "You don't deserve that." He didn't pull away and I didn't take my hand from his.

The gentle motion sent a charge through me. My senses heightened—the moonlight brighter, the wind cooler, the ocean waves louder. On my next breath, I was immersed, swimming in ocean and pine...he smelled so good.

His fingers grazed my wrist, up and down, a soothing fire. The energy shifted and held, powerful, intense.

I leaned in. Each breath. Closer. Closer. His lips pressed to mine. Pillow-soft warmth, a question waiting for an answer. All I wanted was to say yes.

But. This was Logan. And Penny. Penny! *No.*

I pulled my hand free and shoved him hard.

"You know what? You're the asshole." I left him out on the balcony alone, standing there, with the ghost of our moment dissipating in my wake.

The rage was sudden. How dare he! I was in a vulnerable state, and he took advantage of me.

But a small voice whispered: *Did he? Really? Are you so sure it was all him?*

As I stepped inside, a flash of blonde hair drew my

attention to the hallway mirror—*Penny's* reflection. I went still. She was farther down the hall, not looking at me, talking to someone. She walked away as I approached her. I had no idea if she knew Logan was out there, or what she had or hadn't seen, but my insides flipped and bubbled like a boiling cauldron when Penny slipped out of my sight. I should have gone after her and told her right then what happened.

But I didn't.

I should have called her that night. Or the next day. Or heck, any morning, afternoon, or night after. Before she was locked away.

Instead, I avoided her like the coward and horrible friend I was.

Just like I am avoiding the boy standing in front of me now.

"I thought maybe you'd let me explain," Logan says.

"There's nothing to explain."

"So, it's going to be like that?"

"Look, I'm not one of the Tremaine twins. I'm sure they'll be more than happy to play your games."

Logan squares his shoulders, looking down at me. "Never mind. I thought you were different, but I was clearly wrong."

He walks out of the gym leaving me holding the ball and my guilt—and an unexpected twinge of regret. I should've been relieved. I had gotten what I wanted, to not have this conversation and for Logan to go away. So why does it feel like I swallowed a bite of a poison apple and the prince walked away instead of waking me?

CHAPTER 10
SWEET LIES
AARYA

"Nothing like paper autumn leaves, taped to palm trees to tell you it's fall." I take in the decorations adorning Seashore Boulevard and flutter my hands in front of my face as if trying to place a wonderful aroma. "Can't you feel the clean, crisp...eighty-nine degrees and three thousand percent humidity?"

Raven inhales a Zen-like breath to torment me. "I like the autumn flare."

"More like solar flare," I complain.

"Come on," Raven says. "The Sugarcane Festival is a tradition."

"So is stuffing yourself at Thanksgiving. I feel equally ill right about now."

"It's not that bad!" Raven says. "I'm on Pumpkin Patrol today."

"*Pumpkin Patrol*. How do you know that? We haven't even checked in at the volunteer booth yet."

"I asked. At school."

"You are *that* excited."

"I am."

"R.I.P. This is the day I lose you."

Raven makes her cadence singsong to counter my monotone. "I happen to *like* handing out adorable tiny pumpkins."

"Gourd bless you."

Raven cracks up. "Terrible."

Laughter comes with an ache. We'd made this big pledge to figure out the poems almost three weeks ago, a declaration that *felt* like action. But it was only words, at least, so far. Time is adding up with festivals and bad jokes. Lunch. Doing homework. Going shopping. Brushing teeth—all the routine actions that tie us to normalcy in small habitual ways. Because you can't just stop. Life goes on, even with someone missing from it. But the truth is we haven't made any progress with the letters, which means we are no closer to finding Penny.

"I dub this attempt to be seasonal a fail." I hold my ground, against the guilt that we haven't been able to do more.

"I get it," Raven says. "You'll have to smile at strangers. I know how hard that is for you."

"Not all of us are armed with beauty queen dazzle we can fire up on command."

"Psshht." Raven tries to brush me off.

"No, come on, let's see it."

Raven pauses mid-step, tosses her shiny midnight black hair, dips her chin, and smiles—magazine-cover worthy.

"Yup. There it is. You're going to win again."

Raven holds up her fingers in an X at me.

"No doubting yourself! You're going to demolish Vera's historic reign so hard her Botox will break."

"I don't care."

"You should. There's not enough collagen in the world for an ugly heart."

Raven tips her head back and laughs. "Love you."

"Love you, too. So much that I'll even pretend to also love this day."

"Consider it a means to an end. It's not the worst way to get community service hours for school. Do it for the college applications," Raven says.

"I'll do it for the chance to see how Logan's acting," I say. "Let's go get our stuff."

Raven leads us over to the Honor Society's booth and picks up the volunteer assignment sheet.

I peek over her shoulder. "Noooo. I cannot believe I have to oversee *apple bobbing*. I don't think an Ivy League is going to be impressed by this."

"I would think you'd enjoy watching everyone bob for apples," Raven says.

"Hmm." I hold up a finger like I'm actually considering it for a moment. "No. A bunch of people making donkey teeth faces while plunging into water full of other people's donkey mouth germs."

She looks thoughtful for a moment. "You *do* kind of have to make a donkey face to get the apple with your teeth, don't you?"

"I'm not wrong."

"Well, I'll come visit you after Pumpkin Patrol before I go get ready for the pageant." Raven is back to her singsong voice.

"There's something not right about your level of happiness. It's like it's directly proportional to my misery." I notice something on the sign-up sheet. "Hold up. Raven! Guess who's on Pumpkin Patrol with you? Logan! Thank you, universe."

I spin around so excitedly I knock Raven's bag right out of her hands.

"You're hawking pumpkins and spreading fall cheer together all morning. This is your chance to find out everything you can about him and Penny."

"How exactly am I supposed to do that? *Oh hey Logan, Penny's still missing, any secrets you're keeping you suddenly want to spill?*" Raven squats to pick up her purse.

A couple things have fallen out. I bend down to help, grabbing a lipstick, a pen and...a small pill bottle.

Raven snatches the bottle out of my hands. "They're anti-anxiety meds from Vera. Between Penny and my dad leaving and the pageant tonight...the panic attacks... they're happening more often, you know?" She looks at me like it's a confession, but I already knew they'd ramped up. "But I haven't taken any yet."

I touch Raven's shoulder. "It's okay if you did. I'm not judging you. This isn't eighth grade. You're not the same person. You've got this."

Raven regards the bottle in her hands. "Okay."

"So, will you?" I ask. "Try to get Logan to talk?"

She shifts her weight foot to foot. "I'm not good at this sort of thing."

"I'm pretty sure that's not true," I say. "Send that signature beauty queen smolder in his direction and you'll have him eating out of your hand."

"You have too much faith in me. But I'll try." Raven hugs a small pumpkin to her chest before blowing a kiss at me. "See you in a bit."

"Think of me drowning my pain in a barrel of apples." I stumble away in a dramatic trudge and run right into Elle.

"Candied apple?" she says loudly, holding one up,

overly chipper. Then, under her breath to me, "This is... quite the event."

"I know right? Welcome to Everbeach."

"I'll take one of those," someone calls out.

One of Logan's crew, Ryan, points to the apple he wants. He and henchman-bro number two, David, flank Logan as they walk toward the booth.

Logan scans the sign-up sheet on the table nearby. "*Pumpkin* Patrol? Where are the pumpkins?"

"Raven already picked them up." I point. "She went that way."

"Hey, can I get an apple or what?" Ryan waves money at Elle, and she gives him one.

He unpeels the plastic around it and lets the wrapper fall to the ground and presses his lips against the sticky caramel. "Mmm." Ryan licks it suggestively before sinking his teeth in and slurping up the juice. "You never know if something tastes as good as it looks, you know?"

David bursts out laughing. Logan rolls his eyes.

Elle points at the plastic by Ryan's feet. "Why don't you pick up that trash?"

"Pretty sure that's exactly what he's trying to do," Logan cuts in. "Pick up some *trash*."

Elle glares. "I do not know what Penny *ever* saw in you."

Logan flinches. Barely. But I notice.

"Don't let my brother's toxic masculinity bother you. He just acts tough to impress our dad." Hunter picks up the wrapper, tosses it with gusto into the garbage can and takes a bow. "Hey Logan, breaking news, picking on girls doesn't make you CEO material."

"Seriously," Elle says loud enough to make the statement pointed, "Penny should have stayed with the guy from the beach."

Guy from the beach? I feel my face scrunch in confusion.

"What guy?" Hunter asks.

"Yeah," I ask. "What guy?"

"Screw that guy," Logan says in a low voice.

"No, screw *you*." Elle pops off.

"I'd love your thoughts on how Penny wound up in Hightower. Ever consider whether it's your fault for messing with her so much? All the head games, *let's break-up, let's get back together, I love you, just kidding*."

I thought *I* was blunt. This girl goes straight for the jugular.

"Whoa," Hunter interrupts. "I'll make fun of Logan faster than anyone. But watch what kind of accusations you're making."

"Whatever. There's a reason Penny warned us about you Logan!" Elle says.

Shock passes over Hunter and Logan's faces, and I curse inwardly. The *big* thing we promised to keep secret. I grab Elle's arm and turn to leave but Nikki Tremaine steps directly in our path. Kat is right beside her. I take a step back and trip over a small brown spaniel wearing a pink tutu. It growls.

"Watch it!" Kat scoops up the pudgy dog protectively. "Itsie bitsie little Britsie." She kisses the dog on the nose, letting it lick her invasively. "Baby Britsie, it's okay."

"Why would Penny warn you about Logan, Elle?" Nikki smacks her overly lined lips.

Logan points to Elle. "Don't listen to her. You saw her punch me like some trailer park chick on a daytime talk show."

"Loww-gan," Nikki trills, running her hand down his arm. "Don't be so un-woke. It's *mobile home park*. That's what we call them now, right...*Elle*?"

Elle doesn't respond and tries to step by them.

"Don't leave. We want to hang out," Kat coos, putting her hands on her hips in a wannabe boss stance, one foot jutting in front. It makes her look like she's about to fall over.

Nikki squeezes Logan's arm and leans against him. "Logan, did you know Elle's dad is dating our mom?"

It takes a lot to surprise me. But I'm surprised. Floored, in fact.

Logan shrugs like he could care less.

Kat pipes up. "It's so cute. They're, like, in *love*. So that makes Elle our new bestie. Right, Elle? Maybe we'll be sissies someday, aw."

"Riiiight." This time Elle succeeds in sidestepping the twins and just starts walking. But Nikki and Kat fall into step with her.

Not about to let those birds of prey descend, I'm quick to follow. They round the corner away from the boys just as Nikki links arms with Elle and puts her lips close to Elle's ear, whispering something. I hurry to get closer but only manage to overhear the last part of their exchange.

"Tell your dad to end it," Nikki says. "We know what people like you really want."

The twins are clearly not okay with their parents dating and Elle is paying the price. When the Tremaines don't get what they want, they try to peck out your eyes.

Kat folds her arms across her chest. "Yeah. We *know*. We're not stupid. We are pretty much the opposite of stupid. Our emotional intelligence is very keen according to our therapist."

"Somehow I doubt that," Elle says.

"We're *not* stupid," Kat says like she didn't just say it a second ago.

"Right. Got that. Opposite of stupid." Elle rolls her eyes. Nikki glances around, noticing me and a few other students watching them. She leans in and plants a gooey, lip glossed kiss on Elle's cheek. "Besties forever."

Elle gets away from them as fast as she can, ducking down one of the narrow alleys of booths selling art and jewelry and novelty foods, but I manage to trail her.

I tap her shoulder. "Hey are you okay?"

She flinches under my touch, wiping the gloss off her face with the back of her hand.

"I'm fine." She touches the amber beads of a necklace for sale, not making eye contact.

"You look like you're about to cry," I say.

"I don't cry. This is my resting murder face."

"Elle...you practically told everyone about the poems." I say it as gently as I can.

"I know, I know. I'm so sorry. It just came out. Logan makes my blood boil." Elle plays with the beads.

"You're burying the lead here. Your *dad* is dating the Tremaine twin's *mom*!"

Elle massages her forehead. "I only put two and two together in drama class when you said the thing about their mom owning a trailer park."

I remember her stricken expression.

"I knew his new girlfriend owned one...Ashmont Village," Elle continues. "I didn't know she had kids. He never told me."

"But why do the twins have such a problem with it?" I ask. "With you?"

"They think my dad is just after their money..." Elle's voice trails off.

"*Their* mom married for money. Why can't your dad?" I ask. "I mean, you're at the Academy, so I'm sure you all are doing just fine without the freaking Tremaines."

Elle shudders. "Ugh. Please *never* let them get married." She looks positively miserable.

"Hey. Wanna go watch the apple bobbing?" I ask because that's what Penny would have done. "I promise you'll laugh."

Elle nods gratefully.

I might not know her backstory, but Elle is Penny's friend. And that, for now, is enough.

CHAPTER 11
PAGEANTRY
RAVEN

The pumpkins are gone, and so are all my ideas. After we sold out an hour ago, Logan and I have been walking around cleaning up the grounds to finish our volunteer hours, and I'm still not any closer to getting information from him than when we started.

With nothing resolved from our standoff on the court the other day, our conversation is like political pleasantries between enemies. I keep feeling Logan looking at me but every time I look back, he's already shifted his view.

I have to shake things up.

We've wandered into the area with all the carnival games. Time to step up my game...

An older man dressed in overalls and a short-sleeved flannel thrusts a Ping-Pong ball in front of me. "Only one dollar, six chances to win. Don't you want a goldfish to take home?"

"Want to play?" I ask Logan, an idea sparking.

"Why not?" He takes out his wallet, but I hand the guy a dollar before Logan can pay for me.

"And why don't we make it interesting?"

Logan furrows his brow. "What do you propose?"

"You miss, you have to answer a question. I miss, I'll answer one for you."

"Any question? Nothing is off limits?"

"Nothing."

"I'm in."

The man hands me six balls. The top of the bowl is like the rim of a basketball hoop. Easy. I aim, shoot, and miss, the ball ricocheting across the top of the sea of goldfish before dropping to the ground.

"Ouch, I'll have to work on my follow through," I say.

"You owe me an answer to a question."

"Fine. After the game." I hand him a ball. "Your turn."

Logan throws his and it sinks right in. I miss my next one, and the next, while Logan makes both of his.

The man hands Logan a goldfish swimming around in a plastic bag.

"I feel like I just got conned," I say.

"What? Shocked your basketball skills didn't transfer?" Logan gives me his crooked smile and I refuse to acknowledge how it makes my heart pound.

"Yeah, a little. How did you do that?"

Logan shrugs. "My dad always brought us to the festival, and each year I'd get all excited thinking this time, he was going to hang with us. We'd come here. I'd ask him to play, and every single time he'd say, *after this quick call*. Then, he'd hand Hunter and me a wad of cash and send us on our way with our security detail in tow. His quick call would end hours later. I guess it gave me plenty of time to work on my carnival game skills..." Logan's voice trails away as a little girl tugging on her mom's skirt wanting to play the game catches our attention. The mom is texting on her phone, ignoring her daughter.

The hopeful light in the little girl's eyes shifts to a crushed expression when her mom doesn't even acknowledge her. When I look over at Logan, I can't help but think of his face falling that same way at that same age, waiting for a dad who made no time for him.

"Be right back," Logan says to me.

He walks over and shows them his prize. The little girl blinks a few times in confusion, but Logan hands her the goldfish bag.

"Momma, can we keep it? Can we please?" She's bouncing on her toes looking like she's about to take flight. Her mom easily gives in, thanks Logan, and walks off with her daughter.

"That was sweet of you," I say.

"Well, don't let it get out. Wouldn't want anyone knowing I might *actually* have a heart." He repeats my own words back to me, his voice flat.

"Hey, you can't blame me for being surprised."

"I can't?" Logan crosses his arms and cocks his head. "Anyway, my turn for a question."

Instead, I blurt out, "You seem to be adjusting well to Penny's absence." Not smooth at all.

"That's a change in subject."

"I mean, it's not really. Penny's still missing. It's hard *not* to think about her." Although, for a moment there, I had lost myself a little with him—or maybe a lot.

"Yeah, well I can imagine, especially given that Penny supposedly *warned* you about me," he says.

He's not supposed to know about that. "Wait...what are you talking about?"

"The new girl said so."

"Elle? Why would she say something like that? What did *you* do Logan?"

Logan starts to protest. but I keep my laser stare on him. "My friends were being jerks."

I raise my eyebrows. "Your friends?"

"And me."

"Mm-hm. That's what I thought. What's your deal with her anyway?"

"Um, she punched me."

"You deserved that."

"I told you. I say stupid things when I'm upset."

"Are you upset? Really? Because from my vantage point, it doesn't look like you care that your girlfriend is missing."

We've stopped walking and are facing off, like when we were on the court. The expression he gives me is pained. "Of course I care about Penny, and I *am* worried about her," Logan says. "I will always love her, you know. But we were done. Had been...for a while."

This time, my brow furrows. "I thought you were still together when she went to Hightower?"

"Doesn't matter now."

"What do you mean it doesn't matter?"

"Raven, drop it. I've tried to talk to you, but you've repeatedly shut me down. So, I'm done. I'm not having this conversation now."

"So, you're just refusing to tell me what was going on with my friend before she disappeared?"

He has the nerve to look pissed off at me. "*You* refused to have a conversation the other day—in fact, you've refused to talk to me for weeks."

He's right. But I'm not about to admit it. "Never mind. Forget I asked." I storm off and curse myself for letting Logan Steele get the upper hand.

CHAPTER 12
COLLAPSE
RAVEN

Vera tugs on the strings of my corset.

"Don't you think—it's a little tight?" I struggle to get the words out.

"This is how it's done." Vera finishes her cinching and buttons the back of my dress.

I try to breathe deeply. "I'm not kidding. I feel lightheaded."

She hands me a cup of tea. "Drink this, it will help with your nerves." I take the hot mug and sip. Vera and her natural remedies. She calls this tea the holy grail of calm, but to me, it's just another bitter thing I've learned to swallow.

"If that doesn't work, you have your medicine in case you need it, right?" Vera asks.

"I have it, but I think I'm good. It's really the corset. It's tight."

Vera stares at me like she's trying to solve one of my AP calculus problems.

"What? Why are you looking at me like that?"

"It's just...are you doing okay?"

It always throws me when Vera has these human-almost-mother-like-moments. "I'm fine. Really."

"Well, I *really* think it's your anxiety, but if you say it's not...how about we give it a few minutes with the corset the way it is? We all have to make sacrifices for beauty." She starts fiddling with my hair next and makes a tsk sound. "Did you get your keratin treatment like I mentioned last month?" This is the Vera I'm used to, which feels oddly comforting.

"Several weeks ago," I say, suppressing an eye roll.

"Your hair is frizzier than I would expect."

"We live in Florida. Humidity: the heat that sticks to you like water? You've heard of it, right?"

Vera presses a bobby pin into my hair, and it pokes my scalp. I look at her flat eyes in the mirror and know she's pissed. *Dammit*. I need to watch myself. I'm not thinking clearly—the tight corset, the snake in the car and the accompanying texts, the almost fight with Logan. And Penny...always Penny—it's all simmering right under the surface.

In a monotone, Vera says, "Such a shame you got this kinky hair from your mother."

I drop my eyes. I knew something was coming after my smart-ass comment, but it always hurts more when it's about my mom. I go to touch my necklace, forgetting it isn't there. Not for the pageant. Vera planned my attire, and my mom's necklace would never be included.

Vera tucks in the last piece of my hair in a half-up style. "Everything I say or do is for your betterment. I might not sugarcoat things, but I do tell the truth, which will only help you."

Now she sounds sincere again. I hate this; trying to figure her out. Every year, this pageant is the one thing Vera really does help me with. I want to think she means well, but I also know she's all about appearances. The annual Sugarcane Pageant is a big social event for Everbeach. The daughters of all the Who's Who enter, and while maybe Vera doesn't think of me as her daughter, everyone in town does. Plus, this is Vera's moment to show off. Pretend to be something she isn't.

Or I'm just being petty and unforgiving.

"Are you ready?" Vera's smiling—like a real smile. Nothing tight-lipped. She almost seems proud. "I think you're going to be pleased with the results. Turn around."

I face the mirror and barely recognize myself.

The bodice of my dress has a sweetheart neckline covered in hand-stitched Chantilly lace made personally by a top French designer. It shimmers from the silver thread embroidered in a looping floral design. Ribbons crisscross the back of the dress, creating an intricate pattern that culminates in a bow studded with Swarovski crystals. The A-line skirt flares out at my hips, with spirals of mirror-like fabric tumbling down to the floor. When the swathes catch the light, it's an explosion of twinkling stars.

I love the gown, despite what it represents. My dad could never have afforded it. It's one more thing indebting me to Vera. However, if I win, it's one more scholarship, one more step closer to being free from her grasp.

"Raven, that is a lovely dress." I recognize the voice instantly. Even his compliments carry a command, and I feel like I should curtsy. Harvey Steele stands tall in a black expertly tailored suit, white button-down without a tie, cuff links glinting.

"Thank you—" I don't get to finish because I'm cut off by Vera.

"Harvey, you made it!" Vera says, warm and musical, a contrast to the ice and drumbeat reserved for me.

"I got a call from the city, and I need my chief counsel to do her thing. Raven, mind if Vera puts on her lawyer hat for a moment?"

"Not at all," I say, relieved for a little space.

Vera motions for Harvey to step aside with her just as someone lets out a long, low whistle. Hunter Steele walks up with Logan trailing behind.

Logan's staring at me, intense, smoldering. "Wow."

I stay calm on the outside, but with his full attention on me, I can't stop the unwelcome butterflies in my stomach. "What are you doing back here?"

"I came to wish you luck, but I don't think you need it." He offers me the lemonade he's holding. "And I brought you this. Fresh squeezed from the finest of food trucks around."

I look down at the drink but don't take it. "You brought me a lemonade." It's not a question but my tone holds a hint of confusion.

"Looks like I did."

I look up at him. "Why?"

"Why do you think?"

I gather my skirt and step toward him, wobbling slightly, still feeling a little lightheaded from the corset. Logan goes to grab my hand but Hunter pushes his brother out of the way, and puts an arm around me. "Whoa, steady. You alright?"

My breath is shallow, but I think I'll be okay. "Yeah, I'm good. Thanks."

"What have you done to get my brother so worked up he's buying lemonade?"

"Knock it off. She has to be on stage soon," Logan says, glaring at Hunter's arm wrapped around me.

"Jealous?" Hunter raises his eyebrows.

I laugh and wiggle out of his embrace, glancing at

Logan. He clenches his jaw but doesn't respond to Hunter's taunt. Instead, he lifts the lemonade and says, "Truce?"

"Only because it's my favorite."

"Good. Mine, too." He hands it to me and our fingers touch. Instant heat. I want to douse it with the lemonade.

"I'll catch up with you later?" Logan asks, and I nod in agreement. "Come on Hunter, we need to get to our seats."

Hunter blows a kiss to me while Logan drags him away.

They step past Punkaj who's on his way in. He approaches, gesturing toward the lemonade, raising his eyebrows. "So, is this your secret to winning?"

"The lemonade? No secret, but it's my favorite. Logan brought it for me." I take a sip and set the drink down. "I didn't know you were covering the pageant."

"Apparently the star intern gets the annual 'Fairest of Them All' article."

"Aren't you the *only* intern?"

"Details." Punkaj relaxes a bit, but then his expression changes again. "Was it hard to prepare? It must be hard to focus on something like this with all the developments in Penny's abduction."

I play dumb. "What do you mean?"

"Any word from the police?"

I look at Vera still talking to Harvey. She's out of earshot, but I whisper anyhow. "Not here. Not me. If you have questions, please just talk to Aarya."

Punkaj looks where I'm nervously glancing. "Understood."

A man with wire-frame glasses carrying a camera and notebook rushes over at the same time Vera reaches us. "Sorry I'm late." The man turns to Vera. "I'm Charlie

Perot, photographer." He turns his attention to me. "Look at you, all grown up. Do you remember me?"

I take in his stout frame and glasses. There's something about him—the timber in his voice, an echo from the past.

"The first ever 'Junior Fairest of Them All' article? I almost didn't recognize you. What happened to your beautiful curls?"

That's how I know him. I was seven, right after Vera and my dad married. Leading up to the pageant that year, *The Mirror* decided to pick a 'Junior Fairest of Them All,' and I was their pick. Vera argued against it, saying I was too young for the attention. But my dad, seeing the hollow shell I'd become since my mom's death, thought it might help.

After the article was published, the praise poured in, everyone commenting on my beautiful hair—just like my mom's.

It was the last time my hair was curly.

The next week, Vera had me in the salon for my first straightening treatment. The stylist hesitated as though Vera asked her to shave my head, but she did as she was told. When the straightener glided down section after section of my hair, I pretended my tears were from the sting of the chemicals, not from watching one of my last connections to my mom going up in smoke.

"She wears her hair straight now." Vera bites the words out, arms tight by her sides.

An announcement sounds over the loudspeaker. "Five minutes! Five minutes! Ladies wrap things up and get in position."

"We'll have to get the pictures after," Punkaj says.

Vera leads me over to line up. I was getting used to the corset but hurrying after her like this makes it feel like there is a noose around my lungs. I take short breaths, feeling like I ran five miles.

"Raven, you're pale," Vera says. "You look frightful. Did you take the medicine I gave you?"

"It's the corset. I keep trying to tell you. I feel dizzy."

"I'll check it again, but I'm tying it the same as always." Vera unbuttons my dress and fiddles with the laces. I expect to feel relief, but instead my ribs constrict.

"Vera, that's making it worse."

"I haven't done anything different. It must be your nerves. I wish you'd taken your medicine." Vera buttons my dress up again, and I feel like I'm in a straitjacket of lace and glitter.

If there's nothing wrong with the corset, why is it so hard to catch my breath? And my heart rate is speeding. I stare at the runner lights illuminating the path to the stage, and they're blurry, almost like halos around them.

"Maybe yourr-ight." A giggle escapes.

Vera snaps around, eyes wide. "Are you slurring?"

I shake my head no, stifling a laugh. I'm not sure why everything is so funny now, but my head feels light, my feet heavy. "I...it's just...think. I feel off." My name is called from the stage. I look to Vera hoping there is a way out. "I...I can't go out there."

"Nothing we can do about it now." Vera walks me to the curtain. "You can do this. Shoulders back, give me a smile. Now get out there and win for us." With a light push, Vera sends me out. I go from backstage dim light to open-air sunlight. It's like stepping off steady ground onto a Tilt-A-Whirl.

The crowd spins. I feel trapped. Heart racing. Stuck.

My vision is hazy, all black at the edges. The clapping slows. The last thing I hear before everything goes dark is an audible gasp from the crowd.

CHAPTER 13
AFTERMATH
AARYA

t's like Raven vanishes into her dress. She tumbles off the stage and her giant skirt swallows her up like a taffeta sinkhole.

I push past Elle, tripping over bags and feet to make it down the aisle toward the stage. But before I get there, Logan leaps from his seat in the front row, Hunter close behind, waving at everyone to give Raven space. Logan stretches her flat on her back, her head cradled in his arm. How convenient he's right there to catch her. And so gently. For everyone in Everbeach to see.

Paramedics swoop in, lifting Raven onto a stretcher and out of sight.

A hand clamps onto my shoulder. Vera steadies herself, trying to keep up in her stilettos. "Aarya, honey, wait, please." She leans so close I can smell her perfume. "Raven's been off all night. And right before she went on stage, I thought she was slurring. She's not drunk or on something again, is she?"

"What? No!" I answer automatically.

"You were with her earlier..."

I shift my weight from foot to foot. I swore I would never let Raven get in over her head again.

"The more the doctors know the better," Vera says.

She's right. I can't risk Raven not getting the right care. I grit my teeth and then say it. "She had some pills in her bag—"

Vera gasps.

"She said they were from you."

"Oh, okay. Those are just mild anti-anxiety meds. My mind went to the worst place." The tendons in Vera's neck relax for a moment, but then tighten again. "Although, if you take too much of anything... Raven was so nervous backstage, and I kept encouraging her to take the pills. What if she did? And took too many?" Her eyes fill with tears. "It's all my fault. What will I tell her father? He's going to think I haven't been watching her closely enough."

Were any of us watching her closely enough, considering her past? Seeing Vera like this certainly has me questioning things.

We reach the medical tent, and an EMT pokes out his head. "She's come to, ma'am. But she's extremely disoriented." He waves Vera in but stops me at the entrance. "Sorry, family only."

Because that's who Raven would want inside right now. *Vera.*

Elle and Dawn rush toward me with questions—where is she? Did she come to?

"She's awake, that's all I know. We have to wait for Vera to update us." I try not to pace. "Dawn, was Raven acting strange or anything backstage?"

"She kept complaining her dress was too tight. That's it," Dawn says.

"She wasn't...you know...drunk or high or anything

right?" The question tastes bad in my mouth, but I have to ask.

"You don't think..." Dawn trails off.

"*I* don't! Vera brought it up."

"All right!" Vera emerges from the tent. "Raven is going to rest another few minutes. Girls, are you sure you haven't seen anything, *anything* that would explain what happened to my Raven?"

My Raven. *Please*.

When silence greets her, Vera frowns. "She's been *so* upset about Penny. I worry, you know." She bites her bright red bottom lip. "How are you girls doing? How are you holding up?"

"Fine, Vera." My voice is clipped.

Elle nods her agreement.

Dawn adjusts the straps of her gown. "I mean, it seems like Penny was pretty devastated over her breakup with Logan. We're all working really hard to see if there's something more— Ow!"

She shuts up when I pinch the back of her arm.

"Mrs. Snow?" A medic steps out of the tent. "We've cleared your daughter to go home."

Vera lingers for a second, like she wants to say more. I hold my breath willing her not to pick up on what Dawn said.

"I'll be right back." Vera ducks inside.

Dawn scowls at me, rubbing her arm. "What was that for?"

"We agreed not to tell the adults anything. Especially Vera." My tone is sharper than I'd like, but I can't help it. "Do you want to help find Penny, or not?"

A shuffle of footsteps from behind makes me turn— Logan and Hunter.

"Any updates on Miss Sugarcane?" Hunter asks. "I

mean, it's not like she didn't already have our attention... she had to go and faint."

The joke falls flat.

"We're all waiting," I say.

Awkward silence falls.

"Thanks for helping her," Dawn politely offers them.

I sigh loudly as the medical tent door flaps open dramatically and Vera re-emerges, trying to support a floppy Raven against her while walking on the soft dirt in six-inch heels.

"Sorry," Raven mumbles. Her tone has an odd singsong quality to it. She's clearly messed up.

Disappointment and worry snag my throat.

"It's fine, honey," Vera says. "Let's get you home to rest."

"Shorry, I fell down." Raven giggles and repeats herself. "*Shorry*. Ha!"

"You didn't fall down dear, you fainted." Vera sounds more annoyed than concerned.

"Okay. Shhorry."

Raven is *slurring*. Badly. I take a step toward her, but Vera is between us.

"Logan, Hunter, can you help me get her home? There's no way I can get her upstairs and in bed by myself."

Hunter and Logan immediately step in, supporting Raven, as Vera walks ahead toward the parking lot and her waiting limo.

"We can help!" I interject. "Right, Elle? Dawn?"

Elle looks ready to help, but Dawn gestures a bit helplessly at her own pageant gown and heels.

"It's okay, we've got it," Hunter says.

"Since when are *you* in the fold anyway?" I can't cloak my indignation anymore.

"I'm Vera's intern remember? My job is to be in the fold," Hunter says.

"Raven passed out right in front of us, Aarya," Logan cuts in. "Am I not allowed to check on her?"

I push past him to give Raven a hug. "Call me when you get home."

Raven nods blankly and I'm forced to watch the *Steele* brothers guide her to the waiting car. Atrocious.

"I have to go," Dawn says. "Grayson and my parents will be looking for me. But please keep me posted."

She gives a last worried wave before she turns back toward the pageant stage.

I head toward the parking lot to leave, and groan. Notebook in hand, walking a purposeful path straight for me is Punkaj. I can tell even from a distance he's in full-on reporter mode.

I sigh. "First Logan, now Pulitzer Punk. It's like cyanide frosting on a shit cupcake."

"That's...evocative." Elle checks out Punkaj as he gets closer. "He's pretty hot for cyanide."

"Ew." I try for a split second to see Punkaj the way Elle must, his dark, thick hair angled to the side, brushing against an eyebrow, velvet black eyes, wide strong shoulders, the confident walk, annnnd, still no.

Punkaj holds out a hand for Elle to shake. "I'm Punkaj Grimsley with *The Mirror*."

I mouth the words along with him. Why not, *hey I'm Punk, nice to meet you.* But no, he's got to show up like a walking resume.

He turns to me. "Hey...what happened to Raven tonight?"

"She didn't feel well."

"Yeah. I could see that. All of Everbeach could. I mean, what's going on with her?"

"I said she didn't *feel* well." I draw out the words.

"I get that you're sticking up for her. But passing out?"

"Who are you? Our parents?" I glare at him. "Judge much? Whatever, Punk. Choose the grown up's side." Punkaj holds his hands up in surrender. "I was just asking."

"Why? To write an exposé on my best friend? I don't think so. Does your mom know you're prancing around trying to steal Emmy's out from under her?"

"That's why you look so familiar!" Elle says. "The news lady, Gita Grimsley. You're her son."

"Yes. The main anchor, the one married to the pro-golfer." Punkaj fills in the blanks. He sounds a little tired of saying it. "Aarya, for real. I told you. I'm not out to get anyone. I'm trying to write a good story."

"My friend isn't a story," I say. "Just because you have a press pass doesn't mean you're suddenly winning."

Punkaj fiddles with his pen. "You win everything okay?"

"I do. I can hold my breath longer," I poke his arm, deliberately changing the subject away from Raven. "And roll a *pitay* better."

"I don't even like pitay. I hate coconut and molasses separately let alone pressed together in a little soggy cookie," he answers. "Can we not do this? I'm on the clock."

"Yes, of course. But wait until I tell my dad the golden child doesn't like pitay."

"Seriously, come on. I have questions," Punkaj says.

"And I'm *not* answering them."

"Yeah, your foray into pitay made that obvious," Punkaj says. "Don't you care about what happened to Penny?"

"Penny?" I pause. "You mean Raven."

"No, I mean Penny. Sure, I have to cover the pageant for the paper, but Raven collapsing is not the story I'm working on. I told you what I think. A place like High Tower doesn't just lose a patient. So, no, 'grown-up's' side." He makes air quotes with his fingers. "If anything, it's the opposite. I'm here to talk to all of *you*. To everyone who knew Penny best. Including Logan Steele."

Now he has my attention.

"And you think snooping around the Sugarcane Festival is going to help?" I ask.

"I think watching Logan could help," Punkaj says. "He was Penny's boyfriend for a long time. She's missing, and now he's hanging around with Raven, and she's acting weird."

"What do you mean hanging around? They were on Pumpkin Patrol, that's it."

"He went backstage to see her before the pageant," Punkaj says.

"He *did*?"

He nods. "Brought her a lemonade."

Elle's eyes narrow. "Could he have spiked it?"

Punkaj shrugs. "Maybe they were drinking together? On their pumpkin thing?"

"As much as Pumpkin Patrol would drive *me* to drink, Raven loves that stuff. Besides, Raven doesn't drink."

I think.

"I don't know," he says. "But I feel like Logan knows more than he's letting on when it comes to Penny."

Elle clears her throat and gives me a pointed look. I ignore her.

"I wanted to tell you, I'm heading to Hightower tomorrow," he says.

"Because you'll find something the police didn't?" I ask.

"I have my sources." A sheepish look crosses Punkaj's face as soon as he says it. "That sounds cheesy. I know. But for real. I actually have a source or two." He holds out two business cards. "Anyway. Call me if you think of anything okay?"

I roll my eyes. "I have your number, Punk."

Elle puts the card in her pocket, giving me the say-something look.

"Well, use it. If you think of anything. And let me know how I can help. Really. I mean it."

"She wrote to us," Elle blurts out.

If I could fry her with my eyeballs right now I would. "Elle! Again? What the hell!"

"What?" She points at Punkaj. "He *says* he wants to help. If he's going all the way to Hightower, he should know everything."

"What's everything?" he asks.

I tug at a red streak in my hair.

Elle just plows ahead. "Penny wrote us poems. And no one believes us that they're important. But it's obvious there's more to this because why else would someone put a snake in Raven's car and—"

"Hold on! Stop." I cut her off.

Punkaj is processing this with a furrowed brow. "You think the snake was deliberate?"

"Punk, you can't tell *anyone*. For real." I stare at him hard.

"But if someone is trying to scare you...or hurt you," he says, "that's serious."

"Our parents made us promise to leave it to police. And the police say the poems aren't one hundred percent traceable to Penny. Or even if they are, they don't seem to hold any valuable info."

"Do *you* think they do?" Punk asks. "Can I see them?"

I cross my arms, unsure.

"Look, I want to write this story," Punkaj says. "So... you're a source now, too. Real reporters don't spill their sources."

I don't budge.

"Ever."

I let out a stream of air, still tugging on my hair, twisting the red around my finger. Punkaj is nothing if not capital J journalism. He doesn't break rules.

Maybe it's the stress of the night. Maybe Elle is just super convincing. Maybe it's the sincere look in Punkaj's eyes. But I take the leap. And fill him in.

As I do, his brow does the furrow thing again. When I'm done, he glances at his phone. "I have to go file this stupid story about the pageant before I miss my deadline. But text me copies of the poems? I'll think on it."

"Fine. But remember." I point a finger at him. "We're special top-secret sources now, all confidential and stuff. Promise."

"Promise."

"For real," I say.

"I said I *promise*."

"Fine. Thank you. And..." I tilt my chin up. "I hate you."

Punkaj doesn't miss a beat. "Hate you, too."

"Hate you more."

"Hate you the most."

I steer Elle away.

"Are you two always like that?" Elle asks. "It's exhausting."

"Our parents are best friends. I've had no choice but to hang out with Punkaj Grimsley—elite scholar, medical intern, legal intern, reporter prodigy—my whole life. Cruel and unusual punishment."

"He sounds like he truly wants to help."

"Somehow, I think you might be right," I say. "Maybe it's just for the story, but I do think he's on our side. I'll trust him...for now."

"What's with the *hate you* thing then?"

"Oh, we've done that forever. My parents have always dangled him in front of me as the shining example of a perfect kid. It's like they don't even see what *I* do."

"So, you're mad at your parents and hating Punkaj Grimsley solves that," Elle says.

"No, hating him is just fun."

Elle raises an eyebrow. "I think he likes not liking you, too."

"Ew, no."

I pull out my phone to text Raven. "I can't believe Logan and Hunter took Raven home. What was Vera thinking?"

"Couple of tall, strong dudes in flat shoes," Elle says.

"Raven shouldn't have let them do it. That's not like her."

"She seemed too messed up to really protest," Elle says.

"Also not like her. Well, not anymore."

She glances at me sideways. "Did she used to have a problem?"

I give a curt nod, even though I don't think Raven would want Elle to know.

"Could she still?" Elle asks gently.

"No." It feels wrong, talking about Raven like this. But...the pills in her bag. The slurring. Maybe Raven *isn't* telling the truth.

I pull out my phone again. Still no answer. I fire off another text.

Coming over now.

> This is Vera. Raven is asleep. She needs
> to rest.

I'll come keep her company.

> No need. We have it covered. We will
> get to the bottom of what happened.

I let out a frustrated huff and show my phone to Elle.

"Do you want to try anyway?" she asks. "I'll go with you."

"I don't really think we can just show up."

"So, what now?" Elle asks.

"I guess, see you in school on Tuesday," I say shrugging.

"I guess," Elle echoes, sounding equally defeated. "Text me when you know how Raven's doing."

Once Elle is out of sight, I stop walking toward my own car.

My face burns with the sting of it all. Vera calling all the shots is bad enough. Raven so out of it that she's letting it happen—that's the bigger problem. What if Raven is addicted again? What if she doesn't even realize she is? Or worse, does, and lied to my face. Wouldn't be the first time. I didn't know Raven had a problem before, until she was whisked away for the summer to rehab. I swore then I'd never miss warning signs again.

But maybe I am.

I abruptly turn and walk back toward the fair, veering off to the carnival rides. Tinny music loops through the air. A clown juggling bowling pins moves close and then away, making me feel like my own vision is sliding in and out of focus. *Step right up. Over here. This way.*

I find myself trailing toward the Ferris wheel. Just a quick break from it all.

A man with waxy skin, bloodshot eyes, hands me a ticket for cash. "Just you?"

"Just me."

I climb onto the ride, sliding to the center of the wooden bench. The metal lap bar clicks into place.

I whoosh into the sky. Even as I sit still, I'm spinning. The colorful tents below blur. Everything is as out of focus as the patchwork below. Penny. Logan. *Raven*.

On the ground below, the clown's juggling beer bottles now. I've never liked clowns. They're liars, the paint on their faces telling a story that may or may not match their eyes. Or heart. Or soul. They can be a threat in disguise. Anyone can. After all, Penny was abducted.

Darkness can come in garish colors. A nightmare can look like a carnival. Like all the ways we perform for each other and lie that we're okay.

CHAPTER 14
GIRLS LIKE YOU

RAVEN

"Come nuh." A man standing before me holds a machete, beckoning with his other hand. I'm not afraid—not even with the big weapon in his hand. He's familiar. Hard lines sprout from the corners of his eyes, but there's a softness in the way he regards me. I know this man. I trust him.

He puts one finger to his lips. I know to stay quiet as he leads me around a corner, behind a concrete wall—a dividing line from the rest of the property. I smell jerk chicken cooking on the grill. We must be in someone's backyard.

Loud voices. Shouting. One woman's voice rings out above the others—one voice I'd know anywhere.

"Momma—" The man's hand is around my mouth. "Shh. Shh." He makes soft, calming noises. "Please, quiet." His pleading wins. I stay silent. Listening.

The voices escalate. My mom screams. I take off running, too fast for the man to stop me. I kick up dirt and rock. I stumble, arms out to brace when I hit the ground, but my hands and knees touch nothing, my body in free fall.

My mother's scream echoes while I spin through the darkness.

I shoot up straight, the scream still on my lips. Clutched tightly to my chest is a silk comforter. My bed. I'm in my bed in my room.

It was a dream. *The* dream. My recurring nightmare.

It's back, for the first time in four years.

It always ends in the same place: my mother screaming and me falling into nothing.

I still hear voices. They aren't shouting though. They're coming from downstairs.

Swinging my legs over the side of the bed, I wait a second to stand, the quick movement making my head throb. I'm in sweatpants and wearing a loose t-shirt. When did I change?

The last thing I remember is a bright light. Spinning crowd. Onstage. *Oh no, no, no.* I passed out. Didn't finish the pageant. I didn't win or even place, which means... The scholarship is gone.

I launch out of bed and my right knee buckles, pain shooting up my leg as I crumble to the floor. What the hell happened?

It must have been a bad fall. A *really* bad fall.

This injury might be serious and basketball starts in a few months. If I can't play, I'll lose my scholarship offers and I'll never be free from Vera. I'll be trapped in this life like I was trapped in that corset.

I'm stuck. It's over. My breath starts to catch.

Accept.

What I cannot change.

Courage.

To change what I can.

Wisdom.

To know the difference.

Out loud. I need to say it out loud.

"Grant me the serenity to accept the things I cannot change." My voice, hands, legs shake. But I grab my dresser and hold tight. "The courage to change the things I can." I can do this. I hold tight to the dresser and push up with my good leg and stand. "And the wisdom to know the difference."

I don't believe the game is over when we're down three points and there are only five seconds on the clock. I refuse to believe it's over now.

I repeat the Serenity prayer—the gift from my twelve-step program. The pain throbs, but I push through it, making my way from my room to the hall to the stairs, and lead with my good leg all the way down.

Logan sees me first. There's something in the way his sandy hair is tousled more than normal, the way his brows wrinkle.

He's worried...about me.

Vera narrows her eyes before smiling, more prison warden than adoring stepmother.

"She's alive!" Hunter says with more gusto than I'm prepared for, making me stumble a little. "Whoa, careful, we don't need a repeat of earlier." He glances sideways at Logan. "I think his knight in shining armor moments are tapped for the day."

"I have an endless well, actually." Logan turns to me. "You should still be in bed."

"I don't think that's your decision to make." Logan's shoulders slump. I'm being too harsh. Remembering the lemonade truce, I soften my tone. "Sorry, I'm struggling here. How did I injure my knee?"

"You fell off the stage," Hunter says.

"Off the stage? Like all the way off?" Brilliant. That's great. No wonder my leg hurts like this.

"Like timber. Boom."

Logan glares at his brother. "Ignore him. Maybe we should go sit down, talk about it?"

Vera steps forward. "The boys were just leaving, weren't you?" It's phrased as a question, but she clearly gives them no choice in the matter.

"Right, yes," Hunter says. "All right Logan, you ready?"

"I think I'll hang back a minute, if that's okay?" Logan asks me, not even glancing in Vera's direction.

I nod. I can't avoid him any longer. It's time to get this talk over with and move on.

Hunter, the dutiful intern, looks at Vera and says, "That all right? He can call our driver when he's ready."

"Very well. And thank you, boys, truly. I don't know how I would have gotten her home without you." She turns to me. "Please don't wear yourself out. You need your rest, so don't keep the poor boy out longer than he needs to be."

Logan holds out his arm and helps me into the library. When we touch, I feel an unexpected rush and pull my hand away.

"I'm good."

I hobble in, and we sit down on the couch. He's close enough that the cushions tilt us toward each other ever so slightly.

"Raven...what happened out there? What's going on?" he asks.

"I...I don't know. The corset was tight, I felt light-headed...but passing out...I'm mortified, collapsing in front of the entire city like that."

"Everyone in Everbeach couldn't have been there. Maybe *half* the city," Logan says, smiling lightly.

"That doesn't make it any better." I slouch on the couch and let my head rest back. "How do you come back from this? And *The Mirror* was there. Punk is going to put this in his story, isn't he?"

"Anything is possible. But I can make a call."

"What do you mean you can *make a call*?"

"My dad," Logan says. "You know he owns the paper, right?"

"Oh yeah. What doesn't your dad own?" I shake my head. "Thanks, but you don't have to get involved," I say.

"I'll handle it." Logan glances over and our eyes meet. The gray is brighter, accentuating the light blue tones. And he smells good. Like, really good. No, not going there. I know what I need to do and getting lost in his charm is not going to help. I need to be direct, shut him down.

"I can handle my own messes. Just drop it, okay?" A fall off the stage is nothing compared to rehab and group therapy digging up all my buried memories.

I shudder. *My darkest memory, my nightmare.* It clawed its way back today. The gunshot echoes through me. My fists clench. Unclench. Stay present. Breathe. "I don't need your help." I bite the words out. I'm not the little girl in my dream or a damsel in distress.

"Fine." Logan sits up straight and leans away from me. "I'm going to head out."

We stand together and walk to the front door.

This is my chance to stop avoiding and deal with what happened on the balcony. To conclude it was a terrible mistake and move on. "Wait. Before you go, we should talk."

Logan raises his eyebrows. Only the overhead chandelier is on, casting the foyer in low light. Shadows accentuate his chiseled jawline. We're standing close, so close, I feel the heat radiating from his body.

"Thank you for coming here and helping. But...I think we need to keep our distance." I should step back, but when I see the sincerity in his gaze, I pause.

"Is this about earlier? When you asked about me and Penny? I shouldn't have shut you down like that. Raven, I—"

"Don't."

"Will you let me explain?"

"Here's the thing: I don't know if it matters. Penny's one of my best friends and you're the love of her life."

He makes a face I can't quite read. "I wasn't though."

"I don't know how you can say that. You were together since freshman year."

"We weren't together. Not anymore. Not when she went to Hightower. We broke up before that. Before the balcony."

Before the balcony. The words sink in, but I know better. "You would have been on again soon enough."

"Not this time."

"That's what she said every time, and then a week later you were back together." I steel myself. "I'm not one of your girls to be used and thrown away until you want to go back to Penny, destroying our friendship in the meantime."

"It wasn't like that. She was done. And so was I. We both were ready to move on." Logan steps closer to me.

I put my hand up against his chest.

"This doesn't change anything, then?"

Even if I don't have to ache with guilt anymore, Logan is still off limits. Penny put him in the poems for some reason. Until we figure out why, I need to stay a million miles away from this.

"No, nothing has changed," I say.

Neither of us move.

"I should go," he says.

"Yeah, you should." But a voice inside whispers, *Stay, please.*

"Hey." Logan's tone is a gentle caress. "Remember this at least." He twirls a piece of my hair, bending down to bring his lips to my ear. "You were absolutely breathtaking today."

I close my eyes, fighting the urge to give in, to lean in and let his lips brush my skin, to fall into his chest, to finish what we started that day on the balcony: the kiss that would consume me.

But I can't.

"Thank you," I say stepping back, but Logan pulls me into an embrace. In the seconds that pass, my fight gives out, and I reluctantly rest my head on his chest, trying not to drown in a single word. *Breathtaking.*

"Okay," he says into my hair. "No more talk about that night. Or us. I can take a hint."

I nod. If I speak, I don't trust myself to let him go.

"Good night, Raven." Logan releases me and walks out the door.

I make the slow climb back to my room.

Vera sits straight-backed on my bed. "You're alone. I wasn't sure if you'd invite him to your bed or not."

I go completely still. "What are you doing in here?"

"Waiting for you, of course." Vera stands, ethereal and cold.

I back up, carefully on my injured knee, while Vera advances toward me, until my back leans on a smooth pane of glass, the frame pressing into me—the mirror on my wall.

"I see now, you're just like your mother."

"What are you talking about?"

"Don't think I didn't overhear you down there. Going after Penny's boyfriend. And you pretend you're so concerned about finding her."

"I do want to find her. You won't let me!"

Vera grabs my arm tight, nails digging into flesh, and yanks me toward her, spinning me around to face our reflection. The angles of Vera's cheekbones are sharper in the waning light, shadows accentuating the crevices.

She keeps her hold on my arm, but with her free hand, light as a plume, drags a bright red nail down the contours of my cheek, a prickling chill following in its wake.

"Such an island beauty, they say. So exotic." Hatred oozes out of her. "Where does she get it, everyone wonders." Vera motions to my face. "I know the truth. You look like your mother. And now I know you act like your mother. You are exactly like your *whore* of a mother."

Something on my dresser catches my eye, and I twist away from her. A coffin-like box with a blood-red ribbon tied around it. Inside are letters, faded and yellowed around the edges, Vera's present to me on my thirteenth birthday. Letters addressed from Ebony to Clive, Clive to Ebony—my mom and dad's love letters.

Vera and Clive were high school sweethearts and went to college together—*Everbeach's sweethearts*, engaged and then not. My dad left Vera for my mom because she was pregnant with me—a truth I didn't know until I read those letters.

And you, Raven, are a daily reminder of that betrayal. How your whore of a mother stole my husband-to-be.

The letters were never a gift—the sole intent was

punishment. After Vera revealed her miscarriages, she gave me those letters, driving the dagger in deeper, forcing me to crack.

Every day I look at you, all I see is her. And what he did. You are a curse on my marriage and my life.

That was when my panic attacks ramped up and I was prescribed anti-anxiety pills. Within a couple months, I couldn't function without them, and I was sent to rehab.

Vera's flinty voice slices through my thoughts. "I brought those letters up because I think you need a reminder."

"What do those letters have to do with tonight?"

"Boys like Logan never stay with girls like *you*. You're the trash they use for fun, until they go back to where they belong."

Tears pool in my eyes. I try to blink them back.

"I'm only trying to help you understand the ways of this world. Look how it turned out for your mother." Eerie calm spreads across Vera's face. Her callous reference to my mom's death makes me feel nauseated. "What kind of stepmother would I be if I didn't prepare you for the real world? And help you see exactly what you are. And will always be."

She pats my cheek. "We'll have to talk later about what happened at the pageant. If you're drinking or overdoing your meds again, I'll find out. Just like I found out you all aren't listening to what I told you about the poems. Dawn let it slip today. You're not as clever as you think." She looks down at my leg. "But it looks like I don't have to take basketball away after all, you've ruined that all on your own." Her smile pulls tight. She walks out of the room, leaving me alone, staring at myself in the mirror.

My heart feels like it's been hacked out by an axe. I find my purse on my dresser, my hands shaking as I fumble through it until I find the plastic bottle. *Control the things you can, let go of what you can't.* I push the top down and twist.

Hands trembling, I drop the bottle on my dresser. Pills spill out. Little blue ovals dot the surface—giant lakes I can drown in. *No, no, not now.* I cover my eyes, rubbing my temples. I breathe in deep, bringing my hands to a prayer position in front of my mouth and nose.

I can't go back to that place where I needed one to get out of bed in the morning, another and another to make it through the day, and yet another to sleep.

I collapse on my bed. I don't need them. Not now. Not again.

The sting of Vera's grip lingers on my arm, nail indents still there—a physical reminder of how worthless I am. And the box is still on my dresser, another reminder I shouldn't exist.

But something else happened tonight.

I turn out the light and etch the feeling of Logan holding me into my memory—because it can never, ever happen again.

Girls like me don't get a happily ever after.

But tonight, I will let myself dream.

CHAPTER 15
THE REAL BEACH
AARYA

"Aarya! Where are you going?" My father somehow has a sixth sense that alerts him whenever I am leaving the confines of The Maharaja.

"The beach with my friends. I told Mom."

He plants himself in front of me, arms crossed. "What about your studies?"

"Tonight."

"Why not now, and do your relaxing after?" It's phrased like a question, but I know it's a command. Heaven forbid I have fun before every last thing on my to-do list is checked off.

A ragged sigh escapes my lips. I *need* to see that Raven's okay, truly okay, after the pageant. If any of us fall apart, this whole effort to help Penny falls apart. My father's eyes scan my face and soften. "I understand this time is hard. With Penny gone. But tomorrow, you will catch up?"

"I always do."

"You must start applying for internships for next

summer, too." My father strokes his mustache. "Punkaj has already been accepted to an internship at Everbeach Hospital with one of the preeminent doctors in neuroscience. He is working on some great projects in the hematology department."

"I know, I know. He's going to be a brain surgeon and win a Pulitzer and be in the Olympics. He's ah-mazing. Best kid ever."

"No need for being sarcastic. He works very hard."

"So do I."

"Punkaj wouldn't be doing play time on the beach," he says.

"He wouldn't even if he didn't have work to do. Punkaj is the most boring human in America."

My father surprises me by laughing. "Most people who work hard leave that impression." He gestures to the chandeliers, the golden ceiling accents, the aquarium. "You don't build all this by taking weekends off. Believe me. Every day I wake up ready to work, and I ask Ganesha to remove any obstacles. *You* should ask him for wisdom."

Here we go.

"He can guide you toward the sort of discriminating intellect that one must possess to attain perfection in life."

"Must have that discriminating intellect," I say flatly, then switch into a deep, meditative priest voice. "I *bowww* to the elephant faced deity."

"Only sarcasm from you." My father looks upward as if hoping for divine intervention.

"They say it's the most intelligent form of humor."

He shakes his head. "Go have your fun, rascal. But remember, there is no such thing as second best. Only first and last."

I watch him disappear down one of the vast hallways from the lobby, but I still feel his judging eyes on me. Or maybe it's the statues—the giant deities carved in the walls and their stony expressions. One more place where I have to ask for permission. Please let me get good grades, win the race, be the best.

I touch the marble fingers of the goddess Sarasvati, the lute she cradles; a trophy I'll never hold. Divine patroness of music. *Hey Sarasvati, a little help here...how about convincing my parents that singing isn't failing?*

I turn to my favorite instead. Kali. Blood from her battles streaks her face. Fierce destroyer of all evils. Including *ignorance*.

I don't believe anything will actually change. My parents will keep projecting restrictions and rules from their closed-minded corner. Prayer feels like begging. Asking for things you'll never have. To pray is to wait. Not do. Not move. It's drowning while you sleep like a shark gone still.

I drive too fast to the beach. A light drizzle coats the banana and palm leaves. It's the sort of early morning rain that will turn into a searing blue sky within the hour.

Raven texted she didn't know what happened at the pageant, blaming stress, exhaustion, her dress. I hope that's the truth; I'll know once we talk more.

I pull into the lot to wait, scanning Sugar Sand Public Beach.

The Real Beach. All the mansions and pools and private beaches at her disposal, and Penny always picked here. There is nowhere I can think of that's more Penny. Maybe being here together will spark some sort of break-through for us with her poems.

I hear the choking growl of a truck engine kick off and a rusty door groan open.

"I appreciate this god-awful junk truck is some sort of

hipster ode to your affinity for art, but even shabby chic has its limits," I say.

Elle wags a finger at me. "Don't hurt Pumpkin's feelings."

"Pumpkin must die." My joke stalls though.

Elle and I stand shoulder to shoulder looking out at the beach.

"It's so weird being here...without Penny," she says.

"I know." I look at the foggy horizon, taking it in. "Every second of every day feels weird without Penny."

Dawn pulls up, with Raven right behind her. Raven winces as she steps out of her car. I hurry to help.

"Are you alright?"

"My knee. It's really messed up from falling off the stage."

No. Without her basketball scholarship she can kiss her freedom goodbye. Pills or no pills, this is the only thing that matters right now.

"How bad?" I ask.

"At least it's my left one, so I can still drive. But it hurts to stand. Can we go sit down?"

"Of course." I help her down the wooden boardwalk to the beach.

"This is it." Elle points to a spot by the volleyball courts. "Penny's favorite spot."

We set up our chairs. Dawn adjusts her ruffled high waisted bikini. Elle pulls her baseball hat low over her aviators. She's dressed in a bright turquoise and lime green paisley bathing suit with all sorts of cut outs and ties and textures. "I'm surprised your dad let you come to the beach today." Raven knows Sunday is usually homework day.

"Oh, I had to hear it all. *Punkaj won't be doing play-time on the beach.*"

Elle pokes my arm. "Maybe you *should* invite Punkaj to do playtime with you on the beach."

"Not this again!" I swat at her with my hat and kick sand over her feet in protest.

"It's too easy." Elle grabs the hat and tosses it out of my reach. I get up to grab it and notice a group of volley-ball players glancing our way, a couple guys, couple girls, not anyone I know from Everbeach Academy.

Recognition flashes across Elle's face. "Oh my gosh. You guys! That's *him*. Penny's boyfriend."

"I don't see Logan," Dawn says.

"Not *Logan*," Elle says. "Ansel."

The guy from the beach. "Is this what you were giving Logan a hard time about at the Sugarcane Festival?" I ask Elle.

"She didn't tell you about Ansel?" Elle looks surprised. "End of last school year. After she broke up with Logan—"

I cut her off, trying to piece this together. "Let me get this straight. Penny broke up with Logan, not the other way around?"

I spin to Raven for her reaction. Her face is far too composed.

"You don't seem surprised," I say. "Why aren't you surprised?"

The answer is plastered all over her guilty face.

"You already knew."

Raven hesitates, the tension on her face clear. "Logan told me last night," she admits. "But he didn't say Penny was with someone new." She scans the group playing volleyball. "Who is this guy?"

Elle points and we all follow along. "Ansel is uh, third to the left...there."

"Holy hotness." I take in his chiseled chest and arms.

Ansel's eyes are an even deeper brown than his skin, with an intensity visible all the way from here.

"Oh, my word, you all are gawking," Dawn says.

"Sorry not sorry," I say. "And so are you."

"Oh, shush," Dawn says. "I can't believe Penny had a *secret boyfriend*. How did they meet?"

"Here on the beach," Elle says. "It's funny to me she likes coming here when she lives on a private beach."

"She always complains it's boring," Raven says.

"Exactly. She wanted to go to the *real* beach. The one with the *real* people. We saw Ansel playing volleyball. He came up to talk to her and even though the sparks were instant, she said it would never work between them."

"Why?" Dawn asks.

Elle lowers her sunglasses and gives us a look, like we should know. "Not rich enough or connected enough for her dad. Not old money or new money enough. Not educated enough. Not enough, period. I'm pretty sure his whole crew is from Belle Grande. Can you imagine?"

"I didn't realize Mr. Zale was so judgmental," Raven says.

"*Please*. You're giving him too much credit. Her dad's as elitist as they come," I say. "It's the first law of being a social climber: decide where you want to be, grab a coattail, kiss every ass, and make sure to shake off any possible impediments to the destiny that you deserve."

"Mr. Zale seems like he works pretty hard for Mr. Steele," Dawn says.

"Oh, he does," Elle agrees. "But like Penny told me, hard work and climbing aren't mutually exclusive. She said she was sure there was a Venn diagram that could illustrate the overlap pretty nicely."

"What is a Venn diagram exactly?" Dawn asks. "I mean I know in general, sort of."

"I had to look it up after Penny mentioned it," Elle answers. "It's a chart that normally uses circles to show what something has in common with something else. Where the two circles overlap, that's the things they share."

I need facts and timelines, not charts. "So, Ansel and Penny...they dated. For how long?"

"All last summer," Elle says. "He was crazy about her. And she seemed really happy with him, too." She stops. "Wow, um, they're *really* staring. I should go say hello."

Before Elle can get up, one of the girls in the group stalks over. She has the muscular body of an athlete, braids pulled up into a high ponytail, and the same rich brown eyes and skin as Ansel.

"You Everbeach Academy princesses have a lot of nerve coming to our beach," she says in a raspy voice.

Elle looks caught off guard.

"You mean the *public* beach?" I immediately interject.

The girl glares at me, and oh it's a good fiery glare. She speaks slowly. Deliberately. "Your *slutty* friend cheated on my brother."

"Allllright." Elle stands up.

I jump up beside her. "You can leave. Now."

"No. *You* can leave." She gets right in our faces. "*Now.*"

"Hey, hey, hey." Ansel runs over. "Come on Greta. Chill."

She gives him a scathing look. "Frickin' pushover."

They regard each other for a moment in a sort of stare down, then, with a huff, Greta storms back to their friends and sits down, deliberately facing the water, her back to us.

"I'm sorry she said that. My sister is...protective," Ansel says. "Elle. It's good to see you."

"Good to see you, too." Elle fiddles with her hat. "This is Aarya, Dawn, and Raven. They're friends of Penny's."

Ansel nods a greeting.

"How are you doing?" he asks.

"We're, um, hanging in there. You?" Elle answers.

"Same."

"I didn't see you at the vigil," she says.

"I wasn't exactly on the list."

She gives him a shrug. "Neither was I."

"Yeah, well, I don't think I need to be around Logan," he says with a bitter looking smile.

"Logan didn't know about you?" I ask.

Ansel rubs his brow. "Nah. It was the other way around."

He touches Elle's arm. "Anyway, um, nice to see you. Sorry again about my sister."

My mind races as he walks away. *This* is who can fill in the blanks. I hurry after him, catching up at the water line. "Hey, wait." Foam swirls around our feet as the waves roll in. "Can I ask you something?"

"Shoot."

"Was Penny seeing you and Logan at the same time?"

Ansel presses his lips together. "I don't think so."

"Were you still together when she went to the hospital?"

"She'd gone distant even before her parents put her in that place. She kept trying to tell me she needed space, that it was for my own good."

There's a question that's burning. I go for it. "Do you think Logan did something to her?"

"Thought crossed my mind." Ansel lets out a long exhale. "She told me *'Steeles have a habit of getting their way and I don't want you to get hurt because of choices I make.'"*

His words hit like a rogue wave. *Steeles have a habit of getting their way...* I repeat the back half out loud to make sure I have it right. "And she didn't want you to get hurt because of choices she made."

"Penny was convinced that bad things would happen in my life if she was in it, which is the absolute opposite of anything I experienced. She was...the best thing that ever happened to me." Ansel's eyes meet mine. "Has there been any news about her case?"

"I wish the answer was yes."

His eyes glass over, reflecting hints of amber. "It doesn't seem real, you know? I thought she'd have turned up by now, reached out to someone. To *me*." He pauses for what feels like a long time. "I'm worried there's no way this ends the way I hope it will."

"Same."

Ansel's gaze shifts. "I should uh, get back to my friends."

I watch his retreating back. Would Penny be with Ansel now if she were here, or would she be back with Logan?

I step into the water and wave for the girls to join me so we can talk without anybody walking by us and over-hearing. We wade out until it's up to our shoulders, our faces islands in the sparkling, green ocean.

"Ansel is totally freaked out. I was asking him about Penny. And he said she told him that Steeles get their way. And people in their way get hurt."

Elle treads water as a little wave laps up at our faces. "Maybe that's what she's trying to tell us in my poem," she says. "*Hearts...turned to steel...a long time ago. To survive, walk on glass, pretend you don't know the deceit.*

Maybe Logan threatened to cause problems for Ansel if Penny didn't dump him."

"That's *absolutely* what happened." It makes perfect sense to me. "Logan wanted Penny back and manipulated everyone to get his way. It's probably what led to her nervous breakdown and forced her into Hightower in the first place."

"Doesn't explain an abduction though," Raven says.

"Unless Logan saw Penny as the problem, not Ansel," Dawn says.

I clear my throat. "Maybe Penny didn't *walk on the glass* carefully enough."

Elle frowns as she considers this, and twists her wet hair in a bun, glancing back at Ansel on the beach.

I notice a circle on her neck. No, two. Overlapping.

"You *do* have a tattoo," I say, remembering the game from drama class. "Don't you have to be eighteen to get one?"

"If you go somewhere legit." Elle immediately drops her hair back down, but I reach over and push it to the side.

"That's a Venn diagram. Just like you were talking about," I say.

"Um, yeah. It is."

"Why tattoo that on your body?" Raven asks.

Elle looks off to the horizon. "Penny's the one who encouraged me to come to Everbeach Academy to study art. I felt like...without her here, it was the least I could do. The Venn tattoo...it was like...possibility, overlapping with reality, it felt like a promise there's a space where she does return."

"So, the tattoo is new?" I ask.

"I know it probably seems crazy...anyway," Elle says

softly. "I'm going to go." She gives a weak wave and hurries out of the water.

Elle is only in our lives because of the Venn that is being friends with Penny, the overlap where we come together through her. But what is becoming more apparent as time goes on is that in that overlap, there are too many shadows.

Elle Glass is hiding something, and it's about time we found out what that is.

"Let's follow her."

CHAPTER 16
FOLLOWED HOME
RAVEN

We maintain a fair distance from Elle on the road, but it still feels painfully obvious what we're doing. "She's going to notice."

"No, she won't," Aarya says.

Elle's truck rumbles off to the left—Ashmont Village.

"Why is Elle going to the trailer park?" Dawn asks.

"Sooo yeah," Aarya says. "Elle's dad...dates the Tremaine twins' mom."

"When did you find this out?" I ask. "How do we not know?" What I really mean is, *How did you not tell me immediately?*

"Yesterday, at the Sugarcane Festival. The twins were messing with Elle. I overheard them say something about their parents dating. They don't seem happy about it."

"Maybe she's meeting him here?"

"I don't know. But we're going to find out."

Elle parks in front of a mobile home with yellow siding and brown trim around windows with bright brocade curtains. Orchids bloom on the porch and a plumeria tree with multicolored petals, bold pink fading to yellow, frame the entrance. It's a beautiful home—you can tell whoever lives here takes pride in caring for it. Elle walks in without knocking, and Aarya pulls into the parking spot next to Pumpkin.

"Now what?" I ask.

"We're bona fide stalkers." Dawn looks around, her eyes darting from left to right. "Maybe we should just go."

"Not an option." Aarya gives Dawn her you-have-to-be-kidding-me glare. "We're here, and we're getting answers. There can't be secrets between any of us."

My secret twists my gut, even though it shouldn't. After all, I shut Logan down. I didn't do anything wrong. But if that's the case, then why haven't I told Aarya about what happened? And why hadn't she mentioned Elle's dad dating the Tremaine twin's mom? That should have been an immediate text or phone call. Instead, she told me only because she had to.

I stare out the window, avoiding eye contact with Aarya in the rearview mirror when I say, "Do we go right up and knock?"

"That's exactly what we do. Let's go," Aarya says.

We unload from the car and walk up to the home. A flag blowing in the wind catches my eye. A golden *X* surrounded by green and black—Jamaica, my home country, where my dad has been for weeks. Not answering any of my texts or calls.

"That's a Jamaican flag," I say, stepping closer. "I'll take it as a sign I'm the one who's supposed to go to the door." My desperate yearning for a connection with my dad outweighs the messed-up reality that I'm grossly invading Elle's privacy.

Aarya and Dawn wisely wait in the driveway.

The door opens, and a woman with braids twisted into a bun greets me. She wears an apron with palm trees and a sunset painted on it, the phrase *Irie Mon* sprawls across the front. "Wah Gwaan? Can mi help yuh?"

What's going on, how Jamaicans greet each other, and her accent—proper cadence, clipped words, quick pace— it makes me blurt out, "Are you Jamaican?"

"Tell me dis. You in da habit of walking up to stranger's houses and asking where deh from?"

"No. Not at all, ma'am. I'm looking for my friend, Elle. It's just...your accent. It threw me."

"Ah. You're a friend of mi Elle. Come nuh, pickney. She's right over here."

Pickney. Familiarity surges in my bones. I haven't heard that word in years, and now it's all I can hear—a sweet, melodic sound, my mother's voice, calling me *pickney child*. My mother always said the two together, despite *child* being redundant, since *pickney* means exactly that.

"Raven?" Elle appears in the doorway, eyes wide. "What are you doing here?"

"Where's your manners dem?" The woman sucks a breath of air loudly in through her teeth at Elle, just like my mom always did. "Aren't you gonna introduce before you interrogate mi guest?"

"*Your* guest? This is someone I know from school."

"Over at dat fancy academy?"

"Yes, that's exactly where," Elle says. "All right. Fine. Raven, this is my godmother, Titania. Titania, Raven."

"Nice to meet you." I hold out my hand to Titania, but she pushes it away and pulls me into a hug which feels like a warm cloud of fresh pressed cotton with the crisp scent of witch hazel.

"Let me look at you, pickney deh." Titania studies me before her mouth drops open and she says, "Raven. Could it be? You Ebony Snow's daughter?"

"You knew my mom?"

"Gyal, I'd recognize dat face anywhere. But your hair." Titania holds out her hands as if reaching for something missing. "Where's your mane?"

"My what?"

"Your curls, gyal. Your momma was a lioness."

Suddenly self-conscious, I pull my hair back into a ponytail, "How did you know her?"

"We grew up together in Belle Grande. A force of nature, dat one. I knew your father, too, before deh took off back to Jamaica."

A flash of adrenaline skims the surface of my skin. A memory. The one time I visited Belle Grande with my mom it was warm and welcoming, like this woman—like being here. I want to stay forever, hear all her stories, find out everything she can remember about my mom and dad. The ripe smell of fried bananas wafts toward me. "Are you cooking plantains?"

"Yeh mon, I am. And rice and peas."

"No way!" I actually jump up and down and clap at my favorite childhood meal. My dad still makes it on the rare occasion when Vera is away for an overnight business trip. "It's my favorite!"

"You wanna stay for lunch? Mi got food for you to nyam."

Elle immediately interjects. "Raven, you don't have to stay. I know you must be as tired as me after everything."

Instead of taking the hint, I say, "No, I actually wouldn't mind staying."

Elle steps past Titania and joins me outside. "Really, it's fine. You don't have to be polite. Titania understands."

Titania puts her hands on her hips. "No. Mi say you

can't leave, you know. You haven't seen what I've got for dessert. Tamarind balls!"

"I'll walk you out." The look on Elle's face is a mixture of resolve and something else I can't place—shame? I let her lead me to the driveway. "My godmother may think I invited you over, but I know I didn't. You followed me."

I hesitate. Elle looks past me and does a double take. Aarya and Dawn sheepishly wave.

"You *all* followed me? What the hell?"

"We can explain," I say, but Elle's accusatory stare stalls my response.

Dawn noticeably hangs back, but Aarya steps forward. "You were acting weird and abruptly hurried off. Again. At the festival, the Tremaine twins threatened you—"

"And that gives you the right to follow me?"

Aarya opens her mouth to answer but pauses. "You know, that sounded better in my head."

"You think?" Elle has a point.

Maybe I can smooth this over. "While I get you're annoyed because we totally invited ourselves—"

"Stalked me," Elle interrupts.

"I told you all." Dawn almost sounds smug.

"Call it whatever you want," Aarya says, "but we're here now. And I have some questions."

Elle waves her hand at me, gesturing toward my designer bag. "If I'm not mistaken, girls with fancy purses don't hang out in trailer parks."

"Who cares if your godmother lives in a trailer park?" Raven says.

Elle lets out a bitter laugh and points to a silver trailer next to Titania's. "Don't you get it? I live here, too."

"Oh my gosh." Dawn's hand flies to her mouth and

then she looks chagrinned. "I'm sorry. I didn't mean anything by that. I'm not judging. I'm just surprised is all."

Elle pulls at her shirt, fidgeting with the hem. "Yeah. I didn't move to Everbeach from Ashville. I've lived in *Ashmont* for a long time, way before I ever stepped foot on the academy's campus."

I don't ask her why she lied. I don't need to. I know what it feels like to walk into a world knowing I'm not like the others.

When I went to my first cotillion class, I was so excited to wear the dresses I'd brought with me from Jamaica. In layers and layers of bright colors, wrapped and twisted, I marched right into the dining room, only to freeze under gawking stares. Boys dressed in button-down shirts, with too big coat jackets and too long ties, and girls in their cardigans wearing pearls and pencil skirts. It was a sea of khaki and navy and baby pink. I knew I didn't belong.

"So, this is why the twins hate you," Aarya says.

Elle nods. "Their mom's the queen of the park and my dad a mere peasant. They can't stand that their mom is dating a truck driver that lives here. They say they'll tell everyone where I live if I don't get our parents to break up."

I laugh realizing a truth that will save Elle a lot of drama. "You do *not* have to worry about them spilling your secret."

"How so?"

"Because they're climbers," I say. "They latch onto everything and anyone that can raise their social status. You know how ashamed they are of how their mother came into her money. And now she's dating one of her trailer park's residents? Your secret is safe with them."

"You think so?"

"One hundred percent. But I don't think it needs to be a secret. At least not with us."

"Well." Elle shrugs. "You're not exactly...on my level."

"I'm on your level more than you might realize," I say.

"Sure, okay." Elle crosses her arms after pointedly gesturing to my purse and shoes.

"Did you miss the whole Titania grew up in Belle Grande *with my mom?* The tension between Vera and me. It's partially related to that. So, I get it, I do. It's different but the same."

Elle seems to consider what I say, but her face hardens, the layers of armor almost visibly clinking back into place. "I know what people say. *Trashmont.* Trailer trash. The redneck Riviera. I've heard it all."

"Not from *us,*" Aarya says.

"There's a reason we're all friends," Dawn says.

"It's like the Venn diagram," I say. "We're the shaded area where things that don't seem to match come together."

Elle touches the back of her neck. "Maybe there's more to being similar than what's on the surface."

Aarya tugs on one of her bright red highlights. "Is this what you've been hiding? You didn't want us to know you live in Ashmont?"

Elle holds up her hands, and I catch her eyes. There's something in them that says, *Please. Please accept me.*

"Penny chose you to bring us her letters," I say. "She trusted you. So, I trust you."

Dawn and Aarya nod in agreement.

Elle relaxes, her armor visibly coming down.

"No more secrets, okay?" Aarya says.

"No more secrets," Elle agrees.

"I feel like we should hug," Dawn says.

Aarya considers Dawn. "I'll hug, but don't make me talk about my feelings."

I grab Aarya and Elle, and then Dawn jumps in and we do the most awkward group hug I've been a part of. Aarya pulls away and exaggeratedly pretends she needs to brush off the touch. She's smiling though. We all are. It's maybe one of the first real moments of joy we've had since everything with Penny, and it feels like something she would want. To bring the most important people in her life together. Somehow our band of misfits is who she believed in and trusted, who she knew would help.

"Alright. Can we please go back inside and eat some lunch? I'm starving," I say.

Elle looks surprised. "You were serious about staying for lunch?"

"Gyal, you t'ink mi gonna pass up some Jamaican food to nyam?" I say, rich, clipped notes rounding my words.

"Whoa. Where did that accent come from?"

"It's in there. Only needs a reason to come out."

Just then, Titania's boisterous voice calls from the balcony outside her door. "Come nuh, you pickney dem. The food is getting cold."

We follow the decadent smells coming from Titania's kitchen, taking our seats around the candle lit table.

"I love the candles," I say, realizing no actual lights are on. The entire trailer is illuminated by flickering light.

"I don't remember the last time she used real lights," Elle says.

"Fire is real light," Titania says placing dishes on the table. "It mek the world softer. Somet'ing we all need, you know?"

"I like that," Dawn says, then her attention shifts. "Do you sew?"

We all follow Dawn's gaze. There are mounds of clothes on the couch in the living room, a sewing machine set up next to it.

"Ah yes. A likkle t'ing mi do for fun."

"Don't be fooled. Titania is one of the best seamstresses in Everbeach," Elle says.

Titania passes me a plate of chicken, and I instantly recognize the peppery spice. "Jerk chicken. Yum!"

"Shhh. Don't offend mi luv's sensitive ears. We call it 'nice' chicken over here."

"I was five when I said that. I can handle it now," Elle says.

"It's too cute, mi pickney, ah so it set," Titania says. "Come nuh, tek you some of this *nice* chicken before it get cold."

Their rapport is so easy. She's more than a godmother to Elle. They seem like real mother and daughter, what I imagine it could be at least. What I want more than anything and know the chance for is gone.

"So, Elle, while we eat this *nice* chicken, care to tell us a *nice* story, maybe the real story about how you met Penny?" Aarya asks.

"I mean, not if you're uncomfortable. We've already invaded your space enough today," Dawn says.

Elle smiles at Dawn. "It's okay."

Nothing like stalking friends to finally bond us together.

"I told you my mom knew Penny's mom. That's true but that's because my mom worked for her. Cleaning her house." Elle explains when her mother died, Elle had to pick up her jobs to help make ends meet, and Penny's house was one of those jobs.

"Penny was just sitting there at her counter, eating a popsicle when I first met her. She asked why I was cleaning her house when I was her age," Elle says. "I was kind of defensive, you know? But she wasn't making fun of me. She was truly curious. She had this directness and sincerity about her, so I opened up. Told her my story. And then she got up and started helping me clean."

I smile. "That's totally Penny."

"Yeah, she was one of the only people I could really talk to about my mom's death." Elle pauses, the memory clearly evoking emotions. For all of us. Because it is so Penny—no pretension, as real as they come.

"She's the reason I'm at Everbeach Academy." Elle looks around at us.

"Tell dem the whole story, mi inspired one. How you sacrificed deh flowers dem for art," Titania says.

"Listen, your plumeria was fine," Elle says. "But yeah, after the day Penny told me what a Venn diagram was, I went home and sketched a beach where the sun was part of the overlapping sets of circles, superimposed on plumeria petals in the foreground. So yes, I picked a *few*. Anyway, the next time I cleaned Penny's house, I took her the drawing. Penny said she loved it and wanted it to hang in her room. What she actually did was write an essay pretending to be me and sent the drawing off to Everbeach Academy's financial needs program."

"So, you're at Everbeach on a scholarship," Aarya says.

"I'm not working on my art in the art studio during lunch. I'm cleaning. Work study."

"Penny gets you in and then isn't there. You're alone," Dawn says. "That's hard."

Elle starts clearing the table. "Yeah, it's been more than tough, but meeting all of you has made it easier."

"Speaking of how yuh all met, why don't yuh tell ol' Titania where yuh are with Penny's poems."

I should be upset that Titania knows we're investigating the poems—we clearly said no adults—but there's something different about her. She seems like she's on our team, on Penny's team. And now that Vera knows because of Dawn, we need an adult who is on our side. Speaking of, why hasn't Dawn told me about her slip yet? Agitated butterflies dance in my stomach, but I ignore them in favor of getting help from Titania.

Aarya glances at me. I nod, letting her know it's okay to discuss.

So, we take turns filling Titania in, explaining our theory about Logan. I don't dare speak my silent fear: how my poem could be linked to him, that Penny saw Logan and me on the balcony.

Aarya's phone dings. She reads the message. "It's Punk." We all look at her, but she doesn't say anything. Her eyes jump to Elle. "He found something at Hightower."

"Hold on. Why is Punk messaging you about Hightower?" Now both Aarya and Elle are not making eye contact with me.

Aarya completely ignores my question. "He needs to see us *now*."

I tilt my head, scrutinizing her. "That doesn't answer what I asked. Why is he at Hightower?"

"We told him about the poems," Elle says faster than you can rip a Band-Aid off. "After the pageant. He offered to help."

"I thought we weren't going to tell anyone?" I struggle to keep my composure realizing Aarya has kept yet another thing from me—another person knows about the poems—and no one thought it was important to mention this to me either.

"You didn't question just now when Titania knew about the poems," Aarya hedges.

"Elle broke that promise. Not you." I can't help the frost in my tone.

Dawn glances nervously at Aarya. "Now might be a good time to tell you I also told Grayson."

Aarya lets out an exasperated sigh. "Of course you did."

"He's my *boyfriend*," Dawn protests. "And you told Punk!"

I cross my arms, trying to quell the burning in my chest. "So, Punk knows and Grayson knows and heck, maybe we should just announce it over the loudspeaker at school tomorrow. And while we're at it, someone please call Vera and let her know, too. Oh wait." I stare pointedly at Dawn. "You already did that."

Dawn's face turns ashen. "I am so sorry. It was chaos after you fell, and I didn't think before speaking, and—"

I wave a hand toward my knee cutting her off. "It doesn't matter. Basketball is off the table either way. My knee. Vera. It's over."

"Raven, don't be like that. When you fell yesterday—I mean...right after the pageant, it was chaos, and Vera was asking questions. Dawn was only trying to help."

I shift uncomfortably, feeling the embarrassment of what happened at the pageant all over again, and goose bumps spread up my neck and crawl down my arms. "Fine, whatever, but that doesn't explain why you didn't tell me you told Punk."

"This was our first real chance to talk about it," Aarya says, her expression kind, and I feel even more embarrassed because she's right. The pageant was only yesterday, and I need to reign it in.

"Uh, it's fine. Really." I can tell she didn't mean to leave me out, but in a normal world, Aarya would have called or texted me first thing this morning and told me everything that happened when I wasn't there.

I always wondered how friendships broke, convinced it was some cataclysmic, unforgivable event. Something that could never happen to Aarya and me. But now I can see that maybe it's the other way around. Maybe the small things add up until one day it all becomes too much for even the closest of friends to overcome.

But I have to stuff down my feelings about all of it because if Punk helps us with these poems, with finding Penny, my hurt feelings don't matter right now.

Aarya feverishly texts. "He says he'll be here in ten minutes."

"I've got room at mi table," Titania says. "That's enough time for dessert. Mek sure you save the boy some, you hear?" She brings over a plate of little sticky spheres of tamarind mixed with brown sugar stacked in a pyramid on a dish. The smell of the tangy fruit hangs in the air.

I grab several and pop one in my mouth, the sour sweet taste grounding me in the familiar.

Moments later there's a knock at the door and Punkaj whooshes into the room. "You have to see this." He pulls out a file and places the papers on the table. Everyone leans in. "It's a copy of the visitor's log. Someone visited Penny twelve times. Some guy named Ansel?"

We all look at each other. "We know who that is," I say.

"We met him today. Apparently, he was Penny's boyfriend," Aarya says.

Elle looks over Punkaj's shoulder and gasps.

"What?" he asks.

"Hang on a second." Elle hurries out the front door and returns with a large envelope. She places it on the table next to the logs, points at Ansel's name on the log and then her address written on the envelope.

I immediately see the similarity. Block letters. All caps. The handwriting is identical.

Aarya draws back. "*Ansel* sent the poems."

"We have to go find him," I say.

"Go to Belle Grande?" Dawn asks.

Titania puts a hand up. "They don't like people rattling the cage around there. It's not unusual for people to disappear when they a mover and a shaker." Her expression softens when she looks directly at me. "Ebony wanted to change t'ings for da better. She and Clive went back to Jamaica. Left Belle Grande for a reason. But change takes truth, and truth has a price."

She knows more about my mom and dad, and it snags at my heart, beckoning me to ask questions that aren't appropriate. Not right now anyway. "We need the truth, whatever the price. It's Penny."

Aarya agrees. "I think we go to Belle Grande. It's the only choice."

Titania tilts Elle's chin up and says to her, "I know you're gonna go no matter what I say." She motions for us to lean in close and whispers, "You go there, tread careful. Some people you can talk to. Others be scared. And fear can't be trusted. Go straight to Ansel's house. Don't bother anyone else. Ask your questions and you get out."

CHAPTER 17
ROAD TO HELL
RAVEN

T he tattered edges of a weathered, wooden sign greet us at the entrance to the city.

Welcome to Belle Grande
Where her soil is her fortune

Nothing is like I remember it. Five-year-old me saw colorful buildings like mismatched socks, and scraggly bushes I wanted to run through like a maze. Today, everything looks so rundown, and in the distance, smoke billows in the fields, turning the blue sky gray and ominous.

I'm not ready for this. My mind immediately flashes to the last time I was here. My mother and I got ice cream at the corner store and visited an aunt I haven't seen since. My dad never brought me here, not once, after we moved back from Jamaica.

"Muck Town." Punkaj throws on the blinker and hangs a hard left at the exit. "That's what they call this place you know. Because sugarcane grows in swamps."

Even if there's an explanation for the nickname, it still feels rotten. People live here, work hard here, have grown roots here. This is their home. It was my mom's home. I touch my necklace and watch Dawn snap pictures out the open window with her camera. Punkaj enlisted her help for the story he promises he'll find here, so we stopped by her house and grabbed her camera on the way. I want the images she's taking for *my* story—to help me fill in the blanks of a life I've barely known.

Punkaj coughs as a smoky gust of air blows into the car and points to the orange-tinged horizon. "They must be burning today."

"Why do they burn the fields?" My throat is getting scratchy. Not only from the thick, toxic air, but from the ashy taste of loss, of not knowing this place, my mom's history kept from me after she was gone.

"Controlled burns. It's how they get rid of the outer leaves of the sugarcane."

"Black snow," Elle says. "That's what Titania calls it. Happens every year at harvest time. She blames it for her asthma, says practically every kid out here has an inhaler from the day they're born. All sorts of heart and lung disease."

I take in the ramshackle, rain-blanched walls, potholes, chain link, sagging one-story shacks, and the signs—*bail bonds, payday advance, pawn shop.* The smell of sizzling food competes with the stench of rotting trash.

The laughter of children kicking a ragged soccer ball bites back against the silence of the weary elderly crouched in debris-strewn lawns, using old buckets as seats, watching time pass. Underneath it all, a deep and tangible feeling of being unwelcome hovers. It's the energy from the people, glowering in the shadows of stairwells and porches, behind the dirt-streaked windows we pass. Newcomers. Strangers.

Dawn comes out from behind her camera lens like someone surfacing for air. "This is...wow. They don't have very much here at all."

"It's messed up when you think of who they work for and how much *they* have," Elle says.

How much we *all* have by comparison. To think, my mom worked at the Maharaja, serving the haves, coming home to the have-nots. Still, she met my dad, and he left our world for her.

Just like Penny tried to do for Ansel.

I want to leave, too, because it's not even my world. It's Vera's. I touch my constantly throbbing knee. I can recover from this, fight through the pain. I will make my own way. Cut the puppet strings of money and status and power. Empty, meaningless things. For all we supposedly have, it's done nothing in our search for Penny.

You have reached your destination. On the right, the GPS reports.

We pull up to a one-story, mostly gray stucco house, the paint almost entirely faded. "Is this correct?" I ask.

"It's the address I got when I ran public records," Punkaj says.

"It's so..." My voice trails off because *familiar* is what I want to say. I haven't been to this specific house before, just one like it, trailing my mom into my aunt's unapologetically ramshackle home.

The porch awning hangs at a different angle than the tilt of the roof, so it looks like the house got pinched in the middle. The bottom left window is boarded up. But a welcome mat sits in front of the door and potted herbs flourished on the sunny steps—basil, rosemary, sage— next to a rusted metal chair with a dark green cushion.

We pile out of the car, but before we get up the stairs, a curtain in the window moves, and the front door opens.

"Elle?" Ansel recognizes her first. His striking, amber-flecked eyes flash confusion as he sees the rest of us standing there. "What's going on?"

"Sorry to barge in on you like this," Elle says.

"We have some questions about Penny we're hoping you can help us with," Aarya says, putting it all out there in her take-no-prisoners style.

Ansel's chiseled jaw clenches. Even when caught off guard, he's alarmingly handsome. No wonder Penny fell for him.

"I told you everything I knew at the beach," he says.

"Did you?" Aarya asks.

He steps closer to us, voice low. "Coming here is what got Penny in trouble. So do yourselves a favor, and go back to Everbeach."

"Please," I say, leaning in. I sound desperate, and I'm okay with that. Because I *am* desperate and not above begging.

"You all need to get out of here. This isn't a game," Ansel says.

"But are the *poems?*" Punkaj interjects. "Are the poems a game?"

"What poems?" Ansel's expression betrays nothing. "Who are you anyway?"

"I'm a reporter for *The Mirror*," Punkaj says. "The hand-writing on the envelopes sent to Elle match someone's on the guest log at Hightower. Yours, in fact. Want to talk about it?"

Ansel's face immediately closes off.

Elle steps in. "Ansel. He's a friend. He's trying to help. Be honest with us." She looks Ansel square in the eye. "Was it *you* who left me the envelope of poems?"

"I don't know what you're talking about. And this conversation's gone on long enough," Ansel says.

Elle tries to continue, but he's already heading back inside.

I catch the screen door before it closes. "*Please,*" I reiterate, no longer begging but yearning—for my mom, for Penny, for my injured leg to heal. "I know you don't know me. And I don't know you. But I know Penny, we both do. If you're as close to her as I believe you are, then you must love her as much as we do. If you know anything, *anything* at all, please, you have to tell us. Her life could depend on it."

Ansel closes his eyes and lets out a deep, long exhale before stepping back onto the porch, the door closing behind him. "Yeah. It was me."

My tension releases like a giant breath. For the first time since the pageant, I feel genuine relief. "*You* sent the poems. You visited her in Hightower."

"Of course I did." Ansel looks like he could never fathom any other possibility. "I was there every day they let me. But all she did was write poems—different versions, over and over. She made me promise if anything ever happened to her, to make sure you got them. The final version at least."

"There are more?"

"Not more, just more of the same."

"What do you think they mean?"

"If I had any clue what they meant, I'd be out there looking for her myself. But I'm not sure she even knew. She was too drugged up on antipsychotics to make any sense. It was...awful. She was like a shadow of herself."

"Do you still have them?" Aarya asks. "The other versions?"

Ansel nods. "I'll get them for you. But good luck figuring out what she was talking about."

When he reemerges from the house, he has an armful of paper.

Dawn's eyes widen. "All that?"

Ansel shakes his head. "It's all she did."

He places them into Punkaj's open hands, and it looks like it hurts him to let go.

I understand the feeling. It's the only piece of Penny he has left to hold on to, like me with my mom's necklace. If anything ever happened to it, a fissure would crack deep within.

Punkaj flips through the pages.

I recognize some of the phrases from their final versions.

Ansel presses his lips together. "She was so off before they locked her up. I remember one night, she showed up here, sobbing and shaking. Wouldn't tell me why. I tried to get her to talk to me, but she begged me to just hold her and not ask questions. So that's what I did." Ansel pauses. "It wasn't too long after that she was sent to Hightower."

"Where had Penny come from that night?" Punkaj asks.

"Church. Some charity thing her family was into. They do a lot for the sugar workers, especially the new ones coming into the U.S., you know, helping them get set up and stuff. Her dad was renovating the church as a donation from Steele Sugar."

"She volunteered at a church here?" Dawn asks.

"Yeah. Down the way." Ansel looks to the left and right almost as if he expects someone to be listening. "Church of Belle Grand."

Dawn goes still.

"What is it?" Aarya asks.

"I, I..." Dawn is flustered. "I feel like... Hold on." Dawn takes out her poem from her purse, flapping it at Aarya. "Read it for me. Please. I can't."

Aarya reads aloud. *"Go to their church. Wake and ring the grand bell! The taste of success is a spindle from hell... and sweet."*

Dawn's voice trembles. "Grand Bell, Bell Grand. All this time I thought the church line had to do with me, because of my dad. But maybe Penny meant this church, if something happened there that upset her so much."

It makes sense.

"Ring the grand bell," Punkaj repeats. "Church of Belle Grand. Hmmm. It's possible. What could have been going on there?"

Ansel retreats toward his door. "All you can do is go and ask, right? But please, don't mention me, okay? Penny told me to steer clear. I promised her."

"All right." Aarya's voice is too even. I can tell she doesn't trust him, and I'm not sure I do either. Ansel was last to see Penny before Hightower, and the last to visit her before she disappeared.

"You'll still let me know, right? If you hear anything about her?" Ansel asks.

"Give us your number," Elle says. "That way we can get in touch."

Ansel punches his information into her phone and with a curt nod, steps into his house.

"To the church, then," Punkaj says.

It's easier said than done in the congested, looping neighborhoods. The navigation recalculates and tells us to U-turn for a fifth time. Elle points to a soaped-out window, the streaks hiding the inside room from view. "The GPS says it's here."

Dawn scrutinizes the building. "I don't see a steeple anywhere."

"Does it need a steeple to be a church?" I ask.

"I say we try it," Aarya says.

We get out and approach what looks like an abandoned storefront. Elle knocks on the glass door. An older woman steps out, gray hair tucked into a headwrap and colorful dress flowing around her. The woman's gentle tone and smiling eyes ease my nerves. "Can I help you?"

"We're looking for the pastor?" I say.

"You found her," says the woman. "I'm Pastor Dana."

"This is the church and *you're* the pastor?" Dawn asks with confusion.

"You seem surprised," Dana says.

Dawn pauses. "I guess I imagined a big, white building, like my church, with a cross on top. And I've never met a female pastor before."

Dana smirks. "Well, nice to meet you. Why don't you all come inside?"

We step into a room set with rows of folding metal chairs, an electric keyboard set off to the side, a podium with a microphone attached in the middle, and at the front, a cross hanging against the peeling plaster behind it.

"So, what brings you all the way to my doorstep? You don't seem to be from around here."

"We're friends of Penny Zale's," I say.

Pastor Dana's hand flutters to her heart. "Any word?"

I look to Aarya.

"The police say she might have been abducted."

"Oh my." Dana goes pale. "Who would ever hurt that sweet child? We love her here. Truly. She came every weekend to help new workers get settled in, taking care of everything from soap and toothpaste to toys for the kids and canned food. But more than anything, she gave us her time. She spent time with people who sometimes aren't really treated as people. I'm sick, just sick, to hear this."

"Can you think of anyone who would want to hurt her?" I ask.

"We heard she was really upset after leaving here one night," Aarya adds.

Pastor Dana bites down on her lip before answering in a low voice. "I remember that night. I thought it was boy trouble."

"What boy?" I ask. "Ansel?"

"No, no. One of those Steele boys. He dropped her here, and she was a mess."

My whole body is at once electric and heavy. My thoughts evaporate, and I want to disappear with them. This is the most damning evidence against Logan yet.

Aarya's gaze is locked on Pastor Dana. "Logan Steele dropped her here. In Belle Grande. And she was sobbing."

Pastor Dana nods. "I wish I could be more helpful. But that's truly all I know."

"Is there anyone else who might know more?" Aarya asks.

"No one is going to want to talk to anyone from Everbeach."

None of us are surprised she's assumed that's where we're all from, but Aarya still asks, "Why?"

"Because this is the kind of town that keeps their heads down. No one will risk losing the little they have."

Something about her tone makes my skin prickle into goose bumps.

"Questions have consequences in Belle Grande." Her voice carries the same stern warning as Titania's. She walks over to the door and holds it open. Our cue to leave. "You kids take care. Stay out of trouble. I'll be praying for Penny."

We head back to the car, everyone quiet while Punkaj navigates out of Belle Grande.

"What has everyone so scared?" I wonder out loud.

Only the sound of the car engine and the wheels on the road answer.

Titania warned us about trying to find the truth. She left Belle Grande for a reason. My mom and dad had dreams, wanted to change things, yet they left, too.

I look at the sign in the rearview mirror. *Her soil is her fortune.*

No, *her soil is* their *fortune.*

My stomach drops like a roller coaster, my thoughts rubbing against the rails, friction. Muck city for the sugarcane. Sugar for the Steele empire. Logan Steele leaving Penny crying. Penny locked in a tower alone with her poems. Her poems in Ansel's hands. Ansel handing his last pieces of Penny to us, our labyrinth of clues, unscalable walls and poisonous traps, a game leading us nowhere, then...here.

To uncover the truth, we'll have to dance with the dark side of this town and her secrets.

CHAPTER 18
BURNING QUESTIONS
AARYA

Returning to school feels like a crash landing. Back to the buzz and the gossip. A million miles from Belle Grande—even further from answers. Everything that happened at the Sugarcane Festival is waiting to greet us. And it's on me to do damage control. Raven's out today for a doctor appointment to check out her knee and run tests to see why she passed out.

It seems manageable until the tail end of drama class. Nikki—shirt unbuttoned way too low, to show off the diamond necklace from her pageant "win"—stands in the center of her small group of scandal-hungry friends, talking about Raven.

"She popped one too many pills again." Nikki yawns. "It doesn't take a rocket scientist. We *all* remember eighth grade summer."

"Yeah, we sure do." I step into the center of the circle, hoping to scatter it. "When you tried to steal her basketball position."

"I didn't *steal* anything. Raven went on a junior high

bender and couldn't play," Nikki says with an overly sympathetic pout. "Someone had to lead the team."

"Yeah," Kat says, Nikki's ever-present echo. "It's not our fault Raven wound up in like, rehab for tweens."

"I hope she's not heading back down that path?" Nikki cocks her head. "Thoughts and prayers."

Their words land like embers from a burning pile of rancid trash. "Shut up you trilobites! She suffers from *post-traumatic stress.*"

"Well maybe the *extreme* stress of Miss Sugarcane triggered her uh, *PTSD.*" Nikki makes quotes with her fingers. "And she had to *self-medicate*. Either way, I can't wait to read what *The Mirror* writes about her onstage collapse."

I give her a look of disgust. "Punkaj Grimsley covered the pageant. He would never write anything salacious."

I'm surprised to hear Logan's voice. An unexpected addition to the conversation. "*The Mirror* won't write about something like that period. It's in poor taste."

I give him a you-just-grew-two-heads look.

Logan kicks his feet rhythmically against the side of the stage. "You should be grateful Nikki." He hops off and shoots her a scathing look over his shoulder as he walks away. "You never would have won if she hadn't passed out."

Nikki's gooey glossed mouth forms an indignant *O* before she turns away to huddle and whisper with her sister.

On the one hand, I love seeing Nikki taken out like that. But back up. *Logan* defended Raven. Logan defended *Raven*. Wherever I place the emphasis it sounds strange.

The last bell rings.

I head for the auditorium doors with Elle.

The Tremaine twins push by to catch up with Logan.

"Don't be mad at me Logan." Nikki gives him puppy dog eyes. "I'm sorry if I said anything that came across wrong. You know I *adore* Raven and was only worried. Do you forgive me?"

"Sure," Logan says.

Nikki steps in front of him. "Say it like you mean it." She puts her hands on her hips and sticks her lower lip out further, batting her lashes.

"It's cool. We're good." Logan steps around them just as Hunter pokes his head in from the hall.

"You coming or what? Driver's waiting."

"Relax," Logan grumbles.

"I have to get to work. Vera will kill me if I'm late." Hunter scowls at his brother, but his face brightens when he spots Elle and me. "Sea Witch! Slugger! MMA try outs are next week. You should go for it."

"Do you ever stop?" Logan says.

Hunter tilts his head toward Elle. "When are we going on our date?"

"Hard no," Elle fires back.

"I thought we were in a hurry," Logan says, stalking past Hunter.

"All right, all right." Hunter mouths *call me* to Elle, before catching up to Logan.

"Bye Logan," Nikki calls out. She turns to her sister. "He's so hot I can't even stand it."

Elle runs her hands through her hair and lets out a loud, frustrated sigh.

"Aw, was that for me?" Nikki asks.

"It's just gross how you throw yourself at him. You really think he'd want to date *you* after Penny?"

"Maybe mind your own business," Katarina chimes in. "People can date whoever they want."

"Oh, really?" Elle interjects. "Like my dad and your mom?"

"That's different." Nikki narrows her eyes and folds her arms. "Should I tell Aarya *why*?"

"I already know where she lives," I say flatly. "And I don't care."

"Well...we care." Nikki crosses her arms "My mom worked her ass off to get out of Ashmont. I'm sure as hell not getting dragged back by association."

"You know," Elle says. "I suddenly realized I forgot something in the auditorium." She turns on her heels.

She's got the right idea. Why even engage with these two? I let the door slam in their faces and catch up with Elle back on the stage.

"You okay?"

She leans against the grand piano. "I'm fine."

"Don't let them make you feel less-than." I open the piano and play a couple chords softly.

"I certainly have less than everyone here. And that's not easy."

"You have more of a soul." I play a twinkly couple of high notes to match. "And a brain." I rattle off some quick complicated scales. "More than the twins could ever dream of." I hit a bunch of the black keys in a clanging out-of-tune mess at once.

Elle laughs and I smile at her.

Just then, the lights in the entire auditorium dim to an eerie blue with a *click, buzz*.

"Oh my gosh, it's them messing with us," Elle says.

And then, the lights go out. The pitch blackness of the room is so complete it feels like a weight. A bang from the top of the stairs startles me and I jump, then we laugh as we realize we've grabbed onto each other.

"Knock it off," I yell into the darkness.

A spotlight comes on, but the beam doesn't stay still. Instead, it cuts the shadows, jumping from wall-to-wall, meandering in loops across the stage before landing on us. We squint into the light, blinded.

I shield my eyes with my hand. "Who's there?" No answer. The light flicks off again, plunging the room back into black.

"Ha, ha, very funny!" Elle shouts.

I grab my phone for the flashlight, only to have it vibrate.

The message is from a blocked number. I open it and immediately drop my phone at the sight.

Elle scoops it up and freezes, mouth open. "It's the creepy picture of the penny with the blacked-out eyes again."

I take in the picture of the scribbled-on coin. "This isn't the twins. It's whoever keeps messing with us."

I read the message aloud.

"*Lights out. Don't play with fire.*"

The words get swallowed up in the dark room, and land in a pit in my own stomach.

A door slams.

"Whoever it is, they're bolting. Let's try to catch them."

We fumble our way up to the light booth at the top of the stairs. Something smells strange, sort of chemically, plastic, but also smoky as we get closer.

"Is something on *fire*?" Elle asks.

I throw open the door. "Crap. No one is here. We missed them."

The room is empty except for a metal wastebasket. And sure enough, a small fire snaps and licks the edges of the only thing tossed inside.

A picture.

I reach down and grab it, trying to wave out the flames.

Elle leans in. "It's *us*. In Belle Grande."

It looks like a still grabbed from a surveillance camera, the group of us, waiting outside the door of the church.

"Someone knew we were in Belle Grande, maybe even followed us, made sure to get a picture," I say.

"To let us know they know what we're doing," Elle says.

"And they don't like it."

The stubborn flames lick at my fingers, refusing to go out. I drop the picture back into the bin before I get burned. The edges curl in and under. Our faces warp, the picture burning itself out.

"Titania said truth has a price," Elle says. "And the pastor warned us, questions have consequences."

I stare at the smoking embers.

Someone is trying to scare us into not asking questions.

Which means...we're asking the right ones.

CHAPTER 19
WHERE THERE'S SMOKE
AARYA

t is both the last place, and the only place, I want to be—the annual Steele Bro's Beach Bash. As much as I would like a couple of continents between me and the "bros," the can't-miss camp-out on the beach means one thing: a can't-miss chance to dig for answers. After the burned picture in the auditorium this week, this is where we need to be.

"We're getting into Logan's room tonight," I say. "There's got to be something in there that sheds some light."

"It feels a like little déjà vu, doesn't it?" Raven asks. "Back at the Steeles, on a mission."

"How it started, how it's going," I quip.

"And still no Penny."

Still no Penny.

"What exactly are we looking for?" Raven asks.

"There's a saying my parents like. *Focus on the snake, miss the scorpion*," I say. "Think. Who could have known we were in Belle Grande? The Steeles basically run the place." I continue, connecting the dots. "Tonight, we go digging for the snake *and* the scorpion."

"So you have no idea." Raven leans against my SUV, and winces as she takes weight off her leg.

"I want to go through his stuff," I say. "I want to see if there's anything that shows he might be behind these creepy messages."

"I'm sure his burner phone will be right out on his desk." Raven says facetiously, massaging her knee. "I can't believe I'm out for the season."

"There's really no chance of you playing?" I still can't process this.

"A really slim chance," Raven says. "But as much as this sucks for me, it's nothing compared to Penny. Let's just focus on that."

I hear a telltale engine rumble in the distance. "Elle's here." Her orange behemoth sticks out like a forgotten Halloween decoration. Uh oh. So does *she*.

"What?" Elle asks, when she sees my expression.

"What are those?" I point. "And what is that?"

Elle looks down at her flannel shirt and holds up the bag of marshmallows. "The party. You said camping on the beach? It's for s'mores." She gestures to the bulky nylon bag by her feet. "And that's my tent!"

I crack up.

Raven purses her lips to the side, trying to figure out how to say something awkward, nicely. She's wearing sandals, and a tiny, flashy sundress. I'm in black silk shorts and a metal-studded tank top that I had on under a longer dress to get out of the house.

Elle takes note of us versus her. "Okay, so I think I may have been a little misguided in what tonight's party is all about."

"Yeahhh," Raven says. "Our fault. We should have explained the party better. The *camp-out* is not camping."

"Awesome." Elle tangles her fingers into her hair and grimaces.

I reassure her. "There's a job to do tonight. No time for wardrobe drama. Let's get you out of that RV-life ad, and into beach soiree mode."

Raven answers Elle's confused expression. "Aarya always has piles of clothes in her car."

"It's basically a closet on wheels." I hop into my back-seat and pull Elle in behind me.

Raven rummages around the messy floor and pulls out a pair of gold sandals with slim, metallic straps and chunky woven heels.

"I was wondering where those went," I say.

Elle balks as she reads the designer label. "Those are at least four-*hundred* dollar shoes." She shakes her head. "Thanks, but I wouldn't want to mess them up."

Regret prickles through me thinking about barging in on her life in Ashmont, and now here we are flinging expensive shoes at her. "Sorry. This must seem obnoxious."

Elle shrugs. "It's not your fault you have what you have."

"But how could you *not* be mad about it? It's not fair."

"It's not."

"How did you do it? Clean houses? People making messes of all their overpriced crap, not appreciating what they have." I point to the pile of shoes and clothes on my car's floor.

Elle thinks about it. "Titania helps. She tells me poor minds see loss, what you don't have. Rich minds focus on the rewards. We don't have control of the circumstances we're born into, but we can control what we earn, what we work toward."

"Wanti, can't get it. Getti, no want it," Raven says in her Jamaican accent. "My mom used to say that. It's like what Titania is saying. You want something, you can't get it, and those who get it, don't even want it. They become numb to what they have." She looks at the designer heels she'd forgotten in my car.

"Do you really believe that?" I ask Elle. "That you can earn the life you want?"

"Sure," Elle says but starts laughing as she adds, "still sucks ass though. It's a lot of damn work."

"Then wear the damn *shoes*," I say. "You can't control your lot in life. But we can at least control your impending fashion disaster." I emerge from my trunk with a silk sarong and cut off tank. "Put this over your bathing suit. Don't give me that look. Trust me."

Elle considers this a moment. "Thanks, but no thanks. I still want to be me." She takes off the flannel shirt and rips off the sleeves. "Can I borrow that belt though?" She takes a wide leather, silver studded belt from my backseat and loops it around her waist, managing to turn the oversized shirt into a kickass dress in a matter of seconds.

"Wow you even have jewelry just sitting in here?" She grabs a silver bracelet from my cup holder along with a bunch of glass bangles and tangle of earrings.

"Oh, that's my Indian stuff, from an event with my parents. I wore it with a sari."

"Why not with your dress tonight?" Elle asks.

"Um, because...it's my *Indian* stuff?"

"Why do you say it like that? It's beautiful!" Elle trails her fingers over the intricate patterns, pausing where two elephant heads come together, trunks touching at the clasp. "Wow. Heavy. Is this solid silver?"

"No, there's iron inside. It's supposed to protect you from bad spirits."

"What the heck," Elle laughs. "What are you waiting for then? Put it on. Maybe you can protect us from burning effigies of our own faces in trashcans and more reptilian attacks."

"This is your makeover, not mine," I say, but Elle slides the bracelet onto my wrist and hands me the matching earrings and necklace.

"Wow," Raven says. "That makes the whole outfit. Penny and I were always telling you to wear your Indian jewelry more often."

"I didn't think it would look good; a regular dress with my different jewelry," I say.

"What the hell is *regular*? You mean more common. Conventional," Elle says with certainty. "You look like one of the goddesses in your hotel lobby."

I can only see a little slice in the rear-view mirror, but Elle's not entirely wrong. The swing of silver dangling from my ears and shining at my collarbone brings out a glint in my eyes, making them look darker and more alive. "All right, fine. I'll wear it. You win."

Elle holds up the marshmallows.

"Negative," I laugh. "But leave them in my car. They'll make a great snack for us tomorrow."

We head for the pool house gate.

"Let's go get some answers," Elle says.

Raven nods but her voice seems softer than I'm used to when she says, "We hope."

I don't like her ambivalence. But I'm also not surprised. She's always the one to pump the brakes. I guess she's learned to proceed with caution at every moment, every turn, to not erupt Mount Vera.

Music pulses in the distance. Fire pits crackle, with

Adirondack chairs perfectly spaced around them. Strings of lights twinkle between white cabanas spanning the private beach.

"Uh, you weren't kidding." Elle pokes her head inside one. "Beds. Electricity. Minifridges. Fans?"

"You didn't think I'd camp for real?" I shudder to make Elle laugh.

"Wow, look who cleans up nice." Hunter steps up, eyeing us all. "Even you Aarya. You look...extra sparkly or something. Supermodel Sea Witch!"

"Thanks?"

He waves at us to follow him to the bar where he hands out drinks. "Let's go down by the water. That's where the real party is."

As we head for chairs around the fire closest to the ocean, Punkaj falls into step beside me. "Didn't expect to see you here," I say. "Wait 'til I tell my dad you aren't home studying."

Elle leans up against me, her breath too close and too warm as she not-so-quietly whispers, "Plaaay time on the beach."

I bat her away, ignoring the look Punkaj is giving me.

He smells kind of good, like cinnamon and fresh air. I don't think I've ever noticed before.

"You look different tonight..." he says.

"Different." I touch an earring. "Is that a good thing?"

"I think so. Everyone else looks like...everyone else." Punkaj motions for me to walk a little faster to create some space between us and the group. I already know what he's going to ask. "Anything new?"

"Maybe after tonight."

I gesture with my head toward the mansion. "Going to look around once everyone's asleep."

Punkaj brings a finger to his lips, as others approach...

including Nikki and Kat. They're way done up, with perfectly blown out beach waves, and coordinating barely there bathing suits under sheer cover ups.

"Best party of the year!" Nikki gives me a quick scan, taking in my jewelry. "Aw. You're all dressed up Indian. Has anyone ever told you how much you look like your mom?"

She zooms in on Elle. "Nice flannel. Very Paul Bunyan chic."

"Elle, did you know our parents are on a date tonight?" Kat asks.

"That's nice." Elle sips her drink nonchalantly.

Nikki purses her lips. "Is it? I thought we talked about this."

"You know what, tell whoever you want whatever you want about me," Elle says, knocking back the rest of her drink. "I don't care anymore. All I care about is finding Penny."

"At a certain point," Nikki says. "Everyone will have to come to terms with the fact that might never happen." She pauses, letting her words sink in. "I think I'm going to go find Loww-gan. Come on Kat."

Eye on the prize, Nikki hones right in on Logan talking to his friends and grabs him to dance, grinding on him immediately.

That might never happen.

Her words about Penny flicker in my heartbeat like the fires scattered across the beach—dark, hot, dark, hot. Fury and fear.

I look at Raven and Elle, and we all seem to be processing it. I steer us all as far away from the twins as possible. Raven eases herself into one of the Adirondacks, rubbing her knee. Grayson and Dawn join us.

"Have you seen Nikki?" Dawn doesn't even say hello,

she's so scandalized. "She's literally throwing herself at Logan. She's so inappropriate I can't even take it."

Grayson shakes his head. "It's weird. Seeing Logan without Penny."

"It's awful," Dawn blurts out. "It makes me feel like we're never going to see her again." Her eyes fill up and she takes a giant un-Dawn-like gulp of her champagne.

It's hard not to feel hopeless.

So much time has passed. I've watched the true crime shows. Someone showing up alive after this long is not the usual outcome. And here we are, chasing clues like a bunch of Scooby-Doo cartoons. Children.

"Seeing this party, without Penny here..." Dawn's eyes glisten with tears. "It makes me feel like Penny is dead."

"Hey. Don't say that." Grayson touches her shoulder. "Don't even think it."

"No, I mean it." Dawn points. "Last year, that was Penny, dancing with Logan. Now it's Nikki and Penny's *gone*. What alternate reality *is* this?"

I take another sip of my drink and look out across the beach. The campfires scattered across the sand attract little galaxies of people around them. I look at the people in mine. Raven, Elle, Punkaj, Dawn and Grayson.

In *our* galaxy, in *our* reality, we'll find her. We find Penny.

The music pumps louder. But it's not enough to drown out Dawn's words.

What we need is to dance our worries off, if only for a moment.

"To finding Penny." I raise my glass and start to dance.

Elle chugs her second, grabs another, and clinks it to mine.

I hold out my hand to Punkaj for the hell of it, and as expected, he waves me away. I don't think that boy has ever danced in his life. I give him a you're-pathetic look and help Raven to her feet instead. She holds the edge of the chair and moves to the beat with me, but every time I glance over, she's stealing looks at Nikki and Logan.

"It really is like he's forgotten all about Penny," Raven says. But instead of angry, she sounds...sad?

"Let them have each other. Who cares?" I say. "People like that belong together."

"I guess."

"You should have seen her in drama the other day. She was all over him."

"What did *he* do?" Raven asks.

"He actually shut her down. She was talking shit about you passing out, and he told her she was just jealous."

"Really?"

The bonfire crackles. Even in the shadows, I swear I see Raven blush.

Where there's smoke there's fire.

"Really." I pay close attention to her expression. "He definitely seems to have a soft spot for you."

Raven avoids looking me in the eye. "I guess that was the goal, right? Get close. Get answers."

Her face abruptly closes off. I follow her gaze.

Nikki pushes Logan down into a chair like she may do a lap dance. His friends egg him on with hoots and hollers. Katarina is making a stupid duckface and pumping one arm, like go, go, go. Nikki puts a leg on either side of Logan, sliding onto his lap.

With a deliberate look directly at us first, Nikki then turns, takes Logan's face in her hands, and kisses him.

CHAPTER 20
SHOULD HAVE BEEN YOU
RAVEN

Logan starts to pull away from Nikki, but then gives into the kiss, seemingly fueled by the crowd cheering.

When his eyes meet mine, all feeling drains from my face to my toes until my entire body is numb. I let the glass I'm holding fall to the ground, the liquid splashing like my churning insides.

Aarya jumps back.

"Sorry. I'll get something to clean our shoes." It's the out I need. I walk away from the bonfires and butlers and boys.

The beach grows quieter every step I take. When the sprawl of the mansion gives way to rolling dunes and the only thing I can hear is the breaking waves against the shore, I sit down in the powdery sand. I inhale deeply, and the salty air fills my lungs.

I tip my head back, looking up to the sky. The twinkling stars mock me. They see everything; they know the truth—a truth I want to deny but can't anymore because Nikki kissing Logan was like throwing gasoline on a smoldering fire, and now the flames are out of control.

I feel Logan next to me before I see him. Smell his ocean and pine scent, feel the hum of electricity when he sits down, so strong I scoot away—protective instinct.

Logan stiffens when I move. "You ran off."

"I did." Staring at the dark ocean is all I can do to keep myself from demanding, *Why did you bother following me after your little show back there?*

"Right after Nikki kissed me." His voice is matter of fact.

I don't say a word.

"Raven, look at me." It's not a command but a soft appeal, so I turn to him. He catches my gaze with his, eyebrows drawn, head tilted. There's a tenderness in the way he's looking at me.

"You can kiss whoever you want," I manage to say. The words leave a bitter tang on my tongue.

"Yes, I can." Logan tenses. "Penny broke up with *me*. So yeah, I can kiss whoever I want."

My anger surges. I don't want to think about him kissing Nikki...or anyone for that matter. "This party," I say, needing a change of subject, "do you really think it's a good idea? I mean, Penny is still missing. This isn't exactly helpful."

Neither is this conversation.

Logan squares his shoulders and says, "Just because Penny and I are over doesn't mean I don't care what happens to her. I think of her constantly. I can't believe she's still missing and worry every second about where she is."

He's being honest, I can see it in the way his body language softens, almost like it pains him to admit this.

But the vulnerability is gone as quickly as it appeared,

and he's back on the defensive when he says, "Maybe we shouldn't have had the party, or maybe the party is just the distraction everyone needs."

"Clearly you're using the distraction for all you can." I cringe at my own tone.

"What do you want from me?" He points directly at me. "You told me to back off and Penny was the one who didn't need me anymore."

"This is what you call backing off?"

He rubs the back of his neck. "You're impossible."

I pause. "What did you mean about Penny not needing you?"

"In the end, I did what I thought was best for Penny. I second guessed everything and tried to get back together with her, and that's when I found out."

"About Ansel?"

Logan raises his eyebrows. "You know about him?"

"Elle told us." If Logan was involved with the burning picture of us in Belle Grande, why does he sound so surprised I know about Ansel?

"I knew she was seeing someone else, but... Do you remember what I said in drama class?" He hesitates. "You know, what made Elle punch me?"

I roll my eyes. "How could I forget?"

"Well, the whole virgin thing...Penny and I were never together—like that."

"Then that makes you even more of an ass for insinuating it."

"Raven, I'm trying here. Are you really going to be like this? I can leave."

My stomach drops at the idea of him walking away from me. "Don't go." The tension between us dissipates at my request. "I'll listen."

He takes a moment before continuing. "So, my two truths and a lie—there wasn't a lie."

"Then why did you say it?"

"Because I found out Penny was, you know, with Ansel...like that."

"She and Ansel..." I can't believe how serious they were, and I had no clue he existed. It's hitting me now how far apart Penny and I had grown. Long before that night with Logan and I on the balcony, she had stopped returning my texts, waiting for me after school, and had cancelled plans on the regular.

"Yeah." Logan looks into the distance. "I felt so stupid. I was trying to get back together with her, and she'd already moved on."

I knew exactly what Aarya would be thinking if she was here: motive. But that's not the vibe I'm getting. "When did all of this happen?"

"I don't know if I want to say."

"Why not?"

He picks up a handful of sand and lets it slowly sift through his fingers. "I might have tried to get back with her after what happened with us—after you walked away from me on the balcony."

"Might have?"

"Fine, I did. What Penny and I had was so familiar, and what happened that night with us sucked. I know it doesn't help my case with you, but I want to be honest."

"So, what happened?"

"We started texting again, but something was different. She was distant and seemed down. I started to worry that she was in a bad head space," he says. "We met up for dinner one night, and that's when she told me about him. I think I was more shocked than anything, knowing she really had moved on. We got in this big fight, and that's when we decided we were done—like done-done. She insisted I drop her off at the church in Belle Grande. I felt terrible leaving her there, upset like she was. But the pastor came out to meet her, so I felt like she was going to be okay."

I sit up straighter realizing he's talking about the same night that Pastor Dana and Ansel told us about. That was why Penny was so distraught. Logan had never threatened her or hurt her. It was the final goodbye.

We'd been so wrong.

Logan takes in a deep breath, like whatever he's going to say next is difficult for him to speak out loud. "That was the last time I saw her."

We sit in silence for a moment. I think about what the Tremaines said earlier, about the possibility of Penny being dead. My heart fractures realizing we may have all seen her for the last time.

Before I can start spiraling, Logan draws my attention back to him when he says, "I think sometimes when you're with someone for so long, you almost break up in stages. You distance yourself, but it's hard to let go of the friendship. So you go back. And with Penny, there was always this sense of responsibility, to make sure she was okay. You know what I mean?"

"I do," I say softly. There was an ebb and flow to my friendship with Penny, tied to her depressive and manic episodes. We were inseparable at times, sand and ocean mixing, not knowing where one ended and the other began. But then the tide would recede, her storm of emotions dragging her back out to sea. That's when I worried the most about her. "I think it's part of loving someone with mental illness."

Logan nods, then looks at me with a questioning gaze.

"How have you been by the way? With your panic attacks?"

I shrug. I don't need him feeling sorry for me. "It's just something I live with. They don't happen all the time and can be unpredictable."

"Are you okay now?" He's not dropping this like I want him to, but I haven't had anyone to talk to recently, especially with things being off with Aarya.

"They've ramped-up since Penny's vigil," I say hesitantly, leaving out the part about Penny's poems being the initial trigger that started everything up again. "But I've been dealing with them. It hasn't gotten as bad as eighth grade summer at least."

Logan pauses, pushing his hair out of his face. "I don't know if I'd be as together as you are after what you've been through. It's one of the things I admire the most about you." He gives me his crooked smile.

"What? That I freak out randomly?"

"No, your resilience. I don't know if I'd be standing if I were in your shoes." He looks at me with a mix of compassion and awe. "Like how you bounced back after you went away that summer."

"You admire me because of my recovery?" I give him an incredulous stare. "I mean, people use it to mess with me—like the twins, they call me a *pathetic addict, loser, laughingstock with a problem*." I mock their tone.

"I'm not the twins. I see it as brave and determined. You're a fighter." His features soften as he keeps his eyes on mine. "I would never look down on you for that. It's the opposite, really."

"You're not kidding."

"Why would I kid about this? What it takes to get healthy and stay healthy, that's what shows who you really are. Someone willing to do whatever it takes. That's strength."

Warmth expands in my chest. "Thank you for saying that. It was tough coming back after. It was just the summer but everyone—everything—seemed to have changed, moved on without me..." I trail off. That was the summer Logan and Penny started dating. "Anyhow, I've worked hard to make sure I don't have to go away again."

I think about the pills in my room, how I could've taken as many as I wanted after the pageant, when Vera brought my parent's letters back to me, reminding me of my place in this world. I feel an overwhelming sense of gratitude I didn't give in.

I nudge him with my shoulder. "You know, you're not as much of an asshole as you let on."

"Thanks?" Logan laughs, full and hearty, but then he hangs his head. "I wish I hadn't said what I did about Penny in drama class."

"You do that a lot—pretend to be something you're not. And I don't understand why."

"Welcome to being the Steele heir apparent."

"I thought you and Hunter were still competing for that role?"

He laughs. "Now we are. While Hunter was focused on surfing, I was my dad's sole focus. I learned early what he expected of me. Do you remember in the sixth grade when that new scholarship kid Emmet Cooper showed up at school?"

"Of course. He was only enrolled for a few months." I glance at him sideways. "There were rumors about you and your friends bullying him."

"It was Ryan and David. I actually tried to protect Emmet. I got some of the lacrosse guys to help me give Ryan and David swirlies."

I huff out a small laugh. "How are you all still friends?"

"Their parents have business connections with Steele Industries. But Emmet, he wasn't one of us, and so, according to my dad, I shouldn't have taken his side. He called Emmet a nobody and made sure I got detention for what I did to Ryan and David. Said it was a lesson I needed to learn; that we stand with guys like them no matter what they do. We protect the business first. Steele family motto, the right thing to do is always what's right for the business."

"That sounds like something Vera would say."

"I know you get it." He takes a deep breath. "They were worse with Emmet after that, and I had to just stand by and let it happen. He ended up transferring. And I played the game."

"What game?"

"The one we all play. Hunter, my mom, Steele employees. My dad says jump, we say how high, whether we agree or not. She told me I needed a tougher shell. So I did what I had to do. But it's still just a shell, you know? It's not who I really am."

"And no one gets to see that," I say.

"Only the people I really trust." His shoulder brushes against mine again. "And even then, only sometimes. My mom taught me that to the rest of the world, I need to be the son my father expects. It's the long game, one I've been playing ever since."

I raise an eyebrow. "So, you're an asshole by choice, not by nature."

"I guess so. And now you know why. But there will be a day when I'm in charge and don't have to play by my dad's rules." He shrugs, like it's not this huge weight to carry, pretending to be what his dad wants him to be. The same kind of weight I carry for Vera.

"And now I've told you all my secrets again. Your turn: Why did you run off?" His smoky eyes pierce mine, an electric charge passing between us.

No, he's still off limits. *Get up. Get up and leave.*

But I don't move.

And my damn pulse is picking up sitting this close to him. I look away, wrapping my arms around my legs. "I can't believe you kissed Nikki."

We sit in silence for a moment, then he asks, "Do you remember Grayson's end of the year party in eighth grade?"

"Of course I remember." It was the last fun thing I did with all my friends right before my spiral landed me in rehab that summer. "Why?"

"Do you remember that we played seven minutes in heaven?"

"Yeah, how could I forget?" I remember I was so nervous, I didn't even want to play, but Penny and Aarya insisted. I spun the bottle, and it turned and turned and slowed to a stop, pointing straight at Logan.

"I wanted it to land on me," he admits.

"No, you did not."

"Come on, you didn't know I had the biggest crush on you?"

"What? No way." Adrenaline surges through my body at his admission. I tilt my head and pause. When we went back to the room, we sat on the bed, legs not even touching. He told me right away I didn't have to do anything. Instead, we talked for way longer than the seven minutes, and slowly our legs touched, our shoulders brushed against each other and stayed there. He said something funny, and I threw my head back and laughed, and when I looked at him again, he was right there, inches from me, and time stopped. My skin was literally tingling all over and we leaned toward each other, and it happened. It was so tender, so sweet, and I remember how he tasted of spearmint gum. When we walked out of the room, hand in hand, we were greeted by whoops and cheers from all our friends, and I couldn't help but think it was the beginning of something. "That was my first kiss."

Logan sits up taller, takes a deep breath and continues. "I waited for you that summer. After the party, I called, I texted. You never got back to me."

"Things got bad after that, Logan. I couldn't...I didn't even know you reached out." My stomach flutters knowing he wanted to see me again. "After the party, I was grounded for sneaking out, Vera and my dad took my phone, and the isolation escalated everything...my struggle with my addiction...and then, they sent me away." I thought about him every day when I was gone. Told myself when I got better and went home, we could pick up where we left off.

"At the time, I thought you had ghosted me." A flash of hurt crosses his face. "Then I was with Penny, and it's not like I didn't want to be. But it was hard once you came back to school."

"It was hard for me, too," I say quietly. When I got home and found out they were together, I knew Logan was off limits. He was Penny's and that was the end of our story.

"Eventually, Penny and I became something else. She was my best friend. The one person I could trust, no matter what. And when she started to struggle with her mental health, I made the choice to stay with her because I loved her, and I put aside what I wanted..." His voice trails off, his eyes dropping to my mouth before meeting my gaze again.

What I wanted. He means me. All I can do is stare back at him, and the way he's looking at me causes a sudden rush of warmth in my core.

"If I'm honest, this—" he motions between us while holding my gaze, "has always been there."

My lips ache with the need to close the distance between us and...I need space. Now.

I stand abruptly and walk to the edge of the water without glancing back at him. I take off my sandals and step into the shallow surf. The water cools the rushing heat so I can think.

Had I not gone away that summer, there really would have been something between us. I've pushed him away for the same reasons he pushed me away. But if Penny let him go, does it mean he's free to be mine?

What about Elle's poem? It seems to point to him. I may know why Penny was crying at the church now, but it doesn't explain the warning Ansel told us she gave him.

Logan walks up behind me. He's close. Really close. I can feel his breath on my ear. He whispers, "If it wasn't Nikki, who should it have been?"

With a featherlight touch, he grazes my fingers with his, moving up my wrist, then my arm. Tiny sparks trail in his wake, and when he reaches the crook of my elbow, he gently places his arm around my waist, and turns me to face him. He lifts my chin with his other hand, tilting me toward him, our lips a breath apart. "Tell me. Who should it have been?"

The waves crash and hold, reach and retreat, and I say the truth I can no longer deny. "Me. It should have been me."

I can't fight it any longer. All reasoning evaporates.

It's only me and him and this moment. Slipping my arms around his neck, I part my lips—an invitation. He crushes his mouth to mine. My whole body shudders, and I answer with everything I've been holding back: every thought I've tried to stop, every moment I've pushed him away, every ounce of heat I wanted to leave on that balcony—all of it pours into this this moment, and we disappear into the kiss.

A new secret for us to keep.

CHAPTER 21
SNAKING SUSPICION

AARYA

Having an idea is one thing. Executing it, another. Elle's passed out. Dawn's asleep. Raven is nowhere to be found. My sidekicks are sidelined.

Where *is* Raven? I try to push down the unease. Nothing seemed off about her tonight. I call her phone again. No answer. I text. Again. *It's go time.* No response.

I try to get Elle moving, jiggling her shoulder. When she doesn't budge, I pull off the blanket. Elle tugs it back up. "I changed my mind."

"Not an option. This is our only chance." I yank it off again and throw it out of reach. "Hey when did you last see Raven?"

"I haven't seen her since..." Elle sits up and chugs some water. She holds her head. "I think since right before Nikki sucked face with Logan."

The flap to the cabana rustles, and Raven steps inside. Her hair is windblown, eyes bright, clothes splashed with water.

Relief mixes with annoyance. "Where have you been? It's practically sunrise."

"Sorry," she says. "I fell asleep on the beach."

I read her expression for anything off. "I'm glad you're okay. And there's still time if we go right now."

Raven looks at the bed and frowns. "I'm tired. And my knee really hurts."

"You're not going to help?"

"That's not what I'm saying."

"Then what?"

"I'm saying, I'm not sure it's a good idea. We might get in trouble. And for what?"

"Answers! Or have you suddenly forgotten our friend is missing?"

Dawn mumbles and sits up, disoriented. "Is it time? Are you going to search Logan's room? I'm coming, too."

"Our window's closing. If you're in, let's go."

Enough is enough. I head out of the cabana. They all follow. Begrudgingly.

Well, this is going to be awesome—a sketchy Raven, a possibly simultaneously drunk and hungover Elle, and goody-two-shoes Dawn. Not exactly a crack team.

The second we approach the terraced lawn of Logan's house, a thousand motion sensor flood lights blaze on.

A security guard steps out of the shadows. "Can I help you?"

"Um, someone locked the pool house bathroom. Logan told us we could use the one in his wing," I say with confidence. Indian parent problems breed some good life skills, like creative truth-bending on command.

The guard guides us to the left branch of the sprawling mansion, and lets us in. "Third door on the right."

I wait for him to head back outside, then dart around

the corner, waving for the girls to follow. The air in the vast hallways feels like something you must actively step through. Light, elusive fragrances, from candles and potpourri and calla lilies, mix with all the heaviness, leather, and a stillness that comes from thick curtains that aren't opened often enough. I crack a door. Nope, library. Next one, gym. Pristine, shining equipment gleams silver and white. The charcoal gray rubber floor smells like pencil erasers. Then, I step into the crisp bite of an overly air-conditioned bedroom.

A bedside lamp casts a dim glow on an immaculately decorated navy and gray room. You wouldn't guess by the uptight nautical theme a teen guy lives here, but a pair of designer sneakers under a desk, and a couple of textbooks left open and upside down on the bed, tell me otherwise.

"Found it," I whisper.

I go straight for the desk drawers, rummaging through them, quickly and quietly. In contrast to the room, which must be cleaned daily by a housekeeper, Logan's drawers are messy, full of ticket stubs, scraps of papers, chewed on pens, and worn-out notebooks.

Elle searches the closet. Dawn wanders around, touching surfaces but not looking inside. Raven stands staring at a framed photo collage—Penny and Logan over the years. *Happy Birthday boy that I love* is scrawled in silver pen on the frame.

"They look so happy," Raven murmurs, mesmerized.

"It was a lie," I say.

Dawn steps up beside me and studies the pictures. "That's a little harsh. It's more like a wish, like they *wanted* it to work, but it just...didn't."

I take the picture out of Raven's hands and put it back on the dresser beside all the other frames. Logan with Penny as Bonnie and Clyde on Halloween. Logan kissing a crew trophy. Logan, Hunter, and a group of friends with paintball guns posing like they just won a battle. The Steele family in front of their private plane.

"Come on." Dawn has inched back toward the door and glances down the hallway. "I feel like we've been here for too long. Someone's going to catch us."

"I'm not done." I open Logan's top drawer, gingerly examining the contents. "Give me a second."

"I don't like this either," Raven says. "It feels wrong."

"What? You don't like rifling through Logan Steele's boxer briefs?" I grab a pair and dangle them in front of Raven's face.

"Cut it out," Raven tries to push away the underwear, but I shove them into her grip and close her fingers around them.

My amusement abruptly shifts to sharp focus—a small leather case tucked next to Logan's socks. I scoop it up and briefly scan the contents, his passport, a copy of his learner's permit from a couple of years ago, beach parking lot pass, some hunting licenses. And...

My heart starts to pound.

A voice stops me in my tracks. "What are you up to, Sea Witch?"

I quickly shove the paper up my shirt before turning around. Hunter stands framed in the doorway, shirtless and disheveled.

"Logan said we could use his bathroom."

Hunter cocks his head and points to the underwear in Raven's hands. "Did he also say you could use his boxers?"

Dawn opens her mouth as if to respond, and instead, pukes. Divine intervention from my faithful friend.

"Oh man, for real?" Hunter pulls Dawn upright and steadies her. "Someone got the pastor's daughter drunk and it wasn't even me." He motions us out of Logan's room and calls for a maid. "Pee party's over when someone pukes. You can get back out to the beach fastest that way."

He points to his open door and the king size bed. The walls flicker blue and white with television light. "Unless... Slugger? Care to join?"

Elle narrows her eyes at him. "I'm all set."

In Hunter's room, a surfing video plays on a giant flatscreen. I recognize Hunter's floppy hair and muscular stance.

"Watching your own videos?" I tease. "It's okay. We all know you're obsessed with yourself."

"Hardly." He pulls the door quickly shut, but not before the camera catches him wiping out. Hard. His body tumbles and the board flies out, a wave folding him into its mouth.

There's a cloudiness to his expression, one I can immediately place. He's watching himself fail.

"Hunter?"

"Sea Witch?"

"How often do you watch that?"

"Too often."

"I think you should stop," I say.

"I think you're right." Hunter yawns and stretches. "Anyway, bedtime."

My shoulders relax a bit. The folded paper against my skin is screaming to be read.

"Goodnight, ladies," Hunter says. "Dawn, feel better. Find me in the morning. We'll get some hair of the dog."

Dawn blinks. "What dog?"

"Never mind. Get out of my house."

———

I rush everyone back along the beach the best I can, but Raven moves slowly with her knee, and Dawn keeps trying to lie down.

"I feel icky," she says.

"I cannot believe you of all people are hammered." Dawn has a one-drink rule I've never seen her break.

She sits down again.

I haul her to her feet. "Nope. Not doing this. I want to read what I found in Logan's drawer."

"You took something?" Dawn stumbles along beside me. "You should give it back. But also, I want to see."

We finally reach the cabana. I pull out the paper, speed reading the page. I had only spotted one word before Hunter caught us. But that one word was enough to quicken my pulse. *Python*. Now that I'm seeing the whole thing, my hands shake.

"Come look." I gather everyone around.

PYTHON PICKUP PROGRAM: YOU CAN WIN A PRIZE FOR REMOVING PYTHONS IN FLORIDA!

The FWC's Python Pickup Program is an incentive program designed to encourage the public to humanely kill Burmese pythons from the Everglades ecosystem and report locations to the FWC. People who submit proof of

python with location of removal will be entered into a grand prize drawing that will take place in October.

You can submit pythons to the Python Pickup Program that have been killed from any property in Florida where you have authorization to do so from the land manager or land managing agency.

Raven's first to speak. "So, do you think *Logan* put that awful snake in my car. And wrote the creepy message?"

"He was there that day outside the auditorium, too," Elle says. "He could have put the picture in the waste basket."

"And he'd have access to the church surveillance photos in Belle Grande. Steele Sugar runs that town." I have no doubt. "Add this to what Ansel said about Penny warning him to stay away from the Steeles, and this is all the proof we need!"

Raven sucks in her cheeks like she's nauseous.

"He's obviously trying to scare us away from digging around," Elle says.

"We need to go to the police and tell them they have to take us seriously," Dawn says.

"I agree," I say. "They can't blow us off this time."

We rush around the cabana, hastily packing up our stuff, and with bags slung over our shoulders, head out to my car. But Raven hesitates before getting in.

"What? Do you not think this is a good idea or something?"

"Vera is going to be furious. This is her boss's son we're talking about," Raven says. "How do we explain where we got the flyer?"

"I think our transgression pales in comparison to Logan putting pythons in cars and playing arsonist," I say. "We said we'd go to the police when we had some ground to stand on." I hold up the paper and wave it. "This is it."

Raven nods and gets in beside me. "Of course. Sorry."

The level of worry in her voice instantly makes me feel bad. Managing Vera is no joke. "I get it. It's worth being certain before we upset the evil queen."

The Steele estate hovers on the horizon behind us as

we leave, like a shadowy hand on my shoulder. I stop at a light, waiting to merge onto the entrance ramp to the bridge back to town. The first line of light seeps into the horizon. As satisfying as it is to have something that feels like proof, the overarching reality still holds a bitterness. Someone is trying to scare us. Penny is missing, and a boy Penny loved seems to be the common denominator. There is no victory in this.

A phone buzzes.

I fish around in my bag, trying to keep my eyes on the road. "Raven, can you check if that was me?"

Raven pulls out my phone. "Oh my god!"

"What is it?" I ask. But I already know from her horrified tone.

"Another message."

"The psycho strikes again," I say quietly. "What's it say?"

Stay in your lane.

A sudden thwack jolts the car. I jerk the wheel in surprise, swerving. A rat-a-tat-tat of what sounds like rapid-fire rocks pummel the metal.

The windshield cracks, and my hands jump with the impact, the steering wheel spinning out of my control. We veer across the center line.

A horn blares. The guardrail comes at us. Then black.

CHAPTER 22
CRASH AND BURN
RAVEN

Everything still holds a high-speed blur at the hospital. I try to ground myself, but I keep seeing the splatters of color against the windshield and hearing the scream of metal colliding with metal.

We are okay, I tell myself. An ambulance got us. Our parents have been in and out all day. We are safe.

But my thoughts are still crashing.

I think of Logan, his lips, and I'm flying.

I remember the word on that hunting flyer, python, and I'm careening out of the sky.

And then, there's the most damning thing of all—the picture of Logan in his room holding a paintball gun. How could it not have been him?

It doesn't feel possible that the same guy who sat in the sand with me only hours ago—who talked about Penny and Ansel and us, who left fire where he touched and a lingering hum coursing through my body— could do this.

Aarya has a bruised chest from the airbag. Elle, a little whiplash. Me, a sprained thumb of all things. Dawn has to stay overnight to monitor a concussion and we're all crammed in her room, so close it feels like my thoughts are on full display—a lit-up billboard that everyone can read. Aarya keeps looking at me. I swear she can see it, see the kiss burning my lips.

I can still feel the sparks left by his touch as his hand trailed up to my waist. When he spun me to him, I could have melted right then and there even before our lips connected. I stare at the framed posters of oversized flowers in light purples and pinks on the wall, trying to grapple with the possibility that being in this hospital room right now might be Logan's fault.

Forget that kiss. Pretend it never happened. Tell no one.

But I can't forget and it did happen and I'm in way over my head.

Aarya is silent beside me. I know she is trying to connect each discordant piece of what's happened into her version of a symphony of answers, a score I'm sure she's titled "Logan Steele Is Guilty."

There's a soft knock on the door.

"It's for me." Aarya jumps up and opens it. Punkaj walks in. "Things I never thought I'd say: I almost got killed by a paintball and I called Punk for help."

Elle waves him inside. "When you said you wanted to help, did you expect this?" She gestures to our injuries.

Punkaj's face is serious. "You could have been killed."

We could have been killed. The weight of this makes me sink farther into my seat.

"What did the police say about the threats?" Punk asks.

"They said in high-profile cases, sometimes people like to attach themselves to the drama," I explain. "They said it seemed like a game."

"We didn't tell them what we found in Logan's room. We need to present a solid case if we're admitting to trespassing on Steele property," Aarya says. "I think we have enough to tell police what we really think." Aarya turns to Punkaj. "But we wanted your help putting it all together."

"Look, someone clearly doesn't want you asking questions about Penny," Punkaj says. "Whenever you go poking around, that's when you get a threat. The snake and burning picture are one thing. Shooting at your car takes it up a level."

"It all points to Logan," Aarya says. "Whoever is doing this knows where we are and what we're doing at all times. It's someone who is in our daily lives. Logan, Logan, annnd Logan."

"That's one possibility." I ignore the weight on my chest telling me Logan is responsible. "But the motive just isn't there. Breaking up does not equal Logan abducting Penny. It makes no sense."

"I don't think you get a vote on Logan's involvement in this anymore," Aarya says.

I jerk back. "And what's that supposed to mean?"

"Where were you last night? I didn't see you again after Nikki and Logan kissed." Her stare is a challenge.

I sit there for a moment, silent. I refuse to look at anyone else for fear they are looking at me, seeing the imprint of Logan's lips on mine, the lips I still feel.

If Logan is orchestrating the attacks, he could also be manipulating everything between the two of us. I could just be a pawn in his game. "I was with Logan," I admit. "He opened up to me at the party."

"That's where you were," Aarya says.

"Yeah, I was doing exactly what you said to do." But my face burns at the half-truth.

This must be what happens to detectives who go deep

undercover and then end up siding with the bad guys because they lose themselves in the deception. Am I losing myself? I feel like I'm losing my best friend. Maybe that's enough of a sign something is off. Still, I push forward with what Logan told me.

"We keep talking about the poems. 'Hearts turned to steel'—we're assuming it's Penny's heart that was broken. But he told me Penny was the one to break up with him last, for Ansel. Remember the whole incident where he dropped her off in Belle Grande and she was crying? That was because it was their final breakup. She was the one who broke his heart this final time."

Aarya looks excited. "Motive! Again!"

Exactly what I thought she would say the moment he told me. "You're so predictable."

"Can I interject here?" Grayson asks.

There goes Mr. President, ready to play politics. But I have to admit, I'm glad he's intervening.

"Logan can be a dick sometimes. A player, yes. Arrogant, often. I can agree on all that. But do you really think he'd hurt Penny?"

Finally, at least one person who doesn't see Logan as a complete villain. It gives me a few minutes off from being his one-woman cheer squad.

Aarya glares at Grayson. "Why are you defending him?"

"I'm not. I'm just saying, this is a major accusation. You need to be absolutely sure before you suggest the police should investigate Logan. You remember his last name, don't you?"

"Grayson is right. This is another reason why we need to make sure we have hard, logical proof before going to the police about him," Punkaj says.

"Are you two ganging up on me?" Aarya asks.

"No, we're on the same team," Punkaj says. "Us against whoever is trying to keep this quiet. That's why writing this news story is important. The media is the greatest weapon to expose the truth against the rich and powerful. Why do you think hush money is a thing? Do you think people would pay exorbitant sums of money to keep people quiet if telling their story to the media didn't matter?"

Aarya rolls her eyes. "There he goes, Pulitzer Punk."

Elle speaks up. "I think he's right. When it comes down to it, if we have all this information gathered and it still doesn't feel strong enough to go to the police on our own, Punk can break the story."

Aarya looks at Elle and something passes between them. I try to ignore the rip in my heart witnessing their newfound alliance with me on the outside.

Dawn sits up in her hospital bed. Tears well in her eyes. "Penny was isolated, completely alone in a psych ward. What if we're the ones to blame because we were too busy and self-absorbed to support our friend when she needed us most? All I know is we're not any closer than we were when we first got these poems, and now our lives are in danger. How did we get here?"

Grayson wraps an arm around her as Dawn speaks through her tears. "What if I have blind spots, things about me I can't see? And what if the clues Penny sent are elusive to us because we need to be real with ourselves, look deep inside."

Blind spots. Like the one I have for Logan.

Silence falls in the room. We've been so focused on trying to figure out who took her that we lost sight of the reality—Penny was trying to tell each of us something more. Her poems are not only about who took her. They are also about why.

———

I'm the last one to leave Dawn's room. The hallways are dim, and the hospital's slowed to a sleeping pace, visiting hours over, night shift rolling in. I recite Penny's poem over and over on my walk to my car, searching for new meaning.

Nightmares and nearer. Mirrors and discreet.

My recurring nightmare about my mom. Penny knew about it and my PTSD. And my mom is from Belle Grande. But how could my mom's death almost ten years ago be related to Penny's disappearance today?

The other people close to me are Vera and my dad. Aarya and Dawn. Nightmare definitely doesn't refer to my friends. Vera is my nightmare, but there's nothing that links Vera to Penny.

That leaves only Logan.

Even if Penny did see us that night at the gala, maybe she wasn't mad. Maybe she was trying to warn me about Logan. Like Aarya questioning my judgment—she's trying to protect me, too.

A heaviness pulls my stomach to the floor, and it ricochets back up to my throat. I bring a shaky hand to my mouth, like I'm going to stop myself from speaking this out loud to the empty corridor. But I can't stop myself from thinking it.

Logan is the nightmare.

I don't even know if I believe this, but thinking it makes it feel like it is real.

I have tunnel vision when I get to the parking lot: Get in the car and go. I want to go home, curl up in my bed, and sleep away my thoughts.

I grab the car door handle, and someone steps up next

to me. My adrenaline spikes and I let out a frightened yelp.

"Hey, shh, shh, it's okay. It's just me. I didn't mean to scare you." Logan's blond hair falls in haphazard waves around his face, and his button-down shirt is untucked on one side. "You're okay," he says, breathless.

"What are you doing here?"

"I've been worried sick. I've tried calling you I don't know how many times."

"I think my phone's dead." Just as I'm about to ask how he knows, he answers the unasked question.

"The police came to my house and told me...about the accident."

"Why? Why would they do that?"

"Because it's where you all were coming from."

Logan steps toward me. The streetlamp illuminates his face, highlighting the circles under his eyes. Despite my suspicions, his closeness ignites the buzzing between us. I can tell he feels it, too—his eyes sizzle even though he looks exhausted. I lift my hand, craving to touch him, but stop myself.

He seems to read my hesitation. "I was so helpless when I couldn't reach you. Like Penny all over again."

Like Penny. Cold floods through me. "Logan, I have to go."

"But what about last night?"

"Last night..." It's all I can think about and want to do again, but it's everything I need to run from. I force out, "It was a mistake."

"Mistake?" His brow furrows, chiseled jaw taut. His broad shoulders drop. "What do you mean?"

"That night on the balcony, we got carried away. And last night, we were both reminiscing, getting caught up in what if fantasies, things that should have, could have, happened but didn't."

"It was more than that to me," Logan says and little flutters race to my gut, unsettled, wrenching. "I know it was more for you, too."

It was more. My heart begs me to say this out loud, but my rational mind, the one facing the reality that Logan could be involved, won't let me. "I'm sorry. I really am. But we have to stop."

"You're for real?"

I swallow. "It's been a long day."

"And that's a reason to brush me off? What kind of day do you think it's been for me? Not being able to get in touch with you, not knowing if you were okay?"

"What do you want from me? To walk out of a hospital after crashing and do what? Fall into your arms?"

"No, that's not it." Logan takes my hand in his. I should pull away, but I can only stare at our linked hands. "I just want to be near you, to know you're safe. I care, okay?" It would be so easy to get in his limo and ride away with him, to pick up right where we left off on the beach —but not with the very real possibility he is the threat, the thing I should fear.

"I have to go."

He opens his mouth like he's going to say something, but he doesn't. Half of me is grateful, the other half wants to plead with him to try harder.

Logan drops my hand, his stance turning hard and cold. The flame lit only last night blows out as fiercely as it started. I chill to my core. My insides twist watching him walk to his limo and be driven off, leaving me cracked and empty.

CHAPTER 23
TASTE OF REALITY
AARYA

Your car can crash. Your faces can burn in a picture. But you still show up at the Steele Family Foundation's Taste of Success planning dinner to clink glasses, smile politely, and help the less fortunate.

Please, pass the secrets. These lies are delicious. Lovely to see you. Confessions anyone? The flavor is so subtle.

I scan the area for a sign of Logan not sure how I'm going to be able to keep myself from flying at him with accusations.

"You okay?" My little brother's voice comes from behind me.

I turn toward him. "I'm fine."

"You look tired." Raj pokes my arm and then steps around to face me.

"I'm not tired," I say. More like, tired *of*. Tired of no one believing us. Tired of working so hard to unravel clues and then having to sit on them until we unravel some more. How many arrows have to point to Logan Steele before anyone believes us?

Raj's forehead creases in concern. "All week long,

everyone at school has been saying it was on purpose. That someone shot at your car because you're friends with Penny."

"Well, the police say it's just delinquents. A coincidence."

"But you don't believe them."

I shrug. "I don't know if it matters what I think."

"You're not doing something stupid are you?"

"I'm always doing *something* stupid." I ruffle his hair in response, and he immediately combs his fingers through trying to make it lie back in its perfect swoop.

"Listen. I'll be fine. Let's go see where we're sitting."

I scope out the seating cards. I'm next to Raj on one side, the other, Punkaj. Figures. Raven's across from me. And this is new: Elle Glass and her father along with Juniper Tremaine and the twins. Maybe I can move her next to me instead.

I start fiddling with the cards but my mother catches me. "Aarya!"

Raj fades back at the sound of her voice. He's good at disappearing when there's a pending Samudra storm.

"I don't think you should be meddling with anything." My mother leans in, her tone the total opposite of the smile pasted on her face. "You've caused enough stress this week. Not listening, breaking rules, driving dangerously."

"Someone shot at my car." I force myself from continuing. *Sorry we're trying to help our friend. Sorry we're the only ones who seem to care.* My mother still has the plastic smile in case anyone is watching our conversation.

"You could have been seriously hurt. This is the kind of thing that happens when you're out gallivanting at all hours. You run into other people up to no good. You're lucky we bought you a new car."

"You like me driving Raj everywhere."

The smile finally falls off her smooth toffee face. "*Thin*. Ice."

"*Got*. It." I mimic her tone.

She has no idea about why we were out at that hour. No idea that we were heading to the police. No idea that we're planning to accuse a Steele son of a crime. I can't imagine the reaction if she knew what was *really* going on.

Someone taps my shoulder. "Fancy meeting you here."

I give Elle a facetious curtsy and point to the table with an overdone flourish, eagerly steering her away from my mom. "Only the finest for Everbeach's finest."

Elle looks around. "This is...something."

"Yeah. It feels weird, doesn't it? One minute, you're flying into a guardrail, the next your parents are inviting the guy whose fault it is to dinner."

Elle shakes her head. "Fake it 'til you make it. We'll get the proof we need."

I huff in frustration. "'til then..."

"'til then, we show up, smile, and survive," Elle says. She points to Punkaj's card, and her eyes spark with mischief. "Oh look, you get to sit next to your *boyfriend*."

"Do you have a death wish? You *just* survived a car wreck." I narrow my eyes at her. "Anyway, no one else is here yet, so you have a minute to relax."

"I really don't think tonight is going to be relaxing," Elle says. She points to her father back by the bar. "This is the first time I've seen them out together."

Juniper Tremaine drapes herself over Elle's dad, her laugh a little too loud. She is the one who seems out of place—the saucy romance paperback on a shelf of leather-bound books.

"She is *nothing* like my mom," Elle says.

"I wonder what he sees in her."

"I have no idea." Elle's voice is bitter. "I think he just wants to forget."

Her father glances up as if he can feel us watching him, and gives her a little wave, which Elle ignores. "Hey, there's Raven."

She's trailing behind Vera's willowy form. *How are you*, I mouth at her. Raven gives a quick half smile and thumbs up with her thumb still in a foam splint. Only she could still look drop dead gorgeous with a fat thumb and a busted knee. Raven fiddles with her hair, the shiny black curtain swept up and held with a gleaming diamond studded comb.

Vera taps Raven's hand down. "Careful."

"Sorry. It's pinching," Raven says.

Vera reaches over and reangles the comb.

I don't like the sharp slice of Vera's expression, or the nervous look it elicits in Raven. I motion for Elle to come with me, and we step up next to them just in time to hear Vera's low whisper.

"Stop being dramatic. That was my mother's. If you don't want to wear it—"

"No, of course I do. It's...beautiful," Raven says. I hate how she stumbles around for Vera, always trying to please her. "Thank you. For letting me wear it."

"Of course. It looks lovely on you," Vera says sweetly with a glance at us. She passes Raven an iced tea and toasts it with her flute of champagne, then raises her glass to Elle and me. "Girls. I can't tell you how glad I am to see you all out and about after such a scare on the road. Enjoy the night. Take it easy. You've been through a lot."

Everyone's attention subtly shifts as Harvey Steele enters in a light gray suit, holding a drink someone made sure he had upon arrival. He takes the seat pulled out for him by Penny's father. Mr. Zale sits down stiffly, not making eye contact with anyone. He's always been a quiet, uptight man, but tonight the weight of Penny's disappearance seems to seep from his body, sending a chill into my own. Wait, where's Penny's mom? She never misses this dinner. Mrs. Zale is the chair of the committee. This is her event. I search for her, but my eyes land on Raven.

She takes a sip of her tea, eyes focused somewhere else. I follow her gaze to...*Logan*, standing beside his dad.

"Sit, sit." My father raises his arms, waving everyone to the table, and waiters make their practiced circles around us, delivering warm, crusty bread and perfectly arranged salads. Dawn and Pastor Thorne take their seats. The Grimsleys sweep in, but Punkaj beats them to the table. Wherever they go, there's someone who *has* to meet either his dad or mom, get a picture, maybe even an autograph.

"How are you?" Punkaj asks, neatly pulling in his chair, and realigning his silverware.

"You know, living the dream." I narrow my eyes in Logan's direction. My insides may as well be splattered in exploded paintballs at the sight of him. One more thing—one more—and I'll be pushed over the edge. "Easy," Punkaj says, touching my wrist briefly. The gesture actually works, warmth from his smooth fingers a small reminder to breathe.

Logan busies himself with his plate and turns to talk to Nikki on the other side of him, keeping his back to Elle.

"Dawn!" Juniper flashes an open-mouthed smile of delight. "Congratulations to you and Grayson on being selected as this year's Taste of Success student ambassadors. I wish *my* girls had been so lucky. Pastor Thorne, a pleasure."

I literally shudder at Elle's reality. This is her dad's love interest. How?

"Harvey!" Juniper gushes on. "We love what your charity aims to do. I mean, as a self-made woman from humble beginnings myself, I have nothing but sympathy and hope for these young kids in Belle Grande. Showing them a taste of the good life, it gives them something to strive for. I'm honored to stand in for Mrs. Zale, after everything she's been through. I won't let you down."

I try to swallow my shock. Juniper *Tremaine*? Heading this up? Penny's mother must be doing really bad to allow this to happen.

Mr. Steele nods proudly back at Juniper. "Taste of Success has come a long way. You know, their parents work so hard out in the sugar fields, and these kids have never been to a five-star restaurant. It's amazing to be able to take so many of them out to dinner."

"Wait," Elle interjects. "I'm sorry. Excuse me, but help me understand."

Uh oh. Here we go.

Everyone stares at Elle with varying degrees of surprise, or on the Tremaine's part, horror.

"The charity takes poor kids out to dinner. As in one single dinner. That's it? No scholarship? Or internship? Or mentoring or something?" Elle asks.

"It gives them a night they'd never otherwise have," Pastor Thorne says.

"It shows them a *life* they'll never have," Elle shoots back. "I don't get it."

Mr. Steele regards her coolly. "Well, I'm sorry you don't see the joy this brings, young lady. I assure you, if you saw their faces, tasting caviar or tuna tartar, sea bass, a New York strip, for the first time, I think you'd understand what we're doing here. Sometimes all you need is a taste of the good life to light the fire to go after it."

Mr. Steele's voice is a deep and resonant bass, hypnotic in its certainty and even pacing.

Grayson clears his throat. "She has a point, sir."

Dawn's eyes widen next to him.

"I feel like if we got more of the business community from the East Coast involved..." Grayson says, "you know, like the real power brokers, we could create some lasting change."

Mr. Steele shakes his head. "The problem is the leadership there. The city squanders funding. Sometimes you have to cut kids off and say hey, you're not going to get any more cash for candy 'til you learn how to save and spend wisely."

Grayson sits up a little straighter and squares his shoulders. "You're only as strong as your weakest link. We could do a partnership program or something. Business leaders with local politicians, revamping the budget and trying to close the income gap."

Mr. Steele squints. "I admire your spirit, Grayson. I tell Logan he should be more like you all the time. That being said, you'll never close the gap between people like us...and sugar workers." He says it with a tone suggesting the sheer lunacy of such a notion amuses him.

People like us...

Pastor Thorne attempts to smooth the rift. "The church has always believed it's a lovely show of support for our poverty-stricken neighbors to the south."

"And we've always enjoyed the partnership," Grayson's father quickly adds—Mayor McKinley stepping in to couch his son's words. "You know what they say about Belle Grande: Her soil is her fortune. Everbeach believes in paying it forward."

Elle smiles politely. "I'm sure you're right."

The adult's conversation picks up around us, Elle's

faux pas forgotten, dinner eventually winds down, and everyone gets ready to move inside to the bar.

Raven pushes her chair back so hard it tilts.

"You okay?" I ask.

"Of course." Raven steadies herself and walks ahead of us, a little uneasy it seems, but maybe it's just her bad knee.

Punkaj touches my arm. "Is she?"

"I'm not sure."

We follow our parents inside the hotel. Raven zigzags to the wall. No, she is *not* okay.

"Hey." I tuck an arm around her waist. "What's going on?"

"I'm fine," Raven says. "I just need some water."

"Like you were fine at the pageant?"

"Oh come on Aarya, not you, too. I already heard it from Vera tonight. *Do not embarrass me.* Blah blah blah." Raven points toward a beverage station. "Oh look. Aren't the little boats so pretty?"

"They're not boats. It's mounds of sherbet. Raven. Are you on something?"

She ignores me and marches toward the drinks where the rest of our friends are gathered. Her heel catches the edge of the carpet, and she plunges forward.

I pull her to her feet and hurry her away from everyone around a corner. "Seriously. Tell me right now what you're on."

Raven nods slowly, and I think for a moment she's actually absorbing my words, but then she sticks out her tongue. "You don't ownnnn me."

"You're being ridiculous."

"And you're being b—"

"Raven don't." I grab her arm to steady her as she teeters. "Do not say something you'll regret."

"*Do not.*" Raven imitates me and wrenches free. "Bossy. You're being bossy. So—*you* do not. D-o-n-u-t. Because I'm done. Done."

"Fine. I'm a terrible friend for caring. And not wanting you to be on drugs. Which, clearly, you are. And you're not going to tell me. So, fine. You're on your own."

Raven mimics my face with an extra stern expression that looks more like my dad than I care to admit. She squares her shoulders and turns her back, storming off.

I let her go. But as I head back down the hall toward the group, uncertainty tingles against my back. Raven shouldn't be alone right now, even if she thinks she wants to be.

I wander outside to find her. I'm about to call her name when I come to a screeching halt, and tuck into an alcove. Logan leans against a rail next to her, steadying her. Raven yanks her arm away, pulling out of his grasp. Her heel slips, and she's falling, tumbling over onto the ground.

Logan immediately drops to help her up. "Raven, how much did you drink?"

"You know, zero." Raven holds up one finger in front of his face and tries to bend her finger, so it makes a zero with her thumb. "But it sure doesn't feel like zero."

"It's something else then?" Logan brushes her hair away from her face. The gentle gesture smears my face into a suspicious twist.

Raven tilts toward him then sways back. "It's always something. With *you.*"

"Let's get you home." Logan guides Raven down to his waiting limo.

I should intervene, but something stops me. She ran away from me, straight to *him*.

I watch Raven get inside and ride away.

Punkaj appears beside me. "Hey, I was looking for you."

"Raven just left with Logan." It sounds even more unbelievable out loud. The night has slipped into a damp sort of chill, and I shudder.

"And you let her?"

"I know I shouldn't have, but...no one is acting normal, Punk." My teeth are chattering. "Raven, Logan, Penny's parents. Mr. Zale hasn't said one word tonight, and in what world would Mrs. Zale ever give control of tonight's event to Juniper Tremaine?"

Punkaj shrugs out of his blazer and hangs it over my shoulders. "So that means we pay closer attention. When people are acting out of their element that's when they slip up. That's when they spill secrets."

"There are too many secrets." I pull his coat tighter around me. "I wonder about the Zales, what *they* think happened to their daughter?"

"So do what a reporter would do," Punkaj says. "Go to their house, knock on their door, and ask."

CHAPTER 24
SHARD OF GLASS
RAVEN

The incessant beeping needs to stop. My head pounds, light blares through my window, and my phone has the nerve to beep again. I yank the pillow over my head, and while it blocks the light, it does nothing to help with the noise.

I'm exhausted and desperate for more sleep. I tossed and turned through the darkest part of the night, drifting in and out of nightmares over and over. My mother's voice. Desperation. Running. The gunshot. And blood. So much blood.

With the pillow firmly pressed over my eyes, I try to grab the phone off my nightstand but knock it off instead. It beeps *again*. Okay phone, you win. Whoever this is better have a good reason for waking me. I fish my phone out from under my bed and prop myself up with a stack of pillows.

The red bubble in the bottom corner says thirty-nine missed text messages. Thirty-nine? All but one of them are from the same person. Aarya.

> Where are you? Are you ok? Answer
> me. I'm coming over in one hour if I
> don't hear back.

I scroll through her texts, and she's pissed. Like really pissed. Hazy pieces from last night flash—Aarya speaking sternly. Me falling. Logan's strong embrace holding me up.

What the hell happened?

My eyes are itchy, which means I didn't take off my makeup. I glance down and glitter fabric stares back at me. I passed out in my dress. Something is pinching my hair. I pull out a diamond-studded comb, and my messy hair topples down. That's right, Vera gave me this to wear last night. I don't know how to feel about her doing something so mother-esque, *her* family's heirloom for me. Warmth spreads in my chest, but then I remember sitting at dinner and her pushing it in to make sure it didn't come out, pinching my scalp. She is a yo-yo of hot and cold.

It's after dinner when things begin to blur.

I pull the tangled pieces of my hair back up with the comb. It's safer wearing it.

There's a ceramic mug full of cold tea and a water bottle on my side table. I do remember drinking water on the way home, in a limo. Logan's limo. I was in Logan's limo last night.

I glance at the little red bubble with the one last unread message, not sure if I'm ready to hear what Logan has to say after the Aarya text flurry.

I rack my brain trying to figure out how it ended with him. My shoes are neatly placed next to my bed. I remember he took them off for me, one then the other.

When he fumbled with the straps, my stomach did somersaults and made me want him to fumble his way further up my leg, but he was all business, tucking me in under the covers, handing me water when my eyes started to close on their own. "Don't fall asleep yet."

He stroked my hair, and I opened my eyes and he pulled away, going straight for the water bottle. "Drink this first. It will help."

I did as I was told. "What's going on?"

"I was hoping you'd be able to tell me," he said. "But right now, you need water and bed."

"I honestly don't know," I mumbled.

"Sleep. When you're ready to talk to someone, you know you can come to me?"

Come to me. I pushed him away, and a week later he's driving me home, taking care of me, telling me I can confide in him.

I cannot deal with this right now, so I ignore his message, leaving it unread. Time to tackle the immediate problem, the thirty-eight other texts.

Hey.

> You're alive.

Yes I am.

> R u home?

Yes.

> Good. Now that I know you're ok. We're in a fight.

Why?

> You tell me. Oh wait. You're not telling me anything anymore.

Not true.

It was last night.

I don't know what happened last night.

I'm not doing this again. Fight stands
until you're ready to tell me what's
going on. Text me when you want to
tell the truth.

Great. Nothing like waking up to this. I go to stand, but the room spins, and I swallow my breath like it's a lump in my throat, trying not to freak out. I feel hungover but I don't remember taking anything or drinking anything. My knee is also aching more than normal. Did I fall last night, too?

What a disaster. I open my dad's contact, and my finger hovers over the call button. He probably won't answer. He hasn't in weeks, he's not texting me, he's not communicating with me at all. Everything has been through Vera, and who knows what she's told him, but it can't be good if he's been ignoring me for this long.

I can't do anything right.

I'm pissing off my friends. I'm fighting feelings I shouldn't have, thoughts I can't stop. Images dance in my mind—a moonlit kiss, heated blue-gray eyes, a stolen touch in the shadows, waves.

I want Logan bad—but it's bad to want him. I'm stuck in a purgatory with no one to turn to and no good options. I grip my necklace. There *is* someone even if she won't speak back.

I pull out a frame buried in the drawer next to my bed.

As if I could touch my mother's face, I run my fingers over glass. The smooth, cold surface jeers. I tug at a faded memory, unable to fully recall what it was like to stare into those loving hazel eyes in person, but her brilliant smile reminds me to try and smile, too.

The corners of my mouth tug up, but a shadow appears over the frame. My mother's image melts into a reflection, her radiance eclipsed by severity.

Vera's harsh blue eyes and pasty skin jar me from my mother's comforting brown and black. My momentary joy replaced by an acute fear tearing through my gut. If Aarya is as mad at me as she is, I'm terrified to find out where Vera stands.

I close my eyes and open them again, but the reflection is still there. I turn the frame over on my lap. Palms sweaty, I clasp my hands to stop them from shaking and wait for Vera to speak.

"I see you've recovered."

"I don't know what happened."

"Of course you don't. And for some reason, this feels familiar. Does it feel familiar to you, Raven?" The question is rhetorical.

I sink back, resting on the pillows behind me, attempting to disappear. "This is not that."

"You keep saying that. But first the pageant, and now this."

"The pageant was different."

"Was it?"

"The corset was tight. I couldn't breathe."

"You're doing what addicts do. You're lying."

"I'm not lying."

"But you're an addict."

"I'm in recovery. And I've stayed away from everything. Even those pills you gave me. This isn't fair."

"Where are they? Should I count them to see if you're telling the truth?"

"Why can't you trust me and listen to what I'm telling you?"

She seems to consider my plea because a beat goes by in silence before she says, "You embarrassed me last night. Your actions did not go unnoticed, and I had to cover for you with the Steeles." Vera cocks her head. "Speaking of the Steeles, where is Logan? He never made it back for dinner."

"He helped me get home."

"I'm sure he did. And you must have repaid him nicely for the gesture."

Her assumption makes my cheeks light up and stomach tighten into a fist. "It's not like that."

Vera grabs a hand mirror sitting on my dresser. "Sit up. You haven't earned the right to sulk."

Resisting Vera could make it worse. Sometimes cooperating gets the circling hawk to move on to other prey. I do as she says and push myself up.

"Look at yourself." Vera is reflected behind me in the mirror she thrusts in front of my face. "It's a wonder people don't immediately realize you're trash from Belle Grande. You may blend in with your snow-white skin, but I've told you and you just won't listen. People like Logan Steele don't marry girls like you."

My blood turns into little bubbles of anger ready to burst. I look away from the mirror.

"Am I making you upset? It's only the truth. Maybe I need to spell it out for you so you get it this time. People like Logan may hire people like you to work in their sugar fields or serve as maids in their homes, maybe use them for a little fun on the side but, like your dad came back to me, when Logan is done sowing his seeds, he'll drop you and find someone worthy of him."

I can't take it anymore. All reason is gone, my body

overtaken by a tidal wave of frustration and I spit out, "My dad didn't come back to you." Then with slow, deliberate pronunciation I say, "My mother *died*. That is the *only* reason he's with you now."

My head flies back as fast as the words came out of my mouth as Vera grabs my hair and pulls. I scream, each tight strand like a needle pricking my scalp.

"I've already called your father. He doesn't want to talk to you. He's angry and disappointed you're back on drugs. One more slip and I have permission to send you away." Vera holds tight, more and more strands of hair ripping with each second passing. The comb slides out from my hair.

"I don't know why I thought you were worthy to wear this. I tried to dress you up for the Steeles, since so many of your attempts fail. Thank god you didn't lose it in your antics."

Maybe my brain's short circuiting from lack of sleep but I seethe through the pain and say, "I wish I had lost it."

Within seconds my mom's necklace is in her grip. Nails scraping, metal digging into skin, burning when the chain tightens and drags on my neck. One swift yank and she rips it off. The fight drains out of me.

Vera twists the fist still holding my hair, my throat stretched taut. I have nothing left. The tension in my muscles release, surrendering, letting her pull my head back further. Breath hot against my ear, stinking of coffee and mint, she whispers, "You are a shard of glass in my side, that's all you will ever be, and because of your whore of a mother, I'm stuck with you. But not for long. One more mess-up—and I mean if you even look at me the wrong way—you will be someone else's problem." Vera releases my hair. The pain in the back of my head radiates, and I choke down a sob watching her walk out of the room with my mother's necklace.

The mirror glints on my bed. I grab it and throw it hard against the door where it shatters into jagged pieces, a thousand splinters of glass everywhere.

Little fragments of me cracked by her control.

I stare at the pile of glass, entranced by how it catches the light. I pick up a shred of reflective silver. This is what Vera thinks of me. A broken mess. A worthless girl from the wrong side of town. Born from the wrong mother. Wrong heritage.

Wrong, wrong, *wrong*. I don't belong.

I try to grasp my ruby heart, and the space it lives in is empty. I'm empty.

I want to run like I do in my nightmare, and I blink rapidly but it feels like the room fades away and I'm in another place, held back from my mom, and I hear her scream, and I can't do anything. My pulse fights against the cage, a time-warped memory trapping me in this space, heart beating faster and faster, my breath swelling to match it.

I gulp for air, my chest constricts.

Get to the pill bottle.

It's not on my dresser where I left it last. Where is it, where is it? I spin in the room, and my foot kicks something. It's my purse—peeking out of the top is the bottle. Hands shaking, I struggle to open the cap. Push and twist. The lid pops off and the pills spill across the floor.

Count them. Vera wanted to count them. How many are there? One, two, three...I count seventeen. Take one. Take two. Take what I need. Take more than I need. *Need.* Do I need them?

Control... Control the things I can. Let go of the things I can't.

I speak the words out loud. Over and over and over until the pills before me are choices, not demands. Choices I control. I can say no. No, I don't need them. No, I won't take any. *No.*

I put each one back in the bottle, cap it, set it down, and back away. I counted seventeen pills—but that's an odd number. I check the label, which says twenty.

Wait. I don't remember taking any, but three pills are gone. I don't even remember putting the bottle in my purse. Could I have taken them? An old habit so engrained, like driving home on a familiar highway, and suddenly you pull up to your house and don't remember the journey. Was this like that?

One pill wouldn't have made me black out and do God knows what else last night. But three pills would have.

My phone beeps. Logan again.

Hey. Checking in.

Answering him would at least be something concrete, unlike staring at the pill bottle, not knowing if I took any of those pills. I'm afraid of what I might have done. Did I slip and not remember? And if I'm alone any longer, will I be able to resist their pull again?

My phone beeps, and it's him again.

You up yet? Are you ok?

Maybe he only wants one thing. Maybe he's using me and will throw me away when he's had his fun. Like everyone thinks he did to Penny.

Maybe I want to be used. Wrung out like a filthy rag, like the trash Vera says I am.

Or maybe, just maybe, Vera's wrong and my friends are wrong, because in this moment, he's the only thing that feels right.

I leave the pills on the dresser, sure of what I need to do next.

CHAPTER 25
SOFT AS SNOW
RAVEN

park in the circular drive at the front of the mansion, and it hits me how stupid it was to come over here without giving him any warning. I'm glad the guard let me in, which means Logan let me in, which means on some level he's okay with me showing up unannounced.

I check my hair in the rearview mirror. My liner is smudged; a smoky eye that's more you-were-at-an-all-night-rager than sexy glam. I apply some lip gloss and try to wipe away the black from under my eyes. A thin red line circles my neck, and I pull my hair forward to cover it.

I go to open my door, but it opens for me instead.

Logan's wearing a fitted white t-shirt and faded blue jeans set low on his hips. I step out of the car and face the boy who is supposed to be wrong. His expression is a mix of concern and something that feels like longing, and it makes heat rise on the back of my neck.

"I was surprised when the guard said you were at the gate."

I avoid eye contact. "Thanks for letting me in."

"I texted you a few times."

"I know."

"This is one way to respond, I suppose."

"I needed to get out." I ball my hands into fists at my sides, trying to stop the tremors still reverberating from the fight with Vera.

He studies me with an intensity that makes me feel entirely vulnerable, and my core heats. I know how disheveled I look—and how tense I feel. *Please don't ask questions*, I silently beg.

"Okay, then I support your decision since it landed you here."

I almost reach out and wrap my arms around him to thank him for letting it go for now. Also, I need a hug, physical warmth, and strength to borrow before mine gives out, something to make me feel like I'm not crazy. But I resist this urge and follow him inside instead.

The butler holds the door open, and Logan leads me past the sweeping staircase, then through an overly tall archway to a sitting area with a plush velvet couch. He invites me to sit, then lands in the spot next to me.

Immediately, the butler is upon us, asking if he can bring me something to drink.

"A glass of water would be nice."

"Of course, miss. I will be right back."

"That takes some getting used to." I nod toward the hallway the man disappeared down. I'm consciously trying to stop shaking my legs, but my anxiety insists on finding a way out.

"You mean Walter?" If Logan notices my fidgeting, he doesn't acknowledge it.

"Yeah. Walter. Your butler." He seems to see through my attempt to avoid talking about anything real and gives me a *cut the crap* look. "Are you okay?"

I look down at my hands. "I think I'd prefer to talk about Walter."

"You were really messed up last night."

I think about the missing pills and consider telling him but decide against trying to explain something I don't even understand. "I don't know what happened."

"Raven, you don't have to lie to me. It's okay if you're going through something."

My head snaps up and I glare and I'm instantly glad I didn't say a word about those pills. "My life isn't easy like yours."

He runs his hand through his hair and stands up. "Alright. If you don't want to talk, then come with me."

"Where?"

"You'll see." Logan holds his hand out to me, a bridge to somewhere I'm not sure I want to go. I stand up without his help.

He takes it in stride, putting his hands in his pockets. It pulls his jeans down just enough, so his abs peek out over the waist band. I wrench my eyes back to his face, but he totally catches me. "I have something to show you and that wasn't it. So, come on." He says this with a smirk I want to wipe off his face.

I'd always thought I wasn't one to blush, but I'm absolutely sure my cheeks are as red as a stop light. We walk side-by-side down a hall, which is good for me, as he can't see my embarrassment on display. I take in the opulent tapestries hanging between painted portraits of generations of the Steele family and window views of the ocean. He brushes his shoulder against mine and says, "We've talked about this before, but you know I live with the chief executive asshole and you with his second in command."

"Yeah."

"So, this Steele name comes with strings attached. Expectations we've talked about."

"I remember."

"But you haven't talked about what your life comes with."

"You mean with Vera?"

"Yeah. Last night, I went and found you because of what she said to my dad about you."

My stomach sinks. "What did she say?"

"Apologizing for you, other stuff—it doesn't matter. But the worst part was that she saw you stumble outside and instead of helping you, only talked behind your back. So I went after you."

"You didn't have to do that."

Logan holds the door open for me. "I don't do things for you because I have to."

I ignore how my stomach flips. We make our way outside onto a flagstone walkway lined with quaint streetlights like you'd see in an old-fashioned town. Questions about Vera I can handle. Questions about last night, not so much.

"Most of Vera's demands have to do with my mom," I say.

"How so?"

I think of Vera's pure hatred for my mom. For me. "Suffice it to say Vera would prefer if my mom never existed." I don't add that she'd also prefer if *I* never existed, even though I know it's true. "So I go along with what she wants. To keep the peace."

The place where my ruby heart necklace should be burns, reminding me why I have to avoid conflict with her at all costs.

"I get that. It's like that with my dad. It's easier just to play by his rules than deal with the consequences."

"Exactly. So, I don't have pictures up of my mom in the house, not even in my room. And I used to have these wild curls, just like my mom's, but Vera makes me straighten it."

"Wait, what? She controls how you do your hair? I thought you straightened it because you wanted to."

I shake my head. "Vera insists. Gets on me before I even need the next treatment. I'm behind schedule right now, and it feels like a small victory."

This is as much as I'm willing to reveal. I won't tell him what happened today, won't tell him what happened after the pageant. Definitely not what happened on my thirteenth birthday. He can't know, because if he did, I'm terrified it would prove Vera right. I'm terrified he might see me as she does. The product of betrayal. Less than.

"So about last night," he says.

"Do we have to go there again?"

"I just need to know you're okay."

"I'm fine."

"And you're not going to talk about it, are you?"

"I honestly don't know what happened and we're going to go around and around, and I don't want to be in a fight with you, too."

His nose wrinkles. "Who else are you fighting with?"

I clamp my mouth shut, unwilling to say more, embarrassed I said that much.

"Okay, well, then we'll stick with my plan." We reach the end of the path. I gasp at what's in front of me. Logan's full-size basketball court.

"No way!" I run as much as my knee will let me. Walter is waiting on the court with waters and a set of basketballs on a rack. "I need answers."

"As soon as the guard let me know you were here, I

had Walter get everything ready." Logan's eyes look like late afternoon light: beckoning and inviting.

I grab a basketball off the rack to get away from those hypnotic eyes, dribble it a couple times, then jog toward the hoop, coming in on the right side, shooting up off my left foot and banking the ball off the backboard. If I keep the pressure off my healing knee, it might be okay to play a little. Technically, he has the advantage, considering my current state, but my competitive streak kicks in and I can't resist trying. I get the rebound and pivot, throwing the ball right at Logan. He catches it, his lips turning up on one side.

"Watch yourself." I post up in front of him, getting in as low of a stance as I can.

"Is it okay to beat up on you when you're playing with a handicap?"

"What makes you so sure I can't win even with a bum knee?"

"I like your confidence, but you're still going to lose." Logan keeps one foot firmly planted in front of me but twists back with the ball in both hands. He's changed up his strategy since last time when he drove straight to the basket without thought.

I watch his feet, careful not to let his intense, gray eyes distract me. He brings the ball around as if he's going to take off to the right side, but his feet move to the left. I may be out this season, but this move is my signature, and I don't take the bait. I shuffle, keeping step with him.

He sprints toward the basket but doesn't stop outside the paint this time. He drives right in for the layup, and risking the foul, I slap the ball and his hand rather than try to push my knee by running to keep up with him.

"You're playing dirty!"

Hands on my hips, I say, "I'm playing to win."

The ball rolls halfway down the court. We both take off after it, me hobble-running, Logan full-on sprinting. He gets there first and kicks it.

Journeying farther and farther, the ball rolls into the sand beyond. I hobble-run as fast as I can. Logan dives on top of the ball. I tumble down on top of him but manage to keep my weight on my good knee.

He hugs the ball underneath. There's no way I'm getting that ball away from him. Regulation tactics are not working. Dirty it is. I tickle his sides.

Logan laughs hard and rolls, releasing the ball, and flipping over underneath me. He grabs my hands, and our hysterical laughter subsides. Logan looks up at me while I straddle him in the sand. He pulls my hands down to his chest and we both still. My hair falls in a frame around us. Logan brushes away a strand, letting his fingers linger on my cheek. I close my eyes and breathe in the salty air. Silence holds.

I open my eyes. He is so near our breath mingles. "I guess this means..." I pause, his stare its own gravitational force. "I win. Seeing how, you've seemed to...you've lost the ball."

Logan's gaze falls to my mouth. "I'm pretty sure I won this round." He trails his hands up the hem of my shirt and moves up around my neck until he cups the back of my head and pulls me toward him. His fingers, soft as snow, twine into my hair, but when they brush over the raw spot where Vera pulled my hair, I cry out.

Logan lets go. "What's wrong?"

I squeeze my eyes, but an avalanche of tears releases. It all comes back—the shock, the violence.

I slide down into the sand and bury my head in my hands. The sobs keep coming, uncontrollable.

Logan scoops me into his lap and squeezes, holding

me, one hand curled around my waist, the other rubbing up and down my back. "Raven, what's going on?"

I can't say it. No one knows.

"I'm so sorry." I force the words out, not wanting him to think the outburst had anything to do with him. "It's not this. Not you."

"Okay. You don't have to say anything."

The sobs tear through me still, and he continues to hold me. The dam has broken and it's impossible to stop. I cry for the words Vera threw at me, how she ripped hairs from my head. How I don't have any memory of taking anything last night, but I know pills are missing and I know I was messed up and I know she will send me away if I can't get myself together and figure out what's happening.

Logan presses his lips to my forehead and breathes, "Shhhh. It's okay. I'm here."

I bury my face in his chest and he pulls me so tight against him I can't tell where he ends and I begin, as if we were made to be pressed together like this. I let every tear I have pour out of me until I stop shaking, stop moving, stop being afraid.

With salt stung eyes and puffy hot cheeks, I look up at him and speak my truth out loud. "It's Vera."

Logan's brow furrows. "What about her?" I watch him while he processes, his expression goes tight, nostrils flaring. "What did she do to you?"

I don't know if it's how passionately he says it, or if it's how I finally feel safe and grounded sitting in his lap. Maybe it's that I can't hold this burden alone for one second longer or I'll shatter, but I tell him everything. The nail scratches. The degrading comments and demeaning slurs. Vera's hatred of my mom and how she blames me for everything wrong in her life. *Why* she blames me.

About what happened today, before I came over, how the ache continues to throb.

When I'm finally done, Logan breathes heavily. "I didn't know. I wouldn't have—"

"You did nothing wrong," I say.

"Raven, what you're telling me, how she is to you... this is not okay at all." He traces the angry red line on my neck. "You understand how not okay this is, right?"

"I have it handled."

"We need to tell someone," Logan says.

"Who, Logan? Who's going to listen? The police are wrapped around her Steele Enterprises finger because she's your dad's lawyer. Or my dad? Who hasn't returned any of my calls for weeks since he left for Jamaica? I'm sure she's relayed her twisted version of everything to him. The best thing I can do is ride it out until I graduate, and then be gone from her forever."

He sits there in silence for a moment, then takes my hand in his and strokes my arm with his free hand. "I'll talk to my father."

"No, no you won't. Promise me. Please. It will only get worse if you do. I have this handled."

Logan's jaw is tense, and I cup his face in my hands, bringing his gaze to mine. "Please Logan, don't."

"Fine." He swallows like it's painful to say. "I won't. But promise me, if she does something again, you'll tell me. We will figure out what to do."

I nod.

"And, Raven, I'm going to put you on the guest list permanently here. If you ever need to get away from her, you can always come over. Anytime."

I rest my head on his shoulder, and Logan secures his arm around me. His embrace brings me to a place I've been searching for, somewhere to belong, and every lingering fear Vera tried to force—saying he'd never care about a girl like me—every belief my friends hold that he could be involved with Penny's disappearance...it all disintegrates.

At least for this moment, we've found our place. A fleeting ever after.

CHAPTER 26
LET DOWN YOUR HAIR
AARYA

"The blue door." Seeing it hits me in the complete opposite way Penny intended. "Penny told me she wanted the color to feel like a hello whenever she came home."

Elle stares at the door, too. "I remember her asking me what shade of blue a hug was. I told her cerulean and she laughed. Said it sounded like the ruler of a fantasy world. Prince Cerulean."

Today, the cerulean door feels like the sad chords of a goodbye.

Penny's house, with no Penny in it.

The four of us stand on the step together, no one quite ready to knock. I sneak a look at Raven. The Taste of Success dinner, only two nights ago, hangs heavily between us. Penny's mother's voice cracks over the doorbell camera, clearly alerted to our presence on her step.

"Aarya? Is that you? Raven? Dawn... And Elle? Heavens. What are you all doing here?"

"We were hoping to talk about Penny," I say.

The audio clicks off. A moment passes, then the blue door swings open

"Come in."

Mrs. Zale's looks exhausted. Her expensive yoga clothes are rumpled, her hair coming unraveled from a messy side braid.

I've never seen her wear her hair like Penny. It's jarring. A strange, ghostly touch.

"Sorry for the mess. I can make a pot of tea. Do you girls want any?" Mrs. Zale says. "Make yourselves at home."

This is not the Mrs. Zale I know, saying the things you're supposed to say, on autopilot, and the *house*. Papers piled in corners on tables. Dishes covering the counters. Laundry basket turned over on its side on the dining table. A bowl of half-finished popcorn on the entryway table next to a plant in dire need of water.

We all exchange glances and try to find an uncluttered surface to sit.

Raven moves a pair of sneakers and sinks down into an upholstered chair in the corner that swallows her up. Dawn makes room at the long counter. I pull up a stool beside them and rest my elbows on granite, sticky and gritty, cupping the heat of the tea Mrs. Zale hands me.

"So, what's this all about then? How are you girls doing?" Her eyes flit from face-to-face.

"We're okay...ish," I say. "How are you?"

Mrs. Zale gives a little laugh through her nose. "I don't know what okay is anymore."

She focuses in on Elle. "It's nice to see you. And to see that you've met Penny's other friends." Mrs. Zale gives Elle's hand a brief squeeze, her fingers moving away like a fearful sparrow.

"I met them because of Penny's poems," Elle says cautiously. "Have you...read them?"

"Yes of course," Mrs. Zale says. "The police gave us copies."

"Did they make any sense to you?" I ask.

Mrs. Zale purses her lips. "Penny wrote such beautiful poems. I always liked how they sounded, but I'm not very good at understanding poetry."

"We feel like she's trying to tell us something," Dawn offers. "About what might have happened to her."

Mrs. Zale's face tightens. "Oh, Dawn honey. I know there are so many questions around her disappearance. But I don't think the poems are anything more than Penny putting feelings down on paper." Mrs. Zale averts her eyes and gives her head a little shake, like she can't bear to talk about it.

I follow her gaze around the room and notice uneasily that every picture of Penny is either face down or toward the wall. It leaves a coldness in my bones.

We have to fix this. This is no way to live a life. With Penny's face, Penny's *truth*, hidden. Mrs. Zale is crumbling. We can help. The *poems* can help.

"Mrs. Zale...the poems make us wonder if she was trying to warn us about Logan. That maybe he was involved. That he hurt her in some way."

"Logan? Oh my, no, I really doubt that." Mrs. Zale rubs her temples. "Their relationship was...rocky, to say the least. But I don't think she's in any way trying to implicate him in something. All I see when I read her poems is an angry teenager."

"Angry about what?" I ask.

"Honestly? Nothing and everything. Angry for the sake of being angry. She got involved with that Belle Grande boy and started to get all riled up over haves versus have nots. She was always picking fights with her father about working for Steele Sugar. Kept saying they were greedy. Didn't take good care of their workers. But we all know that's not true. That boy, he put ideas in her head."

"Did you not want them to date?" Dawn asks.

"I knew it wouldn't last. Her father though, he wasn't having it. He banned her from going out there, and they fought horribly over it."

Fighting with your dad, something I basically have a degree in, and I had no idea. Sure, Penny chose to be secretive, but when is it on you, as the friend, to figure out something is wrong? When is it your fault for not noticing someone is falling apart?

I glance back over at Raven, hiding in the chair. She is unravelling and won't tell me why. I can't keep making the same mistakes. "Can we ask Mr. Zale about the poems?" Elle asks.

Penny's mother presses her lips together. "He's not here right now. Some things to attend to for Steele Sugar."

"When will he be back?" I ask.

I notice Mrs. Zale hesitates. "Um, he's been staying in the Steele's carriage house. This... It's been very hard on us."

"That's why you weren't at the dinner!" I blurt out. Oops. Way to be subtle.

"Yes. We are um, taking a little...breather," Mrs. Zale says. "You're welcome to try to talk to him, but I don't see what more he would have to say. The poems are the convoluted offshoots of a troubled mind. Penny, you know, was manic depressive."

"That doesn't mean what she wrote is nonsense," Raven says from her corner. "You can't brush someone off as crazy just because something doesn't make sense on the surface."

It's the first time she's spoken since we came in, and I can't help but think she's also talking about herself.

Mrs. Zale's voice gains momentum with each word. "No. It pretty much does. Penny's brain was like fireworks—a pretty show, but explosive. Her thoughts were dangerous to her own well-being. She had some ideas that were..." Mrs. Zale's voice trails away, and she looks off into the distance.

"That were what?" I ask.

Mrs. Zale looks down at her hands, playing with her wedding ring. "The ideas were irrational, which was why they—why *we* put her in Hightower. Spending time in that town went to her head. I blame the boy."

"His name is Ansel," Elle says softly. "In case you wondered."

Mrs. Zale takes a deep breath and closes her eyes. She holds up a finger. Opens her mouth. Closes it again. When she finally speaks, she is firm and abruptly cold. "I wish I could have been more help. But there's nothing to her words...but words."

"Penny's words are never just words," Elle says.

"Yes. They are." Penny's mom's voice is eerily robotic. She stands, escorting us to the door, the house humming its emptiness against our silence.

Mrs. Zale gives us each a quick hug, the equivalent of patting a puppy on the head to encourage it to scamper off.

"Let this go girls. Please." Her breath catches. "It isn't healthy. Penny needs police not poetry readings. Promise me you'll not read into things."

"We'll um, try."

We walk away from the house, a heaviness settling over us.

"I can't believe they separated," Dawn muses. "How sad. You lose your daughter and then your marriage."

Elle frowns. "It can happen after tragedies. Couples can't handle the grief. But it also makes me wonder if she blames him somehow."

"Yes! *Yes!*" I burst out. I gesture for the girls to pause under a trellis cloaked with bougainvillea.

"Did you hear Mrs. Zale say *they* put Penny in Hightower, and then she swapped it to *we*? Who is 'they'? I don't think she wanted to. I don't think Penny's mom agreed with the decision."

"You're making some pretty big assumptions here," Raven says.

"I totally am. But it kind of makes sense, doesn't it?"

"It's not entirely far-fetched," Elle says.

"I wonder..." Raven says. "Elle, can you read your poem again?"

Elle reaches into the pocket of her jeans and pulls out the wrinkled piece of paper. Like the rest of us, she is always carrying around these words. Just in case.

"*Hearts...turned to steel...a long time ago. To survive, walk on glass, pretend you don't know the deceit.*"

"What if," Raven murmurs, "what if it's not Logan she's talking about?"

"She says hearts turned to steel. Logan *Steele*," I say.

"But you heard Mrs. Zale say Penny was angry about a lot of things. And fighting with her dad," Raven says. "What if Penny was writing about him, or Steele sugar, something bigger than her ex-boyfriend?"

No. No way. "Not buying it. The *deceit* is not Penny being upset about what her dad does for a living."

"What exactly does Mr. Zale do for the Steeles anyway?" Elle asks.

We look blankly at one another. "I actually have no

idea," I say.

"Maybe we don't listen about leaving him alone?" Elle says. "Maybe we go talk to him?"

I tug at a strand of my hair. "Because Penny's mom was so forthcoming. I'm sure he'll be an open book. We might be better off trying to spy on him, versus straight up asking him what he thinks."

"No more sneaking around the Steele estate, please," Dawn says. "I really think that's pressing our luck. Look at what happened the last time."

"Yeah. We got answers," I say. "We didn't really know what we were looking for in Logan's room either, but we certainly found something."

Elle squints. It's not going to be easy to just show up there. We had an excuse before. This is broad daylight, without an invite."

"I..." Raven starts to say something, then stops.

We all wait expectantly.

"I think I can maybe get us in?"

"How?" I ask.

She hesitates, takes a breath. "Logan gave me his private code."

My skin prickles. "And you're only telling us this now, because?"

Raven bristles. "Because it didn't come up."

"Was this before or after you went home with him after the Taste of Success dinner? Which also hasn't come up. I saw you leave together."

"What was I supposed to do?" Raven says. "It's not like Vera was helping me. Or *you*."

"I tried! You wouldn't let me."

"Listen. I'm doing exactly what I was supposed to, okay? You're the one who said, get close to Logan, find out what you can. How about thanks, Raven?"

"Thanks Raven, for getting close enough to Logan to get his personal access code and not telling me right away. Anything else you're not telling me?"

"That's not fair."

"I feel like maybe you're forgetting he possibly had something to do with our friend, you know, *disappearing?*"

"I'm forgetting nothing," says Raven. "I'm well aware that he didn't treat Penny well. But that doesn't make him a criminal. He's a kid, like us."

"He is nothing like us. First, he's richer than god. And a total jerk. But for some unfathomable reason, I think you like him," I say.

"What would make you say something like that?" Raven glances around as if looking for a rescue. Elle and Dawn look back and forth between us, discomfort blatant in their expressions.

"*This.*" I point at Raven, who is now blinking rapidly. "How you're acting right now. How you've *been* acting."

"No, I only get frazzled trying to fake it with him," Raven fires back. "We're not all as great at manipulation as you."

"Please don't argue." Dawn's voice is high, pinched.

"We don't have time for this," Elle says. "Raven's got the code. We have questions. This is our chance to get some answers. Are we going to go look around the carriage house or not?"

A quick beat of silence before I say firmly, "Yes."

"Yes," Raven agrees so softly I barely hear it.

"This is a terrible idea," Dawn says. "But, fine. For Penny."

"For Penny," Elle echoes. "If we go in a back service entrance like grounds and housekeepers no one should notice. When do you want to go?"

"Next weekend," Raven says. "Logan and Hunter are surfing on the East Coast on Saturday."

"Of course you know where he'll be."

"Like I said, I'm just doing the job you assigned me."

"Fine." We need to stay focused on Penny, but it gnaws at me, just how well she's been doing her job.

Dawn scrunches her face up like it hurts to say what she's about to. "I know something, too," she blurts out. "The Steeles are meeting with my dad to discuss final touches for the fundraiser on Saturday. They shouldn't be home either."

"Good intel!" I say. "Next Saturday it is. Six days from now, we'll get answers. You're getting good at this Dawn, I'm proud of you. Now go ask for forgiveness and say your hello-Mary's."

"*Hail* Mary's. And for the hundredth time, we don't do that."

"I know. But it wouldn't hurt right? I say I don't believe in Hinduism to piss off my parents, but I'd be lying if every now and then I didn't ask Ma Kali or Ma Durga for a favor. Everyone needs to say hi to a Mary somewhere, sometimes."

My tone is light, trying to smooth the fissures. But my mind flashes beyond the terse exchanges here, and goes back to the empty house, to Mrs. Zale's even emptier gaze. The long braid reminiscent of her daughter. Her nervous hands. How every picture of Penny is turned down or away, as though her own mother can't bear to look Penny in the eye.

I look through the shadows of the thorny vines and deep red flowers to the sky. The cerulean sky.

Hello Mary. Ma Kali. Ma Durga. We need a favor. Help us find our friend.

CHAPTER 27
FALSE REPORTS

AARYA

Saturday. Go time.

School this past week was a blur of going through the motions while Raven avoided me every chance she could, our fight from the dinner last Friday still not resolved. I'm worried about her, but if there's anything I've learned, pushing her to talk when she's not ready will only make things worse.

The guard at the service gate lets us in with Raven's code almost too easily. Dawn hides between two hedges on the terraced garden to keep watch. The rest of us keep our heads down, the curtains of our hair shielding features from any security cameras, and we walk to the door with buckets and mops in hand.

"Housekeeping!" I knock on the door of the carriage house.

No answer. We give it another try, just to be sure, and when it's clear no one is home, Elle punches in the service code she got from her friend who cleans here.

The panel dings and lights up green.

We're in.

The carriage house spans out in rich mahogany, bronze, and reds. Exposed beams, oriental rugs and wrought iron lamps make it feel like we're creeping through a castle room, high in some turret.

"I'll hit the loft," Elle says heading up the stairs to the bedroom.

"Okay," I say. "Raven, help me check every drawer."

"Got it." Raven purses her lips.

I try to focus on the desk I'm searching instead of Raven. "Pens. More pens. Come on, how many pens does one person need? Check the kitchen."

After a few minutes of searching, Raven says, "Nothing other than normal kitchen stuff."

Frustration wedges in my chest. This is going to be a bust. But then I hear Elle's feet thump down the stairs.

"I think I found something."

My heart gives a little skip of excitement.

"This was in his nightstand." Elle holds a wad of papers out and a worn photo.

Raven and I lean in to get a closer look. The photo is of Mr. Zale and a young Penny. Same wild hair escaping from two braids instead of one. Same big grin crinkling her bright eyes. She's holding an ice cream cone covered in chocolate sprinkles.

"Look at the papers," Elle says. "It's Penny's intake forms. From Hightower."

We spread the pages across the table.

A chill creeps across my skin. This is all it took to lock up our friend. Parents, signing away their child.

Wait.

Not *parents.* Parent. Singular.

I scan the pages. *Donald Zale. Donald Zale. Donald Zale.*

"Penny's mom didn't sign it anywhere. Only her dad."

Raven and Elle each take a turn going page by page.

"You're right," Elle says.

"She didn't agree." It's almost like the entire carriage house flickers when I say this, an external shudder of light to shadows. This is the place Mr. Zale has been banished by his wife. A place for someone who did something bad by mistake—or on purpose.

"Why would her dad do something this drastic, on his own?" Raven asks.

My mind starts whirring trying to put the pieces together. "What do we know... Her mom was sketchy last week. And mentioned Penny being upset with her dad, saying the Steele's were greedy. And not taking care of the sugar workers."

"But her mom also said that wasn't true about the workers," Raven says. "And the Zales do the Taste of Success dinner and everything."

"You mean the one night they take a couple of workers' kids out for dinner and do nothing else to help the other three hundred and sixty-four days a year?" Elle's tone is straight mocking disdain.

I give her a look saying this isn't the time. "Penny and her dad were fighting. And we know she was upset about the sugar workers for some reason, even if her mom didn't agree," I say.

"Why would her father commit her though? Why place someone in psychiatric care if they don't need it?" Elle asks.

"To make sure no one ever believed her again," Raven says with a cold certainty. "Think about it. The police dismissed the poems. Penny's own mom called them *offshoots of a troubled mind*. Even Ansel couldn't make sense of them and kept telling us how out of it she was when he visited her." Raven's voice drops. "Who believes the 'crazy' girl?"

"But that would mean she had something to say that someone needed to discredit. Do you think..." The thought lodges in my throat. "Did Penny know something her *father* didn't want to get out?"

Raven tilts her head to one side. "You mean maybe this isn't all about Logan and only Logan after all?"

"Snake hunting flyer. Paintballs. We have some pretty hard evidence he's involved. But I never said Logan's the *only* one responsible for her disappearance." I rifle through the papers some more. "Wait. What's this? *Daily Vessel Log*."

"It looks like some sort of train or bus schedule," Elle says.

I look closer. "No. It's...boats."

Dates along with military time stamps span the left-hand side. Across the top the name of the ships coming in, the agent operating them, size, cargo, and country of origin. All their docking information. *Docks.*

Like an orchestra tuning up and getting in sync, I start to make a connection.

"Hang on!" I grab my poem out of my pocket. "*Take a deep dive...raise your voice in support. Docks clocked by day, false reports that night cheats.*"

I point to several highlighted rows. "These are all times that ships are *docking*! *Docks clocked.* Maybe Penny is trying to tell us something about these ships."

Our pockets all simultaneously buzz with a text from Dawn.

GET OUT NOW.

"Crap! Let's go!" Elle says.

We hurry toward the door only to hear the lock clicking open.

"Hide!" I mouth.

There's no time. The front door swings open, a man's frame outlined against the bright outside light. Penny's dad! No, wait...*Logan.*

He's in swim trunks, and a tight-fitting wetsuit top. He looks around at all of us, gaze landing on Raven. "What are you doing here?"

Hunter steps out from behind him. Raven looks between the two of them and tries to stammer out an answer.

"What are you all doing here?" Logan asks again. This time it's clear the question is for Raven. His tone sounds less angry than...*hurt*?

I step between them. "Relax. We wanted to talk to Penny's father. Her mom said he lived here now."

"Yeah, but he's clearly not here. You've got a handful of his stuff." Hunter sounds more amused than concerned. "And we found Dawn in some shrubs, and she doesn't seem the type to be popping a squat."

Dawn peers apologetically from the door.

"Raven?" Logan's voice is pulled taut like strings wired too tight on a guitar. One hard chord and they'll snap. "The guard said someone used my code to go in the service entrance."

"Oh...well...maybe..." Raven trips over her words.

Logan's eyes flash with anger now. "Why would you use it to sneak in the service entrance, instead of asking *me* to come see Penny's dad? Or calling Penny's dad directly? This is messed up, Raven."

Elle interjects. "You're the one who's messed up. We *know* you put the snake in Dawn's car!" Jeez, this girl is like a low flying plane dropping bombs. She can't ever keep her mouth shut.

Hunter bursts out laughing. "Come on! You girls are losing it. I know my brother's not exactly your favorite, but the python! You've got to be kidding me. It was probably someone's pet once upon a time and got in there."

"Was it?" Elle demands.

Logan explodes. "Are we back to this? Come on! I would *never* do that. To anyone. Raven—"

"Why do you keep turning to Raven to defend you?" It explodes out of me with force. "Raven, is there something you need to share with the rest of us?"

Raven looks from me to Logan. "I, uh, I don't know who put the snake in my car."

"Unbelievable!" Logan shakes his head.

"Says the guy who shot at us with paintballs and almost killed us!" Elle says.

Logan's face twists. "So, you're here, what? Spying because you all think I'm some kind of criminal?"

"Why else do you think Raven would be cozying up to you?" I fire back. "You don't think she actually likes you...do you?"

Raven's mouth opens and closes. But nothing comes out.

"Sea Witch. Come on. Chill." Hunter holds his arms out as if he can transmit calm through the air. "You're accusing my brother of some pretty serious stuff."

"You're right. I am. And I mean it." This time I am not backing down.

"You need to leave," Logan says. He glares pointedly at Raven. "*All* of you."

Raven blinks rapidly, eyes wet. "Logan—"

"Save it." Logan points at her. "You're a liar." And walks out.

Hunter shrugs. "Can't blame him for being pissed. You girls are way out of line here." He snatches the papers out of my hands. "Now do yourselves a favor and leave before my brother calls the cops."

"Fine. But this isn't over," I say. "Wait 'til we call the cops on him for trying to kill us in the car."

"With a *paintball* gun. Please." Hunter's mouth curls with mockery. "It could have been any stupid kid messing around. Take a breath, Sea Witch. You're not thinking rationally. I get that you're upset about Penny. But you're barking up the wrong tree. Logan's a pain in the ass. But he'd never hurt anyone."

I turn to my friends. "Let's go."

Raven doesn't move.

"Come on," I say.

She is fixated on Hunter and Logan walking away toward the mansion.

"I said, let's *go*."

But Raven stays rooted. Then shakes her head.

My mouth drops open, as it registers what Raven is about to do. And Logan, I was right; he *is* more hurt than mad. The abrupt turn. The speed he's walking away. I see it.

I see it *all* now.

There is absolutely something between them. They *care* about each other.

I can't even speak. Raven's been lying to me.

"Wait!" she calls out and leaves me standing there.

To chase after *Logan Steele*.

CHAPTER 28
BROKEN MIRROR
RAVEN

slosh through the dewy grass calling out, "Logan. Wait. Please." Right before the entrance to the porte cochere, I catch up to him and grab his arm.

Logan shakes free but stops. "What do you want?"

"Can we talk?" My heart slams against my rib cage. "I'm sorry."

"Sorry? Sorry for what?" Logan crosses his arms, his storm-gray eyes tight. "Are you sorry for pretending you were interested in me, all to try and get information for some crazy investigation you and your friends are conducting? How you let me trust you? All so you could trick me into giving you access to my house?"

"I wasn't pretending."

"How can I believe a word that comes out of your mouth? After what I just saw and heard over there." His arm flies out when he speaks, motioning toward the carriage house. But then his shoulders drop. I can tell he's thinking by the way he tugs one hand through his hair, stretching it taut.

Maybe, just maybe, he'll come around.

He steps closer to me and hope shoots down my spine. Logan leans in and lowers his voice. "You came here, upset, cried in my lap for god's sake. Tell me, was any of it true about Vera? Or was that another twisted tactic you used to get close to me?"

"I wouldn't make that up." I have to tell him more, try to explain. "Penny left us poems."

"Poems? What are you talking about?"

"She wrote poems and sent them to Elle, and Elle brought them to all of us at the vigil. Me, Aarya, and Dawn."

Logan's frown deepens. "What did they say?"

"Nothing clear. It's all convoluted. But to us, they sounded like clues."

"Clues," he repeats, and the way he says it, flat and dismissive, makes me feel as stupid as he makes the word sound.

"Clues. Messages. Penny was trying to tell us something. And they seemed to point to you."

"In what way?" It's like he screamed the question even though he's unnervingly quiet.

"It doesn't matter. I don't believe it anymore. Not after last week, at your house. I only let them in with the code because I thought we'd find proof to clear you."

"Do you hear yourself right now? *Clear me?* Of what? You just admitted you thought I had something to do with Penny's disappearance. That I was capable of something like that."

"Come on. It's not like you're mister perfect." I squeeze my hands into fists so tight my nails dig into my palms. "You remember what you said in drama class, right?"

Logan flinches. "I told you why I said that."

"Does it excuse it? No. Why wouldn't I suspect you at that point?"

"Right. Because I'm an asshole."

"I used to think that, but not anymore. I don't think you're involved anymore."

"You just said you did *last* week! You came over here and tricked me with your bullshit story about Vera. You're a liar to a level I can't even comprehend."

It's like I've been punched in the gut. My voice shakes when I speak, "I'm not...a liar. I wasn't lying about her, about any of it. I promise it's the truth. Everything between us is real. It's all real for me." I hold his gaze, salty tears stinging my eyes. I need him to know, to *see* how I feel about him, how I'm desperately falling for him, how he's the only thing keeping me from shattering like the mirror when it hit my wall.

"It was real for me, too, Raven." The quiet defeat in his tone, the way he says *was*. "I can't. Not after this."

And then he turns and walks away.

His words cut off my air supply, closing me into a cage of my own making. I go to chase him, but two strong arms grab me tight.

"Hunter, let me go!" I beat at his chest, all control gone. "I need him to understand!"

"Raven. Stop." He's holding me, but gently. "Calm down. Or I'll call security."

"Call security?" I mouth the words after I say them. It's come to this?

"I don't want to. I really don't. But let's think about this for a moment. You and your friends snuck onto our property today, you broke into the carriage house, and you accused my brother of something horrible."

"I didn't accuse him."

"This isn't only about the accusations. You do realize my brother never even gave his code to Penny?"

I blink rapidly and a heaviness expands to my core. "How...I didn't...what?"

This is my fault. I used him. I *used* the trust Logan gave me—for my safety, my protection—and thrust it in his face.

"Let's call this a day. It's over. Okay?"

"Okay." It's the only answer to give, even as I cleave in two.

"Good. You can stay here until your ride comes. I'll let the guard gate know someone will be here to pick you up. But after that, don't come back. If Logan hasn't done it already, I'm going to make sure your name is taken off the list."

Hunter lets me go and leaves. I collapse on the steps, alone and empty.

Logan's right. I am a liar—but not in the way he thinks. Ever since the first moment on the balcony, when I saw a glimpse of the real Logan, I've been lying to myself.

His mask hides an incredible human being. Someone who brought me lemonade and jumped up to rescue me when I fell off the stage. Someone who came to my house to check on me and called me breathtaking. Someone who chased after me when I took off down the beach and kissed me with a passionate ferocity telling me—long before I knew it myself—I was his. When I opened my heart to him and told him about Vera, he made me believe I didn't deserve it, that I was worthy, and offered sanctuary at his place whenever I needed it. And at the first opportunity I got to stand up for him—like he'd repeatedly done over and over for me—I turned into a coward, stared at the ground, and allowed my friends to try him in the court of their accusations.

He has every right to walk away and leave me out here. Because I deserve it. I deserve all of it.

I wipe my soaked cheeks and pull out my phone. I call Aarya. It rings once and goes straight to voicemail. I try again. It barely rings, voicemail.

Great. Even my best friend doesn't want to talk to me.

I could try the other girls, but they'll respond the same way as Aarya and I'm not sure I can take any more rejection.

There is someone who will pick up because my family pays him to—our limo driver. "Roger, can you come get me? I'm at the Steeles. They're expecting you at the gate."

Fifteen minutes later, I'm in the back of our limo on the way home. I need my dad. I call him. Voicemail. I text, but I know he won't respond. And can I blame him? Vera's reporting her version of everything to him, so I'm not surprised he's avoiding me, too.

We pass by a now familiar cement sign, and I ask Roger to turn around. "Take a right, into Ashmont." I direct him to the yellow home in the far back, with the orchids and plumeria decorating the front entrance. Elle's orange truck is nowhere in sight, which is probably for the best. After asking Roger to wait, I walk past the Jamaican flag and knock on her door.

The first thing I see when Titania greets me is her big welcoming smile, but the corners of her mouth turn down when takes in the sight of me. "Pickney child, what happened to you? Why you make up yuh face so?"

My chin quivers and I think my chest visibly heaves as I hold back sobs.

"Oh, dear girl, hush, don't cry. Come nuh. You don't have to say a t'ing." The second after she closes the door, she pulls me into a hug and I break down, tears soaking her shoulder. "Hush, hush. There, there. You're safe. You're okay."

When my sobs turn to quiet and my breathing evens out, Titania leads me over to her couch. Soft reggae music fills the living room. I hear the saxophone, guitar, and piano harmony of a song I've known my whole life. The drums beat and Bob Marley sings, like he's speaking to me. Everything is going to be okay.

Titania's embrace tells me that, too. Her brown arms around me, like my mother's, warm as sunbaked sand, soft as a hummingbird's wings fluttering near a hibiscus. Titania feels like home.

"Tell me, sweet pickney, what happen?"

She holds my hand while I recount it all—Vera's hatred of my mother and how she treats me; everything leading up to the day I went to Logan's, and he gave me his code; to what happened today when my friends and Logan all abandoned me.

"I remember when everyt'ing happen with Vera and Ebony."

"You do?"

"Lawd, yes, pickney child. Mi no forget. It was the talk of Everbeach and Belle Grande a whole year. To t'ink, Clive run off with a quashie, lowly girl from Belle Grande, and leave miss haughty foo-fool."

I laugh for what feels like the first time in weeks. "Never heard anyone call Vera a foo-fool."

"What, that's what she is. And she many other t'ings mi no say, but I should, hurting you like dat." Titania grimaces like she ate something sour. "It break mi heart. I know it would break Ebony's. Your momma loved you somet'ing fierce, you hear me?"

Somet'ing fierce. My hand flickers habitually to where my ruby heart used to be.

Somet'ing fierce. Hearing my mom loved me ferociously, it's enough to start chipping away at the wall inside that Vera forced me to build. I let the warm light from memories trickle in. What it felt like when my mother held me, her soft kisses on my head and the music in her voice telling me I was a good girl, a strong girl, her hand in mine while we danced barefoot on a sunset beach while the steel drummer played. It's like I can still hear the cheerful beats resonating off the drum, like the beat of a heart, *my* heart, also *somet'ing fierce.*

"Hang here. Mi gonna grab somet'ing." Titania gets up and goes over to a credenza covered with knick-knacks and picture frames. She grabs a small canvas and sits back down next to me. "Dis is what I got to show you."

It's a painting with a green, gold, and red stripe across the whole background like a flag, and a golden lion with one paw raised and a crown on top of its head. "Do you know about the Rastafaris?"

"A little, I know it's a religious movement. That it started in Jamaica."

"Yes, good. This painting here, it's of their flag. Ol' Titania don't get caught up in all t'ings, but I t'ink what this stands for, it's you. The colors. They all mean somet'ing. Green is for the land, the connection to it." She squeezes my hand. "Vera try to tek the girl outta the country, she no tek the country out of the girl."

She points to the gold stripe. "The gold, it's what was stolen from the people, and how the people rebelled against the establishment. Vera try to teef your mom from you, but you no let her. You can teef her back. And the red is for the bloodshed, what the people lost who died under slavery. Mi know you lost your momma, and mi know how much dat hurts. I've lost people, too. But you can find your strength and claim back what was done to her. Put your red war paint on and fight back. And you see that lion, honey, mi eva did tell you, your momma with her tall hair, it was a powerful mane. She a lioness. I know dat part of Ebony in you."

It feels like I can sit up taller and breathe deeper than I've been able to in years. "Thank you. For everything. This means the world." Then I know exactly what to say so she knows I heard her. Clipping my words and speaking in the same musical cadence as Titania, I say, "Words cyaah express how tankful mi is."

Titania's laugh is boisterous and full. "You learning fast, mi likkle lioness. Everyt'ing gonna be irie." Titania's thick eyebrows draw together, and she speaks with a softness. "I tell you one more t'ing. Mi Elle won't judge you, and mi know your friends will forgive you. And so will dat boy. May tek some time, but they'll come around. You need to be true to you, know where you come from, show dem who you are. No let that foo-fool woman tear you down. Be the lioness you were born to be."

———

Roger waited for me like I asked, and when I get home, instead of collapsing in bed, my grumbling stomach takes me to the kitchen. Titania offered lunch, but I didn't know how much longer Roger could stay so I had to hurry out of there.

I boil water for pasta. Something I can control.

Nails tap on the counter. A shiver rattles through me.

"Well. Explain yourself." Vera's tone is laced with ice.

"Explain what?"

"Why did you need Roger to rescue you?"

Surprise makes me look up. "He told you about that?"

"He left in such a hurry, and then when he returned, I

saw you fly out of the car. It was easy to put two and two together."

"I don't want to talk about it."

"He picked you up from the Steeles?"

"Maybe." I stare at the boiling pasta, wishing Vera would disappear in a cloud of smoke, never to return. Poof, gone.

"Roger was gone a while, where else did you go?"

"It doesn't matter."

"Why didn't your friends drive you home? Why didn't Logan? Raven. I'm not your enemy. I know you think that, but I'm trying to help you."

Clearly, she has amnesia, because I distinctly remember her latest threat.

Vera drapes her arm over my shoulder in a soft, kind way. "Talk to me, what's going on?" Her touch is meant to comfort, but her arm might as well be made of razor blades. I have zero interest in motherly anything from her, but a stabbing sore spot on the back of my head and my missing necklace remind me exactly what happens when I don't play her games.

Sometimes you're on your own. There's no prince charming riding in on a steed to save you from your horrible life. You have to put on your armor and save yourself.

"Logan and I got in a fight. I think we're done."

"Oh honey! I tried to warn you. But now's not the time to say I told you so. I only wanted to keep you from exactly what's happening now. What about your friends? Where are they?"

"Somehow I managed to get in a fight with them, too."

"You shouldn't sit there and wallow. I won't allow it.

Come on. Get cleaned up, I have a fundraiser tonight at the Museum of Fine Arts. You're coming with me."

This is what my life has come to. "Uh, sure. I guess I'll get changed real quick."

"You can finish what you're doing in here. Meet me by the front door in an hour."

Exactly fifty minutes later, I'm right where she told me to be, in a black dress and heels, my hair swept into a simple half up style.

The limo drops us at the party, and we walk in arm in arm, posing for pictures together at the front. Vera introduces me to everyone, even calling me her daughter.

It prickles against my ears every time she says it. After what Titania told me earlier, this playacting with Vera makes a sickly feeling crawl over me, like my whole body is rebelling against being near this *foo-fool woman*. I smile to myself using Titania's name for her.

On the way to the bar with Vera, I run into Dawn, camera in hand.

I have no idea how to act around her. "Uh, hey."

"Hi." Dawn glances around the room.

"Yeah so, about today—"

Dawn holds up her camera. "I'm working and this isn't the place."

"Working?"

"I got an internship with *The Mirror*. This is my first assignment."

"Are you working with Punk?"

"Not on this article. But others, maybe." She looks like she wants to say more. "I should go. I'll see you later." She turns abruptly, blonde ponytail swinging.

Entirely awkward interaction. None of the warmth I'm used to from Dawn. I hope Titania is right and my friends come around. I'll have to talk this out with her later.

"Did you have a nice chat with Dawn?" Vera hands me a martini glass with green liquid in it and a cherry floating.

"What's this?"

"An apple martini. Non-alcoholic, of course."

I take a sip. The taste is familiar—apple of course, but something else. "Are you sure this is virgin?"

"Of course, I watched the bartender make it."

I take another sip. It doesn't have that bitter alcohol burn.

"Come on. I want to introduce you to more people." Vera takes my free hand and leads me along. The next hour is a merry-go-round of faces and names, all delighted to see Vera's *daughter*. As the hour wanes, the faces start to blur. It almost looks like everyone has halos around them. My heart speeds up.

This is different than a panic attack. Not the thought spiraling, pulse racing, can't breathe feeling I get when those come on. It's like my heart took off on a race, all on its own. My thoughts didn't lead me to this.

I tap Vera gently on the shoulder. She turns to me, breaking away from the conversation. Her eyes widen, and she grabs my elbow pulling me out of the group's earshot. "Are you okay?"

"I don't know. I think I need fresh air. What was in that martini?" I say through clenched teeth. It's like I can't stop biting down on nothing.

"Raven. You're swaying and your pupils are dilated. You look like you're messed up. Don't play games. I know you were upset earlier. Did you take something?"

"No, no, no, not at alllll." Whoa. A nauseous wave

hits. "I'm feeling sick to my stomach, a little tiny bit, like teeny tiny bit, like the smallest of shmall bitsss."

"You're slurring. This is more than feeling a little sick. You're on something." Her tone gains an edge. "Why do I even bother? I told you one more step out of line, and I meant it. Your father isn't going to be happy to hear about this."

"What are you talking about? I'm not stepping on any lines. Look." I point to the ground but it's blurry and I can't tell if there are any lines. But since I can't make any out, I think it's safe to say there are none. "Seeeeee, no lines. None!" My voice rings out louder than I intend. A few people glance over, and Vera grabs my hand, walking me around a corner.

"Do not make a scene. These are important donors." She tips her head back, one hand on her hip, the other pinching the bridge of her nose. "I cannot believe you're doing this to me."

"Doing what?" I sway a little on my heels. I'm on a teeter totter. I don't know what a teeter totter is, but if there was one, this is it. I walk in a direction without necessarily wanting to move, stumbling into someone.

"Ouch. Watch out." The voice is familiar. So is the swishing blonde hair.

"Daaawwwwnnnn!"

"Whoa. Raven. Um, what's going on? You...don't seem okay."

"She's not," Vera says. "She needs to get out of here immediately." Vera points at me. "I tried to do something nice for you, bringing you here. Waste of my time."

"Oh no." Dawn raises her hand to her mouth, focusing solely on Vera, as if I'm not even here.

"Dawn. Can you please take her up front and get our driver to take her home? I'm calling him now."

"Yes, of course, Mrs. Snow." Dawn drapes one of my arms over her shoulder and puts her arm around my waist, leading us out the service door, past servers in black pants and white button-downs, all gaping at us.

We find Roger waiting with the door open. I slump against the limo, missing the door. "Thank you."

From this angle, Dawn is glowing like an angel, a light halo around her head. Why does everyone have white halos? So pretty.

Then Dawn speaks. Cold. Harsh. "I don't know what's going on with you, Raven, but I'm worried. This is the third time you've been completely out of your mind. I didn't want to have to say this, but I need to. I think you need help."

"I'm not on a thing. No. Thing. Nothing."

"Stop lying to me. I can see you're clearly messed up."

I shake my head, and it rattles, making me dizzy. My skin flushes hot. "Oh holier than thou. Holy Dawn. Dawn-hole."

"I saw you drinking a martini!" Dawn's hands are on her hips. "And you're not making any sense. Dawn-hole?"

"Dawn-hole makes sense. To me. Perfect Dawn. Doesn't do a thing wrong." I push off the limo and stumble away.

"Where are you going?" Dawn calls.

I wobble on my heels, pitch forward, but manage not to fall.

"Raven, get back here. I'm going to get Vera!"

"Fiiiinne. Whatever." I think I flip Dawn off before stalking out into the courtyard of the art museum. It's deserted. Great place for me to be. Vera wanted me gone. So I'm gone, far from people. Just me and the statues. There's one with wings, its arms stretched out like it's trying to grab me. In front of me, another statue—a woman in a flowing dress holding two plates in her hands on either side like she's the scales of justice. Now statues are judging me, too. Trees grow up all around the open area, with long limbs and Spanish moss drips around the sculptures.

My heart is still beating fast. My skin feels itchy, and I spin and spin in circles but can't get my bearings. All alone in a garden of statues.

My heel catches on a crack in the sidewalk, my arms flail out and I crash-land, skidding across the ground. My purse flies from my shoulder and the contents spill everywhere.

This is what I deserve. Stranded and alone, crawling on concrete.

Hair falling in a tangled mess around my face, I scramble to collect the contents of my dumped purse. Lip gloss, wallet, phone, prescription bottle.

I pick up the bottle. The last time I saw these pills they were on my dresser. I never packed them tonight.

A wave of nausea swells, and I wretch all over the ground. I heave over and over until there is nothing left. Then I lay on the cool concrete, staring at the pill bottle still clutched in my shaking hand. How did these pills even get in my purse?

There's an odd taste in my mouth. The familiar taste when I took my first sip of the apple martini. I smack my lips together trying to place it. It reminds me of something warm and bitter, but I'm drawing a blank.

I lie there for a while, long enough for my thoughts to feel firmer, clearer, merging into a river of ice, a drifting glacier of awareness...pills were in my purse once before and I didn't remember putting them there. I smack my lips again, and the flavor I couldn't place hits me in a sudden onslaught. It's the *calming* tea. Vera's tea.

The pageant. The dinner. Tonight.

I press into the ground and push myself up to a sitting position, pausing as my vision goes in and out. My head feels light, like I'm going to pass out. I wait a minute, and that's when I see the rashes on my arms. My legs. I *do* need help. I yank on every ounce of resolve I have left to get to my feet.

Taking out my phone, I dial Aarya. No answer. I hit the call button again and again, stumbling away from the museum, into the night.

CHAPTER 29
LOST TRUTH
AARYA

My phone vibrates under my pillow. I turn over, determined to ignore it, but the same buzz shakes me back awake. It's Raven calling again.

When I don't answer, the text messages start.

> Please pick up. I need you.

I sit up. Fine.

> Why don't you call Logan?

I flop back down and squeeze my eyes closed. The phone keeps vibrating. Seriously?

> Need you.
> Please.
> PLEASE. I'm scared.

I frown, concern creeping through me.

"Ha-loww?" Raven slurs on the other end. She sounds worse than at the Taste of Success and Pageant combined.

I can hear the rush of outside air. "Where are you?"

"Where are *you*?"

"I'm at home. Raven, do you need me to come and get you?"

"Yeshh. Hurry."

"I have no idea where you are."

Raven's voice is breathy and faint. "I told you."

"No, you didn't."

Raven giggles.

"Stop. I'm serious. What is wrong with you? What are you on?"

"Ask the person who gave it to me," Raven whispers, all breathy into the phone.

"Did Logan give you drugs?"

"Noooo. He hates me. Even more than you." Raven's voice cracks. She was just laughing and now she's crying?

"No one hates you," I say, while pulling on sweats.

"Yes, they do. Everyone would be better off without me. Vera's right."

Her stoic resolution is chilling. "Raven, you're scaring me. Where *are* you?"

"Um, uh. Hmm. I think I saw Dawn's church. So..."

"So, Briar Rose Court," I say. Great, she's in the road. "Are you walking? Don't move."

"Always so bossy!" Raven snaps. "Don't tell me what to do. Everyone always tells me what to do."

"You need help. I'm coming to get you. Stay frickin' put."

"Whatever you-say-Aarya. Your-rules. As usual." Her words run together.

Laughing, sad, now mad—she must be out-of-her-mind high.

"Raven. You called *me*. I'm not telling you to do anything. I'm offering to *help*. You're the one who went off with Logan Steele. I've done nothing wrong."

"You know what. You're right. Forget it."

The phone clicks and goes dead.

"Raven? Raven? Are you kidding me!" I immediately call back. No answer. I slam down the phone.

I throw on shoes and rush out to my car, speeding to the intersection near Dawn's sprawling church property. I park and jump out of the car, calling Raven's name.

No answer.

I curse repeatedly under my breath. She couldn't have gotten that far in the mere minutes it took me to get here. She must be nearby.

But the minutes collect along with a cold drizzle.

Beyond the road, the campus of Briar Rose Church spans into the distance, swallowed by a thick nighttime fog. Maybe Raven is somewhere in there.

I call Dawn. "Aarya? What's going on?" she asks sleepily.

"Raven. She's gone off the rails. She's literally running around Everbeach alone freaking out, said she was on the road near your church. I need help searching for her."

"It's two in the morning."

"I know. I don't know who else to call."

Silence.

"Dawn... Please?"

"I'll, I'll sneak out my window, I guess? I cannot believe I'm doing this. Okay...okay... Um... Don't drive away until I get there."

"I'm not going to leave you! Just get down here." I hang up and scour the sides of the road calling Raven's name over and over. Nothing. The drizzle thickens to a cold rain.

"Raven! This isn't funny," I holler. The wet air swallows my voice.

A scuffle of sneakers on pavement grabs my attention and I spin around, hopeful. But it's only Dawn, in pajamas and a baseball hat, wielding a flashlight.

"Raven was drinking at the fundraiser tonight," Dawn says by way of a greeting. "I saw her with a martini."

My heart plummets. "Are you serious?" But I don't wait for an answer. I believe her, and questions are for later. Right now, we just need to find Raven.

The grumbling sound of an approaching truck cuts the night. Elle parks and jumps out. "Raven called me," Elle says. "She said you weren't picking up."

"Well, yeah, I was pissed, but then I *did* answer. And she hung up on me."

"She sounded really messed up," Elle says.

"Wait, I hear something." Dawn shines her flashlight toward a muddy ravine on the side of the road.

We hurry over.

Sure enough, a rain-soaked Raven, face streaked with mascara, black dress coated in mud, barefoot, huddles below in the dirt, recognition barely registering.

"I broke my shoe," she says forlornly—then vomits.

It takes all three of us to haul her out of the ditch. Raven wipes her mouth off on the back of her arm, grimacing.

"What's *she* doing here?" Raven points straight at me. "I called *Elle* because. She. Was. Being. Mean."

Raven's trying to hide how far gone she is, but the staccato has the extra effect of advertising her guilt. Her drenched hair and shivering shoulders make her look so frail. Broken. I should have picked up the phone sooner.

"I'm sorry Raven, okay? I'm here." I hold out my hands like a peace offering, but Raven doesn't step closer.

A loud rumble of thunder rakes the sky. Elle glances up nervously. "We should move out of the street. Especially with the rain. It's not safe."

Raven's bad knee abruptly buckles.

"Oh my gosh!" Dawn tries to catch her, but Raven's entire body goes limp.

I step in to help. Her mouth is slack, and her eyes are glazed over. We have to get her help. Immediately.

We try guiding Raven toward my car, but her arms slide off from where I try to drape them around my neck, her head lolling to one side.

"Raven, we have to get off the road. We could get hit by a car. Let's get you to the hospital," Elle says. "Please. My mom was hit on a rainy night. It's not safe."

"No!" Raven snaps out of her fog. "She'll find me there."

"Who?" I ask

"*Vera*. She wants me gone."

"Okay..." I placate, using every bit of my strength to heave her up into the car. I fold Raven's legs inside, and finally get the door shut. "Come on. Everyone get in. We'll get your truck tomorrow, Elle. Right now, let's just get Raven to a doctor."

Inside, Raven is emphatic. "You *can't*. She's trying to kill me."

"Raven..." Is this drugs talking? Paranoia?

"My drinks. She's putting something in them," she says.

"What do you mean?" I ask.

"No one is mad if you took too many meds or something," Elle says. "We're your friends. We want to help."

"I didn't take anything!" Raven starts to cry—hard. "Don't you see? Every time, you think it was me, it was her. At the pageant. She made the corset so tight I couldn't breathe. And gave me tea. Everything tastes like the tea."

"What tea?" I ask. "Logan gave you lemonade that night. How do you know it wasn't him?"

"No. She gave me tea first," Raven insists. "I always feel the same after the tea. It's confusing. Makes my brain fuzzy."

Her breathing is panicky. "She keeps hurting me."

"Hurting you, how?" I ask.

"Like at the dinner. She stuck a comb in my hair—her mother's. I thought it was so special." Sobs wrack Raven's body. "It hurt my head. She jammed it right into my skin, and I felt so strange. And you...you all thought I was on something!"

"But you did! Tonight, anyway." Dawn speaks softly, tentatively. "I saw you drinking tonight."

"Vera told me they were nonalcoholic." Raven's shoulders sink in defeat. Her green eyes ache with desperation. They're reaching for me, flashing ten years of friendship. Begging me to believe her.

I have to hear her out. I have to take this leap of faith. This is what you do for friends. You show up. Even when there's doubt.

"Do you promise?" I ask. Raven doesn't flinch. "I promise."

"If this is true, we should go to the police," Dawn says.

Panic flashes across Raven's face. "You saw how she bossed them around. They'll believe anything Vera tells them. An extension of the Steeles. You know that."

"They can't. They're the *police*. Their job is to help people," Dawn says.

"Oh, go back to Briar Rose and live under your rock!" Raven shouts.

Dawn shrinks into the backseat, her eyes welling with unshed tears. "I'm only trying to help."

"What do you think they'll say? I go in and tell them I think my stepmother is poisoning me? The police aren't on my side. No one is. No one believes me."

Her words crash into me like my car into that guardrail. Raven should never feel like this.

"Then we have to go with proof she can't deny," I say." What that proof is...I wish I knew.

"Wait! What about Punkaj?" Elle asks. "Can he help somehow?"

"Punk's other internship is at Everbeach Memorial Hospital. Maybe he knows someone who can test Raven's blood. If what she's saying is true, her blood should show it? *Then* we go to police. With *proof*."

"Yes," Elle says. "Call him. Now."

I dial Punkaj on speaker. It's already three thirty in the morning, but he answers with an unexpected clarity, like he was born to snap awake and save the day.

"Aarya. What's wrong?"

"We need your help."

———

Punkaj meets us at the back door of the hospital lab as promised and waves us into the empty room. One look at Raven's condition, and he scoops her up in his strong swimmer's arms, her head resting against his broad shoulders. He carries her inside and places her in a chair.

"We're going to take a little blood to test, Raven," he says gently.

"Um, who is?" I interrupt. "*You*? You already know how to do that?"

"Have you met me?" Punkaj says.

Funny how the over-confidence I've hated forever suddenly feels like a hug. The high wire tension lines that are currently every nerve path in my body relax a tiny bit.

"Ready Raven?" he asks.

She nods weakly.

"Nothing other than the virgin martini tonight, right? Which you think got laced with something?" Punkaj confirms the details I hurriedly gave over the phone.

Raven sways a bit in her chair, eyelids drooping like she could fall asleep sitting up while Punkaj expertly draws the blood. I take Raven's hand. Elle lays hers on top. Tentatively, Dawn adds hers. Raven's fingers are alabaster against ours like she's translucent, and I'm seeing the last of her before she disappears.

Punkaj caps off a vial of her blood before inserting IV fluids. "I'm going to run some tests real quick to see if anything pops."

I lean in close to Raven. "I'm sorry." I swallow hard and continue. "I should have picked up the phone the first time you called."

Raven nods acceptance before averting her eyes back down to the table where her arm rests. Her voice is quiet. "Thanks for saying that. But I get why you're mad. About Logan. I wasn't honest."

"Is there something going on between you two? You know, like—"

Raven wrenches her eyes to mine.

But before she can answer, "No drugs or alcohol!" Punkaj announces from his corner.

"Really?" Raven's face twists in disbelief.

"No synthetic drugs. I tested for a lot including gamma hydroxybutyric acid—"

I cut him off. "Wait, pause. For *what* now?"

"GHB?" Punkaj amends. "Liquid ecstasy."

He holds up a hand as Raven starts to protest the impossibility of finding nothing. "Wait. I tested some other known toxins that match your symptoms. You have a ridiculously high level of cardiac glycosides in your system."

"Pause. Again. What?" I ask.

Punkaj frowns and shakes his head, baffled. "Poison... from lilies of the valley. Nearly enough to kill her."

"Flowers?" I ask. "You're telling me Raven was poisoned with *flowers*?"

"Lilies of the valley are one of the most toxic plants out there," Punkaj says.

"So, nothing that should ever be in martinis."

"Not unless blurry vision, throwing up, seeing halos, headaches, rashes, cardiac issues and death is your idea of a good time," Punkaj says. "Do those symptoms sound familiar, Raven?"

"All of them." Raven's green eyes cloud. "Vera grows the lilies in her garden."

She squeezes her eyes closed but tears still stream out. Her breath is going in and out so dramatically it brings the whole room into frenetic rhythm.

"I knew it," she whispers. "I knew it. She was using the pills to mess with me, to cover up what the tea was doing, what *she* was doing to me."

Vera, the only mother Raven has left, is trying to murder her. The realization cuts through the room as heavy and final as the slice of an axe.

"Let's take this to the police," I manage to say into the silence.

"I'll drive," Punkaj says, and I'm grateful.

I sit in the back, holding Raven against me. Like a mother would a child.

We pull into the parking lot of the police station and get out. At the door, a tall, thin, figure is standing like a flagpole staked into the ground to claim it. *Vera*. She's here, *waiting*. Raven shrinks against me.

"Oh honey, you're safe. I was so worried when you ran off. I came right here." Vera reaches out both hands, long red nails gleaming like her lipstick, garish in this light.

"You're lying," Raven says.

"You're intoxicated."

"I know you've been drugging me."

"That's ridiculous." Vera grabs Raven's purse so fast, it's in her hands in one lunge. She pulls out the pill bottle and holds it up. "What's this?" Vera opens the lid. "Almost empty."

"I didn't take any of those," Raven says. "Or even put the bottle in my bag."

Vera cocks her head. "Then who did?"

"You!" Raven says frantically. "You did! You're *evil*."

Vera practically sneers. "You're spiraling. You don't know what's real."

We're part of a dark ballet, a predator dancing in smaller and smaller circles before closing in.

"She does know what's real. We all do," I announce, triumphant. "We have proof."

Vera's low, mocking laughter pulses back like a bow against a violin, sending strings snapping. "Where? In that vial? What is it? Blood?"

A sense of dread spreads through my body as she moves closer. Punkaj opens the lobby door for me, but Vera is too fast. She snatches the vial out of my hands. And then—she lets go.

It drops to the ground. The glass shatters, blood seeping into a small circle. Vera's voice. "Oops. Slipped. Certainly, you have another. No? That's for the best. These games are only hurting Raven's already delicate state of mind. They'll take care of you at Hightower."

Raven's eyes flash fear. "What?"

"You'll be in good hands. Officers! Your help please!"

Before we can do anything, an officer comes outside and gets between us. Another steers Raven toward a police cruiser. They are marionettes dancing under Vera's conducting—one step forward, one step back. Might she have this dance? But of course. They move, like so many others, at the snap of Vera's fingers.

"Take her to Hightower," Vera commands, center stage—her prima ballerina pirouette.

Raven—ripped away, alone, to the same place as Penny.

We have nothing to stop it from happening. The proof that's gone, the stain on the ground, the rage that boils—it's all as red as blood.

PART THREE

Then she was forced to put on the red-hot shoes,
And dance until she dropped down dead.

—*Snow White,* Grimm Brothers

CHAPTER 30
THE TOWER
RAVEN

You are a daily reminder of betrayal and your whore of a mother.

A shard of glass in my side. That's all you will ever be.

It was real for me, too, but I can't. Not after tonight.

Boys like Logan never stay with girls like you.

The symphony of clanging voices echoes. Vera's cutting words. Logan's last dagger before he walked away. How long have I been out? Maybe hours. Perhaps days.

Images flicker. Blood, glass, being dragged away, empty screams, clawing.

My eyes flutter open. Fluorescent light buzzes overhead. I look around. Gray everywhere. I squeeze my eyes shut again.

Muffled voices. A door creaks. Feet tap on the floor. A hand on my face, cold and familiar.

"Raven. Raven honey, wake up."

Honey—the word a tangy acid to my ears.

"Doctor, I thought you said she was coming to."

"She is. Give her a few moments. Her vitals are

showing a spike right now. I think she's nervous. As anyone would be after the state you found her in."

My mind commands my eyes to open. A face hovers over my own, all sharp angles. Tightly pulled back blonde hair. Jarring apple-red lipstick. Vera.

A scream wells up inside, and I have to let it out. "Get away from me!"

I scream again, over and over, the same words. I writhe, trying to move my arms, but they are taut, held down. I try to kick my legs, but those are locked down, too.

"You said she was ready for visitors."

"We miscalculated. Let's give it another day. Get the injection ready."

"Oh, honey, come back to me soon." The voice drips with lies.

A tight pinch on my arm, and the room fades away.

CHAPTER 31
MIDNIGHT MEETING
AARYA

t's for the best. It's for your own good. These are things adults tell you to justify pain. Raven's been locked up for three days. *For her own good.* And there's nothing I can do.

I swim harder.

The laps close in. Sprint to the far wall. Swim back the same way I came. What feels like covering distance is only going back and forth between cement.

The toxin wouldn't have been in Raven's system by the time doctors tested her blood again, if they even tested her. Vera's manipulating this whole thing—always was. And I let it happen. I doubted Raven.

Movement catches me off guard, and I stop mid-flip turn, grabbing the side of the pool.

This is unexpected. "Logan? What are you doing here?"

"I need to talk to you. Your mom said you were swimming." His hair is uncharacteristically limp, and his blue-gray eyes have dark circles under them. "Hunter told me Raven's in Hightower?"

"I watched it happen."

"But *why*?"

Like I'm going to talk to *him*. I climb out of the pool and wrap up in a towel. "Call Hightower if you want information. Better yet, go visit her like you did Penny. Oh. Wait."

"Aarya, when are you going to get it through your head, I'm on your side!" Logan tugs at his hair. "I mean I get it. I've watched enough true crime shows to know how it goes. It's always the boyfriend, right? But I'm telling you, I would never hurt anyone, let alone Penny."

His voice has a raw edge to it that makes me pause. I look directly at him. "What if I told you Raven is being drugged? By her own stepmom."

The angles of Logan's jaw sharpen. "I'd say, I'm not surprised. After the abuse."

"You *know* about Vera?"

"Raven told me," Logan says. "About her...and the poems."

My eyes narrow as I try to process this. She told him everything she wasn't supposed to. And more.

"And Aarya...I'm here because...you're right."

Now he's really got my attention. "I'm listening."

"Vera is up to something, and I think it has to do with Penny's dad."

"There's a reason we were searching his house," I say.

"Which is why I picked up where you left off," Logan says. "It's too coincidental, right? First, Penny is sent to Hightower, and now Raven?" He starts pacing. "It's always a parent sending them there, when to the rest of us, it doesn't seem like it's reached that level."

"Again, why do you think we've been so fixated on this? We know something is off. We knew from the second Penny got locked up."

"All *I* knew is that you girls where in my carriage house. I didn't understand why. So, I started following Mr. Zale." Logan pauses. "And...I overheard something.

"What did he say?"

"He's meeting up with Vera tonight at my dad's office. At midnight."

"They're meeting in the middle of the *night*?"

"That was my reaction," Logan says. "I want to see what they're up to. Will you come with me?"

Everything else that's gone on recently and it may be this question that has surprised me the most. Logan Steele wants my help. I look at his eyes, flicking back and forth. He's trying to read my face. I'm trying to read his. Raven trusted him. But I didn't trust her. And look at what happened. I didn't believe my own best friend until it was too late. If ever there was a moment for a leap of faith...

"Yes. I'll go with you."

———

STEELE—the sign at the top of the tower reads, but it might as well spell *power*. The tall office building is as imposing as Harvey Steele himself—buttoned up, immaculate. The overnight lights seep unblinking and stoic out of the windows.

"Hurry." Logan scans his security card "We need to get inside and hidden before they get here."

The beep of the door clearing repeats in my mind as we sneak inside like the ping of one piano note, a secret soundtrack, keeping me focused, a-sharp, like the sound of a classic suspense movie.

Logan leads us down a few long hallways, up two flights of stairs, and out onto the top level of a rotunda. He crouches behind the base of a wide marble pillar, motioning

294 SORBONI BANERJEE & DOMINIQUE RICHARD...

for me to do the same and points to watch the front entrance. Another beep and the main double doors swing open.

A murmur of voices echoes through the vast room, uncannily clear even from high above thanks to the domed ceiling.

Vera's frosty voice cuts the air. "I don't understand why this keeps happening."

"Collateral damage can't be avoided," Mr. Zale answers.

"Excuses don't interest me." Vera sounds deeply annoyed. "I guess we wait for the numbers."

The front door beeps again.

"You're late," Vera snaps.

A new, familiar voice answers. "By what? Two minutes?"

My eyes fly to Logan's as I recognize the voice.

"Is there any reason we can't file paperwork at ten in the morning instead of the middle of the night?"

Hunter.

"I picked up the logs for you as usual," Hunter says. "Why can't they bring them all the way here?"

"Don't ask questions that aren't of your concern," Vera says. "You're my intern. You do as I say."

"I'm just saying, there's got to be an easier way," Hunter says with a laugh.

"Easy?" Vera says. "That sounds to me like *lazy*. Do you really want me to have to tell your father you don't feel like working hard? Maybe Logan would be a better fit for this role."

Logan stiffens beside me.

"How much inventory came in last night?" Vera asks.

"Umm, twenty-three," Hunter says.

"And how much was lost?" Mr. Zale asks.

"They said four."

"Very well then," Vera says. "Hunter file the paperwork. Donald let's go. There's obviously some work to do tonight."

The main doors swing open and closed and all I hear are Hunter's steps round and round to the top level of the rotunda.

"He's heading to the executive suites," Logan hisses. "Let's get him."

I follow Logan. We keep our distance, spying from the entrance of the executive suites. Hunter puts a small package down and locks some papers inside the top drawer of a file cabinet behind Vera's gleaming desk.

Logan steps into the doorway, an arm pressed to each side of the frame. "What the hell are you doing?"

Hunter jerks back, his eyes narrowing. "Logan?"

He looks past Logan and spots me, prompting a dry bark of a laugh. "Aarya. Snooping around again. What's up bro, you're Sea Witch's sidekick now?"

Logan takes a few steps closer. "What's on those papers?"

"I don't know, man. I'm only doing my job."

"In the middle of the night?" I say.

Hunter shrugs. "Middle of the night. Middle of a Sunday. Middle of the morning—Vera calls, I answer. It comes with the territory."

Logan is locked in on his brother. "I don't buy it."

"What's that supposed to mean?" Hunter frowns.

"Something weird is going on and you know it."

Hunter hesitates for the briefest of flickers. "Bro, seriously. I have nothing to hide. I meet one of Mr. Zale's guys at the gas station off Idlewood to grab paperwork. I bring it here. That's all I know."

"What did those numbers mean? Twenty-three. Four. What *inventory*?" I press.

"That's a little above my pay grade," Hunter says. "I pick up and file papers and lock up the office. Vera says jump, I ask how high."

"Sounds about right," Logan says. "You'll do anything to kiss ass."

"You call it kissing ass, I call it taking care of business. Someone's taking over for Dad one day, and it's obviously not going to be you."

"Right. Because your wannabe pro surfer career prepared you to head up a global enterprise," Logan fires back. He wags his hand with thumb and pinky extended. "Cowabunga. Hang ten, dude."

Hunter responds by cranking Logan's arm down by his thumb, pulling him into a headlock. Logan rams an elbow into Hunter's ribs and ducks out from under him.

"You really want to do this?" Hunter laughs. "Who always wins?"

"Knock it off!" I step between them. "How about we check our fragile, male egos at the door and talk about how Vera got my best friend locked up in Hightower."

"I'm Vera's intern, not her therapist. I don't know what's going on between them. But she told me she *had* to commit Raven. Speaking of, I've got to go." Hunter picks the package back up and waves it with some annoyance. "Because apparently before I finally get to go to bed, I also have to drop off tea at Hightower so Raven can have it in time for breakfast."

My whole body goes cold. I grab Hunter's arm. "Did you just say *tea*?"

Hunter shrugs. "Something Vera said helps Raven de-stress. See? She's trying to take care of her. She's not some evil monster."

"*No*, that's exactly what she is." I'm practically shouting, blood pounding in my ears. "She's been drugging her. Hiding poison in her drinks. In her tea."

Hunter laughs in disbelief. "*Oh*-kay."

"I know it sounds crazy but it's true," I say. "We tested her blood."

Hunter looks to Logan. "Are you buying this?"

Logan's voice is steady. "I believe Aarya."

"You want me to believe this," Hunter holds up the package, "is some sort of poison?"

"It is. It can kill someone. Vera is trying to kill Raven."

"So, you're trying to say I'm about to be an accessory to murder...using tea." Hunter sniffs the packet. "It smells awful."

"Hunter, this isn't a joke! That tea is deadly."

"Bull." Hunter rips open the bag and takes a pinch between his fingers. His face twists into a challenging smirk. "There's no way. Watch."

"I wouldn't do that." I reach for his hand, but Hunter is too fast. He smacks his lips and shoves the dried leaves into his mouth.

CHAPTER 32
MIRROR ON THE WALL
RAVEN

Gentle nails scrape down my arm. A hand sweeps over my hair, my cheek.

"Raven. Do you know where you are?"

I open my eyes. "No," I rasp out, throat raw. Distant screams sing in my memory.

"You're safe now."

I feel anything but. And the voice attached to the promise makes it clear I'm right. Behind my nightmare is a man in a white coat.

"This is so heart-wrenching. You look exactly like Penny did in this bed," Vera says.

How am I in the same bed Penny was in? "Where am I?" Barely a decibel above a whisper.

"Hightower. Only the best for you."

Dread spreads through my veins, slinking through me like a slow drip IV. I'm locked in the tower like Penny. Vera as my keeper.

"If you promise not to thrash again, I'll have them remove the restraints."

I nod yes.

"Say it."

"Promise."

"Okay. Doctor?"

The white coat speaks for the first time. "I don't know if I'd advise that yet."

"She's not going to talk to me if she's tied down like this."

He comes toward the bed and undoes the restraints holding down my wrists and ankles.

"There. That's better," Vera says. "Maybe you can get some real rest. I'll come back in the morning once the tranquilizer has worn off and you've had some time to think. There's so much we need to talk about."

Vera brings her bright red lips down to my cheek for a kiss.

"Oh. And Doctor? Can you please prepare her tea? It's imperative she drinks it."

The tea. No way in hell am I going to drink that again.

The light at the door turns green, the door opens, and Vera leaves the room. The door shuts, the light turns red, and I hear the lock click into place. No escape.

The doctor sits down on the bed, steaming cup of tea in his hand. "Here, drink this. Your mother says it helps with your anxiety."

"Stepmother. Not mother."

He says nothing in reply, just hands me the tea.

I take the cup in shaky hands, weak from jerking against the restraining straps. Deliberately letting my hands shake more, almost violently so, until, *oops*—the entire mug tumbles out of my grip. Liquid spills across the floor, splashing the doctor. He jumps.

I play up the tremble. "I'm so sorry. My hands, they're not working right."

"I'll have the nurse bring another bedsheet."

Once I'm sure he's gone, I swing my legs over the side of the bed and finally have a chance to take in my surroundings. The room is gray and cold—not necessarily by temperature, although it is chilly in here. It's the energy in the room.

Lilies of the valley—the words float into my memory —planted over the five little memorials. One for each of the babies Vera lost. Has she been planning this since I was thirteen? I shudder at the thought.

There's a knock at the door, and a nurse enters with a tray. She sets it down on the side table next to my bed. "When you're done, put the tray down next to the door." The nurse leaves. The door flashes red, locked again. My stomach rumbles. When did I last eat? I pick up the smoothie and gulp it down.

A familiar bitter aftertaste coats my tongue. *The tea.*

I hurry to the bathroom, knowing what I have to do next. The liquid burns as it comes up. I crawl into the shower already feeling weak. I strip my clothes off, turn on the cold water while lie on the floor, and let it run over my body. Small waves of nausea and disorientation come. It must have been a strong dose.

I push off the floor, adrenaline pumping like when I'm on the three-point line, down two points, one second left on the clock.

Eventually, I can stand and take a real shower, then dress in the robe hanging in the bathroom. I towel dry my hair in front of the aluminum mirror. It has a lot of curl again. My last straightening treatment was months ago, before the pageant, before Penny's memorial. I tug at a spiral falling in front of my eye. It springs right back up, alive. My mom's curls, tight ringlets—a part of me I was told was wrong.

"I am Raven Ebony Snow." A whisper at first, saying

my middle name, my *mother's* name—my forbidden other half.

I shake my head freeing my curls from Vera's rotting thought. My powerful mane, like Titania said.

I say it again, louder this time, gripping the sink. "I AM Raven Ebony Snow!"

Vera will never erase who I am with her vile, wicked lies. I am ebony, not porcelain.

A fire burns—a desire to live. A desire to win. This life, my life, is worth the fight. I will get out of here and take that evil witch of a stepmother down. I will make her feel as miserable as she's made me, and I will get my father back. And she will lose him again. Because he, too, will know the truth.

I am no longer a little girl in need of a mother's love. I have *my* mother's love, and it's fierce. No one can force me to forget anymore. Vera will not get away with this. I will make her pay. I have my red war paint on. Let the rebellion begin.

"I AM Raven EBONY Snow!" This time it resonates in my chest, my throat, my heart—like a roar. In the mirror staring back—the resemblance of my mother.

I am the lioness now. And Vera is my prey.

CHAPTER 33
THE SEVEN

AARYA

Hunter Steele is draped across the bottom steps of the Steele Enterprises front entrance, looking at his own hands like he's never seen fingers before. Logan and I are still watching him when Punkaj arrives not long after I texted.

He studies Hunter. "He seriously ate a whole handful?"

"He was trying to prove a point and shoved it in his mouth."

"Is he going to be okay?" Logan asks.

Punkaj nods with a crisp certainty. "I think so. But he's feeling it for sure. He needs to drink water. As much water as possible. We've got to flush it out of his system."

Logan hurries to get more water for his brother. Hunter chugs the whole cup.

"Your head is glowing," Hunter points to Punkaj. "This is fun."

"It's not fun. It's poison," I say.

Hunter's expression shifts from general confusion to

fear. "Am I going to die?" His voice sounds like a little boy about to cry.

"You're going to be okay. Don't worry. If you get any worse, I'm calling 911," Punkaj says.

"Vera...*man*—" Hunter slurs. "She's shady huh? What's she up to anyway? This is getting dark, you know, like, that's messed up, tricking me into helping poison Raven. Like really, *really* messed up. What the hell!" Hunter punches the step next to him. "Ow." He rubs his hand.

I shudder at the similarity to Raven—emotions all over the map.

Hunter slumps. "She even made me scare you."

The blood drains from my face. "Wait...what?"

Hunter throws his arms over his head. "She was all, *you have to protect your family.* She said I had to shut you up before you damaged our reputation. Said it was my job."

Logan sits down next to him. "Hunter. What did you do?"

"Stupid stuff. It was only supposed to scare them." Hunter holds his head. "But when the car crashed... That was a mistake. I never meant for that to happen."

His voice sounds as if it's coming through a tunnel. It was *Hunter*? I swallow, pressure building in my ears, behind my eyes.

"It was you," Logan says. "The whole time. Everything they thought was me."

Hunter nods into his hands.

I point to Logan. "But we found the flyer about the snake hunt in *your* room."

Hunter shakes his head. "I gave him that. I wanted him to go on the hunt with me. Brother stuff. But he didn't feel like it."

Logan is looking at me like *I told you*. I can't meet his gaze.

I feel almost dizzy. I hadn't been totally wrong. It *was* a Steele. Just not Logan Steele.

Hunter holds his head in his hands. "Vera told me you were dealing with Penny's disappearance by trying to find someone to blame. That you were blaming us. She said to shut you up. Show her how much I cared about the company. Show my dad I was the right son to take over the business one day."

My whole-body hums with the revelation. "We have to tell the others." I text Dawn and Elle, careful not to get their hopes up while still making sure they know this is important.

> At Steele Enterprises. Get here. We know who is behind the attacks.

Elle answers immediately, letting us know she's on her way.

> I'll sneak out.

Dawn texts.

> I'll get Grayson to bring me.

Punkaj steps close, lowering his voice. "Hunter will tell us anything at this point. "We need to take advantage."

"Hunter." I try to command his hazy attention. "What was the inventory Mr. Zale and Vera were talking about?"

"Deliveries? Boxes? Sugar? I don't know," Hunter mumbles.

"It sounded like something bad," Logan says, prodding.

"Okay then. Drugs? Weapons?" Hunter starts to laugh. "Gems! *Zombies*."

"Seriously, Hunter," Logan says. "We have to know."

But Hunter is too far gone to make sense.

"Give him a minute," Punkaj says. "Make him walk it off a little."

Logan hauls Hunter off the steps to take a few laps around the lobby. I spot Elle at the door and hurry to open it. Dawn's right behind her with Grayson.

"What in the world is going on?" Elle asks as she takes in Hunter who is barely able to stand up next to Logan.

I quickly fill them in.

Dawn leans against Grayson. "Why would Vera do this?"

"Whatever it is, it has something to do with Penny's father," says Logan. "And their secret inventory."

"What if Penny knew what they were up to?"

Punkaj continues my thought. "And they locked her up in Hightower to stop her from telling anyone."

"We have to get Raven out of there," Logan says. "That's all that matters right now."

"I can help." Hunter's voice has regained some clarity, and his eyes don't look quite as glazed.

"The hell you can," Logan snaps. "You've done enough."

"No, really. They're expecting me, remember? I'm supposed to meet a doctor at the back door. I'll wedge it open so you can get in," Hunter says.

"Why would we *ever* trust you?" Logan asks.

Hunter's voice is soft. "I never meant to hurt anyone."

I fold my arms across my chest. "Prove it."

Silence falls. One beat. Two.

Hunter fumbles in his pocket and pulls out a cheap cell phone from his back pocket. "The messages I sent to scare you. They're all here. Keep the burner phone. If I screw you over, take it to the police. Hell, take it to them anyway."

My face scrunches with doubt. "How do I know we're not walking right into a trap? Hightower security could be waiting for us, and then Raven's stuck in there for good."

Punkaj steps forward, holding out his hand for the phone. "I'll take it. Anything happens to you, I blast everything to *The Mirror*."

———

Hightower Pavilion looms into view against the navy sky, looking back at me it seems, like it has a face, a pulse. Heavy doors glower like narrow, lidded eyes. The cement gate seems to quiver with eager breath. These walls hold you against them with the promise of healing, only to suffocate you quietly in the night. Two long, cement wings span out to the left and right. Front and center— Hightower, reaching for the clouds. A tiny sliver of light from a window at the top blinks.

This building is an angel of destruction.

Punkaj waits in the car, ready to get us out of here at a moment's notice. Dawn and Grayson head around to the front entrance to keep them busy at reception. Elle is the lookout.

Logan and I are going in after Raven.

We duck behind a rusty dumpster to watch Hunter. Step one of this plan is underway.

The back door of the facility opens revealing a guy in a white coat. Hunter hands the doctor the small packet of tea, and a much larger package of money. The doctor peers in and rifles through the cash. Hunter deftly removes chewing gum from his mouth and jams it into the lock to keep it from clicking shut. His move goes unnoticed by the doctor busy counting the bills. The doctor nods curtly before going back inside. Hunter turns to leave.

I take a jagged breath. It's time. Hunter gives a little wave that the coast is clear and walks toward the car, getting in as he normally would.

Elle skulks along the wall, peering in the door, and waves for us to go inside. She gets to the next corner and peeks around it.

"Excuse me!" A voice rings out. "Where do you think you're going? Who are you here to see?"

Logan yanks me back around the corner and out of sight.

A call goes out over the intercom. "Security!"

I need to do something. I scan the long hall desperately. Without a second thought I reach over and pull the fire alarm, the clanging bell sending chaos into the hospital.

We run for the elevator closest to us. I hit the button to the top floor where Hunter said they're likely holding Raven.

My whole-body screams alongside the alarm. This is a wish on fire. A wish that somehow, the seven of us will succeed in waking Raven from her nightmare.

CHAPTER 34
TRUE LOVE'S KISS
RAVEN

The hand clasped around my mouth tightens. I hear the shouts. I wriggle free and run. He grabs me again, making *shhhh* noises. The man. His kind eyes. The machete. All familiar. His uniform with an embroidered patch dragon emblem. Something new. Where is my mother? I wrestle with him, but he holds firm and pleads with me to be silent. Gunshots ring out. A scream. I'm free and running. My mother is hurt. I have to get to her. Tripping in the dirt, strong hands wrap around me and hide me behind a stack of crates.

But it's too late. Because there on the ground, about ten feet in front of me, is my mother's body, her wild mane of ebony curls splayed out into an oozing river of blood.

Sirens blare. I'm dragged back, flailing. Tangled up in something, the sirens are louder and change in cadence; a mess of fabric holds me down.

I wake up screaming, alone. There is no man, no body. Only me and a blaring alarm. I try to find clarity, but the tranquilizer injections thicken my thoughts. A chill shudders through me from my nightmare. It went all the way to...the blood and my mother lying on the ground.

The corners of the room pulse. The blaring siren continues. I swallow the bile rising in my throat while trying to blink back the memory of my mother's lifeless body.

Through fuzzy eyes I scan the room and my gaze rests on the light over the door. It's gleaming green.

I stumble out of bed toward it—a beacon calling me —but my legs are too unsteady. I collapse into a crawl on all fours. *Dig deeper, push.* Like line drills in practice, when my lungs expand to the brink and my heart hammers at the speed of hummingbird wings, I push through.

I drag my body to the door in a full-out army crawl and pull the handle.

The door opens and I collapse into the hallway. I pull myself to my feet using the handle on the door. Adrenaline courses through me as I put one foot in front of the other down the corridor.

Two figures come toward me, fast. I twist, looking for another escape, but there's nowhere to go. I freeze, an animal in headlights. This is it. I'm going to be taken from here like Penny.

The figures close in, and my adrenaline, already in overdrive, spikes making my limbs shake.

I hear a voice say, "Pick her up, we have to get out of here," as emergency lights strobe and my body finally gives out, the darkness swallowing me as I'm taken.

———

Soft fingers trace my face, warm hands cup my cheeks.

"Wake up." A gentle admonishment.

"Is she okay? Please tell me she's alive."

"Wake up, Raven, stay with me."

I catch the scent of ocean mist. Gentle fingers run through my hair.

"Stay with me."

Soft lips on mine. "Please, Raven. Please, wake up."

These lips—I've longed for them every night alone in this tower. He's here.

I open my eyes, and my stare is met by a blue-gray storm. "Logan?"

"Thank god you're okay." He squeezes me and I cling to him. Doors open, and we descend, down, down the stairs. Over my shoulder I see short, black hair swinging. Determined brown eyes collide with mine.

My prince came for me. And he brought my knight.

———

The fresh air shocks my skin with a thick coat of humidity. I welcome the stickiness. We run to the car and the door is already open. Logan slides me across the seat and into Elle's waiting arms. She wraps me in a hug. Logan jumps in behind me, Aarya charges into the front seat.

"Go, Punk!" Aarya says.

The car lurches forward. I lean into Elle while another arm slides over my shoulders.

"We did it." I hear from behind. Grayson and Dawn are in the backseat.

They came for me—*all* of them.

I rest my head on Logan's chest. He wraps his arm around me tighter, and kisses the top of my head. "It's going to be okay. We've got you."

Punkaj drives straight to Ashmont. The familiar yellow home and wildflowers greet us as we pile out of the car. Titania is standing with the door open. She wraps Elle up in a big hug, and then motions to the rest of us. "Come nuh. Bushes have ears, walls have eyes."

I struggle to keep up, leaning into Logan's firm hold.

When we reach Titania's steps, I ask, "Can I just stop here?"

"Whatever you need." Logan helps me sit.

"They gave me more. The lilies of the valley. At Hightower."

"They did?" Punkaj jumps into action. "We need to take your blood again. We have another chance to prove what they were doing. I'll go now and get what we need."

I try to stand up, but I'm dizzy and sink right back down.

Logan sits down next to me. "Can we rest here a second? I'll stay with her."

"Sure. But don't tek too long," Titania says.

The door closes behind her, and we're alone under the streetlamp's dim light. I rest my cheek against Logan's neck, inhaling fresh pine—an intoxicating comfort.

"I thought you were done with me."

He's silent, the only movement the expansion of his chest. He breathes in deep and slowly lets it out.

"Actually, don't answer that. I'm the one who should be talking. I'm sorry." I bury my head in his shirt. "I'm so sorry."

Logan strokes my hair. "You don't need to apologize."

"Yes, I do. I don't deserve you being here."

"Don't say that. I'm the one who should be apologizing to you." There's tension in his voice.

"What? Why?" I sit up and try to pull away, but he holds on, keeping me close.

Logan touches his forehead to mine and lets his hand run over my hair, fingers dancing through my curls.

This is the real me, and he's not running away like Vera said he would—he's pulling me closer and holding on tight.

"I didn't give you a chance to explain," he says. "After I caught you all there at my house. I should have talked to you, but I didn't. I was too angry. When you didn't stand up for me to Aarya, it crushed me."

"I am so sorry for that."

"I'm not looking for an apology. I'm trying to explain myself and how I could have possibly done something as stupid as turning my back on you, letting you walk into Vera's trap."

"You couldn't have known that was going to happen."

"I knew about her; I knew how she treated you. You confided in me, and that night, I turned my back on you..." He trails off, lacing his fingers with mine and pressing them to his soft full lips. "I called you a liar. I didn't believe you. You have no idea what it did to me when I realized where you were, and I was helpless all over again."

Like with Penny. The thought hangs in the air, almost tangible and terrifying.

"Logan, you can't blame yourself. I don't blame you. I mean, we snuck on your property using the code you trusted me with. My best friend made some big accusations. Your reaction was valid."

"Raven, she was poisoning you. Tricking everyone to think you were back on drugs. I can't believe none of us saw it."

"I didn't even know what was going on. She was

calculated. Thorough. She even had me questioning whether or not I had taken anything. We were all deceived."

"I can't even begin to understand how she could do that to you." He brushes a piece of hair out of my face. "All of it. Raven, this is so far beyond...I haven't been able to sleep. To eat. After that night, I ended up following Mr. Zale, and he is up to something with Vera. Actually, Aarya and I went together to spy on him."

"I'm still trying to figure out how the two of you were able to be in the same car, let alone plan a rescue mission together."

"A lot's happened in the past several days. I'll fill you in later. Right now, we need to figure out how to keep you safe from Vera," Logan says.

His grip tightens where our fingers are tangled. Guilt stabs my chest.

"I need you to know something." I tilt his face toward mine to make sure we are eye to eye. "After that day at your house, playing basketball, I knew without question you had nothing to do with Penny's disappearance. I know you trusted me with your code. I never meant to use it against you. I thought if we found something in Mr. Zale's house, everyone would stop thinking you were involved, too."

He sucks in his bottom lip, and I can barely sit there and wait for what he has to say next.

"I forgive you. And it means a lot to know you'd really made up your mind about me, even if you did let everyone in to snoop around." He wraps his arm around my shoulder, bringing me back to him. "We've both messed up here. I'm the one who got punched for saying horrible things about Penny. I mean, I'm lucky you even wanted to talk to me after that. So, if anything, maybe we're kind of evenly matched at screwing things up?"

A small smile tugs at the corners of my mouth. "Maybe we are."

He trails his fingers up my arm, to my hair, wrapping a curl around a finger. "I thought you were beautiful before, but you're stunning like this, Raven."

"I just got out of a psych ward after being drugged for days, and I'm still in my hospital clothes. My hair is all unruly. I'm seriously questioning your judgment."

"Stop it. I love your unruly hair." He brushes a few pieces from my face, and I feel a slight flush of heat on my neck. "You're incredible. You have a light inside that glows despite everything you've been through. Most people would have dimmed to darkness in the face of what you've seen, how you've been treated. Your strength amazes me."

This time, the corners of my mouth turn all the way up and my smile touches my eyes.

"See? You're able to still smile so big it lights up the world." He does a sweeping motion around us. He gets serious again and cups my cheek with his hand and I shiver at his touch. "I wanted you to see through my masks. And now...I feel like you do."

To be seen by another, for them to fully know you, to witness your inner most self, and not run away—this is where I belong. I'm finding my place in the overlap of my worlds, in the shaded middle where the circles meet, the Venn of my life—Belle Grande and Jamaica and Everbeach, black and white and mixed, it all fits together to make something beautiful.

"You see me, too," I say.

His nose grazes mine, our lips almost touch.

A heartbeat and I press my mouth to his. Another

beat, and he responds, a caress of our tongues, tangling and tasting. I savor the kiss as it deepens.

It's different this time, hungrier yet more tender, slower and more deliberate. His breath in sync with mine, electricity humming over the surface of my skin. Our once forbidden yearning is finally released, pushing back the pain and betrayal and heartbreak.

A moment of honesty, two hearts bare. Erasing a stepmother's poison.

The pure magic of true love's kiss.

CHAPTER 35

CRACKED CODES
AARYA

Logan supports Raven as she finds her way to the couch inside Titania's trailer. They're holding hands, fingers linked. I make myself look away, so Raven doesn't think I'm judging. I'm not. But it still throws me—the idea of them together.

I suppose the whole lot of us isn't any less of an odd match up. Elle and Grayson and Dawn at the small dining table. And Vera's sidekick, Hunter, now one of us, sitting on the floor against the couch, with a pile of paperwork he swiped from the executive suite. Anything and everything he thought would help.

Punkaj is back with the equipment to perform a blood test and give saline to Raven. "Take two," he says. "This time we're not going to let evil stepmom destroy the evidence 'kay?"

The needle pokes in. I watch the tiny vial fill up red. "That damn poison from Vera they gave you in Hightower better pop," I say.

"What if it doesn't?" Raven asks.

I wish I knew. We may have saved her from Hightower, but Raven's struggle is far from over. Vera already forcibly committed her; she'll do it again. And she has the law on her side. The seven of us not only have to hide Raven, but keep her hidden until we can get ahold of her dad and convince everyone of what Vera is doing. And if we don't have the proof...

"I feel like Vera is invincible," Raven says. She grimaces as Punkaj inserts the IV to give her the saline to flush her out.

Titania drapes a soft, colorful quilt over Raven. "There's a story we tell in Jamaica," she says. "Everybody knows it. Rolling Calf. It's a creature, look like a bull. But with fire-blazing red eyes, and a chain dragging. He walk the countryside and block da way of nighttime travelers, chase dem with wicked intentions. To get away you gotta drop t'ings, so he stop and count dem, and then run to an intersection so he get confused." She reaches over and tucks a curl behind Raven's ear, cups her face. "You children got evil chasing you. Now is your chance to confuse it."

"Now's our chance to *end* it," I say. Titania's story makes me think of another one. "Hey Punk...do you know Kali's origin story?"

He looks up from where he's carefully packing up Raven's blood sample. "Where she kills all the demons? Yeah, my mom's told me."

I turn to the others. "Kali's the goddess you all thought was scary looking at my hotel. But here's the thing. There was this demon terrorizing the entire universe. Every drop of his blood that spilled turned into a deadly clone of him. Kali stopped the evil demon by draining his blood before he touched the ground and devouring tall of his clones."

Dawn looks horrified. "She sucked his blood? And, like, ate the rest of them?"

"Hell yeah she did. She was brought in when action was needed. The gods decided they needed to work together and come up with a plan to produce one super being that could destroy the demon once and for all. Kali. *We* need to be that super being. It's the only way this story ends with the demon defeated."

"Dats how a likkle axe can cut down a big tree," Titania says.

That's the thing about stories. So many of them share bones. Stories are trees with roots that drink from the same river. Outsmarting evil is the spine of every fairytale. One branch holds a demon, another a calf, another a wicked stepmother.

I have an answer for Raven after all. "We don't need your blood as proof. We have Penny's poems. We need to stop looking at them as clues and start thinking about them as more." I wave everyone in closer. "Penny is trying to tell us a *story*."

We huddle around Titania's scuffed coffee table to pour over the pages. We start where we always do with Elle's. *Hearts...turned to steel...a long time ago. To survive, walk on glass, pretend you don't know the deceit.*

"See why we thought it was you, Logan?" Elle says.

Logan cocks his head. "I can see why you maybe went there, but it's not like it said roses are red, violets are blue, Logan will try to get you, too."

"I mean, it did to *me*," I say.

He answers with a punishing smirk. "I am well aware."

I make a face back. I wouldn't call this the beginning of a friendship but maybe a truce.

Dawn clears her throat. "*Go to their church. Wake and*

ring the grand bell! The taste of success is a spindle from hell...and sweet."

"Grand bell. Belle Grande," Grayson says beside her. "The church."

Raven interrupts, trying to sit up straighter. "Hold on. Now mine. *Portraits in mirrors make it much clearer. They point at nightmares...and ask you who's nearer...and discreet.*" She continues, voice shaky, "Penny was trying to tell me to look at myself, my own life. The nightmare near me. Vera has always hated me because I remind her of my mother. She has been discreetly trying to take me down. She would have, if not for all of you."

Her eyes well with tears. Logan tightens his arm around her.

Punkaj's eyebrows scrunch together before he starts to speak. He's calculating facts. "If we look at it as a story like Aarya said, we need a beginning, middle, and end. Here's the story I see: Vera is trying to hurt Raven, yes, but beyond that, she's dangerous. Something is going on at Steele Sugar that Vera and Mr. Zale are involved in. There's some sort of cover-up, and I think it has to do with their work in Belle Grande."

"What about mine?" I say. "*Take a deep dive...raise your voice in support. Docks clocked by day, false reports that night cheats.*"

Hunter pipes up. "All these files...they're shipping logs like the one you found in the carriage house. But I don't know what they're for."

"Could these be the false reports Penny is talking about," I say. "*Docks clocked by day that night cheats?* Something is going on at night, hidden by day. But what exactly?"

"Who knows?" Raven's eyes fix on some far-off point. "I wonder if these poems are really trying to tell us anything at all, or if they're just a mess from Penny's troubled mind like her mom said. I was only there for a couple of days and look at the effect it had on me."

There is finally some color returning to Raven's cheeks, and Punkaj gently removes the IV from Raven's arm as he offers, "Maybe it's both. Maybe Penny was struggling mentally *and* trying to tell us something. The two aren't mutually exclusive."

Elle goes still. "*Mutually exclusive*," she repeats in a whisper. "Wait. Punkaj, do you have the drafts that Ansel gave you?"

Punkaj rummages in his reporter bag and pulls out a folder with the pages neatly arranged inside. Elle grabs it and dumps the contents across the floor.

It's a mess. Poem verse here. Another there. Another next to it. And whenever they share a word, drawn circles overlap on the papers.

Elle touches the back of her neck, her tattoo. "A drawing of what's in common," she says. "What's not mutually exclusive."

My breath quickens. I feel like I could turn inside out with anxiety and excitement, the line between them blurred. It's all just energy now.

"A Venn," I say.

"A Venn." Elle repeats.

I wonder aloud. "So if she was writing the poem in overlapping circles..."

"They were a Venn diagram," Elle finishes.

We push our poems together, tangible energy now bouncing between us.

"Look for any words they have in common," Elle says.

We keep rotating the papers across the shiny wooden planks, from spot to spot, and trade and switch, left, then right, circle and back. No luck. Defeat settles like dust.

"If you no mash ants, you no find 'im guts," Titania says.

I look to Elle, who gives me a knowing smile. "She means look closer."

"Look closer and closer," Titania says. "Pick 'dem words apart completely."

"Got it. Okay." I rally. "Let's find some guts."

I slide our pages next to each other, grab a pen from Punkaj, and look at the poems again.

"Let's actually circle every word they share," I say, "like Penny was doing in her drafts."

We set them next to each other on the floor, arranging and rearranging until a pattern emerges, circling every word in common. And suddenly we see it.

Running like a vein between the poems are shared words and parts of words.

Elle
Hearts... turned to steel... a long time ago. To survive, walk on glass, pretend you don't know the deceit.

Dawn
Go to their church. Wake and ring the grand bell! The taste of success is a spindle from hell... and sweet.

Aarya
Take a deep dive... raise your voice in support Docks clocked by day, false reports that night cheats.

Raven
Portraits in mirrors make it much clearer. They point at nightmares... and ask you who's nearer... and discreet.

All the branches of this story connect at one root.

GO
TO
THE
PORT
AT
NIGHT.

CHAPTER 36
DEEP DIVE
AARYA

We stay out of the first lines of morning light, weaving our way through towers of stacked crates, piles of buoys, and giant shipping containers. I gauge the distance back to the parking lot and Punkaj's car in case we have to make a fast exit.

Penny went to such lengths to hide this one simple directive. *Go to the port at night.* All of it to bring us here. And now what?

"What are we even looking for?" Logan asks.

"Welcome to every day since we got these poems," I answer. "We know we're looking for something. What that is..."

"I guess it's a we'll-know-it-when-we-see-it kind of thing," Raven says. She's still unsteady so Logan takes her elbow.

Dawn clutches her camera to her chest. "I'm going to go ahead and say this is exactly the sort of thing the police warned us against doing."

"Good," Elle says. "That means we're close."

But each long dock we venture down is a ghost town,

no sign of movement. By dock number six, I'm starting to wonder if we got this right after all. And we're running out of time to figure it out. People will start waking up soon and these docks will get busy.

Raven's pace has slowed down, and Elle's voice is higher than usual when she says, "Can we find something, *anything*, that says we're not wandering aimlessly around?"

A low grumble cuts through the darkness.

"Finally, a sign of life," I say.

Punkaj motions for us to hide behind a row of crates. We crouch in the darkness.

Rubber grates when the boat meets the dock. Men grunt, hauling rope to tie it down. The beeping of a crane cuts the fog, lifting a shipping container from the deck. It settles with a heavy thud on the cement pier.

Wood cranks open. Voices spill out. Someone is crying. Someone asks for water.

A deep voice tells them all to stay quiet, then curses. "Not again."

I put a foot on the edge of a crate and climb to the next one, then tentatively the next, and peer over the top to see what's going on. My body tingles with adrenaline.

People. People stumbling and crawling out of the large wooden container.

"All right everyone, hurry. I know you're tired, but you've got to move. I mean it, move." The voice is laced with urgency.

They're ragged, with cracked lips and soiled clothes.

"You made it this far; you don't want to get caught now do you?" I almost fall backwards off my perch at the sound of Penny's father's voice.

Mr. Zale waves them along. "Welcome to America." When the container is empty, he sends a group of his guys inside. They each emerge dragging something behind them. A sick scrape against the ground. Bodies.

"Good Lord. How many didn't make the trip this time?" Mr. Zale asks.

A muscular woman with hair pulled up in a tight ponytail answers in a gruff voice. "It's bad. We lost five."

More cursing.

"Load 'em up," Mr. Zale orders.

A wave of nausea passes over me. I want to climb down, run from here as fast as I can. But we can't. We need to get proof of this. Whatever *this* is.

I wave Dawn up. I put a hand to my heart and shake my head, trying to warn her silently about what she is going to see. Grayson gives her a boost, and she teeters beside me taking in what's unfolding. A shocked breath hisses out of her, and then the soft click click of her camera, documenting the horror.

The conversation Logan and I overheard between Penny's father and Vera all falls into place. *How many? How many lost?*

They were shipping contraband. But not the kind we thought. Not weapons. Not drugs.

My stomach twists sharply. They are bringing in the next round of workers for Steele Sugar. I'm certain of it. Cheap, illegal labor to run the empire.

Dawn touches my shoulder and gestures that she has to get down. Tears stream down her face. We climb back to our friends.

"What is it?" Raven looks back and forth at our expressions.

"It's *people*." I swallow the gorge rising in my throat. "They're bringing in people."

"Penny's dad looks to be in charge," Dawn whispers.

I speak slowly. "This is what Penny found out."

We let the realization sink in.

Another throat clench and I say, "Some of them didn't make it."

Logan's voice is low and serious. "How many?"

"Five."

Dawn raises her camera. "It's all here. I have pictures."

"I need to see." Logan scrambles up the crates to look for himself.

"Me too," Hunter says.

Punkaj's face is grim. "We should get more pictures."

"I can't go back up there," Dawn says. "I can't see that again."

"Can I?"

Dawn nods for Punkaj to take her camera.

As he begins to climb, the crates beneath the boys start to shift under their weight. All three suddenly pitch forward and collapse in an avalanche of noise.

"Who's there?" Mr. Zale barks.

Logan speaks through a narrow gap. "Get out of here!" We are cut off from each other by the pile of fallen crates.

The sound of approaching footsteps and voices gets louder.

I throw an arm around Raven, helping her along, and we take off, hitting a dead end almost instantly. The only way out is over another stack of giant crates, wedging our feet in the edges of the planks like a ladder and climb. I hear Dawn's panicked breathing. Elle grabs her and pulls her up. We lie flat while footsteps pound below.

Voices echo. Flashlights cut through the gray fog of dawn. I motion for them to climb down the other side. We bend low, running in a crouch, sticking to the walls like shadows through the maze of shipping containers, trying to find the boys and our way back to the car.

I hear panting from behind. Someone is gaining on us. I cut a left and slide behind a barrel, but a woman spots me. "Got her," she yells out.

I back up, hands raised in a sort of surrender. I see the others out of the corner of my eye, forced against a pile of boxes by Mr. Zale—who has a gun.

"What are you girls doing here?" He curses and paces. "*Raven*?" He motions with his head at the woman who chased us down. "Get her to my car. I'll take her to Vera."

When Raven, stricken, doesn't move, he puts his hand on the gun at his waist. "Raven, go."

Raven moves mechanically away from us.

"What did you see?" Mr. Zale demands of me.

"Nothing," I answer quickly—too quickly.

"You're lying." Mr. Zale clutches at his forehead. "You're not going to ruin this. I won't let you."

He gestures toward the very same shipping container that the people were smuggled in on and pulls his gun. "Give me your phones and get in."

Mr. Zale's hand is shaking and his eyes are wide, like he's scared. He is not ready to shoot. He is not ready to harm his daughter's friends.

"What exactly do you think you're going to do here? Lock us up in a box so we don't talk about what we saw?" I ask.

"Just like you did to Penny," Elle says. Her voice wavers, but I don't know if it's from anger or fear—probably both.

Mr. Zale's eyes go vacant. "Penny was safe in Hightower. That's all that was supposed to happen."

Tears stream down Dawn's face. "You wouldn't hurt us."

Something dark flashes across Mr. Zale's face. He points the gun at us—at me "Get in." We step into the mouth of the fetid smelling crate. "I've learned in my life if you want to eat from the garden, you have to pay the price."

He slams the shipping container closed. A bolt slides and clicks shut with sickening finality.

"Start screaming," I say. "Scream as loud as you can."

We scream our throats raw in the muffled air, and pound on the door. The boys have to hear us.

"Shut up!" Mr. Zale shouts but we only scream louder.

He can't do any worse than what he's already done, especially from outside the crate.

"You're making me do this," Mr. Zale yells.

We wait, continue yelling, until there's a groan of metal meeting wood, and the shipping container jerks up, lifting and tilting. We scream, but this time it's involuntary as we trip and slide to one side.

Dawn gasps, "What's happening?"

"He's pushing us!" Elle cries out.

It takes us a moment to realize we're falling.

And with a splash that nearly stops my heart, the container plunges into the ocean.

CHAPTER 37
POISONED REALITY
RAVEN

My hands are tied behind my back and a blindfold covers my eyes, while I ride in the back of the vehicle Mr. Zale forced me into at gunpoint. My physical freedom has been taken from me, but he can't imprison all of me.

Control of the mind is a fragile thing. When you're fully in its clutches you're held by invisible walls, but once you find your escape...you will *never* again be owned.

I listen for every sound, paying attention to each bump and turn, so I can figure out where I'm being taken.

The tires of the car crunch as we drive over rock. The sound of heavy equipment grates in the distance. We come to a stop and the door opens. "Come on out."

"Where am I?" I turn to where I hear the equipment on my left.

"Don't make this harder than it has to be."

Calloused hands grab my shoulder, and Mr. Zale guides me out of the truck, gentler than I would have expected after the gun to my back. I can't gauge how far down the ground is and I stumble, buckling my knee. I lose balance and Mr. Zale loses his grip. I land hard on my injured knee, pain ricocheting through my leg.

Mr. Zale tries to help me up. "We have to go. Now. She's waiting."

"I'm trying." I roll, gripping my knee.

Mr. Zale holds my arm firm. "You can stand. Get up."

I grit my teeth and heave myself up, ignoring as the edges of the rock jab my knee cap. Cold, round steel pokes into the middle of my back. The gun. I walk forward, limping.

"This isn't up to me. I just want you to know that."

I don't respond.

"There are some things I can't protect you from, couldn't protect Penny from."

Mr. Zale removes the blindfold. It takes a moment for my eyes to adjust. We're standing in front of a staircase that winds around a tower three stories high. To my left are rows and rows of tall, reed-like plants.

Sugarcane. We're in the Steele sugar fields.

"Climb."

I step on the rickety stairs, climbing up and around the tower, made more difficult by my knee and inability to hold the railing. Each step up with my right leg intensifies the pain. When we reach a landing near the top, at the end of the platform jutting out from the tower stands a slim figure dressed in a white pencil skirt, tailored white jacket, and red patent leather heels. Her hair is pulled back tight in a bun.

My living nightmare.

Vera looms, apple-red lips taut. "I've been waiting for you. So nice of you to join me."

"Like I had a choice." The gun is pressed harder into my back.

"Thank you, Donald. For bringing her back to me."

She walks toward me, her heels pounding the landing. *Clack, clack, clack.* "Come over here. You'll have a better view." Vera motions for me to join her at the railing.

I hobble to her, Mr. Zale's gun never leaving my back. He guides me to the far side of the railing, putting Vera between me and the stairs. On the other side of the platform another winding set of stairs lead up, which isn't exactly where I want to go. But if I get a chance to run for it, it's my only option.

Vera speaks directly to Mr. Zale. "Let's get this started, why don't we?"

"Yes, ma'am. I'll head down there now. The bulldozers are almost finished, and we'll be ready for phase two." Relief avalanches down my spine when the gun retreats along with Mr. Zale.

When he reaches the stairs, he turns back and looks directly at me. His forehead creases and the skin bunches around his eyes. He feels...sorry for me? For himself maybe? But he obviously won't do a damn thing about it.

Donald Zale descends the steps, his shoulders slumped—a shell of a man owned by others. What was it like to be so enslaved by a lifestyle you'd do anything, even give up your own daughter, to maintain it?

"Right over there." Vera shields her eyes and points into the distance, where the road winds around to an entrance. I recognize the semi-truck from the port. It stops right below the tower. A forklift pulls up holding a wooden crate that must have been about seven feet wide. Several workers unhook the back door.

The bodies from the port.

They're unloading body after body into the field on the right. There were only five dead at the port. How could there be so many more now?

Mr. Zale climbs up onto a tractor pulling a water tank

and drives it down a dirt road between two sugar cane fields.

"You look a little queasy. Don't be. This part won't take long." Vera puts her bony arm around my shoulders.

"How could you?" I choke out, my rage mixing with nausea.

"Why do you look so shocked? I've never been shy about letting you know exactly where you fit. Here's the visual of where you should have been all along. Where I wish your mother had been when she came over, not gallivanting around stealing fiancés."

"All of this because of my mother?"

"Goodness no. We give these people the opportunity for a better life here in the U.S. We give them work. They're skilled and they work hard. And life here is so much better than where they came from."

"*Death* is not better than what they left behind. Do they know the conditions they'll be traveling in when you bring them here?"

"They know there are risks."

Her callous tone forces bile to rise, but I swallow it down, along with any weakness. "Is this what Penny knew?"

"Penny." Vera spits her name. "She stumbled on this when she got involved with that awful boy from Belle Grande. She started volunteering at the church, followed her dad here one day." Vera motions to the site below.

"He does what must be done. It's not his fault. Donald is a good employee. Loyal. But she was hysterical, acting like it was somehow his fault we have collateral damage. She confronted him. We tried everything to get her to calm down, but what she saw...what she knew—it sent her into one of her dark episodes. We knew what needed to be done and we did it, even when we couldn't convince her mother. But we only needed one parent's permission to get her into Hightower. We had no other choice. It was for her own good."

My eyes narrow. "Where is Penny, Vera?"

"You and your friends couldn't leave the poems alone. You had to try and find her."

My lower lip quivers. "What have you done with her?"

"No matter how hard we tried, she just couldn't let it go. She was obsessed. She wrote all over the walls. If I'd known she'd gotten those words down on paper, I would have stopped it before they ever landed in your hands. But the boy from Belle Grande turned out to be more problematic than I thought."

A sudden heaviness washes over me. "What did you do, Vera?" I ask with dread.

Vera's grip around my shoulder tightens and she leans even closer. "You want to know what happened to Penny?" Her hot, sticky breath scalds my ear. "Your friend is dead."

CHAPTER 38
RIDE OR DIE
AARYA

The shipping container lands sideways, cracking on impact. We fall hard against the back corner, landing in a crush on top of each other. Water seeps in from a gaping hole at the bottom. But the container is floating. For now.

Elle curses and kicks the door. Dawn lets out a sob. "We're going to drown."

I push against the wall, every nerve on fire, a stark contrast against the ice of the water. "We can get out through the break!"

The water is filling in fast, hitting our knees, and rising. I kick at the cracked board with force, but it's not enough. I need to push with my whole body.

"The second this thing gives way water is going to come pouring in," I say. "So, when I say swim, you swim."

I suck in a breath, my eyes stinging against the salt. I sink to the jagged crack in the container's wall and kick as hard as I can. It doesn't move. I try again. Elle and Dawn are moving toward me, reaching for an escape that doesn't exist yet.

The girls swim back up for a breath, our air pocket shrinking by the second.

I kick at the boards harder, bubbles streaming from my nose with the effort. I pull at the plank with my hands. Yank it. Shove my shoulder against it.

The board cracks, and the water pressure blasts it right back into my face. A warm rush of blood streams out from where the plank careened into my forehead. Dawn and Elle are pushed up against the top of the crate by the force. They aren't strong enough swimmers to make it out of this hole. I have to find another way. Fast.

I dive down into the dark swirls of early morning water and *swim*. I'm out of the container and up I go, surfacing and pulling myself up to the top of the container. I slide across on my stomach and pull the dead bolt open. I can feel the crate heave a deep bellow and belch of air like a dying animal.

Using the last of my strength, I throw open the door. Dawn and Elle wrench themselves over the edge and out, sucking in mouthfuls of air.

The container moans and glugs as the ocean swallows it down.

We meet in the chop, I tread water with energy I don't have, the reserves pulled from a place of pure instinct.

Dawn is bobbing up and down her face slipping under. I wrap an arm under her, and scissor kick toward the dock, Elle struggling beside me.

"You've got this," I choke out to her. "I can't carry both of you." But no, Elle folds into the water. I grab her too and pull her along, now only left with my legs to propel us forward.

Dawn gasps for air. She's thrashing around, panicked, her arms hitting me in the face, her hands clawing at me. I can't swim like this. Not with her freaking out.

My arms burn. I struggle to hold up my friends. I need more strength. Durga rode a lion and went to battle. Kali slayed demons and wears their skulls as a necklace. Ganesh, with the head of an elephant, Hanuman the monkey god, with the strength of a thousand men. In this moment, I imagine I have ten arms, each with its own strength. In this moment I am part of the water, moving with it, not against. Mythical. A mermaid. A goddess.

I swim. I kick with my legs and drag Elle and Dawn beside me.

There's a loud splash and Punkaj cuts the water toward us. He reaches me and tucks Elle against him and swimming sidestroke beside me.

"Almost there," Punkaj says. "You can do it."

"I...can't."

"Don't let me beat you now. Come on Aarya! Push."

A rope hits the water with a splash and Punkaj grabs it, wrapping Elle's hands then Dawn's. Hunter and Logan start reeling it in from the dock. Punkaj reaches for me. His fingers close around mine, and in a human chain, we are pulled to safety.

My whole body is shaking, as much a delayed reaction from the adrenaline as the cold water. I collapse onto the dock.

Logan's face goes white. "Where is Raven?"

"Mr. Zale...he took her." Hunter looks physically sick. "Has to be the sugar bogs. Vera was scheduled to be there this morning."

"Let's go," Logan says.

Punkaj briskly rubs my shoulders trying to warm me up as we walk. "You're really hurt." He touches the side of my face. "Got sliced open out there."

I wince. "Penny's dad literally tried to kill us."

"We saw, from the shore where we were hiding."

Grayson clutches Dawn against his chest. "My God. I thought we were watching you die."

"We are going to get him." Punkaj points to Dawn's camera on Grayson's shoulder. "I got it all. He won't get away with this."

We hurry to the car, soaked and shivering, trying our best to stay in the shadows.

"Wait." Elle points to two motorcycles in the lot. "Divide and conquer. Punkaj and Dawn, go straight to *The Mirror* and get the story out there. The more people who know, the safer we are. We'll go find Raven. I've got our rides."

"You can hotwire a motorcycle?" Hunter says.

"You can't?" Elle sets to work getting the engines humming.

Hunter looks at Punkaj. "First, you need to stop by Steele Enterprises and raid the files for the story. There's way more than what I grabbed on the fly. I'll take you."

Punkaj pauses before he gets in the car with Dawn and Hunter. "Aarya. Be careful."

"You, too."

Elle throws a leg over the bike. "Get on," she tells Grayson.

Logan grabs the other motorcycle. He answers my questioning look. "I have my pilot's license, remember? If I can fly a plane, I can figure out how to drive this thing."

I get on and wrap my arms around Logan, disbelief flashing that *this* is who I am relying on to help save my best friend.

Penny's dad is the villain. And Logan just might be a hero.

The engine's energy matches something inside me—a churning, primordial rumble. The sound of resolve. The vibration of the fight inside a heart.

I catch my reflection in the small silver circle of the bike's rearview mirror. Blood streaks my face. I look like Kali, wearing the battle against demons like bright red war paint.

An uncanny calm snakes through my body, whispering, *no more*.

No more lives lost to their secrets.

Red is the color of revenge.

CHAPTER 39
WICKED DANCE
RAVEN

let out an anguished cry. Vera clamps her hand over my mouth.

"You need to stop it right now. Get ahold of yourself."

I want to sink to the floor and sob. My body goes limp, Vera and the railing holding me up.

There's no saving Penny. She's been dead all along. My vibrant, carefree, beautiful friend. Gone.

Vera loosens her grip on my mouth. "Are you going to behave?"

I close my eyes and nod. I'm at her mercy.

She lets go. "Think about it. Someone of her status missing this long? Do you truly believe we couldn't have found Penny if she were anywhere to be found?" She laughs, a maniacal look on her face.

I am caught in the clutches of a real-life evil witch.

"It was easy, actually. I only had to make it look like she ran away. It wasn't so hard once I took her hoodie. Cutting off her braid was my idea—to make it look like she'd changed her appearance. She didn't struggle much when I cut it off; the tranquilizers helped, along with my tea. When we walked toward the open window where the maintenance guy had conveniently forgotten to padlock the bars that day, she looked up at me, pleading with her eyes, and I knew I was doing the right thing. She was suffering too much knowing what her dad did. Knowing what was happening to the workers. I helped her."

My stomach roils at her casual justification.

"I gave her one more tranquilizer shot, and when her body went limp, it was easy to push her out of that tower and let her body land in the waiting truck. And then, we brought her here." Vera gestures to Mr. Zale and the bodies below.

I struggle to stay standing knowing this was Penny's final resting place. "You are sick," I spit out.

Vera squints down at me. "Yes, I am. I am sick of living every day with a reminder of the person who destroyed my life. I am sick of stupid girls threatening to destroy everything I've worked for. And I am sick to death of having to pretend that we're one big happy family, and you aren't the poison I need removed from my life. So yes, Raven, I am very sick." Vera's apple-red lips turn up sharply in the corners. "But now, I've finally found my cure."

In a fast, violent motion, Vera slaps me across the face. She grabs me by the chin before I can respond and slams something sharp into my arm. I try to wrench free, but it's too late. An empty syringe falls to the ground.

"It shouldn't be long before the effects hit you. And then, you'll look at me with the same pleading eyes as Penny, and I'll be able to grant you the same peace I gave her. It may be tough on Clive at first, but he'll get over it." Sheer terror courses through me. There is nothing I can do to stop the drug from taking control of my body, my mind. I might have ten or maybe fifteen minutes, but then I will be fully at her mercy.

"Speaking of, let's talk about your dad. Do you want to talk about how he is worth nothing? How his fortune is tied up in a failing company in Jamaica? We would be nothing without me. Steele Sugar would be nothing without me. I am the only one who will do what it takes."

Vera's face twists, her eyes flashing with bloodthirsty power. Her figure blurs. How long since she injected me? Only a minute or two, but the effects are already starting. I have to get away. But what are my options? I could try to run around Vera and get to the stairs heading down, but with my knee, Vera will beat me to the exit. The other staircase is closer, and if I distract Vera, I may be able to get there in time. Anywhere is better than trapped on this platform.

"If you're wondering why he hasn't called or texted you back, it's funny because he's wondering the same thing about you." Vera takes my phone from my back pocket and searches for something. "Ah, here it is." She holds the phone out in front of her, and there in my blocked contacts is a simple three letter word: *Dad*. "You really should keep a better eye on your phone."

"You blocked him from contacting me?"

"And before he left, I blocked you on his phone. Genius really."

The depth of Vera's premeditation sinks in, but I can't linger on how truly diabolical she is. Dizziness is taking over; I am running out of time. I need an out—fast.

Vera puts my phone back in her pocket. *The phone*. If I can find a hiding place, maybe I can call 911.

"The earth gives, the earth takes." Vera motions to where a dump truck drops the last body into the sugar field on the right. Mr. Zale's tractor sprays water on the opposite field, and a worker carrying a drip torch touches his flame down to the base of a stalk in the field with the bodies. "Controlled burns make it almost too easy. Nature can be so cruel."

I hear the crackling first, then the tiny flame explodes into a blaze. The popping intensifies while the fire licks the sky; the inferno a slave to the wind's control, opaque smoke tumbling higher, blocking the sky.

"I almost forgot. I have something for you." Vera pulls from her purse a single, white bell-shaped flower. She tucks the lily of the valley's stem behind my ear.

Vera picks up one single curl and frowns. "You look more like her every day." I guess this is a fitting way for things to come to an end for you. No one will miss you. And you'll get to be buried with your people."

I flinch back from her while rage burns. I am simultaneously terrified and inflamed. My lips tremble. Vera will not win.

Vera's truth is no longer my truth.

I AM RAVEN EBONY SNOW.

True power bursts to the surface—my heritage, pride, the identity I own. I slam my shoulder into Vera, knocking her over, and take off for the closest stairwell, the one behind me, the injury in my knee more dead weight than pain. The tranquilizer is taking over. I haul myself up to the next level.

"You little bitch!" Vera follows me up the metal stairs slowly. "There's nowhere to go." Her voice holds a bone-chilling resolve.

I take in the platform around me. It's a solid metal floor with the same open railing looking over the sugar fields like the level below. Across from the stairs, a door leads to what appear to be offices.

The ground feels like it tilts. The door seems to lean to

the left, then the right. I blink slowly a few times, and everything stabilizes long enough for me to head straight to the door. I jiggle the handle and shove, but it's locked. I pull and shake the door. Banging my fists hard, I scream for help.

"No one is there," Vera says with a twisted joy.

I back up against the door. She's only a few feet away.

"It didn't have to come to this." Vera purses her lips. "You should have stayed in Hightower."

My voice trembles despite my efforts to tamp down my fear. "You were poisoning me, trying to kill me."

"You did this to yourself. I thought you'd get the point when I sent Hunter after you."

"You're a coward making him do your dirty work."

"Everyone does my bidding. That's not cowardice. That's power."

I wriggle my wrists, trying to pull my hands free from the restraints, but the rope is too tight, cutting into my skin. If I'm going to escape, it's going to have to be without using my hands. I have to keep Vera talking while I figure out a plan.

"All I wanted was for you to love me. Why wasn't I enough?"

"How could you ever be a daughter to me? I could never love you, not when you came from *her*." Vera's disdain for my mother radiates venom.

"For so long I believed you, that my mom did something wrong, that I should be ashamed." I shake my head, letting my curls wildly flow and releasing the flower tucked behind my ear. It tumbles to the ground, and I stomp on it, crushing the petals.

Vera's eyes go wide and she straightens. I train my waning focus on her.

"But I know better now. My dad loved my mom

fiercely—as fiercely as she loved me. I'm sorry you got hurt. But nothing justifies what you've done. There's no one to blame for this but you."

"Your mother was a whore, and you are the same trash as her."

"She. Was. Not!"

Rage surges in waves.

The years of abuse.

Five graves with five lilies on my thirteenth birthday.

The way she made me feel worthless, cutting me off from my father. Making me think Logan would never want me.

It has to end here. Tonight. "Her name was Ebony. Say it! Vera, say it! EBONY!" I lunge for her, but this time Vera is ready. She catches my shoulder and shoves me. I go down hard, skidding across the floor and rolling into the railing.

I struggle to keep my breathing rhythmic. A calming sensation floods my mind, my neck limp, and my head lolls to the side.

No. I have to fight it. Get. Up.

For Penny. For the sugar workers. For my mom. *Ebony.*

I push off the ground with my shoulder to come up to my knees—the pain minimal, my body numb. Vera looms, eyes dancing wild. I dig my heels into the ground and lean against the rail behind me, using it as leverage to stand.

Shouts from below catch our attention. Vera's focus falters and she steps back.

I can just make out a group of people approaching below—my friends—hopping off motorcycles and running to the tower with Logan in the lead.

"Raven, watch out!" Logan yells and points frantically

behind me. I turn to see Vera lunging at me like a jackal after her prey. Instinct takes over, and the world slows.

A beat and Vera dives. Another and she stretches toward me. I fake to the right with my body but move to the left with my good leg, like I would on the court, dodging out of Vera's reach. And her momentum sends her flying into the rails.

There's another beat where she's still there on the platform with me, and then she's in the air.

Vera falls, tumbling feet over head to the ground. A sickening crunch reverberates through the early morning air.

Clanging footsteps pound up the stairs. Arms wrap around me.

Logan unties my wrists, and I sink against him. Fading. But alive. And safe.

He grips me tight, and I cling to him like he is the only thing holding me to this earth. His touch melting the ice of my chilled, shivering insides, stopping me from going into shock.

The police lights and sirens pull us back to the ledge.

"It's over," I whisper.

Taking my tattered copy of Penny's poem out from my pocket, I hold it over the railing's edge, the frayed paper fluttering in the wind—and I let go.

The poem zigs and zags, winding and floating through the air until it touches down, Penny's final words finding their resting place next to Vera's lifeless form.

CHAPTER 40
TRUTH AND LIES
AARYA

I watch the evening news as if I'm not part of the headline. Like it happened to someone else. Like I'm up in the helicopter that's getting the sweeping shots of the sugar bogs and was never on the ground, racing toward that tower where Raven and Vera stood framed against the cloudless sky. Like I didn't see a body plummet and not know at first which of them it was.

My parents, Raj, and I perch in front of the television listening to Punkaj's mom. Gita Grimsley introduces a press conference with the mayor. Grayson's father walks somberly to the podium.

"Everbeach has experienced an unfathomable tragedy. The death of Vera Snow, Chief Counsel of Steele Enterprises, exposed an ugly secret harbored in our great city. I can assure you the sort of human trafficking and illegal labor practices that have been uncovered will not be tolerated. I am confident that in partnership with Steele Sugar, we will take all the right measures to ensure this never happens again. And with that, I welcome Mr. Harvey Steele."

Harvey Steele clears his throat and stares toward the camera.

"To the people of Everbeach. I love this community with all my heart. It has been my family's home for generations, and we've dedicated our lives to making it a thriving economy built on integrity. To learn that Vera Snow, someone I trusted with my company, my legacy, was engaged in this sort of activity, as you can imagine, is beyond devastating. Couple that with her monstrous targeting of children, it's incomprehensible. She was deeply misguided to put profit over all else. There is no price on human life. The fact that she'd conspired with one of my most trusted employees behind my back to achieve this evil is salt in the wound. I was betrayed. And I want to apologize to all of you for not knowing what was going on."

He pauses. "Our thoughts and prayers are with the family of Penny Zale, whose father now awaits justice at the hands of the court. And the good people of Belle Grande. Without them there would be no Steele Sugar. Thank you."

The news anchors pick it back up from there. They describe Raven's rescue and Vera's death in the same unaffected lilt, as if these two things somehow hold the same significance. All of it, Penny's *murder*, delivered in perfect pacing.

Everything in life has a rhythm: from the basic things that keep us alive—heartbeat, breath—to daily routines—work, rest. When something disrupts that rhythm so deeply it ricochets into society, there's a rapid response to reign back in the rogue notes and return them to a common refrain. We do not like chaos. Or tragedy.

I can see. From my pretend vantage point in the chopper. From the real one tethered to the couch. From where

I sit, both near and far, part of it and not, I feel like I can physically see the fault lines this scandal is sending through Everbeach.

I realize I've been gnawing on a nail during the speeches. "It's impressive," I say. "How fast a scandal can be managed."

My mother unexpectedly reaches over and cups my face. "*Bheta*, we are so sorry this happened. You don't know how grateful we are that you're safe."

My father clears his throat. "Children should not have been in this position."

Like I need to get scolded after what we just went through. "I could have died you know," I say. "I could be at the bottom of the bay." I'm about to get up and walk out of the room, but he raises a hand.

His tone is gentle. "You've misunderstood me. What I mean is it is a deep failure as parents when our young ones take on a battle like this *alone*." He sits up straighter. "Don't ever hide the truth from us again. Don't feel like you have to. We are on your side. Always."

I don't say anything. The silence in the room feels... warm, a little bit of hollowness filled by my father's unexpected acknowledgement.

My little brother rests his head against my arm. I muss his hair, like I do, just to make him fix it—a small thing I can predict. But then, something about the softness, the smell of shampoo, the sheer fact that I can feel him, warm and full of life beside me—it hits me. What I just said. I could have died. We all could have.

And Penny...

"I can't believe Penny is...gone," I choke out.

My father walks to the window overlooking the bay. He motions for me to join him.

"I know this loss is hard," he says. "And you might

just think I'm spouting words. But words have power. They give a place to house pain, joy, all the extremes the heart doesn't know what to do with. Words are the scaffolding for our souls. They let us build a path through darkness."

I find myself listening to him, in a way I perhaps never have before.

"There are two ways of passing from this world—one in light and one in darkness," he says. "When one passes in light; he does not come back. But when one passes in darkness, he returns. That's from the scriptures of the Bhagavad Gita."

"So, you live a good life, you ascend. A bad one..."

My father puts his arm around me, the physical affection abnormal, and we stand awkwardly connected looking out at the sky. "Penny has passed in light. Her spirit is ascending. Try to find some peace in that."

His words are meant to comfort me. I know that. But it leads to a disturbing thought. If Penny has gone into the light, what sort of evil returns from Vera's dark passing?

I can't shake the sense that a storm gray sea is quietly eroding the foundations of Everbeach, and hurricane waves are coming.

I need to talk to Raven. Hear her voice. Confirm her existence.

"Thanks," I say to my father. He nods, a small acknowledgement, but right now it's enough. I step out onto the balcony and call Raven. She answers on the first ring.

"Hi."

"Hi."

Those two short words instantly connect us, like we share the exhale.

"I...I wanted to check on you. Are you okay?"

"What's okay?" Raven asks. "I'm resting. I'm...alive."

I take a big breath. "I wanted to say I'm sorry."

"No," she says. "*I'm* sorry."

"It's not your fault. Vera was—"

"Not about that." Raven hesitates. "I'm sorry about Logan."

I don't respond.

"There's a lot more to the story than you know."

"I gathered that."

"Normally I tell you everything about everything. And by not telling you this... It spiraled and the next thing you know I'm not even telling you the little things."

"Like what cereals you mixed for breakfast?"

"Yeah, that."

"And what silly thing Mr. Alpine said in class when I was out." I pause. "And that you were falling in love with Logan."

Raven speaks slowly, like it's the first time she's truly accepting this truth out loud. "I've kept it to myself this whole time. And I need to talk about it. It's eating me up that I kept it from you. Never again."

"Never again. I need to know everything. I want every detail, no matter how minor. How can I advise you as your best friend if I don't know every glance, every text, every hang out?"

"Then we need to start with spin the bottle in eighth grade."

When Raven gets to the end of the story, I sink into a deck chair. "There's a whole world of guys out there and you had to pick Logan Steele to fall head over heels for." I sigh melodramatically. "If you're happy, then I'm happy. But next time you decide to fall for our missing best friend's unscrupulous, but-has-now-proven-himself ex-boyfriend, you better tell me. No more keeping secrets. Ever."

Raven laughs. "I think we're safe this won't happen again."

Because it can't.

Penny will never have another boyfriend. Or graduate from high school. Or bound down the beach to meet us with glittering excitement.

We spent months holding on with an iron grip to the idea Penny would be found alive. And in one shattering moment, the metal melted and swallowed up the wisp of hope.

"I'll never know if Penny is okay with me dating Logan," Raven says.

"There was so much we didn't know, even when she was still with us," I say.

Tears choke Raven's voice. "How did we not know she'd left Logan? How did we not know about Ansel? How did we not know what she'd stumbled on? I wish— God how I wish—she'd told us, asked for help—before it was too late."

"I think that's what the poems were," I say. "Words. Her last weapon. The only one she had."

"You're right. They were her way of coming back."

Penny's final outreach to her friends.

I glance back into my house, and a painting over the couch catches my eye. The goddess Durga, her muscular arms fanning out like a sun burst behind her.

"You know," I say, "having friends—really good ones, the ones you'd do anything for—it's like being a Hindu goddess. Each friend is an arm, holding something special to help you survive..."

Raven doesn't speak, waiting for me to finish the thought.

"You make a good arm," I say.

"You too," Raven says.

I feel instantly lighter.

Secrets are kept. Choice words said. Hurt happens between friends. Perhaps the things you fear in friendship —the weaknesses—are actually the strengths. There will be gaps and holes and missteps, but *how* these things are handled makes all the difference. Every friendship requires a different balance, offering a different return, a unique power.

My brother raps on the glass. "Punk is downstairs for you."

"Um, Punk is here," I say to Raven.

"Go."

"It's fine. He can wait. I'll go down in a minute," I say quickly.

"It almost seems like you're excited," Raven says.

"Shut up."

"It's okay if you are. He did help save the day," Raven says, and then, "so did you." She pauses. "And I love you."

"I love you, too."

I hang up and hurry down the stairs. The second the elevator doors open I throw my arms around Punkaj.

"Whoa."

"Thank you," I say. "For knowing exactly what to do. And doing it. The blood was the proof we needed. Now everyone knows what Vera did."

Punkaj steps back. "Guess being a total nerd has its benefits."

"I don't think you're a *total* nerd." But the energy to tease him isn't there today. I am exhausted.

"How are you doing?" His forehead creases in concern. "Now that we know what really happened to Penny."

"I don't know," I say. "There's nothing we could have done to save her, I get that, and Raven is safe. But something feels off—like this isn't over."

"What do you mean?"

I squint. "I'm not sure. I think maybe that news conference isn't sitting right with me."

"Do you want to go somewhere and talk?"

"I...do," I admit. "How about the roof?"

"Why do I have a feeling we're not supposed to be up there?" he says. I manage a small smile, and we walk down the main hall a bit before I stop short. "When I was fighting to get out of the shipping container...I thought of these guys." I point to the statues of the Hindu deities. "It was weird. I didn't know I believed in them. I'm still not sure I do. But when I was the most scared I've ever been, there they were."

I raise my hand to meet Durga's carved one and give it a fist bump.

Punkaj copies me, giving a bump to Ganesh. "I guess almost dying can do that to you. Shows you who you are."

I hold out my fist to Punkaj. "Shows you who your friends are, too."

As he meets it with his own, his big brown eyes fix on mine. "You mean not everyone breaks into hospitals for you? Performs blood tests on your friends?"

"Or jumps into an ice-cold ocean to haul me to shore?"

Punkaj smiles. "It was cold, wasn't it?"

We walk the long line of carvings, fist bumping each one and acknowledging them.

"Thanks for not letting me die," I say to the goddess Lakshmi.

"Yes," Punkaj says. "Thanks so much for letting Aarya

continue to grace this earth with her sweet presence. I'm eternally grateful for the torture."

I fist bump another sculpture. Kali. "Thanks for making me think I had super strength." I fall silent, and touch the side of my face, the cut that stings even as it heals.

"Thanks for making her think she can now swim faster than me." Punkaj cups a hand over his mouth and whispers, "She can't."

His joke snaps me out of it. I laugh. And it feels good. So good. Laughter is like a seed in scorched earth. It is the thing that not only survives disaster but tells you that it did, with every bloom. It says you can't crush us.

Once we reach the top floor, I lead Punkaj to a back staircase, up and out onto one landing, and motion for him to follow me up a ladder to go even higher. We sit on the wide rim of the very top spire of the Maharaja Hotel. We are so high above the horizon, the dark stain of rain swollen clouds seems in line with our faces, like we're a part of the sky.

"We could fall," Punkaj says.

"That's what makes it fun."

"You're right."

I give him a look of scrutiny. "Did I hear you correctly? Did you just tell me I was right? Don't make me fall off the roof."

Punkaj leans into my shoulder. "You're not terrible."

I lean back. "Neither are you."

We sit like that, watching the clouds swell and roll as if they're alive. A sudden crack, like the sky is solid and breaking, sends slivers of lightning racing far on the horizon.

I sigh. "That's a goodbye from Penny if I ever saw one."

Thunder growls in the distance, a comforting thrum moving in the thick air like fingers through fur.

"We should get inside," Punkaj says.

The dark gray line of heavy rain is crawling toward us steadily, but slowly. "We have a minute."

I take out the worn poem and turn it over a few times in my hands. Then, on a whim, I fold it into a paper plane.

Punkaj touches my wrist and shakes his head with a deliberate superiority, but his eyes are warm. "May I?" I hand over the poem, and he undoes the plane to fold his own.

"That's much better," I admit.

Punkaj holds up his hands in disbelief. "Now *I'm* going to fall off the roof in shock. You told me I'm better at something than you."

"Don't get used to it. I'm in a vulnerable, emotional place right now." I don't lean away from his shoulder.

I study the folds of the plane, how Punkaj smoothed and re-creased the paper with such precision. "You're such a control freak."

"Takes one to know one."

Wait. *Wait.* My mind starts racing. Punkaj looks at me expectantly. "You're making an *I just discovered the world is round* face," he says.

"Control freaks!" I exclaim. "I'm a control freak. So are you. So is someone like Harvey Steele. He controls *everything*. How would he not be aware of what Vera was up to? He's the ultimate boss. How would he not have a clue about what was going on at the port and in his fields? I don't buy it."

Punkaj does his slow nod, the one where each up and down tilt of his head is like one thought being absorbed at a time. "Penny's dad was his most trusted employee besides Vera. The two of them were doing this together. I think it's reasonable to question if it was at Steele's direction. And, what's to say it stopped? What's to say there isn't something worse going on?"

"And if that's the case..."

"This story is only beginning." Punkaj looks from me back out to the sky. The rain is getting closer, and I can feel the cold, damp wind bringing the storm to shore.

"You better write it."

"First we have to find it." Punkaj's eyes flash with resolution, catching and holding the waning light like the scaffolding my father was talking about, like he has all the words we need inside of him.

"We will."

I feel it down to my bones, as certain as the tide pushing and pulling the ocean below. Sometimes a feeling is all you need to keep going. We solved the mystery of Penny's disappearance on a raw gut sense that was pushing us along. We have to trust our instincts to get through this next dark sea.

I raise my arm to launch the plane.

"Sure you want to do that?" Punkaj asks.

I lower my arm. I *thought* I was sure. "I haven't recorded a single song since Penny disappeared."

"Aarya. You can't *not* sing." His eyes look like the bottom of a waterfall, the clear pool you land in after the roar.

"You should hold on to that," Punkaj says.

"No." The uncertainty evaporates as it comes to me. "I have every word she wrote to us memorized. I don't need the piece of paper. Penny's poems are forever engrained in me. *Penny* is in me. And I'll put her words into the world by turning them into a song."

That's how someone lives forever—through their words.

My thoughts flash to what my father shared: *Penny has passed in light.*

One step ahead of the rain. One breath ahead of the darkness.

I send Penny soaring into the storm slashed sky.

CHAPTER 41
FAIREST OF ALL
RAVEN

Tragedy leaves in its wake scattered pieces of devastation. And, if you're lucky, hope.

I never have to fear Vera again.

Still, several days after returning home, walking down the hall to the kitchen, an echo of anxiety follows me. I need to create new memories in this house to erase the remnant of Vera's darkness.

"Good morning, my darling." My dad's voice calls to me from the kitchen. He flew home immediately when he got the news, and we've been avoiding the hard conversations since. He takes bagels out of a bag with a tub of cream cheese. Because breakfast will fix things.

"I can't believe she blocked our phones." His opening is blunt. Yet, there isn't a good way to get into this.

I stare at the bagel. "I know."

He places his hand over mine. His eyes flash sorrow. "I am so sorry for what happened."

"I am, too." I focus on keeping my composure, but I can feel my lower lip quiver.

"I should have been here." Yes, he should have been.

He promised it would be different this time, and he was dead wrong.

"Why did you have to go to Jamaica?"

He blinks and sits back. A flicker of something, and then it's gone. "There were some important...business dealings. I had to be there." He looks like he's warring with himself, how much to say, what not to say, when to say it. "I want to tell you more. I really do. But just know, I don't need to go back anytime soon."

I've been through this charade so many times. And every time I stuff down my feelings like the obedient girl I'm supposed to be. Well, not anymore.

"What could have been so important you left your daughter with a murderer?"

My dad stills. The corners of his eyes fold into worried crevices seemingly deeper than just a few months ago. "Raven, I didn't know. God if I had known, do you think I would have left? Would have been with her?"

"I don't know anything anymore. *Why* did you go back to her? After Mom."

He takes a few moments before speaking. "To love Ebony meant to hurt Vera. So, when fate took Ebony away, I thought the right thing to do was to return to my first love." His shoulders tense, and his lips press together in a grimace. There's more he isn't saying. I can tell.

"Darkness took over Vera's heart and almost took us down with her. Remember this, you and I are not Vera. However battered and bruised we are, we are still a family."

Yes, we are a family, but one haunted by her manipulation and his mistakes. He hadn't been here, and Vera made me think he didn't care at all. Vera played us both like puppets on strings. I know now she kept us apart, but

I can't understand why he didn't fight harder, insist she let him speak to me.

Then again, I took her at her word. I believed he was disappointed and upset with me, and I didn't push her to get him to talk to me.

Still, it will be hard to forgive. Like most families, there are skeletons shoved in dusty closets. Only ours tumbled out all at once and landed in a heap at the breakfast table. Maybe that's the key to forgiveness: starting with all the skeletons and sorting through the rubble until the world makes sense again.

"I'm going to need time. And space," I say.

"Take all the time you need. I'm not going anywhere. Ever again." He pauses and stares at me for a moment. "I forgot how much you look like her with your curls. I wish I had seen...realized what Vera was doing, how she was controlling you, manipulating me." His eyebrows furrow and his forehead creases, agony visible on his face. "If you don't want to, you never have to wear your hair straight again."

Warmth blooms in my chest. "Maybe I will. Maybe I won't. But at least I have the freedom to choose."

"Now you sound like her, too." My dad pulls a small velvet box out of his pocket and sets it in front of me. "This is yours. I had it repaired."

He kisses me on my head and walks away.

I open the box, and my mom's ruby heart necklace stares back at me, catching and reflecting the light like it's glowing from within. My heart swells like waves in a storm.

I'm still here and my mom's necklace is back. I can rest in the calm as the eye of the hurricane passes overhead. Recovering from Vera's destruction won't be easy, but we will survive.

I fasten the clasp around my neck, putting my mom's necklace back where it belongs. For now, I know my father is with me, and that's enough for today.

———

The doorbell chimes, and I fling the door open to find Logan, hands overflowing with sunflower plants. We planned this—after we both had time to accept Penny was never coming home. I told him and all our friends, and it was one of the most heartbreaking, terrible things I've ever had to do. The truth was like a grenade—all the hope we lived for while deciphering her poems and chasing down the clues turned to the dusty rubble of grief.

I take two plants from Logan and lead him outside to the garden.

He puts his arm around my shoulders and pulls me close. "Are you ready?"

Instant butterflies from his touch. I inhale ocean and pine, and on the exhale, strength remains because I know I don't have to do this alone. I pick up a shovel and hold it out to Logan. "I think so, but maybe you should start."

Logan doesn't take it. "I could, but I think this is something you need to do. I'll be right here with you."

I nod and bend down to touch the little bell-shaped white flowers planted here. I run my fingers over the surface of the gray stones.

I read the names: Evelyn, Matthew, Jackson, Anastasia, Melanie—headstones for each of Vera's miscarriages. And behind them, the plants she used to poison me.

I sink the shovel into the dirt. It takes a couple scoops to dislodge the plant. Logan takes it from the ground and places it on the walkway. We work in tandem, scooping and lifting, until we remove all five flowers. I cradle a sunflower plant, cut the plastic pot off, crinkle the root ball to loosen it, and place the fresh, vibrant flower in the hole behind the first headstone. Logan fills in the empty space with potting soil, patting down the edges.

One by one, Penny's light washes away Vera's darkness.

"I want to leave the headstones. They would have been my brothers and sisters. Penny can watch over them now."

Logan pulls me into an embrace.

It's going to take time to banish what it felt like when trapped by her on the sugar fields, learning how calculated Vera was, how much control she exerted over those in her orbit: Me, Mr. Zale, Hunter. To think she convinced Mr. Zale to put his own daughter away, Hunter to attack us. "How's your brother holding up?" I ask.

"It's kind of a war zone around the house. But Hunter's guilt; it's eating him alive. He's grateful he was able to help in the end, but I think it's going to take him time to forgive himself."

"I hate that for him."

Logan shakes his head releasing me. "Only you would feel bad for someone who ran you off the road with paintball guns and brought you poisonous tea."

"If anyone understands what it's like to live under the control of Vera, it's me. I can't blame him for following her orders. He chose the right side in the end when it really mattered."

"Well, I'm not letting him off that easy." Logan hugs me again.

I rest on his chest. "I needed this, you. Right now."

"I've needed this for a while. Longer than I was willing to admit."

"We don't have to hide from it anymore."

"I hate that we ever did." Logan strokes my hair. "All I could think when you were in that tower was how badly I let you down..." His voice trails off.

I stand on tippy toes making direct eye contact with him and place my hand on his heart. "We were messy from the beginning, and we did our best, clawing and fighting to find our way. Now that we're here, I don't want to focus on what should have, could have, or didn't happen. It didn't break us; we're stronger because of it."

"It's you and me now." Logan presses his forehead to mine, our lips a breath apart. "I'll never let you break alone."

His words a promise, true and sure.

Suddenly I'm wrapped up in a giant hug from multiple directions. Aarya. Elle. Dawn.

"Where did you all come from?"

Logan steps back, leaving the four of us together. "I meant what I said: you never have to be alone again."

"We have somewhere to be," Dawn says.

"So if we're done with the mushy stuff," Aarya says, her tone softer than her words, "we need to get going."

Elle pulls out her phone. "Thirty minutes until sunset. We have to hustle."

"The limo's waiting out front." Logan ushers us to the driveway and sends us off with a soft kiss on my cheek.

We pull up to the beach—*the Real Beach*. The sun casts the sky in orange and red hues, a warmth chasing the daylight.

"We needed to be together," Aarya says. "When we say our good-byes..." Her voice trails off, eyes drawn to the setting sun on the horizon.

To Penny—what Aarya couldn't finish the sentence with—catches in my throat, making it hard to swallow the reality of why we are here.

We stand where the water kisses the sand, waves lapping our sinking toes.

Dawn whispers, "I had so much hope we would find her. It has me questioning my faith like I never have before. I've done things I wouldn't have a year ago and been places I didn't even know existed in this city and around it. It feels like the eyes of my heart have been opened, which is a good thing. But I'm struggling with what it cost for us to see."

"Penny gave her life to get the truth out," I say.

Dawn pulls out her poem. "I'm going to keep this. Frame it next to my bed as a reminder. Seeing Belle Grande. Pastor Dana's church. There's a deeper purpose I want to find. To honor Penny. Continue her work." Dawn chokes up.

I pull her in for a hug. "I sent my poem sailing down from the sugar tower. It was like letting go of the horror I lived under and didn't fully understand."

"Mine went soaring off the rooftop of the Maharaja. What Penny did, it's as sweeping as the sky," Aarya says. "And I want to turn her words into a song. I want to sing again. So the world won't ever forget her."

Elle is uncharacteristically quiet. We wait for her to speak. When she finally looks up, her eyes glisten with a love and warmth I'm not sure I've seen from her until now. "Penny gave me the gift of friends I didn't know I needed." She looks at each of us. "Remember, we are a Venn diagram, too. Penny is *our* overlap."

Elle looks down at the poem in her hand. "Penny used to tell me that when it came to sadness, anything dark, she would imagine the feeling exploding into tiny pieces. That way it could never take over. You were always bigger than it."

She shreds her poem. "Let's be bigger than this pain.

Let's be stronger." Elle tosses the poem into the air, and it falls into the water churning at our feet.

The gulls make circles against the sunset. The pink sky deepens to magenta, the last of the sun a jagged orange streak.

"Venn diagrams in the sky, too," Elle says. A frown crosses her face. "I can't shake the haunting sense that we're still so blind to all the secrets of Everbeach."

The truth is heavier here now that someone else has spoken it aloud.

"I feel it too. There's more underneath the surface," Aarya says. "And it's for us to uncover. We won't stop until every secret is brought to light. For Penny."

We stand in silence, arm in arm, watching the sun dip below the horizon. The last line of light, where day and night converge is golden, removed from time.

That's where Penny lives on.

"I never knew the end could feel so quiet," Elle says. "But I have hope. In this quiet."

I take a deep breath. "That's the thing about hope. It doesn't have to be believable. You just have to believe *in* it."

And each other. Even when, especially when, there's so much brokenness. Inside. Outside.

Hope mirrors possibility and whispers in the face of darkness that some sort of happily ever after exists.

We will find it.

That's the bigger promise—to uncover the sea of secrets and tightly spun lies that hold up Everbeach like a tower. In a risky balancing act, delicate as dancing on glass, we will get to the heart of what is broken.

Truth is not a fairy tale.

ACKNOWLEDGMENTS

A heartfelt and huge thank you to:

Our publishing team at WiseWolf—for jumping in headfirst and giving all four books a home. Mike Bray, Jake Bray, and Kristin Yahner, we are so excited for this adventure!

Our amazing editor—Rachel Del Grosso whose keen eye, sharp mind, and open heart made *Red as Blood* the novel it was meant to be. Thank you for going hard on us because our writing is better for it. You're a force!

Our agent—Tamar Rydzinski for always believing in Everbeach, even when it was 50,000 words too long. Thank you for cheering us and our characters on and for guiding us all along the way.

Our first editor who slashed and burned this story to its sparkle—Gretchen Stelter. You have a way with words that's a true gift, and we are so grateful for you!

Our early readers, especially the friends who tackled every draft, even the really bad ones—that's you Lisa Aimola and Cathy Holbrook. No more scooby-dooing around.

Our writer's coven—Linda Hurtado Bond and Kelly Coon, for all the feedback and support on this incredible journey. And Nova McBee, you steered us here and we love being publishing sisters with you.

Our magical network—ITW and Thrillerfest, for providing the community that brought all of the people together to make publishing this series a reality.

And to our readers—thank you for letting Everbeach into your heart. We hope Raven and Aarya's journey inspire you to see yourself as the amazing and worthy person you are!

———

Sorboni:

My husband—for doing all the adulting while I disappear to write, believing in me and knowing when to say "let's go"—this book would not exist without you. Neither would I.

My son—for endless support, understanding and faith too deep and strong for your young age. Everything I do is for you.

My father and mother and brother—telling and reading stories aloud with you made me an author.

———

Dominique:

To my partner in every way, my husband—Luke, when I say I couldn't have done this without you, I'm not exaggerating. You believed in me and my writing before I was able to believe in myself. Without your encouragement and steadfast support to pursue this dream, I wouldn't be where I am today. Thank you for being everything I could have hoped for in a husband and more, and for being the best dad and role model to our twin boys.

To my sons—Mason and Gavin, you are my heartbeat, my joy every single day. Thank you for being so understanding when Mommy had to close her office door and write all those long hours (and for only interrupting when it was the most important, like when your iPad freezes, Mason; or when you had to tell me about a new modern house you drew or car you discovered, Gavin). I miss you too, even when we're all here.

To a few special people in my life (you know who you are)—your commitment to getting healthy and staying healthy over the past decade, to work your program and live a beautiful, renewed life in recovery, you are a living example of true strength. Your resilience, bravery, and determination will forever be an inspiration.

To my family—My mom for teaching me to always be proud of who I am and where I come from. My grand-mommy for being the matriarch who kept us all together with your unconditional love. And to you both for laughing when I took notes on our conversations and helping me infuse just the right patois. My dad for encouraging me every step of the way and always being a listening ear. My Auntie Annie for telling me I was a writer before I even knew I was one. My sisters Deann and Danitza for always being on my level (and sometimes even more so). And to my entire Jamaican family who raised me on the island and in the states. It really does take a village, and in my case—a lively, Jamaican one.

A LOOK AT BOOK TWO:
A STOLEN VOICE

The fast-paced, immersive sequel to *Red as Blood*, with more page-turning suspense, forbidden romance, and twisted secrets for fans to devour.

Penny Zale's secret is out. But it's only the beginning.

Her friends, Aarya and Dawn, head to Jamaica to escape the fall-out from Penny's disappearance. The plan backfires when they are contacted by a mysterious whistleblower known only as Dagger. He's being hunted for what he knows and needs their help.

Aarya and Dawn have secrets of their own. Aarya falls into a steamy off-limits romance with pop mega-star Jett John, whose attention she captures after going viral with a song in memory of Penny. Dawn battles temptation when she meets the adventurous islander Keenan King while on a break from her longtime boyfriend. Each of them must come to terms with their culture and faith, even if it means risking everything they've always wanted.

When Dagger's trail goes cold, the group of friends reunite on the island and race to survive Jamaican voodoo, jungle chases, cliff diving, and danger at sea. Dagger has a story, and it's up to them to find the truth and give it a voice.

"An addicting saga that reads like a Netflix series you have to binge."

AVAILABLE MARCH 2023

ABOUT THE AUTHORS

Sorboni Banerjee is a Bengali-American author and Emmy Award winning television news anchor and reporter in Tampa, after spending more than a decade as an anchor in Boston. With a dad from a small Indian village and mom from Maine, Sorboni's experiences growing up "mixed" shape her stories. Fueled by coffee and conversation, Sorboni loves the beach, boating and traveling the world with her husband and son. Other books by Sorboni include Hide With Me.

www.sorbonibanerjee.com

Dominique Richardson is a Lebanese-Jamaican author and CPA who now uses her number-crunching excel skills to plot her stories. She spends her free time passing on her love of unicorns to her twin boys, running in the Florida heat, and drinking all the coffee. Raised between Jamaica and the United States, her biracial heritage finds a home in her books. She now lives in Tampa, Florida with her family.

www.authordominiquerichardson.com

Sorboni and **Dominique** are the co-founders of YA by the Bay, a nonprofit teen reading and leadership festival dedicated to inspiring teens to "be the author of your own life." Learn more at www.yabythebay.org.